ORION

STAR BLOOD

ORION

SOFI AGUILERA

Paperback ISBN: 978-1-63337-837-7
E-Book ISBN: 978-1-63337-839-1

Printed in the United States of America
1 3 5 7 9 10 8 6 4 2

To my family, my unwavering North Star,
guiding me through every twist and turn of life.

Chapter III

Light into a tight Net was spun,
Like a Tree born from the purest Dawn.
Its roots into the Ocean of Life submerged,
And its branches high into the darkest corners took shape.
The Seven Luminous Ones now began to emerge,
Forming out of the great Tree that into a Web had been made.
The Seven realms they were tasked to rule,
To keep the Wheel of Time spinning and a new End to await.
Every edge of the Universe Light held,
Binding together Life with Death.
But Chaos still roamed without restraint,
Into tangles and knots the Web it ensnared.
The Great Dragon of Wisdom this issue pondered,
A new rule of Light and Order it wished to create.
The Seven also took council, and the Wisest One a solution brought forth.
Into Three Wells the Ocean of Life fell,
And into those Wells the Tree of Life its roots interred.
The First Well Wisdom held,
But only those of pure heart its waters could taste.
The Second Well Death contained,
To create new Beginnings from the Ends.
In the Third Well Fate remained,
To guide all Times in the right paths.
Three Weavers would need to take care,
Of each Well and everything they contained.
The First Weaver into Life was fashioned,
She who knew all things Past and who remembered what had befallen.
The Second Weaver was then born,
She who in the Present time all things saw at once.
The Third Weaver was finally made,
She who all Futures could shape.
The Three Weavers a new Universe Weaved into One,
A Universe where they decided how Life would roam Time.
Chaos into Order was entwined,
To make space for new Luminous Ones.
The new beings who would soon be born,
To take Destiny under their control.

CHAPTER 1

I STOOD LOOKING DOWN at the splatter of blood on the floor. It had turned almost black and been absorbed by the wooden boards. It lay a few feet in front of her bedroom door, and I wondered again if she had been coming into the room or out of it when she had been attacked. Not that it mattered much anyway.

I hadn't cleaned the blood—this was the last bit of Zia I had left. The large stain had the rough shape of a half-moon. Smaller drops spread around it like stars against a rugged sky.

My scars burned instinctively, and my inner compass spun, leading me to Zia's location. She was in southern Greece, a few miles north of Athens, in the same spot where she had been for the last month.

I tore my gaze away from the blood and kneeled. I gripped the crowbar tightly, then pulled on a floorboard next to her bed. It snapped in half, sending splinters flying around me. I tossed the broken piece to the side and looked into the hole hidden under it.

Empty.

But it had small bits of paper at the bottom. Zia must have hidden documents here.

I stood up again and carefully stepped on the floor, shifting my weight from one foot to the other. I found another floorboard that bent slightly underneath me with a whining creak. I kneeled and broke that one too.

Another empty hole.

I leaned closer to it as I caught a distinct smell. Gunpowder drifted into my nostrils. She had probably hid some small handguns there.

I continued ripping other loose floorboards free, but found them all empty. Once my arms started burning with the strain, I sat to rest for a bit. I hadn't touched the area around the splatter of blood, but the rest of the room looked like a minefield with blasted holes all over the floor.

I exhaled slowly, then took in the room around me. Zia's black bed stood against the wall. It had been left perfectly made, but after my search last week I had pulled out the sheets and blankets, which now lay crumpled on the mattress like a carcass next to the torn pillows. After night had arrived, I had closed the black curtains. Now the only light came from the lamps on the nightstands at the sides of her bed, and the bathroom light that spilled through the door left ajar. I glanced at the desk in front of the bed. The computers still lay there with a timer indicating they were both disabled for the next thirteen hours—I had tried out too many incorrect passwords.

"Come on," I whispered, as if Zia's ghost would answer me.

I stared at the large bloodstain again. I exhaled, willing myself to walk over to it. My steps were hesitant as I did, as if I would blow up as soon as my foot touched the dry blood. I didn't blow up, but my heart burst with pain. This was the spot where Perseus had attacked Zia and taken her captive. Fury swam through me at that thought. I tested the floorboards, but most of them seemed solid—except for one that cut horizontally through the center of the ragged half-moon.

I kneeled down slowly, gripping the crowbar so tightly my knuckles turned white. The smell of blood wafted into my nostrils, and dizziness shook me like an earthquake. Memories flooded through my mind, and I was back in Greece where I had last held Zia's dead body. I shook my head, cutting those memories away, then gritted my teeth and pulled. The floorboard snapped like a twig, flying to the side.

The hole was empty.

I cursed under my breath, then sat back down, breathing deeply. My phone began to ring. My scars burned—I had left it in the bathroom. I stepped around the broken floorboards to get it, then walked back into the room as I answered the call.

"Hey, Rose," I said as I sat at the edge of the torn bed.

"Hey, baby," she said. "Are we still meeting for breakfast tomorrow?"

"Yeah," I said. "I'll see you at the café."

"Sounds good. Good night."

"Good night."

I hung up and pushed the phone into my pocket. Rose was the only girlfriend I was still in touch with. I had five missed calls from Aster, three from Maia, and two voicemails from Mary. But I didn't have time for them anymore. The only reason I wanted to see Rose again was because, according to Andromeda, she was Perseus's adoptive sister. I intended to use that to my advantage to find, and kill, Perseus.

He was prophesized to kill Andromeda unless she killed him first. He was a threat to Andromeda's life, and I intended to destroy him before he could lay a hand on her again.

My scars burned as I tracked Andromeda. She was still in Switzerland, as she had been for the last two weeks. But tracking Andromeda had become harder since the battle at Palatine Hill. Normally, I could just sense her exact location. But lately her signal had been faulty, as if my internal GPS had lost satellite signal only to connect again a few minutes later.

But as soon as I thought of Perseus, I felt only a void. I couldn't track him, or his giant wolf and flying horse. Which is why I needed Rose to find him. I didn't know if Rose was aware of Perseus's true nature, and if she was, she hid it well. I wondered if Perseus knew that I was still dating his sister. I was playing a dangerous game with Rose, but I was willing to take that risk.

I sighed, then glanced around at the ruined floor and empty nooks where Zia had hidden her secrets but left no trace of them. Perseus had taken Zia captive for a reason. He had wanted something from her. Had he discovered her secrets before he killed her? Or was he still searching for the truth just like I was?

Zia must have known a way to stop Perseus—she had sent Andromeda to kill him even before Andromeda was aware of her Prophecy. Maybe she'd had another plan to kill Perseus if Andromeda failed. That's what I needed to find.

I took a deep breath as I stood up from the bed. I could come back again tomorrow to continue searching. There had to be something Zia had left behind that would lead me to the secrets she had taken to her grave.

I turned off all the lights, but the room didn't plunge into darkness. Instead, pulsing white light shone from my right arm. I'd gotten a nasty gash during the fight at Palatine Hill, about five inches long, running from my elbow to the middle of my upper arm. The light pulsed in tune with my heart, making the shadows around me move in a quivering dance—shadows that almost looked like ghosts. I didn't know if ghosts were real, but decided it didn't matter. The world was already strange enough without them.

●———●———●

"Are you going to eat that?" I pointed at the bagel Rose had left on her plate.

She shook her head, pushing the plate closer to me. "You can have it," she said after she sipped her mocha coffee. I picked up the bagel and began eating it. I had already apologized for not having seen her before, blaming my dying adoptive grandma as the reason I had been away from town.

Rose eyed me with a smile, her cinnamon-brown eyes sparkling under her thin eyebrows. She had ditched her '80s looks, which had been a favorite. She was studying theater in college, and had been working on a play during the semester. She had taken her character very seriously, but now that the semester was over, she had started to dress normally again. Today she wore jeans and a light brown jacket above a white sweater. Her cheeks had turned bright red with the cold outside, but now they were a light pink. Her loose blonde curls spilled around her head like lazy waves. Rose was the longest romantic relationship I'd had. We had been dating for almost a year.

The bell rang as someone entered the café. I startled, but it was just a young man with a shabby dark beard. Not Perseus. I glanced out the window. Few people passed by the snow-crusted sidewalk—a man with thinning hair and circular glasses, a woman with a bright blue scarf and small dark eyes, a tall teenager with a pair of sunglasses and auburn hair tied in a bun.

"Why are you so jumpy?" Rose asked.

I took another bite out of the bagel.

"Every time someone comes in you look at them as if they were an assassin."

I laughed, then smiled.

Rose set down her coffee and placed her hand above mine, tracing small circles on the back of my hand. The bruises on my wrists had faded out, but I worried she might still notice the slight discoloration in my skin. The angry bruise on my neck had also slowly vanished, but the memory still felt tight around me.

I cleared my throat, intending to ask Rose more about her family, but just then her phone rang. She pulled it out of her pocket, looked at who was calling, then placed the phone face down on the table as she rolled her eyes. "It's stupid Leah again."

"Oh," I said.

"Did I tell you what she did now?" Rose asked, her cheeks flushing red with anger.

"What did she do?"

"Well . . ." Rose launched into a long, overly dramatic story that felt stupid to me. "Anyway," Rose said after she was done boring me to death with the gossip. "Do you have plans for the holidays?"

"Not really," I said. "My foster family doesn't celebrate Christmas much. We'll be staying here." I made a short pause. "How about you and your family?"

Rose looked at a passing motorcycle, then back to me. "My brothers are planning our vacation."

Rose never talked much about her siblings. She had mentioned her brothers a couple of times, which meant she had more siblings. I had tried to search online for Andrew Wood's adoptive children, but I hadn't found anything asides from a newspaper clipping years ago that said he had adopted a few children. No names were specified, though. I found it strange that there was no information about them whatsoever, but imagined Perseus must have planned it that way to stay hidden.

"We'll be going to South America," Rose said after a short pause.

"That sounds fun," I said.

I remembered something Draco, one of the other Star Children Andromeda had found, had told me—that Algol would rise three times. The first time had been at Palatine Hill in Rome, and that had been catastrophic. Draco had said that Perseus's second rising would be at the end of the year, around Christmas. What if Perseus's second rising was in South America?

At least Andromeda wouldn't be there. But what if he tried to kidnap her again? What if he tracked her down and discovered she was in Europe? No. I couldn't risk that. I would have to kill Perseus before he left—which also meant I needed to find clues from Zia soon.

"Are you done with that?" Rose asked as she pointed at the coffee I had barely drank.

"Hmm?" I had completely zoned out. "Oh yeah, I didn't like it." I paused. "Is all of your family here right now? Or have some of your siblings or parents already started traveling for the holidays?"

"We're all still here finishing exams and stuff, but we'll leave for the trip together," Rose said.

Good.

"So, what part of South America will you visit?" I asked.

"I think we may go to Peru, Ecuador, and Bolivia."

"How long would you stay there?"

She smiled. "Would you miss me much if I was gone for long?"

I smiled at her. "Of course I would."

"We'll leave right before Christmas and come back a week after New Year's."

That gave me a bit less than a month to find Zia's secrets and kill Perseus. We made small talk for a few more minutes, until Rose glanced at her watch.

"Would you mind walking me back home?" Rose said.

My heart sped up. "Sure." I had walked her home before, but that was before I knew she was Perseus's sister so I hadn't paid much attention. Now could be a good time to scout her house and find ways to break in.

We stood up from the table and walked out of the café. A wave of cold slapped against me. It had begun to snow again. Rose put a white beanie on her head. She held my hand and pressed herself close against me as we walked.

We stopped at a red light. A woman in a bright purple coat elbowed her way past me and scurried into a tall building on the left. I hoped I didn't encounter Perseus at his house just yet. I needed Zia's secrets when I confronted him again.

"Oh, I was also going to tell you." Rose held my hand tighter as we crossed the street. "I already have my class schedule for next semester. All of my classes are Monday, Wednesday, and Friday. So I would be free to see you Tuesdays and Thursdays, and over the weekends."

We passed by a heavily Christmas-decorated store with sparkly white snowflakes covering most of the window.

"We can make that work," I said, knowing that by then I would be far away from here. "Do you have any interesting classes next semester?"

"I have one where we will work on a comedy play during the semester, and there's another one . . ."

My heart began to beat faster. The scars on my back and shoulders burned as if fire had cut through them. Andromeda was on the move. Her signal flickered and I lost track of her for a couple of seconds. My scars burned more painfully as her signal came back. She was next to the lake I had seen on a map, close to the Swiss town of Orbe.

Rose and I rounded the corner and walked into her street. "Oh, look!" Rose said as she pointed towards her red-bricked house. "My dad is back with the Christmas decorations!"

I held my breath as my eyes settled on the black car parked in front of Rose's house. A man who looked to be in his mid-forties came out of the car; I didn't spot anyone else inside the car. Rose pulled me forward—I hadn't realized I'd stopped walking.

"Don't be nervous," she whispered. "He's really nice."

My scars burned as I tried to sense Perseus—but only sensed a hole instead. My pulse quickened.

"Hey, Daddy!" Rose said as we approached the car. "Where are the others?"

The man turned around, looking startled as his eyes landed on me. I smiled in return.

"They stayed at the mall ice-skating with mom." Andrew Wood's eyes traced me up and down, assessing me. I was a full head taller than he was. He had white streaks of hair at his temples, and wrinkles edged his dark brown eyes. He looked like he had recently shaved his beard, and I noticed his nose was a bit crooked.

"Nice to meet you," he said to me.

"Hello," I managed. I realized I had been crushing Rose's hand and loosened my grip.

"I could use a hand unloading the decorations," Andrew said.

"Sure," I said.

Andrew opened the trunk, revealing boxes of inflatables, rugs, calendars, pillows, colorful lights, bells, and all other sorts of decorations. There were more decorations on the back seats. I guessed the Wood family really got into the Christmas spirit. Growing up with Zia, we had never really celebrated Christmas or received gifts.

I picked up a box that showed a Santa Claus inflatable from the trunk and carried it inside. I stopped at the threshold, taking in their enormous house. Above me I counted seven floors that reached up until they met a domed glass ceiling that revealed the cloudy sky. A dozen black orbs hung from the ceiling like dark stars against a white sky. In front of me wide stairs curled up to the upper floor. To my right was a large living room full of boxes. One of them had colorful lights dripping from it so I guessed the boxes contained more decorations.

I made a mental note of all the windows and checked there were no cameras inside the house. I also spotted some good places to hide—behind the large green couch or inside the dark-wooden closet.

I helped Andrew carry the rest of the boxes inside and left them right next to the front door. "Thank you," he said once we were done. "Well, I guess I'll see you around."

"See you around," I said with a smile.

He disappeared down a hallway, his steps fading away.

"How about we meet the day after tomorrow?" Rose said.

"Sure."

Rose stood on tiptoes to kiss me on the lips. I pulled her closer by the waist. "I'll see you then," she said after pulling back. I walked out of the house but turned back as Rose waved me goodbye before closing the door.

Even when I was already several blocks away from Rose's house I didn't slow down. I knew Perseus and I would see each other again soon, but before then I was on a race against time to find Zia's secrets.

Chapter XV, Verse I

The Hunter shall become the hunted,
Chased by those who pretended to enjoy his love.
At night the deed done, with very few words whispered.
The secrets of the dead Queen he will discover,
But into the hands of the enemy they will fall.
Secrets that for so long had been lost,
And now to the Prince of Darkness they belong.

CHAPTER 2

ZIA'S ENTIRE APARTMENT now looked like it had been through a war. Holes punctured the floor and the floorboards were dispersed about like giant splinters, making it look like a bomb had dropped inside the living room. All the couches were upside down and torn into tattered rags. The kitchen drawers lay in pieces on the floor with their contents scattered like debris.

I only had a few weeks before Perseus left, and I didn't know if he would try to seek Andromeda before then to kill her. I couldn't let him walk out of New York alive.

"What were you hiding?" I asked out loud.

Cold rage swept through me as I clenched my teeth. Even after her death, Zia still wanted to keep her secrets. I grunted in frustration. If Zia had been involved with the Star Children, and had known Andromeda and I were part of that world, then why had she kept us away from it? Could she have been hiding us from Perseus? Or from other dangerous Star Children?

I swept my gaze through the room again. This entire apartment was a treasure trove of secrets, but it had been completely emptied.

My phone buzzed, and I fished it out. It was Maia again, but I didn't have time to see her now, although the memories of our last encounter did make my chest warm up with desire. I ignored that feeling and put my phone away. I couldn't get distracted.

I took in a deep breath as my mind searched for answers. If Zia had sent Andromeda to kill Perseus, then she should have known she was about to set off a series of events that could back-fire. What if she hadn't emptied her apartment because she didn't want *me* to find anything, but because she didn't want *Perseus* to find her secrets? This is the place where he had taken her captive, and he could have looked through some of her stuff too.

Then where else would Zia hide her secrets? I had searched the GPS history in her car, but it had been wiped clean. I had also made a list of all the places Zia had traveled in the last few months, but there were too many of them and since I hadn't been tracking her all the time, I didn't know which buildings she had visited specifically.

I exhaled slowly, stretching to ease the pain in my back from having been hunched over the floor for hours. If Zia had wanted me to find something, but not Perseus, where would she go? The answer that came to mind was so simple I cursed myself for not having realized it before. If Zia had left *me* a secret, she would have left it in the place I frequented the most—my own apartment.

Gripping my reliable crowbar from the floor, I grabbed my keys and left.

•———•———•

"Am I something you would eat?" Maia asked.

I looked at the card that she had pasted on her forehead, which read: Chicken.

"Yes," I said. "Am I something you would wear?"

Maia giggled. "Not really."

We sat on the white carpet in her bedroom. Rain fell heavily outside and splattered on the window. Thunder crackled somewhere distantly.

"Am I a farm animal?" Maia asked.

"You are. Am I something you would use as a weapon?"

Maia laughed. "If it was the only thing I had, then sure."

I scratched my cheek, thinking.

Dimples formed in Maia's cheeks as she smiled. The dark blue sweater she wore made a stark contrast to her hair, which curled around her like waves of fire. Her eyes were green like a tree in full blossom under her thick eyebrows.

"Am I a cow?" Maia asked.

I smiled. "Nope."

"Shoot," Maia said. She took off her remaining sock.

"Am I something you commonly have in a house?" I asked.

"Yep. Am I an animal you would have as a pet?"

"Hmmm." I pressed my lips together. "Maybe."

"Am I a lamb?"

"Wrong," I said.

I waited for her to remove her sweater, revealing a thermal shirt underneath.

"Am I a cooking pan?" I asked.

"No."

I cursed under my breath and took off my right sock. I let my bare feet curl into the carpet.

"Am I a chicken?" Maia asked.

"Yeah," I said with a smile. "You win. Let's play another round."

Maia's eyes narrowed. "The game isn't over until you guess your card." She pulled the card away from her forehead, leaving a rectangular mark on her skin.

"Fine," I said. "Am I something you would keep in your kitchen?" I asked.

Maia shook her head.

"Am I something you would keep in your bedroom?"

"Not really."

"Am I something you would keep in your bathroom?"

"Yes!"

I tried to think about an object I would keep in my bathroom that I could use as a weapon if it was the only thing I had. But then again, if I really put in the effort, anything could turn into a weapon.

"Am I . . . a towel?" I could choke someone with a towel.

"Nooo." She pulled off a strand of hair from her face.

"Damn," I said. I couldn't take my sweater off. Maia would see all the scars on my back. Those were wounds that I didn't want, or need, to explain. I should have thought about that before letting her pick the rules.

I took off my jeans, then bunched them next to me. Maia's gaze never left my eyes. I needed to win the game before I had to take off any other piece of clothing. Taking off my sweater was not an option.

"Am I something you use in the shower?" I asked. A heavy shampoo bottle would give someone a concussion if I hit them hard enough. Or maybe I could choke them with a bar of soap? How would I kill someone with a sponge?

Maia shook her head.

"Am I something you would use for your teeth?"

Maia nodded.

"I'm a toothbrush!" Stabbing someone in the eye with a toothbrush would certainly be an effective weapon.

"No."

"Oh, come on!"

Maia laughed. Her face flushed red from the laughter, which only made her eyes look a brighter shade of green. She pointed at my sweater. "It's gotta go."

"I think I'll keep it," I said. She pointed further down. "No."

Maia shrugged. "Rules are rules."

"You didn't take off so many layers!" I complained.

"It's not my problem you're terrible at guessing." She giggled. "Come on."

I hugged my own chest. "I'm cold. I don't want to take it off."

"You have to take something off."

"How about I just keep guessing?" Before Maia could speak, I began to name objects I used for my teeth. "Dental floss, mouthwash, toothpaste."

"That's not how this works," Maia said as she rose to her knees.

"Guess I'll just look at my card."

"No!"

I pulled the card from my forehead, feeling as if it had sucked out some blood from my skin. "Dental floss?" I looked up at Maia, who had her arms crossed across her chest. "How would you use dental floss as a weapon?"

Maia shrugged. "I don't know. You tie it around someone's neck and choke them?"

"Huh," I said. I made a mental note not to be near Maia if she ever got hold of dental floss. "Well, game over. You win."

"Game's not over," Maia said. "You guessed wrong one time before guessing dental floss." She inched closer to me. "Something's got to goooo."

I shook my head. "No. I'm too cold."

Maia leaned forward, making my heart speed up. Her lips hovered right next to my ear. "It's all right. I'll keep you warm."

●———————●———————●

I would have to find another place to sleep, because the torn bed didn't look too appealing anymore. I had spent all night, and half of the next day, searching through my apartment. The landlord would not be happy about it, but I didn't think he would be able to find me once I left.

I ignored my phone as it pinged again—probably another text from Aster. She had already texted me twice today. Ignoring her actually felt hard. Even though I hadn't known her for long, she seemed like a sweet girl, and now she was asking whether I was all right and if I needed help with something. But this was for the best. She deserved someone better than me.

I silenced my phone to avoid any more distractions, then looked through the destruction I had caused. I still hadn't found anything in the bed, couches, or under the floorboards. I had searched desks, tables, chairs, and every other piece of furniture I could think of. Perseus wouldn't know where I lived, and I had never taken Rose here. I knew Zia had hidden something here, and I didn't intend to stop until I found it.

●————●————●

"The movie was great!" Aster said as we exited the cinema.

"It was awesome," I admitted. I had been skeptical to see the superhero movie, but I had liked it.

Aster held my hand as we walked through the streets. It was night already, and I had promised I would walk her back home.

A group of teenagers burst out laughing. They gathered under a streetlamp, smoking and talking animatedly. The smoke drifted towards me, making my nose itch.

Aster rose to her tiptoes and kissed me on the cheek, pulling my attention back to her. "Thanks for the date."

I leaned down and kissed her on the forehead. "Anytime."

Aster flashed her pearly white teeth with a smile. Her skin and eyes were both dark brown, but every time we walked below a streetlamp her skin shone golden. Aster's heart-shaped face had a small nose and thin eyebrows. Her long black hair was always tied in a beautiful braid with blue beads woven into it.

"If you could have any superpower from that movie, which one would you choose?" Aster asked.

I thought about that for a second. I already had a superpower, but wasn't sure what else I would want to do if I had the chance.

"I don't know," I admitted. "Which one would you want?"

Aster looked up at the dark sky.

"I'd like to be like Moth Girl," Aster said.

"Moth Girl?" I said, remembering the horrible creature that had the body of a deformed human and the wings of a moth.

Aster laughed. "Just because she's the only one with wings."

"Oh."

Aster kept looking up at the sky. "If I had wings, I would just fly away from everything and everyone, and it would just be me, the sky, and the birds." Aster smiled. "I've always been more of a loner."

"Me too."

She held my hand tighter. "It's just that . . . never mind. I don't think you would understand."

I leaned down to whisper in her ear. "Try me."

Aster met my gaze. "I have several sisters," she said. "And we're always together. Always. *It's not that I don't like them," she added quickly. "But we always do everything together. Literally. I sometimes wish I could fly off on my own for a while. I guess . . ." She gripped my hand tighter. "I just wish I could do something for myself, instead of always having to do something for my sisters or with my sisters."*

I let her words sink in. "You love your sisters, but you just want to live your own life. There's nothing wrong with that."

"Pretty much." She puffed out her cheeks, her breath misting with the cold. "All my life it has always been about us, *and I've never had the chance to think about* me. *What benefits us as a whole is always more important than our independent wishes."*

"That sounds tough," I said. "I can't relate to that, but it must be hard trying to find yourself growing up like that."

"Yeah . . ." Aster said. Her head snapped back to me. "Never tell my sisters about this."

"I won't," I assured her.

"You must have had tough times too," Aster said. "Living in foster homes all your life."

I shrugged. "I've always had a roof over my head, a comfortable place to sleep in, and food to eat. That's all that matters. Many don't have that."

Aster was silent for a few seconds. "Who told you that was all that mattered?"

"What do you mean?" I asked.

"That sounds more like something you've repeated to yourself a thousand times rather than something you firmly believe." Her dark eyes were looking questioningly into my own.

I shrugged. "No one told me that," I said. "That's simply what matters the most."

"But it's not," Aster said. "What matters is the love you receive from the people you call family. It's not about a roof, a bed, and food." She gave my hand a squeeze. "It's about the people you share those things with."

This conversation was getting too deep for me. I felt my muscles tightening.

"I . . ." I couldn't find anything to say. Zia had given us a house, a bed, and food. Nothing else had mattered. Well, I guess only one thing had really mattered to me all my life. "I do have someone," I finally said. "Someone who's truly my family. But it's just one person."

Aster smiled. "It doesn't matter. Sometimes, all it takes is that one person."

I nodded. "Acid-Man," I said as I tried to ignore the knot in my throat.

"What?"

"If I could be anyone in that movie, I would be the guy who vomits acid."

Aster laughed. "Why?"

"Wouldn't it be awesome if you could just vomit acid on people you don't like?"

"Are there a lot of people you don't like?" Aster asked, her eyes narrowing as she smiled wider.

"Not really, but if I did I would definitely use that power on them."

My stomach growled, reminding me that I hadn't eaten anything since the previous day. I exhaled as I walked over to the fridge, then groaned when I realized I only had an egg, two apples, and a few slices of cheese left. I had mostly eaten out or ordered meals in the last few weeks. Maybe I had some frozen meals that I could quickly heat up in the microwave?

Water spilled out of the freezer as soon as I opened it, splashing onto the floor. I cursed under my breath as water began soaking into my socks and spreading around my feet. I noted a broken section of the gasket I hadn't seen before, which must have slowly thawed the ice. After taking a deep breath, I looked back into the freezer.

I started when my eyes landed on a small metal key.

CHAPTER 3

THE KEY LAY IN THE MIDDLE of the freezer, soaked with water. Where had that come from? Moldy chicken and meat surrounded the key, and the bag of blueberries was still crammed at the very back. All the ice cubes under the ice machine had melted, which is where the avalanche of water had come from.

When was the last time I had opened the freezer? I couldn't remember. I eyed the gasket again. I would have remembered if that had been broken before. Had Zia broken it?

Water continued to drip from the freezer as I stared at the key. Zia could have hidden it inside a big ice cube and left it somewhere in the freezer. It would have easily blended in—or at least not been immediately obvious that a key was hidden here.

The broken section of the gasket was small, so the ice wouldn't have thawed out immediately. No one would have found the key right after she left it there—it could have taken days for the ice to fully melt. That meant that if Perseus, or someone else, came looking through my apartment right after taking Zia, they wouldn't have found the key.

I pulled out the wet key and held it in my palm as my heart sped into a race. It was roughly the size of my thumb. The polished surface reflected the light from the lamps above me. It had a number on its side—749.

I walked to the kitchen counter and placed the key on it, memorizing every little detail. Someone knocked. My scars burned, and I cursed under my breath. I slowly walked towards the door and opened it.

"Hey." Mary smiled at me.

"Hey, Mary," I said, forcing myself to smile. "What's up?"

Mary shrugged. "I had a fight with my dad and left my house. I didn't know where else to go at three in the morning."

That was the only reason I had given Mary my address. Because she had needed somewhere to hide from her abusive father, and since I could relate to having an abusive parent I had felt the need to help her.

"I'm sorry," I said as Mary's eyes settled on the thrashed room behind me. "I really am. But I'm going through something and can't help you right now. I can give you some cash if you want so you can stay at a hotel or something."

"That's okay," she said slowly, clearly disappointed. "I'll figure something out."

She rushed down the hallway, away from me. A pang of guilt beat against me, but I had just discovered Zia's key and couldn't get distracted by anything.

I took a deep breath as I closed the door and walked back into the kitchen. I grabbed the key, wiping away the water with my sweater, and analyzed it more closely. I took in every single detail from the cuts and the shoulder of the key. There was only one lock out there that could inversely match that pattern of cuts, and I visualized it as vividly as I could.

My scars burned fiercer, and I bit down the pain. My internal compass spun. The lock was somewhere in New York. The compass kept spinning as I narrowed down the location. I pulled out my phone and opened my maps app. I could feel that lock so close to me—Manhattan, West Bronx, Morris Avenue—I kept zooming into the map until my scars stopped burning. The lock that fit the key was somewhere in a building that my map denoted with the number 672. I zoomed out again to memorize the route and the exact location. I smiled, already feeling the adrenaline of the chase.

My stomach grumbled again, and I knew I wouldn't be able to ignore it much longer. I could buy some food on the way. Before heading out, I took a shower and changed my clothes. My phone began to buzz as I grabbed my wallet. It was Mary. I sighed, ignoring it, then got a message from her.

I need your help. The message read. I opened it just as she typed another text. *My father is drunk and he hit me. Can you please come get me? I promise I'll leave you after that.*

Damn it. Why had she gone back home? I guess that had been my fault.

"Okay," I said out loud. I could go help Mary, leave her in the hospital or something, go get some food, then find the lock.

I'll be right there. I texted back. *Hide if you can.*

My scars burned as I walked to the drawer next to the stove. I opened it and found my motorcycle keys dangling from a plush monkey keychain. The monkey had a creepy smile that I had never liked, as if he knew something very funny that I didn't. I picked up my jacket from the floor and left the apartment.

My blood boiled at the thought of Mary's father hitting her. I would make sure to hit him harder before I left her house. I hoped he hadn't wounded her too badly.

I arrived at the garage and ran past a few cars. My motorcycle was parked at the end, next to a small red van with a dent next to the back tire. I hopped onto the motorcycle, the seat cold underneath me. The engine growled to life as I turned the key. I liked that familiar sound. Going out on my motorcycle at freezing temperatures with snow and ice covering the street wasn't very safe—but I had left Zia's car at her apartment and didn't have time to get it back.

I quickly rode out of the building. Clouds covered the dark sky like a sheet of iron as the bleak wind scratched my face. Bright colorful lights, Christmas music, honking cars, and rushing pedestrians blurred around me as I rode in the cold. I focused only on my internal compass, telling me exactly where I had to go. Turn left. Keep straight ahead for ten blocks. Turn right.

Before I knew it, I had arrived at my destination. The two-story house had dark bricks and a black-tiled gabled roof. None of the windows revealed any lights inside the house. I could sense that Mary was on the bottom floor at the center of the house.

I left my motorcycle parked on the street and stood in front of the house. I pulled out my phone and called Mary, but she didn't answer. I called her again but it sent me to voicemail. I put my phone away and made my way around the house to find the back door. Bare trees and skeletal bushes surrounded it, forming a dense barrier that edged the property. Snow covered the back-yard entirely, but there were no footprints or disturbances in its smooth surface. I walked towards the back door and tried to turn the knob. As expected, it was locked. I hesitated before forcing the door open, but then realized that I wasn't really trying to be silent.

I pushed the door with my shoulder. It didn't give in on the first try, but on the second the door swung inside and banged on the wall. I left the door open as I walked into what looked like a kitchen. The counter had a thick layer of dust, and there was no fridge, stove, or dishwasher. The faded yellow walls had mostly peeled off. It seemed no one had been here in decades. Light spilled into the kitchen from the open door on the left. I walked through it, passing below a set of stairs, and stepped into a large two-story atrium.

I stopped cold before I had gone more than five steps. Gathered in the large room were Mary, Maia, Rose, Aster, and my old ex-girlfriends Elena, Tay, and Cela.

Chapter XXVIII, Verse II

The Hunter to seduce to unearth the secrets left hidden.
The Seven Sisters will be allies against his charms.
A curse of Darkness they will lay upon him,
One not even the Healer will be able to repair.
Of his Death they may be the cause,
Unless he can listen to the voice spoken beyond this world.
Only by the Bull will he be able to find the true cure.

CHAPTER 4

IF THERE WAS ANYTHING I hated more than my girl-friends finding out I had cheated on them, it was my girlfriends ganging up to take revenge on me. It had happened before. I once had a girlfriend named Lilly, and had dated her cousin Allison at the same time. I hadn't known they were cousins, since they didn't look alike and their last names were different. Lilly and Allison had tried to run me over with Allison's car, but luckily I had escaped unharmed.

I sighed as I looked at the seven girls in front of me—I didn't have time for this. I wondered which one of them had been the snitch. I realized that Mary had probably never been in any danger and I was annoyed that she had managed to fool me. I had fallen right into the trap. Did she even live here?

The floor above me had several closed doors behind the broken railing, and the ceiling was cracked in some sections. On the first floor, a pair of couches covered with a blanket of dust stood behind the girls. But besides that, the house was bare—there were no paintings, rugs, or other furniture.

"Hey, girls," I said with what I hoped was a charming smile. "A surprise seeing you all here."

"Hello, Orion." Rose smiled widely at me.

Mary stared at me curiously, her brilliant blue eyes shining with amusement. Maia fidgeted with the silver bracelet on her wrist. Aster stood with her arms crossed. She stared at the other girls as if waiting for them to strike first. My gaze then turned to Tay. I had broken up with her a while ago, but she was still as beautiful as ever. Her skin was dark gold, and her jewel-like eyes were bright like polished copper. Her catlike face held a fierce expression.

Next to her was Elena with her flowing white hair. Her skin was even lighter, and her eyes an electric purple. She'd grown a bit taller since we had broken up. Cela too was as pretty as she had been a year ago, with her shining silver eyes that made a dazzling contrast to her tanned skin and raven black hair.

"I know you girls must be angry at me," I said, my voice echoing inside the big room.

That's when I realized something was wrong—none of the girls seemed angry. They should have been furious, lunging at me and trying to tackle me to the floor. Or maybe trying to pull out my hair, kicking me places that had been out of limits before, or doing other sorts of things teenage girls could do. Instead, they all seemed happy—excited even. That made the hairs in my neck stand up. The girls looked at each other, as if they were communicating telepathically. Aster took a step forward.

"Just give us the key and we'll let you go," she said.

Rose, Tay, and Mary glared at her.

Aster shot me a warning glance. She extended her hand to me. "Give us the key, and leave."

"What key?" I asked.

Mary stepped forward. "The one that was on your kitchen counter."

I was surprised she had noticed it when she had peeked into my apartment.

"Oh, that old house key?" I crossed my arms. "I gave it to my foster mom."

"Hmmm," Rose said, her gaze sharp as daggers. "That's funny, because from what I know, your foster mom Zia is dead."

My chest caved in, as if my ribs had disintegrated. How would they know about that unless . . . ? Perseus had planned this. Anger swelled in my veins, threatening to make them burst. That boy was Machiavellian.

"Give us the key, Orion," Mary said, balling her fists. "Or we'll have to take it from you."

"We don't want to hurt you," Maia said.

I laughed. I hadn't meant to, but it just escaped from my mouth. Even though the girls outnumbered me seven to one, there wasn't much they could do to hurt me.

"I think I'll just let myself out," I said.

I was eager to disappoint Perseus when the girls returned to him empty-handed. I turned to leave, but just as I took a step towards the door, I slipped and fell flat on my face. Well, that was embarrassing. The girls snickered behind me. I pulled myself up, noticing the floor was unusually cold under my palms. The girls all smiled when I turned to look back at them. I glanced down and realized why the floor had felt so cold. There was a thin, nearly invisible layer of ice covering the floor. It was shiny, reflecting the light filtering through the glass ceiling above us. Had that been there all along?

"Did you really think we'd just let you walk away?" Elena asked with a smile that stretched though her cheeks.

I tried to turn away, but my feet didn't move. I glanced down again. Ice had crept up from the floor and encased my shoes. "What the—?"

Aster extended her hand again. "Give us the key."

"No."

I jumped out of my shoes and raced towards the door. My forehead burst with pain as I crashed against an invisible wall. I crumpled down, but quickly got back to my feet. The door had been blocked by another, nearly invisible sheet of ice. Where was it coming from?

My bare feet began to burn as I stood over the ice. Without glancing back at the girls, I made a run for the door on the far-right corner. A column of ice rose before me, and even though I tried to stop myself, my feet slid over the ice and I crashed sideways against the column. I tumbled to the floor, then hurried back to my feet. My right shoulder felt like . . . well, like I had crashed against a solid column of ice.

The girls hadn't moved.

Aster extended her hand, but Rose pulled it back down. "We gave him his chance," Rose said. "Now it's time to have some fun."

Whatever *fun* she intended I guessed it wouldn't be fun for me. The door I had come through was completely covered, and the one I had run to was partially blocked by a column of ice. I wondered if I could slide through the narrow gap that was left but didn't feel very confident about it. That left the stairs going to the upper floor as my only escape. There were two stairways, one at each of my sides. The stairs on the left were at the opposite side of the room, facing towards me. The stairs on the right, above the door I had used to get inside the room, were facing the other side. The stairs on the left seemed to be a faster exit, but I would have to get through the girls.

Elena extended her hands at either side. Two spikes of ice rose from the floor and reached just below her palms. "If we trap him inside a block of ice, then he'll be easier to take."

"He would be heavy to take," Maia pointed out.

"And he would be hard to hide," Rose said.

"He would also not enjoy being inside a block of ice," I said.

Hadn't I seen a movie, several years ago, about a white-haired girl who could control ice? She had used it to save her kingdom, or possibly her sister, or maybe both? This all seemed like a really bad spinoff. I was guessing that I was the bad guy of the story, since I was the cheater. I knew cheating on my girlfriends hadn't been a very honorable action, but in general I wasn't a very honorable person so I didn't think it mattered.

"Weren't we just taking the key?" Aster asked.

Rose's gaze ate me up hungrily. "No. I want all of him."

A day ago, I would have loved hearing her say that. Now that seemed like a terrible idea. Elena shot her arms forward. I lunged for the partially blocked door and hid behind the column of ice covering it. When I turned around, another giant block of ice stood where I had been seconds before. How were the girls doing that?

I emptied my lungs and wiggled through the narrow gap between the door frame and the ice as the girls shouted at each other behind me. I quickly closed the door and was relieved when my feet stepped over wood instead of ice. The new room had a window right across from me, and another closed door on the left. The door behind me rattled. My bare feet propelled me towards the other door. I swung it open and immediately closed it behind me. Some rags dangled from a rope above an old clothes washer on the side, and a ladder next to the washer led to the second floor. I hurried towards it and climbed quickly. The room at the top had a dirty mattress and some blankets spread around the room like Halloween ghosts.

Opposite the ladder was an open door that led to a hallway. I spotted the railing at the other end of the corridor but couldn't see the atrium below. Footsteps echoed in the hallway, but before I could even move Mary and Maia came in. Behind me, Rose climbed from the ladder and stood in front of it. Ice spread around Rose's feet, but it never touched her shoes.

Mary swung her arms forward and a giant white ball smashed against my chest. I fell backwards, crashing onto the floor. I gasped for breath as snow scattered around me. White ice gathered at my sides. Before I could move away, the ice rolled over both of my arms, pinning them to the floor. Cold seeped into my bones as it penetrated my jacket. More ice spread over my thighs, leaving me mostly immobile.

Rose, Maia, and Mary stood over me.

"Well," Mary said. "I was glad to see that if I'd really been in trouble, you would have helped me." She looked at the other two girls. "I think he may actually care about us."

"Of course I care about you!" I said.

Rose leaned down and sat on my stomach. I grunted. "What?" Rose asked. "You never complain about me sitting on you."

My cheeks burned with rage as the other two girls snickered.

Rose leaned forward. "Just tell us where the key is."

"He might have it with him," Maia said.

"And if not, we can search his apartment," Mary said.

"I want to search him first," Rose said as she smiled. She leaned down to whisper in my ear. "I'll search every inch of your body if I have to."

"I'm afraid you might be disappointed with what you discover," I said.

Rose pulled back. "I don't think I will be." She held my face between cold hands. My chest contracted painfully, as if Rose had frozen my heart. It wasn't the first time any of my girlfriends had touched my face that way—they had done it frequently. But the helplessness I felt in that moment pulled me to the times when I had felt utterly powerless with Zia. Something inside of me broke loose. I felt as if I had snapped out of a dream. A surge of strength flooded through my veins. I screamed in rage, startling Rose.

The ice holding down my legs and arms cracked and exploded in pieces as I shot to my feet. Rose fell to the side. Maia and Mary stepped back. Before they could react, I raced towards the door and into the hallway. The room below was empty as I ran through the corridor. I wouldn't risk going to the lower floor and finding the other girls there. I headed for the window at the end of the hallway instead.

Sizzling, white-purple light crashed into the ceiling above me, making pieces of wood rain down. I covered my head with my hands and risked a glance below. Purple electricity sizzled in Elena's hands and arms.

I kept running towards the window, shielded my face with my arms, and threw myself against it. The window shattered with the impact. Everything seemed to slow down. The sun had started to rise above the horizon. The sky had cleared and was now bright blue, dotted with puffy white clouds that looked like cotton balls. A few daring blades of yellow grass rose above the white blanket that covered the backyard.

I bent my knees before landing on my feet twenty yards away from the house. Snow shot up around me. A jarring pain bolted up my legs and my bare feet burned from the snow. I needed to get to my motorcycle. I turned just as Elena, Tay, Aster, and Cela came out of the house.

Cela turned to look up at the broken window. "Holy cow. Did you really just jump out a window?"

Tay spread her hands to her sides. The snow from the ground swirled around her like it was being sucked by two small tornadoes in her palms. It occurred to me that if the girls could somehow manipulate snow and ice, going outside to a backyard coated in snow had probably not been a good idea. The two small whirlwinds coming from Tay's hands continued to pull in all the snow around the girls. I needed to get around the house and jump on that motorcycle ASAP. That was assuming, of course, that the girls hadn't trapped my motorcycle inside a block of ice. My feet were already numb, and my legs tingled with pain.

"You should have just given us the key," Aster said with a sigh.

I was about to lurch into a sprint when one of the walls exploded and the biggest bull I had ever seen came out of the house.

CHAPTER 5

I HAD SEEN MANY BULLS in my life, at a few farms and in the general countryside. They had always looked cute to me, like overgrown cows with big horns and shaggy fur.

This bull was a different breed. Its white fur seemed brighter than the snow around it. Its chest was so broad it could have stopped a moving car just by puffing it out. Its massive muscles indicated a ridiculous amount of strength, and the golden horns created a crescent moon crowning his head. I was sure, without anyone telling me, that the Bull was a Star Child.

I had no intention whatsoever of becoming acquainted with the Bull, as fun as he seemed to be. The girls had all turned to look at the Bull in surprise. I took that as my cue. I shot forward, towards the right, edging around the house and running through the front lawn. My feet had gone numb but somehow they still worked. My motorcycle, thank the stupid Stars, had not been turned into a giant popsicle.

I jumped on the motorcycle, started the motor, and sped away. A powerful *MOOOO* erupted behind me. I turned around just as the white bull ran into the street. And even worse—Rose was riding the Bull. The Bull mooed again. Fire erupted from its nose. I rode even faster. I was sure Draco wouldn't be happy that there was another fire-breathing monster in town.

At the end of the long street, I swerved sharply to the left, making the wheels whine in complaint. I wanted to whine with them, but there was no time for that now. The Bull turned too and kept chasing after me. It was roughly thirty feet behind me, and he didn't seem to be tiring.

In retrospect, nearly getting run over by a car had been much better than getting run over by a flaming bull. Why were all my girlfriends maniacs? How could they control ice and snow? How had Elena thrown electricity at me? My first thought was that the girls might be Star Children too, but the only female Constellations were Andromeda, Virgo, and Cassiopeia. Wasn't the Bull a Constellation too? The zodiac sign Taurus?

I hadn't been looking at my surroundings until a scream pulled me out of my thoughts. A woman who had been crossing the street jumped out of my way, dropping a grocery bag with apples and bananas. I rushed past her and turned to look behind me again. The white bull was just rounding the corner as more people screamed and fled. I swerved to the right, riding between two cars. A few seconds later more screams erupted behind me.

I wasn't sure what the people of New York City would make of this—a girl riding a bull chasing a guy on a motorcycle. Maybe they would think we were all part of a circus? Their opinion wasn't important, but I did assume that someone would call the police.

I kept riding between the cars as fast as I could. How had the girls managed to plan all of this without me noticing? I had never sensed them in the same place together, had I? I would definitely have remembered if I did. I didn't track any of them as much as I tracked Andromeda, but I always knew the places they routinely visited. I had the feeling that Perseus was behind this, and that he could have hidden their locations from me.

My leg grazed a taxi and I nearly knocked down its side mirror with my elbow, but I leaned to the other side just in time. I needed to lose the Bull quickly. I didn't want the girls to follow me where the key led.

The light in front of me turned red, but I didn't care. I raced past the other cars and turned left. A black car nearly crashed against me, but stopped just a few feet away. It blared its horn at me. The Bull mooed behind me, and I turned as it tore through the sidewalk.

Sirens began to blare somewhere in the distance. The police wouldn't take long to find us. I wondered if they would just go after the Bull, or if they would come after me too. At the end of the street I turned left, then kept straight. I glanced behind me but didn't see the Bull among the cars. I didn't want to push my luck. I turned onto a long, empty alley.

A *MOOO* exploded behind me, making me startle and lose my balance for a second. The Bull raced forward, nearly catching up to me in a few seconds. My heart seemed to beat out of my chest. Flames shot out of the Bull's nose and a wave of scorching heat blasted me. The back wheel caught fire, the flames almost licking my feet and slowing me down. I couldn't see Rose behind the Bull's head but knew she was there. The Bull's eyes were two pools of black ink as he glared at me. He lunged forward and his head hit the motorcycle, leaving me right in between its horns.

The Bull turned his head to the side, and his horns twisted the motorcycle violently to the left.

I was shot off the motorcycle. Pain wrapped around me and black stars danced in my vision. Sirens blared somewhere in the distance; a few seconds later, the sound died down as the black stars pulled me into them.

●———————●———————●

The Roman Colosseum stood behind me, bathed in the red light from the blood moon. The sky was pitch black, as if it had drowned every single star.

Orion.

Her whisper echoed around me, making me turn away from the ruins. The Colosseum was surrounded by dozens of ambulances, but they were all silent and their lights turned off. Where had everyone gone? The ambulances had been full of wounded civilians, but there was no trace of them or of the dead bodies that had been left on the sidewalk. There was no emergency personnel either, and I couldn't hear any of the police cars that had been driving around the city.

I walked closer to one of the ambulances. The back door had been left open, and I took a peek inside. A body covered in a white sheet lay on top of a metal table. I stepped into the ambulance and inched closer to the body. Red dots stained the blanket. They rapidly began widening into large bloodstains. I hesitantly gripped the edge of the blanket, then pulled down.

There was nothing.

"You could have saved her." Arianna said. I whirled around. She stood beyond the ambulance door, hovering over the ground.

Her eyes shone blue on her pale face. *"If only you would have taken my Darkness, you could have saved her from Perseus."*

I turned back to the metal table. Andromeda lay there, lifeless.

"No!" I screamed.

My fingers went to her neck, but she had no pulse. Her skin was cold, her eyes staring at me blankly.

I shook my head. "No," I said. "She's still alive."

"You left her to die," Arianna whispered. Tendrils of Darkness curled around me.

"No, I never left her!"

The Darkness wrapped around me, and Andromeda's body vanished from my view.

I was walking home during the night, trying to stay under the light of the streetlamps. Smoke from a cigarette drifted in my direction, but I couldn't tell where it was coming from. Tall buildings stood around me, their windows dark. No cars had been left parked on the sides of the streets, and no one else walked on the sidewalk. Where was I?

I tried to use my power to sense my apartment and head in that direction, but my scars didn't even itch. My heart lurched, and I stopped abruptly. Why wasn't my power working?

"Because you didn't take my Darkness," Arianna whispered.

I knew she was standing right behind me—I could feel her cold breath on my neck. I closed my eyes.

"Orion," she whispered. *"My handsome boy."*

My eyes flew open as I turned. Zia stood in front of me. The knife still stuck out from her chest, and blood streamed from the wound like rivers. Zia's eyes were milky white.

"The Darkness has always been inside your heart. It's only a matter of time before it consumes you." She opened her mouth to scream, but only Darkness tore out of her like a beast.

•————•————•

I startled awake. Metal clanked. I groaned as I tried to move my arms, but a jolt of pain traveled from my wrists to my shoulder. It took a few seconds for my blurry vision to adjust. The metal clanked again as I realized my wrists were chained above my head and the two chains were attached to the ceiling. I stretched my legs in front of me as my head pounded with a sharp ache. The small square room was dimly lit, the only light coming from a very narrow window at the top of the left wall. A closed door lay in front of me.

A shiver ran down my spine, and I realized I was shirtless. I looked down at my torso in confusion, discovering some bruises on my ribcage, and a couple of cuts on my left arm. Where were my shirt and coat? And who would have chains stuck to the ceiling in their basement? My scars sizzled with electricity—the inflatable Santa Claus I had unloaded from Andrew Wood's car was one floor above me and a few yards to the left. I clenched my jaw hard.

I was in Perseus's house.

I muttered a curse under my breath. He must have known I was dating Rose and had used her against me before I could make my move. He had used *all* of my other girlfriends against me. The question was: Did Rose know the truth about who Perseus was? A day ago, I would have assumed that she didn't. But Rose, and all the other girls, had been able to control ice and snow. They were involved with the Star Children somehow.

I pulled at the chains above me with all the strength I had, but they didn't budge. My heart went into a sprint when I didn't feel the key in my jean pocket anymore. My scars lit up. The key was a couple of floors above me. I shouted another curse. Perseus had played me well. I would make sure to return that favor. I pulled the chains downward again, grunting, but only managed to make my wrists throb painfully. I pulled on them once more to stand up, but as soon as I did my feet flared with pain. I fell back on my butt and stared at the soles of my feet. They were swollen red and had a couple of blisters.

I took a few deep breaths and closed my eyes, letting my arms hang limply above me. My scars burned with electricity. Andromeda was still in Switzerland. I exhaled with relief. I would keep Perseus away from her at all costs.

Footsteps echoed outside the door, and I opened my eyes again. The door slowly swung open, and my seven ex-girlfriends walked in and spread around me. From behind them, Perseus walked through the door and stood before all of them.

"Hello, Orion," Perseus said. He was exactly as I remembered him. His flaming red hair spread around his head like a lion's mane. Perseus was tall and athletic, but not nearly as strong as me. His black eyes were dark as his rotten soul. He wore black leather gloves that reached up to his elbows, which made him look even more sinister.

"Perseus," I said.

He motioned at the seven girls around him. "I assume you've already met my sisters, the—"

"Your *sisters?*" I shouted. I had known Rose was his sister, but what about the others?

Perseus smiled widely. "Yes. My Seven Sisters of the Pleiades."

Chapter XIII, Verse III

The curse of the White Queen shall follow the Hunter,
Into the depths of the Maze and the gardens in the Castle.
A mighty weapon to reclaim, or the curse to remain,
Only by blood shall the matter come undone.
A secret born from love and a sin created by envy,
Will chase the Hunter until the truth he has discovered.
No ashes will remain of the one who by many was once well loved.

CHAPTER 6

THE NAME MADE MY BRAIN itch. I had heard about the Pleiades before. It took me a couple of seconds to remember their myth. The Hunter Orion had fallen in love with the Seven Sisters and had chased them until they had escaped to the sky to live as stars. So they *were* related to the Star Children. I remembered Corvus had told me that only Constellations could materialize into Star Children, but now I knew that Stars could too—at least those seven Stars.

The irony hit me in the face like a slap, and I burst out laughing. Perseus regarded me suspiciously, as if I had lost my mind. I probably had. The funny thing was that, in the myth, Orion had hunted the Pleiades. But now, it was the Pleiades who had hunted *me*. Funny how life worked out. I stopped laughing, and Perseus looked at the girls with a confused frown.

"You played me from the beginning," I said. I began connecting the dots. "You knew Andromeda, Zia, and I were here as soon as we stepped in New York."

"We did," Perseus said. He turned to look at Elena. "And you made our jobs so much easier when you started dating Elena."

I sighed. Well, well, well. I was *boo boo* the fool and I had caused my own doom. My heart turned heavy in my chest. The girls had never dated me because they liked me; it had only been so they could spy on me. Somehow, that hurt more than all the injuries I had suffered that day, making my entire body throb with pain.

Perseus looked at the girls. "Could you bring him some food?" He turned to me. I was about to say that I would have rather starved to death, but my very treasonous stomach growled like a zombie cow.

"I'll get him some food," Aster said, walking out of the room.

Perseus looked at the other girls, who hadn't moved. "I want to talk to Orion. Alone."

One by one, the other six girls filed out, and the last one closed the door with a loud clank. Lucky for Perseus that I was chained, or I would have bashed his head on the floor until it exploded.

Perseus sat next to the door with his back against the wall, ten feet away from me. He was silent for a few seconds. "Is Andromeda all right?"

"You mean is Andromeda all right after you nearly killed her?" I said.

Perseus examined his gloved palms. "Is she all right?"

"I don't know," I said.

Perseus looked up then, as if trying to discern the lie on my face. Had he really expected Andromeda to come back to New York? Perseus looked down at the floor, his gaze landing on a tiny hole the shape of a spider.

"I do care about her," Perseus said, meeting my gaze with his black eyes.

I chuckled. How could Perseus spit out lies like that and expect me to believe them? He had a very macabre way of caring for people.

"Aside from the key, did you find anything else that could lead us to the secrets Zia hid?" Perseus asked.

"If you wanted to know more about Zia's secrets then maybe you should have asked her instead of killing her!" The words flew out of my mouth in a torrent. Fury boiled inside my veins as the memory of Zia's body flashed in my head—the white knife sticking out of her chest, her vacant stare. I tried to block that image as best as I could, my eyes focusing solely on Perseus.

"I *had* to kill her," Perseus said.

"Why?" I asked.

Perseus remained silent for a couple of seconds as he stared at me, his dark gaze intense. "You and Andromeda would never have been free as long as she lived."

I instinctively pulled down on the chains, making them rattle. I wasn't sure what Andromeda had told Perseus when they were together. Perseus must have at least known that Andromeda hated Zia, and that Zia had been violent sometimes.

"Just because Andromeda always felt like a prisoner doesn't mean that we actually were," I said.

"I did you a favor," he said.

I huffed.

"I know what she did to you."

"The scars aren't that bad," I admitted. "I could have probably avoided most of them, but I didn't keep my mouth shut."

Perseus shook his head slowly. "I'm not talking about the scars."

I felt like Perseus had landed a blow on my stomach. My lungs shrank inside my chest. "How would you—?" Zia must have said something that hinted at what she had done. Or had Perseus read something in the Prophecies?

"I don't blame you for defending Zia," Perseus said. "You and Andromeda have been abused psychologically, emotionally, and physically all of your lives. Those types of scars take a long time to heal."

I jumped to my feet and felt a sliver of satisfaction when Perseus instinctively pressed himself against the wall. My feet were screaming at me to sit back down, but I didn't care.

"Don't you dare talk to me about what I should think or feel towards Zia," I spat out.

Perseus's eyes were two bottomless lakes of pity. He stood up and glanced at the door. "The girls don't know about it," Perseus said. Was I supposed to thank him for that? Perseus exhaled, rubbing his hair. "I need your help, Orion."

"And you actually expect me to help you?" I almost laughed again.

I sat back down, my feet burning in pain, and let my arms hang above my head again.

"Do you know what I'm fighting for?" he asked.

"To destroy Fate, Destiny, and Prophecy," I said, remembering what I had learned after the fight in Palatine Hill. "And destroy all Order in the Universe."

When I said it out loud it sounded ridiculous. But Perseus was actually trying to achieve that.

"I'm trying to free us," Perseus said. "Why should we live in a world where our lives are guided by Destiny and Fate? Where the only thing that leads our future is Prophecy?" His eyes gleamed with passion—he truly believed his own delusions. "Right now, everyone is cursed to face a specific Destiny—even if it's horrible. There is no way to escape the future the Stars have chosen. And the Weavers ensure that you meet your Destiny through Fate." He paused. "Fates are the different paths that will lead you to your Destiny, so while there are a few different roads, they will all eventually lead you to the same place."

"I know that," I said, recalling my conversation with Virgo. "But as Star Children we don't have Fate or Destiny, only Prophecy, so why would you care?"

Perseus smiled. "We each have a few different Prophecies, true. But they're all horrible. Don't we deserve to live good lives too? I want to help you, and Andromeda. I want all of us to be free from the terrible Prophecies that will lead us to our inevitable deaths." He paused. "There will be Chaos, but Chaos is simply another word for probability, for randomness, for liberty to live as we choose."

I opened my mouth to respond, then shut it. I wasn't in the mood to argue with a madman and didn't care too much about his plans. I only wanted to kill him because I knew he intended to kill Andromeda. The rest of the mission seemed silly to me.

Perseus took a deep breath. "Zia was a lot older than you think." He was baiting me, trying to give me crumbs of information he knew I desperately wanted. Perseus leaned against the wall. "Most Star Children are older than us. The real mystery is why *we* are so young." Perseus flexed his left hand. "You, me, the Pleiades, Andromeda, Corvus, Virgo, Draco, and the Gemini Twins—we were all born around the same time." He paused, tracing circles on the floor with his foot. "Every other Star Child is centuries or millennia older." He turned back to me. "Zia lived a very long life, and she knew many ancient secrets that she took to the grave with her. Those are secrets we need."

He eyed me expectantly.

"I won't help you," I said.

"You will."

I huffed, which only made him smile. "Have you forgotten I have the Prophecies of every single Star Child?" His smile widened. "That I can predict what will happen? I used your Prophecies to make sure that you ended up here." I felt an electric chill sizzling down my spine. For the first time, fear settled inside my chest. "No matter what you do, in the end it will lead us all into the future I have planned for."

CHAPTER 7

I HELD ON TIGHTLY *to Zia's dead body. Night had already fallen, and the stars had begun to twinkle in the cloudless sky. Tears silently rolled down my cheeks as I kept my gaze focused on the ground. The damp blades of grass reflected the silver light of the moon.*

The Wolf let out a small growl, but I didn't dare look at it. The creature roamed around me, its eyes never leaving me. I could have escaped Perseus, but I knew I couldn't escape the paralyzing gaze from that beast. Even though I had shot the Wolf hours earlier, it hadn't affected it much. Perseus had simply bandaged its side, and now it was up and about. It would tear me to pieces if I made any menacing move.

I buried my fingers in Zia's cold hair as the blades of grass before me bent with a sudden gust of wind. Perseus had pulled the knife from Zia's body a while ago, and her blood had already dried around her chest. I hadn't bothered to wash the blood from my own hands, and my clothes were smeared with it too.

I had closed Zia's eyes earlier—they had been staring blankly at the sky—so she seemed to lie in a peaceful sleep. Her cheeks were pale in the moonlight, and her pale blonde hair looked almost white. My heart bled as more tears streamed from my cheeks.

Perseus shifted somewhere behind me but I didn't even bother to look at what he was doing. He hadn't spoken to me since I had woken up in the clearing after getting shot with the dart gun. I was glad about that—I would have knocked the teeth out of his face if he had tried.

Something stirred ahead of me, and the Wolf stopped walking, standing still at my side. The Wolf's fur, which was the color of a fierce storm, stirred with another sudden burst of wind. It took me a second to realize that there was no wind. But the trees still shook, and the blades of grass bent with an invisible force.

A pale face materialized in front of me, and I blinked in confusion. Then the rest of her body came into form, pulling itself out of the shadows. The tall woman wore a long black dress made of a starless night, and her skin was so pale it could have been carved out of a full moon. Her eyes were a brilliant blue, like two glittering jewels.

"Hello, Arianna," Perseus said behind me.

"You lost the girl," the woman said in a voice that was like a chant.

I turned around. Perseus held the ragged pieces of parchment in his hand. He met Arianna's gaze for only a second. "I'll get her back." Then he looked down again. I didn't know what could have been so interesting about those stupid pieces of parchment—Perseus had spent all day reading them and taking notes.

"Cassiopeia," the woman said.

I stumbled backwards as she slid closer to me. I looked at the ground and realized the woman had no feet. She was a living shadow. The woman's brilliant blue eyes focused on Zia, and I pulled her closer to me. The woman smiled, showing perfect white teeth.

"I met Cassiopeia long ago," she whispered. "I had a different form then—I was the Shadows that bred from the Night." She cocked her head to one side. "Now I have come as something different."

My numb mind couldn't process what she said. I was having a hard time accepting the truth of my new reality. Only an hour earlier I had seen the light pulsing from Perseus's stomach. He was like Andromeda and me—someone who bled light from their scars. I still didn't know what that meant, only that I lived in a world much stranger than I had thought before.

"Do you know what Zia means?" Arianna asked. "It means Light." I clutched Zia tighter, burying my head in her hair, ignoring the woman. "She controlled the Light. She manipulated it to create realities that were only illusions. That's why you never saw her for what she truly was, because she made you see only what she wished." Arianna began humming. "She had too much power. Great power that came without sacrifice, and in the end, it consumed her. Too much Light can blind, but she never understood that. She was never willing to give anything for all that she received." Her hum died down.

I looked up again, but the woman was gone. I heard Perseus walk up to me from behind, but didn't turn to look at him. He dropped something next to me—a shovel.

Hot tears slid down my cheeks again. I wiped them away and finally lay Zia on the ground. Her muscles had already gone stiff. I stood, my legs steadier than I expected them to be. I looked at Zia again, at the hair spread around her head like a halo. The large stain of blood on her shirt was black now.

I picked up the shovel and began digging. I didn't even feel the burn of my muscles, the strain of the effort. It was just a mechanical *task that my body could do without the help of my mind, so my thoughts just slipped away. Two feet, three feet. I knew bodies were usually buried six feet beneath the ground, so I kept digging. The rhythmic sound of the shovel piercing the ground soothed me somewhat.*

Before I knew it, I had already created a hole nearly as deep as I was tall. The smell of wet earth wafted into my nose with a sudden current of wind. I placed the shovel outside the grave, pulled myself back onto the ground, and walked over to Zia. I picked her up gently, her hair raining down from my arm. I slowly walked back to the grave, then jumped into it. I lay Zia on the ground, then pulled myself back up again.

I stood at the edge of the grave, looking down. The moon illuminated Zia's body in a silver glow. Her hair was purely white now, like threads of snow spread around her head. She also had wrinkles in her face like cracks cutting through porcelain. I would have liked to cremate Zia instead of burying her. That seemed more appropriate—I could have spread her ashes anywhere. I didn't like that she would be buried in a random forest in Greece, but this was the best I could give her.

I stepped to the side and filled the shovel with dirt. I hesitated before dropping the dirt into her grave. I wanted to say something to Zia, maybe "Goodbye," but no words came out of my mouth, as if I had lost my tongue. This wasn't a goodbye though. Zia must have left something behind in New York. She had been acting very strange for the last couple of weeks leading up to her disappearance. She had been hiding something from me—something related to all of this mess. I would find out whatever it was once I managed to escape Perseus and find Andromeda again. Yes, that seemed like a good plan.

I let the dirt drop into the grave, and it covered her feet. I took one last look at Zia's face, but the face staring back at me wasn't the one I had known. The Zia lying in the grave looked ancient, as if hundreds of years had caught up to her in a few minutes. This wasn't my Zia, I thought as I shoveled more dirt into the grave. The Zia I knew was back in New York—inside all of the hidden nooks and crooks of her apartment where I knew she hid weapons and files. My Zia was back there, waiting for me to hunt down the truth she hadn't had time to reveal to me.

I didn't look back at Zia as I let more dirt drop into the grave, slowly filling it up. It seemed like only a couple of minutes had passed before the grave was full again. My scars burned instinctively, and I winced. Zia was at the bottom of all of that dirt, and I knew that every time I tracked her, she would lead me to the same place.

I crumbled to my knees, as if they had suddenly turned to dust, and let the shovel drop right next to me. Shouldn't I have been feeling more pain? The woman I had known all of my life, who had taken care of me for so many years, was dead—murdered. But my heart was numb. Was there something wrong with me? I should have been crying more, feeling more. Maybe I would, sometime later. Once reality hit me in the face I would feel the full force of my emotions.

I took a deep breath. Zia was dead, but her secrets were alive and waiting for me—I wouldn't stop until I found them all.

•———•———•

Perseus left the room without sparing me another look. Fury boiled in my stomach so fiercely it made my gut twist painfully. I didn't know how much the Prophecies revealed about each of us, but they must have said enough about me for Perseus to maneuver my future. Maybe I did need to start believing in Prophecies. I clenched my teeth in frustration. The metal chains clanked as I unconsciously tried to pull my arms down.

I wondered why Perseus wanted to uncover Zia's secrets so desperately. But regardless of his reasons, I needed to keep her secrets away from him at any cost. If Perseus had been any smarter, he would have waited until I found something with the key before kidnapping me. But he hadn't. So I could still steal the key, find where it led, and then escape.

I instinctively tracked Andromeda again and felt a wave of relief when I sensed her at that lake again. She wasn't moving, and I pictured her sitting next to the water. At least one of us was having a nice day. I took a deep breath, my bruised ribcage aching. Maybe I could find Andromeda again after I escaped, even if I had promised her not to. If I was with her then I could better protect her from Perseus—she would surely understand why I had broken my promise.

I took another deep breath. First, I needed a plan to escape from Perseus. Then I could worry about the rest. The chains rattled above me as I shifted, trying to get into a more comfortable sitting position. My scars burned as I tried to track Rose, but only found a dark void instead. I balled my palms into fists. I tried tracking each of the seven girls, one by one, but they were gone, as if swallowed by a black hole. I had been right. Perseus could somehow block people from me. I tried a different approach and instead of tracking Rose I tried to track the golden heart necklace she always wore—but again, there was only a cold emptiness that greeted me instead. How was Perseus doing that? If the Pleiades were sisters, then they must have lived together, but I had never sensed them in the same place. It was as if Perseus could just wrap people with a veil of darkness and . . .

I knew Perseus was working with Arianna, the physical manifestation of Darkness. Could *she* be the one veiling people from me, and not Perseus? I had never been able to track Arianna. How does one track Darkness if it exists all around us? Arianna must have been the one behind this strange occurrence. Was that also the reason I was having trouble tracking Andromeda? It was as if she momentarily got wrapped up in that Darkness too but then resurfaced seconds later. But it was different with Andromeda—I never felt a void; it was more of a momentary glitch. I sighed. There were too many things I didn't know.

The door swung open. Aster walked in, then quickly closed the door behind her.

"I just wanted to check if you were all right," she said.

I huffed. "I'm doing great."

Our stares met for a second. Aster stepped closer to me, eying the chains above my head, then tracing through the bruises on my torso. Silence settled between us for a few moments.

"None of you ever cared about me, did you?" I asked. It was a stupid question, but I couldn't stop the words that tumbled out of my mouth.

"Does it matter?" Aster asked.

It shouldn't have mattered. Yet it did, for a reason I couldn't quite pin down.

"Did *you* care about any of us?" Aster asked. "I guess you wouldn't have tried to save Mary unless you did," she said slowly, almost as if speaking to herself. "I do care about you."

"Why?" I asked. "This was just Perseus's plot. And you knew I was cheating on you with your sisters."

"I don't know," Aster admitted. "I liked being with you, talking to you. I felt that you understood me." Our eyes met again, her dark stare like an open black wound. She opened her mouth to say something else, but just then the door burst open.

Maia, Mary, Elena, and Tay walked in. Tay handed Aster a bowl of steaming soup after shooting her a questioning glance, and Mary held a plate with meat and mashed potatoes. Once again, my treasonous stomach growled.

"Awww." Maia walked closer to me and kneeled down a few feet to my left. "Our boy is hungry."

I didn't trust myself to answer. Aster sat at my other side and plunged the spoon into the soup, then pulled it out and put it right next to my lips. I opened my mouth hesitantly, and she guided the spoon inside my mouth. The tomato soup tasted good, although I didn't say that out loud.

"Is Aster even your own name?" I asked her.

Aster nodded. "It's Asterope, but everyone calls me Aster."

I looked at the other girls, who sat in a semicircle in front of me.

"Maia is my real name."

"I'm not Mary," she admitted. "My real name is Merope."

"I'm Electra." Which explained the electricity in her hands.

"I liked Elena better," I said.

"Taygete."

Tay got to her knees and crawled around me to look at my back. I could feel her copper eyes tracing my scars. "So *that's* why you never took off your shirt."

Aster stared intently at the scars on my shoulders as she fed me the soup. I met gazes with Merope. She was the only one who had once seen my scars—during the day of course. She'd had an abusive father, or at least that's what she had made me believe. I had felt that I could trust her with the scars. My heart squeezed in pain.

"You could have hit her back," Electra said, pulling her white hair into a ponytail. "You're bigger and stronger than Cassiopeia. Why didn't you ever fight her?"

I didn't answer, and instead let Merope feed me the meat. I had asked myself the same thing many times. I could have hurt Zia, but I never had the heart for it. She had raised me as her own son, given me everything I had, taught me everything I knew—she had been abusive, but she had also been caring. I didn't think any of the girls would understand what I had been through.

I was halfway done with the meat when Rose and Cela walked in holding a tray of gingerbread cookies. Rose sat next to me, her eyes digging into my scars too.

"And what are your real names?" I asked her.

"Celaeno," she said as her silver eyes focused on the chains above my head.

"Alcyone."

"What?" I asked. "Where did Rose even come from?"

At least the other girls' names were similar to the real ones.

Alcyone shrugged. "I just liked Rose."

I took one last mouthful of meat and Merope fed me the mashed potatoes. Cela sat on the right, behind Aster, placing the tray on the floor. She picked a cookie with a bright red dress and ate it in one big bite. Rose, who was sitting a few feet in front of me, whispered something into Electra's ear as they stared at me. Both girls laughed.

"What's so funny?" Aster asked.

Rose and Electra shared a devious glance, then Rose nodded and looked at me.

"We were just wondering, Orion." Rose smiled, her eyes gleaming. "Which one of us is the best kisser?"

Electra burst out laughing, and all the other girls turned to look at me.

"I don't think that's something you want to know, Rose," I said.

Maia raised a brow, pushing her red hair out of her face. Her moss-green eyes trained on me. "I would like to know that too."

"We'll feed you all of these cookies if you tell us," Cela motioned at the tray.

"Maybe you just need a reminder," Rose said. She leaned closer and pressed her lips hard against mine. I tried moving away, but her hands on my face held me firm in place.

"Ohhh," one of the other girls said, then laughed.

I abruptly pulled back. "Stop that!" My tone was a lot sharper than I had intended, but it made Rose immediately step back, and the other girls stopped laughing.

They criticized Zia but they were no better than she was.

Perseus entered the room again. He eyed Rose as she sat at my side.

"Pack your things," Perseus said. "We leave tonight."

My stomach twisted. What if Perseus wanted to use me as a bait again to lure Andromeda to him? He must have wanted to kill Andromeda before his next rising so she couldn't stop him. I couldn't let that happen. I needed to find a way to escape, fast, and I needed to figure out how to kill Perseus.

Rose stood up, and the other girls did the same. They began exiting the room.

"If you have to know," I said, "Aster is the best kisser."

Aster swung around, staring at me incredulously. Electra huffed, and Rose's jaw hung open. I smiled widely, chuckling. Perseus looked petrified, as if he had just realized that if I had dated all of his sisters, then that probably meant I had kissed them all. His face turned as red as his hair, and it gave me an odd sense of satisfaction to see him like that. He had kissed Andromeda—I was sure of that. It seemed fair that I kissed his sisters. After a few seconds, Aster finally smiled shyly at me, then Merope pulled her out of the room.

Before stepping out of the room, Maia looked at the chains hanging from the ceiling, then at me. "You better not try to escape," she warned.

"Or what?" I asked challengingly.

Maia pulled something out of her back pocket and threw it at me. The small object hit me in the chest before clattering on the floor. It was dental floss.

"Ha-ha, very funny," I said.

She smiled wickedly at me, then left the room. Perseus closed the door after all the girls had exited, eying the dental floss suspiciously. Then he looked at the abandoned tray of ginger cookies to my right, but wisely didn't try feeding me one.

"Where are you taking me?" I asked, although I didn't expect him to respond.

Perseus smiled. "You'll see soon enough. We'll need your help with what comes next."

I chuckled. "I already told you. No matter what you do to me, I'll never help you."

Perseus looked at me with something like sadness in his eyes. "I know you hate me, Orion."

"That's an understatement."

"But I don't," Perseus leaned against the wall. "I really don't hate you." He paused. "Algol is out of my control," Perseus said. He cocked his head to one side. "I don't think it ever *was* in my control. The reason I planned to sacrifice Andromeda in Palatine Hill was because her blood was the only thing powerful enough to free me from Algol." At the mention of Andromeda my heart went into a race. "If I had killed Andromeda and spilled her blood, then Ara, the altar, would have granted me any wish I wanted—and I would have destroyed Algol myself."

"But you didn't kill her," I said.

Perseus shook his head. "I couldn't." He looked down at me with his black eyes. "Algol is Prophesized to kill every single Star Child in the end," he whispered. "Unless I destroy Destiny, Prophecy, and Fate, I'll end up killing everyone I love."

I wasn't sure if Perseus was telling the truth. He could have been lying to convince me to help him, but the anguish on his face seemed authentic. So he was either a great actor, or he was being honest.

Either way, Perseus would end up killing all of us—unless Andromeda killed him first. He didn't have to destroy everything, and could have just sacrificed himself for the people he loved if he really cared about them. What he really wanted was to have the power of the future in his hands. I could see it in the gleam of his eyes whenever he talked about the Prophecies. He said he wanted to escape them, but he reveled in being the only one who could manipulate our futures.

Perseus leaned forward. "We don't deserve to experience the Prophecies that have been written for us. I've read yours too and your end won't be pretty either, even if I don't kill you."

I remained silent.

"I *will* destroy Fate, Destiny, and Prophecy. I will set us free and allow us to choose our endings. And I will protect the ones I love, no matter the cost." Perseus clenched his jaw, his eyes two swirling ponds of dark madness. "I don't want to hurt you, Orion, but I won't let you get in my way."

Perseus turned around and left the room, slamming the door shut.

The room grew darker, as if a cloud had passed over the sun. Perseus truly was mad. There was no such thing as absolute freedom—that led only to Chaos. It was like living in a city with no laws. Physics, chemistry, biology—nature itself had laws that couldn't be violated unless the Universe fell into destruction. Not that I cared too much about science or theology, but logically his plan made no sense. Perseus would doom us all.

Unless Andromeda killed him. The chains rattled as I let my arms fall limply above me. What if the Prophecies were real, and I couldn't kill Perseus? Was Andromeda truly the only one who could? I didn't like that. Not a single bit. I wanted Andromeda as far away from Perseus as possible. If she tried to kill him, then he would try to kill her too. There had to be a way to destroy Perseus that didn't involve Andromeda.

I took another deep breath as the shadows around me stretched longer with the fading light. I stood up, ignoring my aching feet, and looked up at the chains. Andromeda would have been able to unlock them in seconds. I didn't have her power, so I would have to rely on my strength. I jumped and held each of the chains with a hand, my feet dangling in the air. My ribs felt as if they were stabbing into my lungs, but I ignored the pain. My arms strained a bit, but I was used to supporting my own weight. I placed my hands about midway through the chain link. Then I pulled down with all the strength I had. Nothing happened. I needed more force. I gripped the chains tighter and took a deep breath. I pulled myself up with a surge of strength, my head coming up dangerously close to the ceiling for a second, then I let myself drop, pulling down at the chains with as much force as I could muster.

I was surprised when my feet painfully hit the floor and metal clanged loudly around me. I stood in silence for a second, then looked up. *Ha!* I had broken the links, and now two shorter chains dangled from the ceiling, clanking with each other. I still had the manacles around my wrists, and a small chain dangling from each of them, but I could worry about that later.

I needed to get out of the house *pronto.*

I hurried to the right, kneeled down, and pushed three gingerbread cookies into my mouth—they were deliciously crunchy—then walked to the door. I didn't have any weapons, but I guessed that the manacles and small chains would serve. I wrapped the chains around my knuckles, then opened the door and bolted out of the room. I stopped dead on my tracks when I heard the gagging. I turned to the side.

Corvus sat tied to a chair with tape covering his mouth.

Chapter VII, Verse I

The Silver Circle spins into many shapes,
A Crown made of tall Spires, and a Castle that encircles her head.
Once inhabited by the Generation of Old,
Then only ghosts shall roam in its halls.
When one is imprisoned in its bed,
Poisoned dreams and cruel nightmares will take shape,
To fill the space that was once full of faith.

CHAPTER 8

CORVUS GAGGED LOUDLY as he squirmed in the chair.
I rushed to his side and pulled the tape from his mouth, then
quickly began untying his hands and feet.

"He'll be back soon," Corvus whispered.

"How did you get here?" Maybe I should have been keeping
better track of Corvus, Draco, and Virgo.

"Perseus kidnapped me a couple of weeks after you left," Corvus
whispered, which sounded like an accusation. I had initially planned
to stay with Corvus and his friends to help them fight Perseus, but
after Andromeda had left, I hadn't found the motivation to go back
to them. Guilt snaked through me but I pushed it away.

I finished untying Corvus, but he remained sitting. He looked
back at the room I had come out of, then at the manacles on my
hands, then at my bare chest. "I saw them dragging you here but
couldn't do anything while I was gagged."

I remembered that whenever Corvus told a lie, people
believed him. I guessed that the first thing Perseus had done when
finding Corvus was gag him to suppress his power.

Corvus stood, then stretched his back with a groan. He was
sickly thin, as if he hadn't been fed in two weeks. Maybe he hadn't.

His brown skin seemed tinted grey, and his dark eyes had sunken into his face. He'd shaved his short beard, and his black hair was shorter than I remembered.

I scanned the room around us. The cement walls seemed solid enough that I wouldn't be able to break through them. There was nothing I could use as a weapon. Old furniture and other random objects lay strewn around the room—a couple of dusty couches, a few chairs, an abandoned teddy bear with a red bow on its neck. The bear had a thick layer of dust on its head that looked like white hair.

"We have to get out of here," Corvus whispered, his eyes wide.

"Wait," I said. "Did you see Perseus or the girls with a key?"

Corvus shook his head.

"I won't leave without that key. We can't let Perseus have it."

"Why?" Corvus asked as his eyes settled on the door at the far end of the room, which I assumed led out of here.

"It was Zia's," I said. "It's important."

Corvus looked at me for a second, then nodded. "I can lie to the girls to give us the key." He looked at my bare chest and then down at my feet. "I could also ask them for a shirt and pair of shoes."

"That would be great," I agreed.

Just then the door opened and Rose walked in. Her eyes widened and she opened her mouth.

"You want to keep quiet," Corvus said.

Rose's mouth snapped shut. Her gaze took on a dreamy expression.

"You want to quickly bring us the key you stole from Orion, a shirt, a pair of socks and shoes for him, and a coat for each of us.

If anyone asks, you're dressing us up before we leave." His voice didn't falter, and Rose simply nodded. "Oh, and bring us a key to free Orion from his manacles."

Rose nodded again and walked out. I had seen Corvus use his lies a few times before and knew they were effective, but my heart still hammered against my chest with dread. Would Rose wake up from the lie? Would Perseus realize that anything was wrong with her? Corvus took a couple of deep breaths, as if he had forced himself to run a race.

"So what's the plan now?" he asked.

"We need to contact your friends," I said. The two of us wouldn't be strong enough against Perseus, the girls, the Bull, the Wolf, and the Horse.

"Do you know where they are?" Corvus asked. "I haven't seen them since Perseus took me."

My inner compass spun. "They're in the middle of the Atlantic. Huh. Maybe they're in a boat? They seem to be heading here."

Corvus's hands trembled slightly. The poor boy must have had a terrible time here. Why had Perseus taken Corvus? And why hadn't his friends already come to save him? They knew Perseus lived in New York—they had tried to kill him in a park the same day Andromeda had. It seemed strange that they would be sailing to America only now.

Rose came back after a few painful minutes. She dropped the shoes, shirt, and two coats at Corvus's feet, then pulled out two keys. I immediately took Zia's key and pocketed it. Rose used the other, smaller key to free me from the metal manacles and chains. I dressed quickly while Corvus put on his coat.

"You want to help us escape without anyone else noticing," Corvus lied. "You will draw the others away from here while Orion and I escape through the front door. Then you will forget we had this conversation."

Rose simply nodded.

"Now," Corvus said.

Rose began to walk out of the room, and we followed her. We slowly climbed the stairs. Muffled voices and laughs echoed above me as we neared the door at the top. Corvus and I stayed on the steps while Rose walked into the hallway. I couldn't make out what she was saying to the others, and a few seconds later the voices faded in the distance.

Corvus motioned to me and I pushed the door open. We stepped into a long hallway that stretched to both of our sides. The smell of gingerbread cookies hung heavily in the air and seemed to come from an open door on the left. Corvus and I silently rushed down the opposite side and arrived at the main entrance. The railings from all seven floors above me were full of Christmas decorations—wreaths, colorful lights, Santas, reindeers, stockings, bells, and snowflakes dangled from the railing, making it look like Christmas was spilling from each floor. Corvus opened the door and we both stepped outside, into the frigid night. I was thankful Corvus had asked Rose for those coats. Corvus silently closed the door behind me. The giant inflatable Santa glowed brightly on the front lawn, swaying with the cold breeze.

"We should run," Corvus suggested.

I didn't need any further encouragement. I sprinted forward, my feet slipping dangerously on the snow-covered ground.

Corvus rushed behind me, and I remembered he probably wasn't going to be as fast as me so I slowed down. The snow crunched under my feet as we hurried forward. I risked a glance back but the house was silent. The giant inflatable Santa Claus watched us go with a brilliant smile. His right hand was frozen above his head waving us goodbye. Corvus and I turned into another street and I lost sight of Santa. We raced through a few empty streets until we found a young man opening the door of his blue car.

"Hey," Corvus shouted. The man turned to look at us as we approached him. He had small eyes behind his rectangular glasses, a long beard, and shaggy brown hair that poured out of his red beanie hat. "You want to give us your car. You can take a taxi back home."

The man eyed us with a lost expression, as if he had strayed into a daydream. "Yeah, I want to give you my car."

"We'll give it back soon," I said. "We'll leave it . . . somewhere."

The man nodded.

"You want to give us the car keys," Corvus said.

The young man pulled them out of his pocket and handed them to Corvus, who in turn gave them to me.

"I don't know how to drive," Corvus said.

I took the keys from him and we climbed into the car. I started the engine and sped away, leaving the young man standing on the sidewalk. He was still watching us with that dreamy expression as I swerved to the right and lost sight of him. Even at eleven at night, there was a bit of traffic on several streets, and I expected it would take us about half an hour to reach our destination. My scars burned as my internal GPS guided me to the lock that matched the key.

"Thank you," Corvus said after several minutes of driving.

"Thank *you*," I said. "It would have been hard to escape without you."

Corvus didn't smile, his expression somber. I didn't remember him being so serious. I wondered what Perseus had done to him these last couple of weeks.

"How did Perseus kidnap you?" I asked, curious.

I knew Virgo, Draco, Sirius, Aquila, Leo, and even Maera wouldn't have let Perseus take Corvus without a fight.

Corvus sighed. "You missed a lot."

"I can see that," I said as we stopped at a red light.

Corvus stifled a yawn. I glanced behind me to make sure we weren't being followed, but I couldn't spot Perseus or any of the girls in the cars behind us. The traffic light turned green and I drove forward. I had been stupid to let Perseus fool me with the girls, but he wouldn't fool me again.

●————————●————————●

I wasn't sure why, but a nagging feeling deep inside me told me that something was wrong with Andromeda.

I had immediately stepped into the car, which Zia had gifted me, and driven to Andromeda's location. She'd escaped from her foster home, but Zia didn't seem to know that—yet—or else she would have already told me. Andromeda wasn't in her "secret lair" either, where she now liked to spend most of her time. I had gone to visit it a couple of times while she wasn't there. It was just an old warehouse with an empty room Andromeda had appropriated.

I stopped at a red light. Rain splattered on the windshield as the wipers furiously cleared it away. Something nudged at me, dreadful. Andromeda simply felt wrong.

I sped forward as the light turned green, following my inner compass. Andromeda was in a building under construction where she had met with Zia a few weeks ago, after I had found her in the forest and taken her back.

I'd had to cancel my date with Rose to go check on Andromeda, which made me furious. Couldn't I enjoy myself for a little while without having to worry about Andromeda? I had rented a very nice cabin for the weekend on the outskirts of the city. Rose had said that she couldn't stay for the entire weekend because her parents probably wouldn't give her permission. But still, we would have hung out for a while and then I'd have a nice little cabin for myself away from Andromeda and Zia.

Cars honked angrily at me when I made a sharp swerve into the right lane—I ignored them. I arrived at the building a few minutes later, parking on the side. Raindrops pounded on me as soon as I stepped out of the car, drumming loudly as they hit my head. The building before me was dark, and it still had a construction fence around it. I walked to the fence—a lock lay on the muddy ground. The front door had been left wide open too. I shook my head in desperation. Was this another attempt from Andromeda to get arrested and go to juvenile jail? Probably.

I stepped into the building and let my scars burn as I sauntered up the stairs to the fourth floor. Lightning flashes, entering through narrow windows, illuminated my way as I climbed up the stairs. I followed the trail of open doors until I made my way into a bedroom inside an empty apartment.

Lightning flared through the large window, and thunder reverberated through my bones a second later. Fury burned inside me as I walked into the next open door, then stopped cold before walking in. My mind seemed to fragment my vision into pieces. A bloody knife lay under the sink. Blood flowed from Andromeda's wrists and onto the white floor. Andromeda's eyes were closed. A disfigured red puddle lay around her.

I acted on pure instinct, feeling detached, as if someone else was moving my body and I was just watching. I took off my raincoat, then pulled off my shirt. I grabbed the bloodied knife and tore my shirt into a long, thin strip. Both of her wrists were bleeding in a steady flow, but there was no pulsatile bleeding, which meant that Andromeda hadn't severed any arteries. She hadn't cut deep enough. I bandaged the piece of cloth tightly over Andromeda's right wrist, then bandaged her left wrist after tearing my shirt into another strip. I checked her pulse, which was probably the first thing I should have done. It was steady, if a bit slow.

I wrapped Andromeda with my raincoat and hauled her up into my arms. I rushed out of the apartment, down the stairs, and was out in the rain again. Cold drops splattered against my bare skin like tiny prickles of a needle. I placed Andromeda in the passenger's seat and then climbed into the car, soaking wet. I started the engine and drove off. I needed to take Andromeda to—

I definitely couldn't take her to Zia, and I didn't want to take her to the hospital. If the hospital saw her scars glowing for any reason . . . Even if they didn't, they would want to know how I had found her. That would cause trouble. No, I could take care of Andromeda on my own. I glanced at her bandaged wrists, which lay limp on her lap. Blood had already begun soaking through.

I was barely aware of driving onto the highway and realized I had instinctively headed for the cabin I had rented. If I went back to my apartment Zia would find us there after getting a call from Andromeda's foster parents that she hadn't returned. We would come back eventually, but I would make sure that Andromeda recovered a bit before we did. The cabin was probably the best place we could go to, even though it was an hour away. Would Andromeda last that long? I looked back at the bandages, which were stained red but not dripping. That was good; the blood flow had slowed down. A larger stain soaked through the bandage on her left wrist, probably because she had slashed that one first. I was unsure if I needed to make a tourniquet above her wrists, maybe below the elbow, or if I should just leave the strips of shirt tied as they were. I glanced at her chest and let out a relieved sigh when it moved with each slow breath.

I drove absently, only alert enough to avoid crashing but focusing mostly on Andromeda. After some time, the blood darkened, showing it had dried a little, and it never dripped down from her wrists. The rain had stopped, but some drops still clung stubbornly to the windshield and the windows.

I arrived at the cabin and parked the car at the front. I grabbed the first aid kit from the trunk, and carried Andromeda inside. I lay her on the bed and untied her left wrist first. Blood swelled from her wounds, but it had started to scab. I sprayed alcohol on the wound. Andromeda stirred, jerking her head and legs, but didn't wake up. I probably should have disinfected the wound as soon as I could, but hadn't thought of that. I cleaned the wound with a sterile gauze, then bandaged her wrist again. I did the same with the right wrist, then just sat there.

It was already dark outside, but I didn't move. Andromeda breathed deeply, and I let myself breathe out too. I needed a new shirt, and I should probably put some logs in the fireplace to make the room warm. But I didn't want to stand up—I didn't want to be more than a yard away from Andromeda. I held her limp hand, her skin cold and clammy. I forced myself to pull away and walk to the fireplace. It already had some logs there. I rushed out to grab my things from the car and quickly went back inside. I lit a fire. The flame was weak and frail at first, but eventually it spread over the logs.

I walked back to the bed to check on Andromeda. She was still breathing, and the bandages had a small dark stain. I grabbed a new shirt from my backpack and put it on, then settled on a chair next to the bed. Exhaustion crawled through me, but I stayed awake even though my eyes stung with pain. I could sleep later, once Andromeda awoke.

Why had she hurt herself? I would have to ask her when she awoke because I couldn't think of any logical answer. Fury blazed inside of my heart. She had almost killed herself and left me. That thought sent a nauseating wave of panic through me. I had to take a few deep breaths to avoid vomiting my lunch.

I closed my eyes. Had she even thought about me? Had she considered the pain that this would cause me? I wasn't the one with slit wrists, but the pain that flared inside my chest was like a stabbing blade. She probably hadn't thought about any of that—Andromeda just cared about herself. She only focused on her own "suffering" and had never noticed everything I had done to keep her safe. I opened my eyes again and took a deep breath as I stared at the wooden beams in the ceiling. I couldn't hang that on her. I had made my choice, and that was not something I could blame her for. I had tried so hard to keep her safe from Zia, but had failed to keep Andromeda safe from herself.

I rubbed my forehead, closing my eyes. What could I do to prevent this from happening again? Maybe I could spend more time with Andromeda, something I hadn't done since we had been sent into foster care. I could take her out for lunch sometimes so she wouldn't feel like I had abandoned her. Andromeda had said that she wanted to be able to spend more time alone when she escaped. Maybe I could let her roam free for longer before I brought her back to Zia? But how would I know she wouldn't hurt herself if she was alone? I couldn't watch her day and night.

Frustration tore my heart apart. I gently pushed Andromeda's hair away from her face. Her chest rose and fell. I placed my hand on her cheek. Her skin had started to warm up. The flames bathed Andromeda's pale face in a gentle glow. I leaned down and kissed her on the forehead. What would I do if Andromeda was gone? I couldn't even bring myself to think about that.

I checked her wrists again and was happy to see there wasn't much blood. I would find a way. I wouldn't let Andromeda die—I wouldn't let her abandon me. I looked back at her sleeping face as I let out another sigh. She couldn't glare at me when asleep. She couldn't hate me, or shout at me, or run from me.

I stood from the chair and pulled the blankets down, under Andromeda, then gently covered her up to her chin. I wished I could look at her eyes, even if she only glared back at me. I didn't care how much she hated me, as long as she was safe. I leaned forward again and pressed another soft kiss to her warm forehead.

I wouldn't let her leave me. Ever.

CHAPTER 9

A TALL BUILDING loomed before us. A huge FOR SALE banner hung above the entrance. Trash littered the steps leading up to the main door. I spotted empty glass bottles, plastic wrappings, and even a rotting bagel.

The cars parked on the street behind us had a thin layer of snow on top of them. We had parked the stolen car in an alley a few blocks away in case Perseus decided to track us down.

Silence hung in the air like thick fog.

My heartbeat pulsed faster as my inner compass spun—the lock that matched the key was inside that building, somewhere on the first floor. Corvus and I made our way up the steps and towards the main entrance. The glass door had metal bars crossing before it in a diamond pattern. I really wished Andromeda were here—I had always relied on her to open locks.

"Can you sense if anyone is inside?" Corvus whispered.

I shook my head. "That's not how my power works. I can only track people I have seen."

Corvus nodded. I thought I had already explained that the first time we had met but maybe he had forgotten. I inched closer to the metal door to peer through the glass, but it was so dirty that I couldn't make out anything inside.

"We could try a back door," Corvus suggested. "The building seems abandoned so I don't think it will matter if we break in."

I nodded. We walked down the steps and rounded the building, entering a narrow alleyway. I didn't spot any back doors, but a window had been left ajar on the fourth floor. Corvus followed my gaze.

"I'll get in through the window and see if I can open a door or one of these first-floor windows for you to climb in," I said.

"Sounds like a plan," Corvus said.

I exhaled, white mist swirling out of my mouth like smoke. I carefully stepped on the ledge of the first-floor window. I took a deep breath, bent my knees, and jumped up. I extended my hands upwards and barely gripped the edge of the window above me. Both of my legs dangled in the air, and my muscles strained. A pounding pain flared through my ribs as they reminded me they had been bruised recently. The snow on the ledge started melting under my fingers, and my hands numbed. I pulled myself up and placed my feet on the ledge. It bent slightly under my weight as I stood again. I climbed the same way to the third floor, and then finally to the fourth.

Corvus had his head pulled back to look at me. He gave me a thumbs up and I returned it. I didn't think Perseus would know where to find us, but it still made me uneasy to leave Corvus down there. With his lies, though, he was probably better prepared than I was to face Perseus and the girls.

I peeked inside the window. The sink right below it was infested with dark moss, and so was the toilet across the room. To the left hung a shower curtain that looked like it had been ripped apart by a very angry cat. I tried pushing the window to open wider, but it didn't budge. I didn't want to break the glass—it would make too much noise.

I took a deep breath, then pushed the window with my shoulder. It screeched loudly as it swung inside. Once I had opened it all the way, I jumped over the sink and landed on the floor. Dust rose around me like a cloud and I covered my face with my sleeve, coughing.

I walked out the door and came into an empty room with a large population of dust bunnies. The opaque windows had slashes of paint like scratches on a wall, and large holes dotted the ceiling above me. I stepped over a few rumpled blankets as I made my way to the front door. It didn't budge with my first push, so I had to use my shoulder to ram it open and step into the hallway. The closed door before me had small cracks under the peephole. An elevator and curling staircase stood at each of my sides. Dim light came from a window next to the stairs.

Before I could walk to the stairs a hiss shot through the room. My heart thundered inside my ears when something moved at the corner of my eye. The snake that had been lying still next to the door slowly slid towards me. I took a step towards the stairs, and the black snake hissed louder in warning.

I didn't have time to deal with snakes, so I kicked it away. The snake hissed again as it flew in the air and hit the door in front of me. I rushed down the stairs before it could recover and hoped it wouldn't follow me.

My heart rate sped up as I sensed I was approaching the lock. But first I needed to get Corvus. At the bottom floor I was greeted by a double door with a chain around the two handles. My heart galloped wildly. *There,* my inner compass told me.

Two hallways stretched out on either side. I walked through the left corridor until I came across a door that had been left open and I stepped into the room. Several cardboard boxes arranged in piles still lay pressed against the walls. I made my way to the window, removed the latch, and pushed it open. The cold winter air howled into the room. Corvus stood a few feet to the right. He had been looking to his left, eying the alley carefully, but as soon as I opened the window his head snapped to me.

"That was fast," he said.

Corvus quickly climbed through the window and coughed as he stepped into the dusty room. We made our way back to the double doors, where I broke the handles and pushed my way inside.

The spacious new room stretched two stories up. Chairs and circular tables had been pushed to the sides. A long window at the top of the wall on the opposite side illuminated our surroundings with dim light, and right below it stood three rows of small, square lockers. I walked towards them and pulled out the key from my pocket.

"Do you need help?" Corvus asked.

I shook my head as my scars burned. I walked to the left until I felt a surge of adrenaline shoot through me. I crouched down and my eyes settled on the same number as the key: 749.

I inserted the key, my heart pounding like a giant drum, then swung the locker open. A satchel waited inside. I pulled it out, my hands numb. My throat dried up as I opened the satchel and grabbed the first thing I saw—a white carved knife. The handle was smooth and cold to my touch.

Corvus kneeled next to me, holding a small flashlight. "Found it in the corner. I'm not sure if it works."

He turned it on and the white light blinked unsteadily. I kneeled too and set down the satchel. I pulled out a folder and opened it to reveal a stack of pictures. Corvus flashed the light over the images. My heart twisted. The first picture showed me and Andromeda. We were very young, probably younger than ten, standing in the middle of a field. Andromeda and I were still the same height. She smiled at the camera, showing a missing front tooth. Her black hair was tied in a ponytail, and her blue eyes were the same color as the sky above us. I smiled too, a bit awkwardly, as if I wasn't sure how to do it. I turned the picture; the date read *April 9th*. It didn't specify the year, but I felt sure it had been soon after Zia had found us. She had also written both of our names below: *Andromeda & Orion*. I couldn't remember taking that picture and wondered why Zia had kept it. She had never wanted to leave any trace of our existence, so it surprised me that she had left this behind.

I looked at the next picture, which was in black and white. The paper felt thicker too. It showed Zia and another man from the shoulders up, standing before a bare wall. Zia still looked to be in her early thirties. Her expression was somber as she stared at the camera, her hair tied in a braid at her side. The man with dark hair and full beard stood a head taller and had one hand on her shoulder. I couldn't make out the exact color of his clear eyes. He had high cheekbones, a straight nose, and a big forehead. I turned the picture: *Cassiopeia and Cepheus*. My blood turned to ice when I read the date below the names: *June 12, 1889*.

Chapter XLIV, Verse III

The secret of the Forgotten One he took to his grave,
Until the Liar his memories once again regained.
A final stand the King will make after his death,
Against the one whom he chased until the end.
His last moments will be spent in grief and sorrow,
Knowing he couldn't save the young one he so dearly loved.
The secret of the Shadows shall never again be discovered.

CHAPTER 10

"WHAT IN THE STARS?" Corvus asked. His brows drew in together as he leaned closer to the picture.

Zia is a lot older than you think. How had Perseus known that? I stared at the date again, then turned the picture to look at Zia. The man next to her, Cepheus, was another Star Child—I recognized that name from the Constellations, but Zia had never mentioned him. Anger stained in my cheeks red. Andromeda and I had been Zia's children, we had lived with her most of our lives, yet we seemed to be the ones who knew the least about her.

"Have you seen him before?" I asked.

Corvus shook his head. "No, but in mythology Cepheus was Cassiopeia's husband and Andromeda's father."

Corvus carefully began arranging the other pictures in rows over the floor, but I didn't take my eyes away from Cepheus. My scars burned intensely as I tracked him. I had sensed him before, I realized with a start. A bit over a year ago, Zia had drawn a sketch of Cepheus and asked me to locate him, but she had never revealed his name. It wasn't uncommon for Zia to draw sketches and ask me to track those people down, so I hadn't thought him important.

I had found Cepheus in London—dead. I could tell he was dead because he didn't move an inch during the days Zia had asked me to confirm whether he was still alive. He had been near the British Museum, close to where I sensed him now. Maybe Zia had moved his body after she had flown to London to find him, which is why I sensed him somewhere different now. She'd never mentioned the man again.

I looked at the picture again. Cepheus's arm rested comfortably on her shoulder—they had been a couple. I had no proof of that but also no doubts. That meant that at some point before Zia had found Andromeda and me, they had separated. Then Zia had decided to contact him again a year ago, but it had been too late.

Another thought struck me—Star Children could only be killed with very specific weapons or by another Star Child, unless we were drowned, burned, or choked to death. It seemed likely that Cepheus had been killed by a Star Child. Could it have been Perseus? If he had been capable of killing Zia, then I didn't doubt he had killed Cepheus too. But I couldn't rule out the possibility that it might have been someone else.

I was only sure of one thing—Zia and Cepheus had shared many secrets, secrets that Perseus was now desperate to find. Strength surged within me—I had a new target. I just had to make sure Perseus didn't follow me.

"Orion," Corvus whispered.

I followed the flickering light as Corvus guided it over the pictures he had neatly arranged next to us. A lot of them showed me and Andromeda. The pictures had probably been taken the first couple of months we were with Zia. It still surprised me that she had kept pictures of us when she had been insistent that pictures were prohibited, and she had never let us own any. I counted a total of five pictures of Andromeda and me, including the first one I had seen.

One showed us at the beach next to the ocean. Neither Andromeda nor I faced the camera. I was frozen just as I jumped over a wave that hit Andromeda's side. Another picture showed us standing outside with bright red raincoats. I was gazing up at the sky while Andromeda stared at a puddle at her feet that blurrily reflected a brightly lit building on the side. In another picture Andromeda and I lay on the snow face up and smiling. The last picture showed us in a pool, with only our heads poking out of the water. The pictures specified the day and month, but never the year. I still couldn't recall any of those memories. It had been so long ago, almost in another life, when Zia had loved us and we had felt loved.

I kept following the light as it passed over other pictures. One picture in black and white had been ripped in half and taped back together. It showed Zia standing on the docks next to the ocean. Her back was to the camera as she looked up at a cargo ship with dozens of boxes stacked on top of it. White bobs of clouds dotted the sky. *Argo and Cassiopeia, December 21, 1901.*

In a full-color picture Cepheus sat behind Zia on a horse, holding her waist tightly. Cepheus wore a coat and Zia a cream-colored dress with long sleeves. My eyes fixed on Cepheus's left hand, which rested on Zia's leg—he had a wedding ring. I immediately looked at Zia's left hand as she held one of the reigns—she wore a matching ring. The light from the flashlight extinguished for three seconds, plunging the picture into darkness, then turned on again, blinking madly. *March 3, 1920. Equuleus, Cassiopeia, and Cepheus.* They had been married for decades, maybe longer. Had he left her? Had she left him?

Corvus pointed the flashlight to the next picture with a rip at the edge. Cepheus sat on a dark wooden chair, the background behind him blurry. He held a pure golden crown. *Cepheus and Corona Australis, 1931.*

One of the last pictures showed Zia kneeling next to a pool, her hand patting a dolphin's head. *Cassiopeia and Delphinus, 1967.*

The next picture showed Perseus. He looked nearly the same as he was now. The picture could have been taken anywhere in New York. Perseus was walking past a store, looking at a mannequin with a bright yellow dress. He seemed completely unaware of the camera right in front of him. I had already figured Zia had moved to New York to be closer to Perseus, but now I had evidence that she had been tracking him.

I turned to the last picture. The left side was damaged, as if water had been spilled over the picture, but I could still make out a pair of male twins who looked around nineteen. They wore dark sunglasses, which reminded me of Draco. One of them had long hair tied in a braid, and the other had short hair. Their long faces ended in pointed chins. They stood on a dock in front of a large white yacht. *The Gemini Twins and Argo.* The yacht behind them looked nothing like the cargo boat in the earlier pictures. Maybe it was another Argo?

"They're all Star Children," Corvus said. "But why would Zia keep pictures of them?"

I shrugged. These pictures gave me new leads to follow. I put them back in the folder and placed them inside the satchel again.

I opened zippers and pockets to see what else I could find. I was sure Zia hadn't gone through so much trouble just to hide some pictures and a knife. After some searching, I found a piece of cloth inside a smaller side pocket. I grabbed it, feeling something solid wrapped inside of it. I quickly unwrapped the cloth from the object. My head pounded with pain as I looked at it, and Corvus let out a groan—it was a ragged piece of black metal that reflected the light too brightly. My head kept pounding until I wrapped the metal inside the cloth again. Corvus squeezed his eyes shut and grunted, letting the flashlight fall to the floor.

"Are you okay?" I asked.

Corvus didn't answer. His breaths quickened, and his hands began to shake. I quickly picked up the flashlight and aimed the light at his eyes. His pupils were too dilated. I wasn't a doctor but I knew that was not a good sign. His eyes rolled back and he collapsed to the side. I let the flashlight drop and caught him by the arms before his head hit the floor. Corvus's head hung backwards. I placed him down gently on his side. I felt for his pulse on his neck—it was steady and strong.

Had the metal done something to Corvus? It had made my head throb with pain, although I wasn't sure how a metal could do that. Was it emitting radiation?

I took a deep breath. I would have to carry Corvus out of the building and back to the car. We needed to get out here and hide for a bit before I came up with a plan to kill Perseus. The satchel hadn't exactly given me the answers I had hoped for to destroy Perseus, but maybe searching for some of these other Star Children would give me those answers. Zia had left these pictures for a reason—she had wanted me to track them down. My scars burned as I tracked Cepheus's dead body back to London. I would start with him.

I pulled the satchel's strap over my head and let it rest across my shoulder. I was about to carry Corvus when my scars burned. I bolted to my feet and spun, facing the door. A young man blocked the entrance. The snake I had kicked earlier stood at his side.

The flickering flashlight was pointing the other way, but the light from the streetlamps coming through the high windows was enough to see the man. He seemed older than me, around twenty-five. His curly black hair reached just above his ears. His tanned skin made a sharp contrast to his brilliant grey eyes. He had high cheekbones, a straight nose, thin lips, and thick eyebrows. He had a slender physique and was a head shorter than me. The man wore a long black coat and snow boots.

He walked forward, stopping ten feet in front of me. He might have not been strong or tall but the look in his grey eyes was dangerous, like a twisting snake waiting to strike me. The young man eyed the satchel carefully, then he looked straight into my eyes. "I knew someone would eventually come pick that up." His voice was deeper than I would have imagined. "You have thirty seconds to give me that satchel," he said.

"You have ten seconds to step out of my way." I balled my fists, my muscles tensing.

The snake hissed, sliding forward. Its skin expanded to the sides right below its head, like a cape flowing behind it. The snake's belly turned light brown, and its back became lighter with white stripes like rings encircling its body. The snake hissed again, its black tongue waving dangerously at me. I took a step back, standing protectively in front of Corvus.

A smile crept up the man's lips.

More hisses echoed around me as dozens of snakes slithered out from underneath the old tables and chairs. They slowly slid over the floor, and I could feel their gazes on me. I risked a glance behind me. Corvus didn't look like he would wake up any time soon. I stood still, trying to figure out my options. The snakes continued to advance, and I took another step backwards, my shoes grazing Corvus's arm. The man stared at me intently with that devious half-smile. I really wished Corvus was awake.

"Ten, nine, eight," the man began.

I gripped my satchel tighter.

"Seven, six, five."

I pulled the satchel over my head and held it with both hands—it would probably be a good shield.

"Four, three, two."

A snake on my left lunged forward, aiming at my chest. I batted it away with the satchel and it landed somewhere behind the man. Another snake slid at me from the right and I kicked it away. I hit another snake with the satchel as it flew at me.

Sharp pain stabbed my right calf. I let out a scream and crumpled to my knees, my breath getting caught in my throat. The rest of the snakes backed away as I fell to the side, my muscles cramping painfully. I let out another ragged breath as I rolled to the side and lay face up. The young man stood right above me, looking down. He pulled a little vial with clear liquid from his coat.

"The bite from a king cobra will kill you in less than five minutes unless you drink this antidote." He shook the vial lightly. "That means you have only a few minutes to tell me exactly who you are and how you found that satchel."

CHAPTER 11

THE PAIN STABBED ME like jagged daggers digging into my flesh. I began to shake violently, and my vision swam with agony.

"Come on," the young man said as he continued to stand above me. His grey eyes held as much warmth as a glacier. He kneeled at my side and pulled the satchel from my grip. My numb fingers curled painfully into my palm. Sweat trickled down my back and brow. The young man held the vial with clear liquid a foot above my head. "Most people can't bear the pain of the venom for more than ten seconds. You're determined—I admire that."

I knew the venom would kill me—the snake must have been a Star Child too. How else would it have been able to change shape? That meant the man must also be one of the Star Children, but I couldn't guess which one. I gasped for breath as the pain continued to squeeze the life out of me—I didn't have enough air in my lungs even to scream. The man was calm as he continued to stare at me, his snakes hissing somewhere behind him. To my side, Corvus still lay unconscious, and thankfully the snakes hadn't touched him. The pain spread to my groin and stomach, and searing agony burned my bones to ash.

"Orion," I gasped.

The young man raised a dark brow. "How did you find the satchel?"

"I . . . found the key . . . in my apartment." I could barely force the words out as my lungs shrank inside of me. My heartbeat slowed despite the wild panic running loose inside of me. Spots danced in my vision. The man pulled his hair back with one hand. His curls were so twisted they could have been made of tiny snakes.

"Cassiopeia . . . she had the key . . . before," I couldn't say anything else as a sharp pain erupted in my heart, as if it had been ripped out of my ribcage. I would have clutched my chest if I could move my arms.

A bitter tase washed over my mouth before I realized the man had forced the antidote down my throat. My heart stopped for five beats as I lay immobile—then it began hammering rapidly against my chest. Air rushed into my lungs and I took a deep breath as the man searched through the satchel. He pulled out the folder and carefully looked at each of the pictures. His gaze darted to me at one point and he analyzed my face, then he became absorbed by the pictures again for a good five minutes. He put them back inside the folder once he was done. My body remained numb, as if I had anesthesia running through my veins instead of blood. The man pulled out the white carved knife and eyed it for a few seconds, then pocketed it in his coat. Lastly, he pulled out the strange metal that was wrapped in the cloth.

As soon as he looked at it his eyes opened wide, like two full moons at midnight. I couldn't tell if he was surprised, or excited, or scared—it could have been all of those at once. He looked at the metal as if it were the most precious piece of gold he had ever held. Carefully, as if dealing with a bomb, he wrapped the strange metal with the cloth again and pocketed it too.

Then his gaze fell on me again. There was a strange glint in his eyes, something the rest of his face hid carefully behind a neutral expression. Madness. As if he was a scientist who had just made a world-changing discovery. His gaze became drunk, almost intoxicated, detached from reality and living in a wild dream.

The young man left the satchel a few feet from my head. Then he pulled out a bandage from his coat and walked over to my leg. He pulled up my jeans and bandaged my leg tightly. Once he was done, he crouched at my side. He pulled out another small vial and placed it on top of the satchel.

"Drink this in a couple of hours, when you're able to stand." His voice was steady and deep. "You'll have a headache that will last for a day, a bit of fever, and you may have convulsions. Try to wash the bite twice a day with clean water but don't use alcohol. Drink a lot of water and don't worry if you vomit and feel nauseous, that's normal unless you vomit blood." He paused. "You should be back to normal in a couple of days."

"Who . . . are . . . you?" I forced those words out of my numb lips.

The man eyed me carefully as he stood again. "My name is Ophiuchus."

His footsteps echoed inside the room as he walked away from me.

"How did you . . . find me?" I asked.

He didn't respond.

I couldn't move my head to see him walk out of the door; my gaze fixed on the metal lights hanging from the ceiling. I wondered if the snakes had left too. I couldn't hear them any longer.

I exhaled slowly. Had the man known Zia? How had he known she had hidden something here if I had only found out about this place the day before?

I remained lying on the cold, hard floor, waiting to recover from the venom. Seconds stretched out into eternity. Needles stabbed at my body—a pain similar to when my leg or foot went numb and I tried walking again. Rivers of sweat trickled from my skin, but I shivered with the cold. My vision blurred and I closed my eyes, which made the pain a bit more bearable.

Who was Ophiuchus? His name was strange enough to belong to the Constellations, although I didn't remember that Constellation specifically. He hadn't been interested in the pictures, and the knife had probably been an extra prize for him to take—Ophiuchus had wanted that strange metal. I had been right—that metal was important. And I had lost it less than five minutes after I had found it. I couldn't even ball my fists in frustration. Zia had gone through a lot of trouble to hide it, and this man had almost killed me to get it. Is that what Perseus had been after? It didn't matter much, because neither he nor I had it now. I was sure the man wasn't with Perseus, or else Perseus himself would have shown up here.

I opened my eyes again and stared at the dark ceiling. I noticed a red heart-shaped balloon hanging limply from one of the lights. The flashlight finally extinguished—I had forgotten it was still on. The room was plunged into a deeper darkness, broken only by the dim light from outside.

Corvus breathed slowly next to me, and I wondered how long it would take for him to wake up again. Slowly, I began to gain mobility in my body. I moved my head to the sides, trying to look for any trace of those snakes. The tables and chairs stood just as they had before—immobile and without a trace of any reptiles. I breathed deeply, my lungs straining.

After a few more minutes I began to move my fingers, my hands, then my toes and feet. It was a painfully slow process. I needed to find that man again. What if the metal *was* the key to destroying Perseus? I clenched my teeth in frustration.

I tried tracking Ophiuchus, but my scars didn't even burn—the poison had numbed my power. A new wave of panic swept through me. I couldn't sense Andromeda and didn't know if she was safe. Nausea swam up my throat and I had to force myself to take deep breaths. I didn't want to die choking on my own vomit. Andromeda would be all right—there was no way Perseus or the girls could have gotten to her if they had all been here a few hours ago. I closed my eyes again, focusing on the rhythmic pounce of my heartbeat. Every breath I took became easier, and although I was still numb, the pain lessened.

At some point, Corvus groaned. I opened my eyes again as he sat up. He rubbed his eyes, then blinked a couple of times. It took him a few more seconds to realize I lay right next to him.

"Orion!" Concern washed over his features as he hovered anxiously above me. By that time, I could move my legs somewhat, but it took me much effort to do it, and I didn't want to waste my energy. "What happened?" Corvus asked as he looked me up and down, as if trying to find a bleeding wound.

Slowly, as fast as my lungs would let me, I told Corvus about Ophiuchus and how he had attacked me. Corvus remained silent as I talked, his face pale and his eyes wide in fear.

"I don't think we've ever met Ophiuchus," Corvus said after I was finished. "And I don't know anyone who has met him either."

I sighed, but I wasn't surprised to hear that. Zia had managed to hide from other Star Children during my entire life. I assumed other Star Children would have their own reasons to remain hidden.

"What happened to *you*?" I asked.

"I . . ." Corvus was so pale I worried he would faint again. "I remembered something . . ."

"What did you remember?" I asked.

"It doesn't matter," he said cuttingly, which startled me a little. Corvus looked around the room as if trying to find the snakes that had been here earlier. "We should leave."

I opened and closed my hands, then tried to pull myself into a sitting position. The pain in my back was so excruciating that I couldn't raise myself more than an inch. "I can't move," I whispered.

Corvus began breathing faster, and I worried he was having a panic attack. His eyes were wide with terror as he looked at the door, as if a giant snake would slither inside the room and swallow us both. His breath calmed after a few seconds and he muttered something under his breath.

"We'll have to wait then," he said.

I didn't like that option, but Corvus wasn't strong enough in his current state to drag me all the way to the car. Even if he did, he didn't know how to drive, and I didn't think tonight would be the ideal time for him to learn.

"What should we do next?" Corvus asked.

"We need to go after Ophiuchus," I said.

I needed that metal to figure out how I could use it to destroy Perseus. It had made my head throb and had made Corvus pass out. Maybe stabbing Perseus with it would kill him.

"What about Cepheus?" Corvus asked.

"What about him?" I asked.

"If he was married to Zia then she could have left something at his grave," Corvus said. "So you want to find him first."

Corvus was right. Tracking down Cepheus could reveal secrets about his past with Zia. Those secrets could be the key to destroying Perseus.

"Yeah." I breathed out, my lungs contracting painfully. "I need a map of England so I know exactly where we can find him."

Corvus nodded. "There should still be people walking around New York at night," he said. "I could convince someone to give us their phones and we can do a quick search."

"Sounds like a plan," I said.

After some time, I regained more mobility, and Corvus helped me sit up, then stand again. My body felt weak, and I was still sweating despite the cold. Corvus handed me the vial Ophiuchus had left and I drank it. I wasn't sure if a few hours had already passed but I would rather drink it now than wait for another catastrophic encounter where I might lose the vial. The taste of the liquid was so bitter I nearly spat it out, but forced myself to swallow it.

Corvus grabbed the satchel and helped me make my way back to the window. Climbing out the window felt a lot harder than it had been before, as if I had to climb down a cliff. My body was so numb it didn't even react to the freezing cold out-side. I leaned on Corvus for support as the ground beneath me swayed. He was more than a head shorter than me, so he made a very convenient crutch. I walked for about ten steps before I doubled over and vomited. It didn't worry me much, since the serpent guy had warned me it would happen. I was glad when I didn't spot any blood in the vomit, only some green from the frosting of the gingerbread cookies I had eaten earlier. Corvus managed to pull me up again, and we slowly made our way back to the car.

It occurred to me that if Perseus wanted to attack me, now would have been the perfect time. In my current state, I couldn't have even batted away a fly. The buildings around me shifted up and down, the snowy sidewalk and road rippling like the surface of a dirty ocean. I closed my eyes. The blackness was somehow better, more comforting.

"We're here," Corvus said. I opened my eyes again. The sto-len car was in front of us. Corvus looked at me with a pale expres-sion. "Are you sure you can drive?"

"Yeah," I said.

I opened the door and got into the driver's seat. Corvus climbed in next to me. I sat in the car for a couple of seconds. My power still felt numb, so I couldn't track anything. My heart shrank inside of me—I had never been without my power before. It was like walking blindly. I held on to the wheel to prevent my hands from shaking. My power would come back when the venom faded. Everything would be all right.

I shook my head and willed myself to focus on our plan. We needed to find someone with a phone. I clicked the GPS icon and looked at the streets around me. I moved the map until I saw Richman Park a few blocks away. Corvus gripped his seatbelt tightly when I started the engine. I slowly drove out of the alley and onto the street, accidentally knocking a trashcan somewhere behind us. I drove a lot slower than normal, but I just wanted to be safe. The streetlights at my sides were unusually bright, so I squinted my eyes.

"Orion!" Corvus yelled.

I instinctively stepped on the pedal to go faster. "What?"

"You just ran a red light!"

I hadn't even seen it. I slowed down again as we continued forward, and hoped the police didn't track us down. I made a right turn. The road ahead of me twisted left and right, so I maneuvered to the sides to follow it.

"Why are you driving in a zigzag?" Corvus asked in an alarmed tone.

"I'm not."

I tried to keep the wheel steady as I continued forward. A car honked behind me, then sped past. Corvus gripped his seatbelt even tighter, although I wasn't sure why he was so worried. Taking everything into account, I was driving just fine. I did see the next red light and stopped. In front of me, the streetlight bent forward, twisting. I blinked a couple of times and the streetlamp went still.

"It's green now," Corvus said, and I stepped on the pedal again.

At least my arms and hands didn't hurt anymore, but my legs began to tingle as if someone were tickling them. I giggled, and Corvus pressed himself so hard against his seat I worried he might knock it backwards. The tickling climbed up to my butt and I accidentally stepped on the pedal. The car surged forward for a few seconds until I slowed down again. I continued driving with Corvus letting me know of any red lights or stop signs until we arrived at our destination. I parked the car in an empty spot and turned off the engine.

"Is there any particular reason we're at a park?" Corvus asked.

"There's always people in parks at night," I said.

Corvus didn't seem excited. I opened the door and tried to step out of the car but something dug into my flesh. I groaned, then realized I had forgotten to take off my seatbelt. I unbuckled it and finally got out of the car. Corvus stepped out the other door and together we walked into the park.

A couple of teenagers sat on the stairs that led up a small hill, kissing. I walked over to them, Corvus hesitantly following after me.

"Hellooo," I said as I stopped a few feet in front of them.

The teenagers broke apart and stared at me wide-eyed. The girl's blonde hair had been dyed blue at the tips. Her large eyes blinked rapidly as she looked at me. The boy had short black hair and a crooked nose that had swollen red and purple. He stood up, his hands balled into fists. "What do you want?" Before I could even answer, he lunged at me. I pushed him backwards with ease, and he landed on his side a few feet in front of me.

"André!" The girl shouted as she rushed to his side.

I turned to Corvus. He looked at both teens. "You want to give us your phones," he said.

The expression of both young teenagers turned blank. The girl fished into her pocket and pulled out a phone.

"You want to unlock the phone and give it to us," Corvus said.

The girl did as Corvus instructed and handed him the phone. Corvus gave it to me in turn. I looked for the maps app and clicked on it. I dragged my finger to the UK and then zoomed in on London. Before my body had gone numb, I had sensed exactly where Cepheus was, so I didn't need to use my power again. After finding the British Museum on the map it didn't take me long to find where Cepheus's body was—Kensal Green Cemetery.

Cepheus hadn't been there when I had tracked him a year ago. I would have remembered the cemetery. That meant Zia had buried him there, and I knew that she must have left something behind with him.

I smiled. Now I knew where I was going for Christmas. There was nothing better to do to celebrate the holidays than digging up a dead guy from a cemetery. I was sure that was illegal, so I would have to do it carefully, which just added to my macabre holiday spirit.

I gave the phone back to the girl, and Corvus and I walked back to the car. I put my seatbelt back on and started the engine.

"So Cepheus is buried at Kensal Green Cemetery," Corvus said.

"Yep," I said. "I think we should—"

"You want to drive to Central Park," Corvus said.

What a great idea. That was my favorite park in the city. I looked at the map and began driving southwards. I hadn't been to Central Park in a while, and I had never visited it at night. Excitement warmed my chest. The park must look beautiful at night, and even more so with the snow.

I was feeling a bit more awake than before, but the streets still blurred around me. We arrived at Central Park a while later and walked for a bit. The snow looked beautiful on the bare trees and shrubs, as if they had wrapped themselves in a thick white coat.

"You want to lie down to sleep for a while." Corvus said. Another fantastic idea. I was so tired, and the venom had left me so weak. The grass seemed so inviting, with clumps of snow everywhere like fluffy pillows. I kneeled down and lay on my side with my head in my hands.

"You just want to sleep."

My eyelids closed at his command, and sleep immediately overtook me.

Chapter L, Verse I

The Crab remains hidden inside the Ship,
Abandoned when the King and Queen broke their promise.
A witness the Crab will become to the true horrors the Lion escaped from.
Alone and forgotten the Crab prefers to remain,
Until by the Twins it is discovered again.
Many secrets it will keep away from the tombs of those put to death,
Only out of spite it will fight the Prince in the Night.

CHAPTER 12

I DROVE FULL SPEED on the highway, a thrill of adrenaline coursing through my veins. The dark trees on the sides blurred past me like fleeing shadows. The headlights broke through the empty lane like two bright lasers.

I welcomed the burn of my scars as I sensed Andromeda nearby. She had escaped to Wyantenock State Forest in Connecticut. I had no idea how she had gotten there.

She had only lasted a month in her new foster home, which made me furious. Couldn't she have stayed there for a little longer? Every single time she escaped she knew I would bring her back, but she still ran away. Defiance was just in her nature. I had left her alone for a week, until Zia had asked me to bring her back. Andromeda had spent that week in random motels as she moved northwards, and only today had reached the state forest.

I dreaded taking her back to Zia. Andromeda would suffer a beating, and Zia would lie and say she had found Andromeda with those wounds. At first, when we had entered the foster care system Zia hadn't dared touch us, but she had become more comfortable now. She had started beating Andromeda again, although it was never too bad. Andromeda would just get a couple of lashes this time while I . . .

I didn't even want to think about that as the car raced along the highway, the engine a rhythmic roar inside my ears. I would worry about that later, but even as I pushed those thoughts away the cold began to creep into my chest. I let the adrenaline burn it off.

After a few more minutes, I slowed down and parked on the side of the road, driving over the grass. I turned off the engine and exited the car. I took a deep breath and trotted into the forest. The long branches intertwined with each other in a tight embrace, forming a dense canopy that only let fractured rays of moonlight filter through.

The weight of the gun at my side was a familiar companion as I made my way over the muddy ground. I didn't plan on shooting anyone but had brought it just in case. I also had a few knives strapped at my belt. A soft breeze brushed past me, making the rustling trees sound like they were whispering to each other.

Adrenaline jolted inside of me as my scars burned. I crouched down behind a tree. I still couldn't see Andromeda, but knew she was walking towards me. I waited. I could see better in the dark than most people. So while the forest seemed bright to me with the dim light of the moon, it might have been dark for Andromeda's eyes. A leaf broke from a tree and landed next to my foot. It had pointed edges, and I could perfectly make out the veins cutting through its smooth surface.

A snap echoed in the distance, and my muscles tensed with anticipation. Andromeda was right ahead, behind the thick tree with one large, bare branch. My hearing sharpened. I heard each soft crunch as she stepped over dry leaves. Her silhouette appeared a few seconds later. She carried a backpack, and wore a dark brown jacket, jeans, and hiking boots. My scars sizzled. Those were my *hiking boots. I* wondered how she had stolen them from my apartment, and intended to claim those back as soon as we returned. I wondered what she had done to make them fit.

Her midnight-black hair fell loosely around her head, reaching a bit above her elbows. My heartbeat slowed, but my muscles remained tense, ready to sprint into action. Andromeda actually seemed calm, as if she were strolling through a meadow.

I waited patiently until she was passing right in front of the tree where I hid. I sprang forward. Andromeda screamed as I tackled her to the ground. She fell backwards on her backpack, which I hoped had cushioned her fall, and I fell on top of her. Andromeda kicked me in the chest. Even though it only hurt a little, I let her think that she had surprised me with the kick and let myself fall backwards. Andromeda scrambled to her feet and ran away, heading to the right. I stayed on the ground for a couple of seconds. I looked at the bright moon above me, its white surface cracked like broken glass as the branches cut through it.

I jumped to my feet and raced after Andromeda, feeling the thrill of the chase. I liked how the wind felt on my face as I ran and enjoyed the jolt on my legs every time my feet hit the ground and propelled me forward. I was a lot faster than she was and could have caught up in less than a minute, but I didn't. I knew I would eventually catch Andromeda, and she knew it too, but she liked to believe that she could outrun me. I let her have that—even if it was only for a few moments.

I slowed down when I was twenty yards behind her. The backpack bounced up and down as she ran, and her black hair waved behind her. She abruptly turned to the left, almost falling as she stepped out of balance. I slowed down and let her get ten more yards *ahead of me. Andromeda didn't even look back to see if I was still after her; she didn't need to.*

I slowed down a bit more, then hid behind a thick tree. A few seconds later Andromeda stopped. She was at least sixty yards away from me, but I could still hear her heaving. She was getting out of shape—she should have kept training in her foster homes, but I knew she hadn't.

I let her run for a good five minutes, until I sensed her stop again. I stepped away from the tree and raced after her. It was as if the forest conspired with me, making sure I didn't step on any dry leaves or fallen branches. I was just another shadow moving among the trees. The light dimmed as a cloud passed over the moon, but I could still see perfectly well. I ran until I caught up to Andromeda, then stopped, breathing slowly.

She hid behind a large rock ahead of me. I approached it very slowly. My muscles burned with exertion as I crept closer. I sat on the other side of the rock, which separated us by a few feet. Andromeda breathed fast, and I could almost feel the thump of her heart against her ribcage. She kept peeking up from the rock, but I knew she couldn't see me, not unless she leaned forward a bit more and looked down, which she never did.

She shuffled with the backpack, the zipper purring loudly in the dark. Andromeda fumbled with a plastic wrapping, and then began to munch on something. I couldn't smell what it was. She finished her meal a couple of minutes later.

I pushed myself up to my knees and faced the rock, gripping the ragged edge. My muscles tensed again before I jumped over the rock and fell on the other side right next to Andromeda. Fury flashed across her face as she widened her eyes. I pulled Andromeda closer to me, her back to my chest. She clawed at my arm but I didn't let go. I wrapped my legs around hers to avoid her kicks. She tried hard to wriggle out of my grip, but her strength didn't match mine. It took her about two minutes to finally give up, and she gave one last frustrated growl.

"I hate you," she said, her gaze cast down.

"How did you steal my boots?" I asked.

Andromeda didn't answer, tensing in my arms. I was about to ask her to give me the boots when we got back, but they looked good on her. I would let her keep them, even though I knew she would throw them away at some point, which meant I would have to retrieve them from the trash if I wanted them back.

Andromeda didn't try to escape again as I let go and stood. I extended my hand to her but she stood on her own. She slung the backpack across her shoulders again. She didn't look at me as we walked away from the rock, heading back to the car. I knew Andromeda didn't understand why I kept coming after her, but it was my only way to protect her, the only way to keep Zia moderately content. I wondered if she would beat Andromeda this time. She probably would—she had asked me to take Andromeda back to a building under construction. She probably didn't want any evidence in her apartment.

My heart twisted painfully when I thought of Zia beating Andromeda, but I knew the beating wouldn't be as bad as they had been before. Just a few lashes. In any case, it was Andromeda's fault for escaping again. Zia would have left her alone if she just stayed in her foster homes. I didn't understand why she kept running away if she was already out of Zia's reach. Probably to piss her off, and to piss me off too.

I hated Andromeda's escapes. I didn't mind chasing after her. I hated every time she ran away because that meant I had to see Zia again too and deal with her. Zia didn't beat me much anymore—she had found other ways to punish me, and every time Andromeda ran away Zia made sure to make me pay for that as well. But that meant Zia wouldn't take out all her rage at Andromeda, so Andromeda would be safe from any significant damage.

I pulled out of my thoughts when a leaf fell on Andromeda's hair. I brushed it away, and she flinched slightly. Andromeda finally looked up to meet my gaze. The anger was gone from her clear blue eyes, replaced by resentment. She hated me, but she was safe from Zia's rage. As we kept walking through the forest, I kept telling myself I could live with that.

●———————●———————●

I felt a sense of déjà vu when I heard the clanking metal. My head felt heavy as a boulder as I slowly came back to my senses. I was in the same room where I had been chained just hours before. Had I dreamed about my escape with Corvus? I looked up at the ceiling where the broken chains hung limply, clanking with each other. My leg seared with pain, reminding me of the snake bite. Faint light came in through the window on the upper left wall, indicating that morning was finally breaking through the night.

No, I hadn't dreamt anything. I tried to stand but realized I couldn't move. Thick ropes tied my hands and feet together. Another rope bound my arms and torso tightly. I wanted to scream in frustration, but the gag prevented me from making any noise.

My mind spun as I remembered the last few moments before I had lost consciousness. I had fallen asleep on the ground in Central Park. Why in Hell had I done that? Because Corvus had suggested it. My stomach twisted. No, Corvus hadn't *suggested* that—he had *lied* to me. Why?

The door burst open and Perseus walked in. He closed the door behind him and looked down at me.

"Where's Corvus?" I tried to ask, but I was sure he hadn't understood me through the gag.

"I just wanted to thank you," Perseus said. "For being so cooperative with us and helping us find Zia's satchel."

My blood turned to ice. Perseus's eyes glinted like two black lakes beneath a full moon. Corvus had not been on my side, and I wondered if he had ever been. What about Draco and Virgo? Had he betrayed them too? I strained against my bonds, the rope digging painfully into my flesh.

Perseus smiled. "So, Kensal Green Cemetery. Raiding a cemetery was not something on my bucket list, but it needs to be done." Corvus must have told him everything. Rage boiled in my veins. Perseus took a step to the left, towards the gingerbread cookie tray. "And the best part is that you'll be helping us dig up Cepheus." Perseus's smile dropped. "I did try convincing you the nice way. But you refused, so now Corvus's lies will have to make you more cooperative." My chest caved in with fear. I'd had a taste of Corvus's lies already, and I knew I wouldn't stand a chance against them. Perseus would use me as his puppet. "We were planning to leave before sunrise." He looked at the faint light coming in through the window. "But unfortunately, we've had some complications that we need to take care of first."

I growled in frustration.

Perseus scratched his cheek. "We'll talk more later. There's a lot we need to discuss."

I let out another growl.

"You deserve to know the truth about Zia, and I can give that to you."

Perseus walked out of the room, leaving me alone once again. I hated him. I squirmed in the thick ropes, but they just dug deeper into my flesh until I felt they would cut off my blood flow. I heaved a sigh. At least this time they hadn't taken off my shirt, and I was still wearing the coat.

Even though it was cold, I began to sweat again. Nausea swirled through my chest. I let my head rest against the wall. Perseus had played me like a fool, not only with the girls but also with Corvus. I had fallen into every single one of his traps. I felt so stupid.

I tried to stand, planting my feet on the floor and pushing myself up with my legs, using the wall for support. I felt like every muscle in my right calf was ripping apart with the poison, but I managed to stand again. I wouldn't be able to move much further unless I cut through the ropes. I looked around the bare room, but there was nothing I could use except the tray of cookies. I glanced up again. The bottom link of one of the chains was broken. It wasn't very sharp, but it might be able to cut through the rope. But it was too high for me to even attempt to reach with my arms bound at my sides.

My eyes searched the floor again, more carefully this time. My gaze settled on the far-right corner. Another broken metal link lay on the floor. I hopped to the corner, trying to keep my balance, then kneeled down once I stood above the chain link. I had to lean forward, with some effort, to grab the link with my bound hands, then pulled back. The broken link had another ragged edge. Like the one still hanging from the ceiling, it wasn't very sharp, but it was better than a cookie.

Sweat trickled down my brow, and the floor swayed below me. My head pounded with pain, and my hands began to tremble. I gripped the broken chain tighter—I would not allow myself to feel sick and weak. I began cutting the ropes around my wrists. It didn't help that my hands were trembling, but the rhythmic process of sliding the broken link back and forth made my headache recede into the background.

I had been cutting the rope without much progress for only a couple of minutes when the wall under the window at the other side of the room cracked. I stopped, looking at the crack.

Was it an earthquake? Panic flared in my chest as my memories reeled me back to the terrible earthquakes in Rome that Perseus had caused. I took a few deep breaths. The ground wasn't moving, so it couldn't be an earthquake. The crack on the wall extended from the bottom of the window at the top of the wall, to the floor. The crack widened and little cracks appeared on the sides, as if someone were pushing the wall inside with incredible strength. The window shattered to pieces and broken glass scattered onto the floor.

I dragged myself backwards as a snake slithered out of the crack. My heartbeat roared inside of my ears. Then I realized it wasn't a snake but a tree root sliding into the room. More dark and twisted roots moved into the room. They dripped mud as they slowly snaked above the floor, inching closer to me like gnarled limbs. The roots reached me, and one of them wrapped around the rope in my wrists. I tried to pull backwards but the root pulled me forward with surprising strength. I toppled over and fell on my stomach with a grunt. My ribs burst with pain as air was knocked out of my lungs.

The tree root began cutting the rope that bound my wrists as if it were a knife. In less than a minute, the thick rope fell to the floor. My wrists itched, and I scratched them as other tree roots began cutting at the ropes around my torso and legs. In a few more minutes I was completely free. I ripped out the piece of cloth tied around my mouth, then pushed myself to my feet as I licked my dry lips.

The roots retreated back into the crack, and I took in a few ragged breaths as I wiped the sweat off my brow. The wall crumbled down a second later like a pile of dust collapsing on itself. Only damp earth and a dense network of roots lay on the other side. At the very top, where the window had been, was a hole big enough for me to climb through. I wasn't sure what was happening, but I wouldn't ignore my opportunity to escape. I stepped over broken pieces of concrete and glass as I made my way to the other side of the room. I gripped the edge of the hole and pulled myself up with some effort. I wriggled through the hole, which was barely big enough for me to slip through. I dragged myself over the snow, away from the hole, and pulled myself to my feet. The world spun for a moment, and I took a few deep breaths. Withered shrubs and tall, bare trees stood motionless around me.

I took a step forward, then stopped when something moved behind me. I whipped around, ready for a fight. I was expecting Perseus, the Pleiades, Corvus, or even that stupid bull to jump out from behind the trees and attack me. But the only person standing next to the house was Virgo.

CHAPTER 13

VIRGO LOOKED DIFFERENT than when I had last seen her. Before, she had been sickly thin, as if someone had vacuumed out half of her muscle mass. She was still thin, but now as any normal person would be. Her freckles were dark on her rosy cheeks, and her gentle brown eyes seemed more brilliant. Her cheekbones didn't look like they wanted to cut through her skin like sharp blades anymore, but they were still prominent. A white strand of hair stood out starkly from her brunette hair, and I wondered where that had come from.

Virgo grabbed my arm. "We have to escape, quickly," she whispered.

I didn't move as Virgo pulled me forward. What if this was another one of Perseus's tricks?

Virgo swiveled around but didn't let go of my arm. "Orion, come on!" she whispered. "Perseus and the Pleiades will be back any minute!"

"And how do I know you're not working with them?" I asked.

Virgo exhaled slowly. "Corvus tricked you, didn't he?" she asked.

"How would you know that?" I asked.

Her eyes welled slightly with tears, and I assumed he had tricked her too. "You'll just have to trust me. Come on, we need to hurry."

I debated that for a second. Corvus could have forced me to do anything with his lies, so Perseus didn't have any reason to send Virgo to "save me," right? I exhaled, hoping I didn't regret my decision, and nodded at Virgo.

The snow crunched under our feet as we made our way around the house. Virgo raced to a car parked right in front of the house. She immediately climbed into the driver's seat, and I opened the door of the passenger's seat and got in. Virgo started the engine, and I expected her to race away, but instead she looked intently at the open front door. She rolled down the window next to me, and the one behind too.

"Cancer!" Virgo shouted at the house.

That seemed like a very strange thing to shout. Was Virgo killing Perseus with cancer? Was that possible? A few seconds later a giant crab walked down the main steps of the house and towards our car. I blinked a couple of times, but I had seen it right. A crab, probably a yard wide, raced towards us. Its dark brown and orange shell had a couple of white spots. It snapped its claws once as it approached us—they seemed big enough to chop my entire hand off.

The crab jumped into the back seat through the open window, its long legs poking six holes in the leather seat. I had never seen a more terrifying crab, or ever considered crabs to be terrifying. Its eyes stuck out the front like two black orbs.

"What is *that?*" I asked.

"That's Cancer the Crab," Virgo said.

Of course that was Cancer the Crab—how could I have missed that? Virgo stepped on the pedal and the car surged forward. I quickly put my seatbelt on as the car sped through the street. Virgo rolled the windows back up to shut out the cold wind.

"I promise I'll explain everything when we get back to Argo," Virgo said as she ran a red light. She changed to the lane on the right, nearly crashing into a taxicab, which honked loudly at us. "I imagine you must have a lot of questions."

"Just a few."

Virgo nearly drove onto the sidewalk, then sharply turned the wheel to the left, almost bumping against the cars on the other side. We drove past another red light as honks erupted behind us.

"Do you know how to drive?" I asked.

"No."

"Well," I said, "you're doing great."

"Thanks," Virgo said as she nearly knocked down some pedestrians trying to cross the street.

"Perseus won't let us escape this easily," I said.

Dread clutched at my chest. Before bumping into the blue car in front of us, Virgo swerved onto the left lane.

"It's okay, we made a plan to distract him while I rescued you," Virgo said.

I turned back to see if we were being followed, but instead the Crab stared back at me—I had momentarily forgotten it was there. I turned again. Snowflakes stuck to the window as it began snowing again. A triangular flake had circles inside, and a round one next to it looked like flower petals. A square snowflake had lines twisting inside it like a circuit board.

The snow looked so soft on the sidewalks as people walked over it. I noticed the snowflakes on the window. There was a round flake that looked like flower petals, and—

"Cancer!" Virgo shouted. "Stop distracting us or I might get us killed!"

I pulled my gaze away from the window. We were escaping from Perseus, I remembered. I shouldn't be looking at snowflakes. I turned behind us to see if we were being followed, but only saw the giant Crab, which I had momentarily forgotten about.

"What did the Crab do?" I asked.

"Cancer distracts people, and can make you momentarily forget what you were doing," Virgo explained. "He got inside Perseus's house to distract the Pleiades who stayed behind."

I wasn't entirely sure how that worked but was thankful that the crustacean's distracting abilities had helped me escape Perseus.

After a few more minutes we arrived at an area with several rusted warehouses. Virgo parked the car in between two buildings and we both climbed down after she turned off the engine. Virgo opened the back door and the Crab jumped down.

"Hurry," she said.

I wasn't sure where we were going but followed Virgo. Snow gently drifted onto my hair and coat. I spotted the ocean behind one of the warehouses. The water stretched before us as far as I could see until it met the horizon. Virgo raced to the edge, but my hopes sank after I realized there was no boat waiting for us.

I was about to ask Virgo what her plan was, but just before I did, a dark object surged from the water. My first thought was that a giant whale had just jumped out of the ocean. Then the dark object settled on the surface, and I realized it was a submarine. It stopped right in front of us, and the hatch at the top opened, revealing a ladder that led down. Virgo smiled. The Crab was the first to jump onto the submarine and drop into the hole. Virgo and I followed after it. The metal rungs were cold to my touch, but the ladder didn't shake with my weight. I stepped away from the ladder when I reached the bottom and stood in a carpeted hallway.

Footsteps thundered at the end of the corridor, and my muscles tensed instinctively. A second later Draco came into view. He rushed towards us, smiling.

Draco nodded at me, the vertical slits in his reptilian orange eyes expanding. "Nice to see you again, Orion."

"Likewise."

"We managed to distract Perseus and make him think we had docked further south," Draco said as he looked at Virgo. "But I wasn't sure if we had given you enough time."

Virgo nodded. "We managed to escape just fine. Did Perseus attack you?"

"The Pleiades tried to freeze us into ice cubes, but they weren't very successful," Draco said.

I wondered how much Draco and Virgo knew about the Pleiades. More footsteps echoed down the hallway and two more guys rounded the corner and walked over to us. I recognized them from Zia's picture—they were the Gemini Twins. Just like in the picture, one of them had long blond hair and the other had cut it short. Both of their eyes were grey-blue like the ocean outside.

"You see," the Twin with a ponytail said as he pointed at me. "I told you he was hot."

The other Twin nodded thoughtfully.

"And look at those eyes," said the ponytail Twin. "They're yellow, like pee."

"What's wrong with them?" I asked Virgo and Draco.

"We're not sure," Draco said with a shrug.

"There's nothing wrong with us," the Twin with long hair said as he grinned. "I'm simply admiring Orion's aesthetically pleasing physical attributes."

I wished I could show them how my physical attributes could choke them both to death at the same time, but I refrained from doing that.

Virgo sighed. "Let's go grab some lunch. I'm hungry."

"We need to get to London," I said to the others. "Can you sail this submarine there?"

"Not London again," the Twin with long hair sighed.

"Why London?" Draco asked as his vertical pupil narrowed.

"Long story," I said. "I'll explain on the way. We need to get there before Perseus does."

Perseus knew where Cepheus was buried. I couldn't let him get there before me and discover Zia's secrets.

"Okay then," the Twin with short hair said. "Argo! Take us to London. Again."

I wasn't sure if there was anyone in the captain's cabin who had heard him. I looked at the metal walls but couldn't spot any microphones or cameras. The others began walking down the hallway, so I followed them, hoping we were already on our way. I couldn't feel the submarine moving, but assumed it was.

"Why London?" Virgo asked.

"Cepheus's tomb is there," I said. "I think Zia might have buried something important with him, and Perseus is interested in discovering what it is. He knows the location, so we need to beat him to it."

"Hmmm." The Twin with long hair undid his ponytail, his hair falling right above his shoulders. Just like Virgo, he had a white strand of hair. "Specify what *something* means." He collected his hair into a bun. "I mean, aside from the dead body, what are you expecting to find?"

"I'm not sure," I admitted.

"This is actually a good lead," Virgo said as she eyed a painting on the wall that showed a fruit bowl. "We never found out where Cepheus's body was, only that Typhon murdered him."

"Who's Typhon?" I asked. At least now I knew that Perseus hadn't murdered Cepheus.

"We'll explain in a bit," Virgo said.

"And you said Perseus will also go there," the Twin with short hair said.

I nodded, swallowing the lump in my throat. "Corvus tricked me to get that information to Perseus."

The mention of Corvus had the same effect as if I'd given everyone a slap in the face. Virgo pressed her lips into a very thin line.

"Was Corvus all right?" Draco asked, his gaze cast down.

"Looking a bit sick but fine."

Draco nodded. "A lot has happened since we last saw you." What he most likely intended to say was: *A lot has happened since you left us, saying you would return, but then you never did.* Part of me felt ashamed that I had never gone back to help them, but another part of me knew that I'd needed to come back to New York and find Zia's secrets.

"I'm guessing that it wasn't very good."

"No," Virgo said, her voice tight.

The Crab stepped around me and walked down the hallway, past the Twins. I had forgotten it was here.

"Hey!" The Twin with long hair said. "Where are *you* going?"

The Crab ignored him, as most crabs would, and disappeared as he turned left in the hallway.

"It would have been useful to know you guys had found Cancer." Draco glared at the Twins.

They simultaneously shrugged.

"We forgot he was here!" said the Twin with short hair.

"How can you forget a giant Crab inside your submarine?" I asked.

"He made us forget he was here so we would leave him alone," said the Twin with short hair.

If I was that Crab, I would have done the same.

"We discovered him a few days ago," Draco explained. "When he was stealing food from the kitchen."

"He ate most of our tacos!" the Twin with long hair said. The other one looked equally as distressed at the loss of their tacos. I wondered if tacos were healthy for crabs.

"But how could Cancer have stayed here all along?" Virgo said. "Argo turned into a raft in the underground river in Egypt."

"We're not sure," said the Twin with long hair. "Everything that's inside the submarine seems to stay the same no matter how many times Argo shifts, as if all of his forms exist at once."

"Wait," I said. "This is *the* Argo?"

I remembered the boat from Zia's pictures.

"Yes," said Virgo. "The Ship can understand us, and it can shift into any marine vehicle it wants."

"How—?" I began asking.

"Could we please save all the questions until after lunch?" said the Twin with short hair.

"Fine," I said.

"I'm Pollux, by the way," said the twin with long hair.

"Castor," said the other twin.

"You knew Zia, I mean Cassiopeia." I looked at both of their faces.

"Oh yes," said Castor. "We met her a couple of times."

"How did you know her?" I asked, then realized my voice had sounded a lot more intimidating than I had intended it to.

Castor smiled. "Let's eat first. Then we'll talk."

Chapter LII, Verse II

A secret in the bowels of the Ship the Twins hide,
One that will not be discovered until the River is sailed.
Only the Crab will have been a witness,
To the promise made to the Prince of Darkness.
Stone and flesh one of each shall remain,
As punishment if the promise they break.
The Ship will advise them too late.

CHAPTER 14

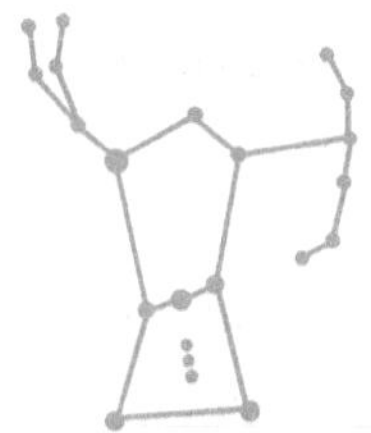

TRUE TO THEIR WORD, the Twins finished their fish and chicken tacos before we started talking. We all sat on a large U-shaped couch facing a floor-to-ceiling window that revealed the dark sea beyond. The Twins sat directly in front of me, and Draco and Virgo were on my left. While we ate, the others kept glancing outside, as if a killer mermaid might swim by. At that point I assumed that mermaids were real—it seemed like a logical conclusion after everything else I had experienced. Even though I'd felt hungry before, my appetite seemed to leave me once I started eating. I drank a lot of water instead.

"So what happened since I last saw you?" I asked once the others were done with their food.

"You first," said Pollux, his dark blue eyes staring at me a suspiciously.

"I went back to New York," I said, setting my plate, which still had two tacos, on the glass table in front of me. "I knew Zia must have left some secrets behind that could be useful to kill Perseus. One of my girlfriends is his sister, so I was using her to track him since my powers don't usually work on Perseus."

"Wait." Castor's eyes widened. "*One* of your girlfriends?"

"Ex-girlfriend now," I said.

"Yeah, but," Castor continued, "does that imply you had more than one?"

"Maybe," I said.

Virgo's jaw dropped, and Draco's face remained neutral. Both Twins burst out laughing.

"Let me guess," Pollux said in between hysterical laughs. "Your girlfriends—oh, sorry, your ex-girlfriends—are the Pleiades."

"How would you know that?" I snapped.

"Having the Pleiades seduce you seems like something Perseus would plan," Castor said as he howled with laughter.

"But there's seven of them," said Virgo. She gazed curiously at me, and not in a good way. I shrugged. The Twins burst into another round of laughter, as if my love life was so funny. I wondered if *they* had ever dated anyone. Probably not.

"Did you discover anything from them?" Draco asked over the laughter.

"Rose, I mean, the one with the weird name that starts with A," I said. "She told me that they were planning on vacationing in South America for Christmas and—"

"That's where the solar eclipse will hit," Virgo said. "This confirms that Perseus will be there for Algol's next Prophesized rising. The solar eclipse will give Algol enough strength to rise to full power again."

"Which means we have a bit less than a month to prepare," Draco said.

The Twins sobered up a bit. Their faces remained stained red, and their eyes glittered with tears, but they stopped laughing. Pollux glanced at the table, realized I had left two tacos, and picked up my plate. Castor grabbed one of the tacos, and Pollux took a bite from the other one.

"And how did you end up in Perseus's house?" Virgo asked.

I leaned back on the couch.

"Let me guess," Pollux asked. "The Pleiades lured you to a place where no one would be able to help you and used their water-and-ice powers to trap you."

When I didn't respond, they exploded in another fit of laughter. After that passed, I gave everyone a summarized version of everything that had happened from the time I had returned to New York up to the satchel I found in the abandoned building.

"Why would Zia have pictures of other Star Children?" Virgo asked.

I shrugged.

"Who was in the pictures?" Draco took off his coat and set it next to him on the couch. The discoloration on his neck was still slightly visible.

"Uhhh," I tried remembering all the names. "Argo." I motioned all around us.

"We knew that Argo had been owned by someone before us," Castor said. "Maybe it was Cassiopeia and Cepheus."

"There was also a dolphin," I said. "And Corona Austrina or Australis or something." I looked at the Twins. "She also had a picture of you."

The Twins exchanged a worried glance. "What kind of picture?"

"You were standing in front of Argo as a yacht," I said. "Was there supposed to be another picture?"

"No," they said simultaneously.

Draco eyed the Twins carefully as their faces reddened.

"How did you know Zia?" I asked.

Castor swallowed a piece of taco. "We found her about a year and a half ago."

Pollux nodded before he pushed half the taco into his mouth. "We discovered that she flew to London frequently and visited the British Museum quite often," he said in between bites.

That must have been because of Cepheus. But why would she go there so often if he was already dead?

"What else did you find in the satchel?" Virgo asked.

"One of those strange bone weapons," I said. "And a weird black metal. It made Corvus pass out. I had never seen anything like it."

"Oh my Stars!" Castor exclaimed. "Zia and Cepheus must have each had one!"

"That means the metal we found in London isn't the only one!" Draco said, his eyes bright with excitement.

"She might have known that eventually Typhon would break free from his prison, so she had another piece of metal to imprison him again," Virgo said.

"What?" I asked, completely lost.

"Wait," Virgo's head snapped to me. "Please tell me Perseus didn't steal that metal from you."

"He didn't," I said.

Virgo let out a relieved breath.

"Ophiuchus did."

"Ophiuchus the Serpent Bearer?" Pollux's brows drew together.

"I think so." I explained how he had attacked me.

Draco turned to the Twins. "Have you ever met him?"

"Only a couple of times," Pollux said. "He's a very weird dude."

Castor nodded in agreement. "He's one of the only Star Children that we know works alone."

"What did he want from you?" Virgo asked.

Pollux scratched the back of his head and his bun loosened. "He was looking for Centaurus a couple of years ago, but he never said why."

Draco rubbed his cheek. "We need to get that metal back from him. It's the only thing that we know can imprison Typhon again and possibly kill him."

Wait . . . hadn't my original plan been to find Ophiuchus first to retrieve the metal because it could help me defeat Perseus? It had been, I realized, until Corvus had lied to me and made me want to search for Cepheus first. That meant Perseus must have been more interested in Cepheus than in the metal, but the metal still seemed important.

"We still have some time until Perseus's next rising." Virgo twirled a strand of her hair as she leaned back. "We should be able to go to Cepheus's tomb and then retrieve the metal from Ophiuchus."

"Digging up an old dude sounds exciting," Pollux grinned.

"Hopefully we'll get there before Perseus does," Draco said.

"Perseus doesn't know the exact location," I said. "So most likely he'll wait for us to discover Cepheus's tomb and then attack us to steal whatever we find there."

"That sounds like a Perseus thing to do," Castor said.

"Our only hope is to get out of there before he arrives," Virgo said.

"We have to assume Perseus will find us and be ready for a fight," Castor said.

There was a second of silence.

"So what happened to you guys?" I asked the others. "And who the hell is Typhon?"

Virgo and Draco took turns sharing what had happened since I had last seen them, with Castor and Pollux adding some comments.

"So, in summary," I said as my brain spun. "Perseus and Corvus are brothers, but Corvus erased his memories to find Crater. You found Corvus shortly after that, and he was with you for a while. Then after the battle at Palatine Hill, Perseus took advantage of Corvus's memory loss and tricked all of you into retrieving Crater, a Star Object that can either kill or heal and revive someone who drinks from it. And Corvus's memory loss was the only way he could hold the Cup and use its power?"

"You got it," Pollux said.

"And we forgot to mention that in the process of retrieving Crater we killed Hydra," Castor said proudly.

"Is that the monster with multiple heads?" I asked.

"Yes," Castor said. "It was a very badass fight."

I respected the Twins slightly more for that.

"And we also forgot to mention how Zia was involved in the hunt for Crater," Draco said.

My muscles tensed.

"Corvus had met Zia," Virgo said. "He interrogated her and found out about Cepheus and Typhon."

"Who's Typhon?" I asked, annoyed no one had given me an answer yet.

"Cepheus discovered that there was a forty-ninth Constellation that had disappeared from the sky because it had been destroyed by Darkness," Virgo said.

"But not before the Star Child of that Constellation, Typhon, was materialized into life," Draco said. "Which makes Typhon the most ancient and powerful Star Child."

"Cepheus trapped Typhon within a black asteroid metal," Virgo said. At least now I understood why the metal was so important. "But Typhon fatally wounded Cepheus and he died shortly after imprisoning the monster."

"So when Zia went to London to find Cepheus," I said, "he was already dead, but he must have left something behind for Zia to know that Typhon had killed him, and that the monster had been imprisoned."

"Yep," Draco said. "And you just found out that Zia had another piece of that asteroid metal." He paused. "Maybe she wanted to imprison Typhon to buy herself more time while she found Crater to eventually kill him."

Zia would definitely go after the monster that had killed Cepheus. But why would Ophiuchus want the metal? Was he also after Typhon?

"Corvus remembered what Zia had told him—that he needed the Cup in order to kill Typhon," Pollux explained. "But then Corvus remembered Perseus was his brother and went back to him." Pain laced each of those words.

"We thought that Perseus wanted to destroy Typhon," Virgo said. "But instead of killing it, Corvus and Perseus used Crater to heal it."

That took a second to register into my brain. "Why would Perseus heal the most powerful and dangerous monster?"

"We assume that the Prophecies state that Typhon will help Perseus, so they're most likely working together." Virgo clutched her sweater again.

"Which means we'll eventually have to fight the monster," Draco said.

"Yeah. In any case, after Perseus and Corvus healed Typhon, we tracked them down." Pollux redid his bun.

"We found them, and the Pleiades, on the coast of Greece where Cetus was attacking them," Draco said. "So we helped them defeat the monster."

"Wait, who's Cetus?" I asked.

"The Sea Monster." Castor said. "The one that's five times as big as any cruise ship and is part whale, part snake, part octopus, and totally hideous."

"Why did you help them fight Cetus?" I asked.

"We weren't going to let it kill Corvus," Draco said.

"And we weren't going to let Cetus roam free either." Pollux balled one of his fists. "That monster has been chasing us for a long time. We knew that the only chance of defeating the monster was joining forces with Perseus."

It was hard for me to think that, only a couple of weeks ago, Virgo and Draco had teamed up with Perseus and the Pleiades.

"How did you defeat Cetus?" I asked.

The temperature seemed to drop as if the Pleiades had just walked in. "Corvus defeated him," Virgo said. "Cetus wounded me and I nearly died. Corvus realized that the only way to kill the monster, and to save me, was to use Crater, but—" Her voice cut out, and she cast her gaze downward.

"But the only way to use Crater's full power was to erase every single memory he had," Draco finished. "So that's what he did."

Even though Corvus had technically betrayed his closest friends to help Perseus, in the end he had given up everything to save them. Perseus must have taken Corvus after the battle. Since Corvus didn't remember anything, Perseus had bent the truth to his advantage, and had turned all of Corvus's friends into his enemies.

"Argo was hurt during the fight," Pollux said. "So we couldn't go anywhere for a couple of weeks while he repaired. That's why we didn't set out to find you earlier."

"But once Argo was healed, we immediately sailed for New York," Draco said. "We didn't know what else to do after we lost Corvus. We thought you might help us."

I hadn't even considered the possibility that they would be looking for me. I cleared my throat.

"What can Typhon do?" I asked. "Do we know the mythology from its Constellation, even if it disappeared?"

"In the Greek myths Typhon nearly killed all of the gods," Virgo said. "And he bore several children who are in the Constellations, including Leo, Hydra, Aquila, Draco, and Cerberus, which is one of the aspects of Canis Major."

"We're still not sure of what he can do specifically, since we haven't met him yet," Draco said. "But we assume he's very dangerous."

I exhaled slowly. Algol, Perseus's malevolent star, was going to rise to full power again in less than a month. Perseus had Lupus, Pegasus, Taurus, the Pleiades, and Corvus. He owned a

Star Object that could literally kill or heal anyone. On top of all that, the most dangerous and powerful of all of the Star Children would help Perseus destroy all order in the Universe.

Fighting on our side were Virgo, Draco, and the Twins, and I imagined that Leo, Aquila, Sirius, and Maera were around somewhere. We also had the help of Cancer the distracting Crab, whose existence we might forget later. I took another deep breath—I wasn't liking our odds at all.

"We need your help," Virgo said.

"Yeah, I'll help," I said.

I didn't have another choice. If I wanted to destroy Perseus so he wouldn't be able to hurt Andromeda ever again, I would have to join forces with this group.

"I'll stay," I repeated again. "I'll fight Perseus."

Andromeda was the one Prophesized to kill him, but I would do everything in my power to destroy him.

CHAPTER 15

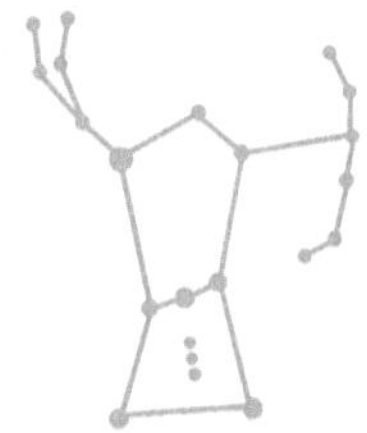

I SAT ALONE, staring out the window at the dark water outside. After catching up with the others, we had talked about what to do once we arrived to London. It was a simple plan—go to the cemetery, unearth Cepheus, get whatever we could find, run away. But we had to be prepared in case Perseus and his friends showed up.

I pulled up my legs onto the couch, hissing as my right calf throbbed painfully. I had washed the snake bite with clean water, as Ophiuchus had instructed, and Virgo had given me a new bandage. The Twins had also found an ointment for my burned feet that had helped relieve the pain. Then they had guided me to a room inside the submarine, next to Draco's. I'd taken a hot shower, but instead of taking a nap, like everyone else had said they would do, I had come back to the living room. I wasn't tired, and knew I wouldn't be able to fall asleep.

My scars burned as I sensed Andromeda. She was still in Switzerland, somewhere close to the lake she now liked to frequent. She must have been having a nice time, taking walks every day, completely unaware of what else was happening. I wondered if she worried about me, just as I worried about her.

Fire flared through my back as I turned my attention to Ophiuchus, who was now in Ireland. I dreaded our next encounter. I gritted my teeth as my scars continued to burn, but when I tried to sense the Pleiades, I only felt a void. I exhaled and the scars stopped hurting. It was strange that I couldn't sense them—I had grown so used to knowing where people were.

A growl thundered behind me. I turned around with a start. Leo stood in front of the stairs. I had forgotten he was nearly as tall as I was. His golden-brown fur was the color of the sun, which contrasted beautifully with the dark red and brown mane that looked like fire flowing around his head. He had three scars on his right side and one on his chest. They had already healed into white lines, but I still remembered the gaping wounds bleeding heavily after the battle in Rome. I met Leo's gaze, and my muscles tightened. Leo's eyes shone like gold, so bright that they seemed to be slices of the sun. The Lion walked closer to me.

"Hey, Leo," I said as the Lion sat next to the couch, looking intently at me.

I couldn't read anything from his feline expression.

"I'm guessing you don't want to take a nap either," I said.

"Sleep has become harder to find these days," Virgo said behind me. She had changed into a purple sweater. She had another sweater folded in her hands. Sirius was at her side, and as soon as he saw me, he wagged his tail.

"Hey, boy," I said as the Dog walked over to me. He smelled my bare feet, tickling them with his nose. They must have smelled funny with the ointment. Sirius pulled back and sneezed, then stepped forward again and let his snout rest on my leg. I caressed him in between the ears.

"Can't sleep?" I asked Virgo.

She shook her head and sat next to me, placing the sweater at her side. "I haven't been able to lately," she sighed. "Sometimes I slept with Draco and Corvus, and that made me feel safer." She paused, and her face reddened. "I didn't mean it like that!"

I laughed. "I wouldn't judge you either way."

Virgo's face turned purple, mimicking her sweater. "I mean, after the earthquake in Rome, Draco, Corvus, and I slept in the same room because we didn't have anything else. And afterwards Corvus and Draco would come over to my room to talk and they would end up falling asleep on the couch."

A long silence stretched in the room. "You guys must miss him a lot," I said.

"Yeah," Virgo cast her gaze down, looking at the bare metal floor. "I should have done more to—" Her voice cut off.

"You couldn't have known who he really was if he didn't know that himself," I said. "You did everything you could to save him."

Virgo bit her lower lip. "I *did* know who he was," she said, almost in a whisper. Her gaze turned distant as she glanced at the window. "I met Perseus and Corvus years ago."

I kept scratching Sirius's head as Virgo talked.

"I was kidnapped when I was younger, but I was never able to escape. After a year, Corvus and Perseus were kidnapped by the same men, and we escaped using Corvus's lies." She held onto her sweater, gripping it tightly. "We could have just run away, but instead I used my power to kill all the men, and nearly killed myself in the process. The only reason I didn't die was because Perseus and Corvus saved me. When Draco and I found Corvus in the hospital, I knew exactly who he was."

"You wanted to repay the favor," I said.

Virgo shook her head. "I saw an opportunity." She lowered her voice. "Perseus will destroy the Universe. He's fanatical about his ideas." She pulled her hair behind her ears, and again I noticed the white strand of hair. "Corvus is his closest friend, his brother. They have known each other for most of their lives. I knew that the only person who could possibly convince Perseus of anything was him." She paused for a few long seconds. "If Corvus could see the other side of the story, the importance of Destiny, Fate, and Prophecy, then he would be able to make Perseus see this war from another perspective. If there was anyone who could have brought a balance between Perseus and us, who could have made us all work together to find a path in between, it was him."

"But he forgot everything," I continued. "And now the only truth he knows is whatever Perseus has told him."

Virgo's eyes glistened with tears. "He lost all of his memories to save me and kill Cetus." Her voice cracked and she absently wiped a tear from her cheek. "I didn't want him to save me, because I knew what we would lose, but he did it anyway." She wiped more tears from her cheeks. "I never imagined we would become so close."

"Is there a way to make him recover his memories?" I asked.

Virgo shrugged.

"When we found the strange metal in Zia's satchel, I think he remembered something." I turned back to Virgo. "Maybe that could work."

She shrugged again. "Even if he recovered a memory, it won't be enough. We need Corvus to remember *everything*, and I'm not sure how we can do that."

Sirius pulled away from me and shook himself. He walked over to Virgo and placed his snout on her leg instead. Virgo gently caressed his head.

"He's going to be there," Virgo said. "I know Perseus will find us at the cemetery, and he'll take Corvus with him. But I—I can't fight him." Virgo looked down at Sirius, and the Dog wagged his short tail. "I'm scared."

I didn't know what to say. I wasn't even sure why she was confiding all of this in me. Not that I minded, but I would have guessed Virgo would rather discuss this with Draco, whom she seemed to be close friends with, instead of me.

"We'll find a way to make everything work," I said. "And it's all right being scared of Perseus and—"

"I'm not scared of him," Virgo said.

Sirius threw back his ears.

"I'm scared of myself." She looked towards the stairs, as if wanting to make sure no one was listening.

"Why would you be scared of yourself?" I asked.

Virgo looked at Sirius as she scratched him behind the ears. "When Corvus healed me, he healed me completely." She raised her head to look at me. "Corvus restored my full power."

"What's your full power?" I remembered the tree roots in Perseus's basement that had helped me escape. At that moment, I had overlooked that strange occurrence, since so many strange things had already happened to me. But now I realized that had been Virgo.

"I don't know," she whispered.

"You can control the earth," I guessed.

"It's more than that," Virgo said. "There are only three female Constellations in the sky. Cassiopeia is the Queen, Andromeda is the Princess, and Virgo is the Goddess."

"Which goddess?"

Virgo tensed. "All of them."

I let that sink in. I wasn't an expert in mythology, but knew that the power of *all* goddesses combined would make Virgo incredibly powerful, more than any of us could imagine.

"I feel much more powerful than I've ever felt. Crater not only healed me physically. It's as if it unlocked all my powers at once." She clutched her sweater again. "I'm afraid of what I might be capable of."

I nodded. "You're scared you might hurt us accidentally."

"I'm scared I might lose myself in that power," Virgo said. "I—" She took a deep breath. "Last time I used my power, I was fueled with anger and vengeance. It nearly killed me, and I could have accidentally killed Corvus and Perseus too. I killed so many men that day."

It was hard for me to imagine Virgo being capable of that.

"You experienced something extremely traumatic, and things like that take a long time to heal," I said. "So don't be too hard on yourself."

"But how do you get over that?" she asked. "Those men are dead, but they still haunt me. No matter how fast I run, my memories are always after me. How do I escape them?"

I exhaled. "I'll let you know as soon as I figure it out myself."

A gentle smile extended over her lips. I couldn't completely understand what she had gone through, but I knew what it felt like to have memories hunt you. Zia, the men Virgo had killed, they were dead, but they still lived inside of us; just like our scars, they would never go away.

She looked behind us once more. "I don't want Draco to know about this."

"About your powers?" I asked.

"He doesn't know I killed a lot of men, and I just . . ." Sirius climbed onto the couch and lay next to Virgo, half of his body on top of her legs. That didn't look very comfortable, but she didn't move him. Instead, Virgo hugged his neck. "I don't want him to be afraid of me. The thing is, I feel like Crater gave me infinite power." She paused. "It's dangerous to feel power without any limits or restraints. That's what nearly killed me last time."

Virgo's gaze was distant, staring at a horizon that didn't exist. It must have been strange to have her power again after so many years without it. I tried thinking of losing my own power, and my bones shuddered. Tracking people, just knowing where things were, had become part of my nature. Losing it would be like becoming deaf or blind—I didn't think I could live like that.

"So you're afraid of feeling invincible when you're not and accidentally hurting the people around you or letting that power drain you again," I said.

Virgo nodded.

"The only way to know your true limit is to find it before it's too late. And you have to use your power to know what that limit is. Suppressing it won't help anyone," I said, which sounded easy in theory, but I didn't know how Virgo would be able to figure that out. "Next time you use your power, try to get rid of all your emotions, as hard as that may be. Let your mind rule your power, not your heart."

Virgo was silent for a few moments as she considered this. I wasn't sure this would solve any of her problems, but it somehow seemed like the right thing to say.

"Yeah," Virgo finally whispered. She turned to face me, eying me carefully. "We'll need to find Andromeda before Perseus's next rising."

I didn't trust myself to answer so I bit my tongue instead.

"I know you want to protect her from Perseus, but it's inevitable that they'll fight each other again. And she's the only one who can truly defeat Perseus."

I focused on that shapeless darkness outside, one full of secrets and mysteries.

"If Andromeda doesn't kill Perseus in his next rising, then he's Prophesized to triumph in the last one and kill us all," Virgo said slowly.

"Let's find Cepheus first, then Ophiuchus," I said. "Then we'll worry about Andromeda."

Virgo nodded, although it wasn't a very convincing nod. She looked at the sweater she had brought, as if remembering she had it. "Oh, I brought you this sweater," she handed it over to me. I unfolded the dark blue sweater—it seemed to be the right size.

"Thanks," I said in heartfelt appreciation.

"It's a special sweater," Virgo said. "No bullets or knives can tear it, so it should protect you."

"Thank you," I said again. That would definitely be useful. I folded the sweater again and hugged it close to me.

She stood up. "Anytime," she said with a smile. "I'll see you later."

"See ya."

Sirius followed after her, and Leo remained sitting next to the couch. Once Virgo was gone, he stood up to face me and let out a small growl. It wasn't menacing, but more of a frustrated growl, as if there was something he wanted to tell me but couldn't.

"What?" I asked the Lion.

He growled again. His eyes boiled like a storm of golden fire.

"You want to tell me something?"

Growl.

"Is it about Perseus?"

Silence.

"Virgo?"

The Lion's glare was so intense my own eyes stung. I knew Leo had enough intelligence to understand everything we said, but it still felt strange to try to communicate with him.

"Zia?"

Growl.

It seemed funny to me that not so long ago I had played a similar game with Maia, except this time I wasn't enjoying the guessing as much. At least it didn't involve stripping. I wondered if Argo had a Scrabble game or some alphabet blocks so Leo could spell out a message.

"Did you know Zia?"

Loud growl.

I widened my eyes in surprise. He hadn't been in the satchel pictures, but that didn't mean they hadn't met at some point. I wanted to ask how he knew her, but that wasn't something a growl could answer.

I exhaled. "I really wish you could talk."

Leo growled again, setting one of his paws on the couch, right next to my leg. His claws were as long as my thumb. I was glad Leo liked me. He growled again, showing me his white teeth. His meaty breath nearly made me choke, but I didn't dare cough in front of him, out of respect.

"What about Zia?"

Leo let out a long growl, as if trying to form words. He was silent for a second, then gave an exasperated roar that made my bones vibrate. He looked intently at me, as if he could telepathically send me a message.

"I'm sorry," I said. "I have no idea what you're trying to tell me."

Leo let out a frustrated huff. Why would the Lion only want to talk to *me*? And why now?

"Does it have anything to do with Zia leaving something behind in Cepheus's tomb?"

Growl.

Leo hadn't been here when we had discussed Cepheus's tomb, but Virgo or Draco might have told him where we were heading.

"Do you happen to know what Zia buried in his tomb? I mean, aside from the dead body."

Loud growl.

"Is it another Star Child? She buried a Star Object there?"

If Perseus had been after Crater, he might be hunting down his next weapon.

GROWL.

"Which—?" My scars burned before I could finish the sentence. I thought back to the only Star Object I had seen in the pictures—the one Cepheus himself had been holding. Fire burned inside of me, my inner compass spinning wildly.

"Corona Australis is buried with Cepheus," I said.

Leo pulled back his lips into what looked like a terrifying smile and roared.

So *that's* what Perseus was after. He might not even care about the asteroid metal. Perseus had known that Zia would leave me clues to find a powerful Star Object that could help us defeat him.

"Leo," I said. "How do you know Zia buried Corona Australis in Cepheus's tomb?"

The Lion didn't respond, his eyes burning with an intelligence that I felt surpassed my own. Leo walked out of the living room, but I knew that our conversation wasn't over. I wondered how Zia had met Leo, and why the Lion knew so much about her. It seemed like another secret that she had taken to her grave.

Chapter XIX, Verse II

After the curse of the King was laid upon him,
His power lost and not even a voice to mourn.
The Lion shall keep his secrets from his new friends,
Until with a new voice he can speak again.
The sorrowful places of his past he will revisit,
To discover the treasures left by the Queen.
Then to lose his voice once more in a storm of darkness.

CHAPTER 16

ARGO HAD TURNED into a small boat to sail through the Thames River, leading us deeper into the city and directly to the cemetery. I stood on the outer deck. The water reflected the grey sky above us, making it look like cold, molten silver. It rippled in waves as Argo cut through it. Virgo's sweater was surprisingly warm against the brisk weather, and I also had a thick coat over it.

Trees lined the narrow river on one side. The skeletal branches leaned into the river as if trying to scoop up some water. On the other side of the river was a narrow path, but there wasn't anyone on it. I looked at the clouds again, and wondered if it would rain later in the day.

"How close are we?" Virgo asked as she stepped up next to me. She wore a dark brown jacket over her knitted sweater.

"Less than a mile away," I said, sensing Cepheus's presence closer than before.

Draco walked over to Virgo and stood at her other side. He wore a pair of dark sunglasses and a black leather jacket, making him look like a cool biker.

"What will we do with Leo?" Virgo asked. "He'll attract a lot of attention."

"Well we can—" Draco didn't finish.

I knew what he had been about to suggest. *We can lie to people and tell them he's a cat,* as they had always done, but Corvus wasn't here anymore. His presence hung alongside us like an uninvited ghost.

"The cemetery is right next to the river," I said. "So we won't have to walk through the streets of London."

"That's good," Draco said.

We were all silent then, not mentioning that someone inside the cemetery might see Leo. Dread and anticipation pulsed inside of me with every beat of my heart. I had already told the others that I had discovered Corona Australis was buried in Cepheus's tomb, but I didn't tell them Leo was the one who had dropped the hint. I wanted to know how the Lion had discovered that information first.

I had asked Virgo about Corona Australis because I didn't know much about that Constellation. She had said that the Crown, along with Corona Borealis, had more obscure myths. In Greek mythology they were both associated with Dionysus, the Greek god of wine, ecstasy, and madness. None of us were sure of what kind of power that would give the Crowns, but we certainly didn't want Perseus to have it.

Virgo let her gaze rest on the water below, while my eyes kept searching the trees for any movement. My heart went into a sprint as my scars seared with pain.

"Stop here," I said.

Argo immediately veered to the right, heading to the edge of the river. As soon as the boat was right next to the path, I jumped out. My muscles knotted with tension. A wall that presumably edged the cemetery rose eight feet above the ground. A chaotic spray of colorful graffiti decorated it.

My scars lit up in flames—Cepheus was close. My inner compass pointed to the left once we crossed the wall. Draco and Virgo walked up next to me, followed by the Twins. Castor had two swords strapped across his back, and Pollux had a spear in one hand and an axe at his back. Aquila was already in the sky, flying in circles above us. His golden-brown wings made a stark contrast against the grey sky, like a fragment of the sun cutting through the haze. The Eagle was silent, so I assumed he hadn't detected any immediate danger around us.

Leo, Sirius, and Maera jumped down from the boat, followed by Cancer. I had forgotten about the black poodle until it happily made its way towards me. I had never seen the small dog do anything, and wondered why he was here—he always just seemed to be accompanying the other animals. Leo let out a low growl as he walked up closer to me. The Twins immediately stepped to the side. Virgo pulled down her sleeves to cover her hands as she looked nervously around us. I hadn't seen anyone near the river, and hoped our luck would last.

"There must be an entrance somewhere," Draco said as he looked at the wall before us. It seemed to extend as far as I could see to our sides, and I didn't spot any doors or gates.

"Let's just climb," I said. "It will be faster."

I stepped forward. The wall was only two feet taller than me. I bent my knees, jumped, grabbed the edge, and pulled myself up. I crouched at the top and glanced down at the others.

Leo crouched down five feet in front of the wall, his tail wagging. Then he lunged forward, flying over the wall and landing with a thud on the other side. Sirius barked, then gave a low whine.

"Come here, boy," Draco said to the Dog.

Sirius hesitantly stepped up to Draco, then looked up at me with big, bulging brown eyes. Even though Sirius was quite a big boxer dog, reaching almost to Draco's waist, Draco easily carried the Dog and raised him towards me. I grabbed the Dog and hugged him close. I jumped down from the wall carrying Sirius and then gently lowered him to the ground. I helped the others climb to the other side while Cancer used his pointy legs to climb the wall. A minute later we were all inside the cemetery. I didn't spot anyone around us, for which I was grateful. But it did make me slightly uneasy that the cemetery seemed empty.

We all walked towards the path ahead of us. Slabs of stone rose out of the ground like ragged waves in a grey ocean. Fresh flowers had been left at most of the graves. I spotted some white roses next to a slab with two paragraphs inscribed on it. Next to it was a white marble cross with a jar underneath it. I could tell which slabs were older because their inscriptions had worn away into unintelligible text that looked more like ancient hiero-glyphs. A few tall trees stood between the stones, their naked branches reaching down as if wanting to pull the dead out of the earth.

"Let's stay alert," Virgo said. "Perseus may be close."

My scars burned like electric wires running through my skin. I tried to sense the Pleiades, or Perseus, or Corvus, but they had been swallowed into a dark hole. I sensed Andromeda. For one terrifying moment, her signal disappeared, but then resurfaced a couple of seconds later. She was still in Switzerland. I exhaled in relief. I began walking through the path at a rapid pace, letting my inner compass guide me. Cepheus was less than a mile away.

"Let's hurry," I said.

Leo walked right next to me with big strides. Sirius and Maera trailed behind him, wagging their tails excitedly. Draco and Virgo were right at my heels, and behind them were the Twins and the Crab.

We passed by countless more graves. A few of them had more elaborate designs. I walked by a marble tomb with a cherub at each corner kneeling in prayer. I found it ironic that people spent so much money on their burials. Death didn't care about wealth. Yet some people still found it important to let the living know they had lived an affluent life, as if that would make any difference once they got to the other side.

My internal compass told me to keep going straight, so I did. Patches of green peeked out in between the graves, defiant to the winter cold. Yellow daisies clustered close together next to a black cross. On my right, in front of one of the slabs, someone had left a white envelope under a rock.

The path curved to the left, and we followed along. Birds chirped happily above us, flitting between the branches. The birds on a tree to my left dispersed before a large raven landed on one of the lower branches.

"That's a bad omen," Virgo whispered behind me as she stared at the raven.

"Our entire lives are a bad omen," said Pollux. I was tempted to agree with him.

The raven flew away as Aquila appeared above with his bright golden wings. He still didn't give any warning cry, but that didn't make me slow down. My scars burned as my inner compass pointed to the right. A path a few yards ahead of us turned in that direction. The trees became denser around us. The overgrown grass at our sides covered some of the graves. The stone crosses looked centuries old—broken and eroded white with age. No flowers or other offerings had been left here.

We kept walking straight until the path turned left. This section of the cemetery seemed a bit livelier. The graves were dotted with colorful flowers around them. Green, red, white, yellow, blue, and purple decorated our surroundings as if a rainbow had shattered above us and scattered around the graves.

We reached a crossroads. Dividing the paths was more overgrown grass as tall as my knees. The trees were so densely packed they seemed to be huddling together for warmth. Most of them were bare, but a few willow trees had branches drooping down like torrents of rain with withered leaves like twisted raindrops. I spotted several Egyptian obelisks rising from the ground like white spikes. I counted four of them, one at the side of each path. One of the obelisks had been smashed at the top. Large stone tombs covered in dark vines took up the rest of the space. A tall angel seemed to be guarding one of the tombs, its wings spread wide at its sides.

"Where to?" Draco asked.

My scars burned again. *Right.* We were almost there. Everyone followed behind me. The naked branches swayed above me with a sudden gust of wind that howled around us. More tombs, a few obelisks, and other statues lined our path.

After another minute I set my gaze on Cepheus's grave. It was fifty yards away from us, right next to one of the crying willow trees. I quickened my step so much that I was almost running, my heart thumping against my ribs. A pile of black stones, like a cairn, marked Cepheus's resting place. I stopped as soon as I reached them.

"He's here," I said.

"Oh, shoot," Pollux said as he pulled back his hair. "I just realized we forgot to bring a shovel."

"Damn," Castor snapped his fingers. "I don't suppose we'll just find one lying around somewhere?"

Leo roared and stepped forward, making us all startle back. He looked at the rocks, his teeth bared at them. I removed the rocks and set them close to the tree. Once all the rocks were gone, Leo sniffed the ground right above Cepheus. He began digging with his big paws. Sirius barked, then joined him. For the first time, the Dog seemed somber. His ears were thrown back and his eyes glistened, although I wasn't sure if dogs could cry. The Crab just snapped his claws in encouragement and Maera gave a cheery bark. Virgo might have been able to move the earth with her powers, but she didn't volunteer so I didn't push her. Aquila settled on a branch behind us, eyeing our surroundings. Castor and Pollux unsheathed their weapons and faced the path we had just come through.

One foot down, two feet down. The memories of Zia's grave poured back into me, but I pushed them away. A growing mound of earth rose behind both animals. The hole was like a gaping mouth, waiting to swallow me. Leo's golden paws soon became dark with dirt, and so did Sirius's white paws.

The seconds ticked by fast like water slipping from my fingers. Four feet. Five feet. Leo stopped with a low roar, and Sirius stopped digging too. The Dog jumped out of the hole, and Leo pushed himself out of it. I still couldn't see anything sticking through the earth. Maybe Leo was afraid of scratching Cepheus's body or whatever else was in there. I jumped into the hole, my feet hitting the solid ground. It was icy, as if the cold wind had pooled inside the hole.

I kneeled and began brushing away dirt in different places. Less than a minute later, I uncovered a white patch. I cleared the earth around the patch, and it took me a few seconds to realize it was a forehead. Cepheus's skin was soft and smooth as I cleaned the dirt from his face, as if I were unearthing a marble statue. He had a high-bridged nose, bushy eyebrows, and a shaggy black beard that didn't want to let go of the dirt.

"Gross," one of the Twins commented above me.

As far as dead bodies went, this one didn't look gross, which struck me as odd. Cepheus had been dead for over a year, yet his face looked like he had died seconds ago. His skin had become more transparent, revealing dark veins under his cheeks and forehead. His hair and beard were still a very deep shade of black, like the raven we had seen earlier. His eyes were closed, with long lashes edging his eyelids.

I kept brushing the dirt from the rest of his body. The others didn't volunteer to help, which didn't make much of a difference to me. I uncovered Cepheus's neck and something gleamed—a chain with two rings hanging from it. One golden ring was considerably smaller than the other. I remembered the rings from the pictures I had seen in Zia's satchel. I carefully pulled the chain off his neck and held the two rings in my palm. I had never seen Zia wear the small ring, but I knew it was hers. The others were silent as I hung the chain around my own neck and dropped the rings inside my sweater—the metal was painfully cold against my chest as I continued digging.

I uncovered Cepheus's bare upper chest. He had dozens of white scars cutting through his skin. I started uncovering his lower torso, then stopped. Someone gasped behind me.

"Oh, that's truly gross," one of the Twins said.

A foot-long hole cut straight through Cepheus's stomach. The skin around the hole was rotten black, green, and blue. Cepheus's bones—his spine and some of his ribs—were still there, gleaming white, but his skin and organs were not. It seemed as if some kind of poison had eaten through his flesh.

Leo emitted a lamenting roar. I glanced up at the Lion. I wasn't an expert in feline facial expressions, but his eyes seemed to drown in sorrow. They drooped down, about to let rivers of fire flow from them. Leo made a sound somewhere between a moan and a roar. Sirius's big brown eyes bulged and he howled in anguish, making my bones shudder.

I forced myself to look away from the grieving animals. My scars burst with fire. The cold earth pushed into my nails as I dug above Cepheus's head. My palms touched something smooth, and I brushed the dirt away from the Crown. It was made out of solid gold, and even though there was no bright sun above us, it still gleamed brightly. I pulled the Crown away from the earth and held it with both hands. It was surprisingly light.

"Do you feel anything?" Virgo asked.

"Nope," I said.

Leo emitted an urgent growl. Our gazes locked. He growled and his dirty paw pointed at a spot at Cepheus's feet. Virgo eyed the Lion curiously but didn't say anything.

I unzipped my coat and placed the Crown inside the large pocket under my left breast. It felt uncomfortable once I zipped my coat back, but I wanted to keep the Crown safe with me. I stood up, then walked to Cepheus's feet where Leo had pointed and kneeled again. I began digging. My nose itched, but I refused to scratch my face with my dirt-covered hands.

"We should take Cepheus too," Castor said behind me.

"Why would we?" I asked.

I glanced up as Castor motioned at his swords. "What do you think these are made of?"

I stopped digging for a second and looked at Cepheus's dead body. His ribs protruded from his flesh like gleaming white spikes. "Bones," I whispered. I didn't have time to think about those implications as I kept digging.

"We already have a lot of big bones from Cetus," Virgo said.

"There is no such thing as enough bones," Castor said.

"So you just cut away the skin from dead Star Children and carve the bones into knives and other sorts of weapons?" I asked.

"Yeah," Castor said. "We've gotten really good at carving knives."

I knew I wasn't entirely sane, but the Twins seemed to be at another level. My fingers finally touched a smooth surface. I dug frantically as everyone else stared in support. I brushed dirt away from a leather object. For a moment I thought it might be a book or notebook with a leather cover, but as soon as I pulled it out, I realized that it was a pack tied with a thin cord. The black leather seemed to be in good condition after having been buried for a year. It was only a bit bigger than my hand, and I wondered what was inside. Maybe more pictures or a letter? I would find out soon enough. I was about to unzip my jacket again but stopped. It wouldn't be wise for me to have both the Crown and the leather pack.

I stood up. "Hide this," I said as I reached up and handed the pack to Virgo.

She nodded and tucked the pack away in her jacket. Then I turned to Leo. He gave me a single nod. I wondered how he had known about the pack at Cepheus's feet. I would have to ask him later and try to piece an answer from his growls. I placed both of my palms on the grass and pushed myself out of the hole.

"Can we take the body?" Castor asked. His bright, stormy blue eyes gleamed with excitement.

"No. Let's go," I said as I walked back to the path.

Aquila jumped from the branch and flew into the air.

"Are we just going to leave the grave like that?" Virgo asked as she kept pace with me. The others followed quickly behind me. Sirius gave one last look at Cepheus, whined, and then raced back to us. Leo growled as he stared into the hole, which sounded like a sorrowful goodbye, and then jogged towards us.

"We don't have time to bury him again," I said. But even as those words left my mouth, guilt climbed into my chest. I hadn't known Cepheus, but he had given up his life trying to imprison the most dangerous Star Child. He had been married to Zia once. I felt like we owed him a decent burial. If Perseus hadn't known we were here, I would have buried him again. Virgo also seemed conflicted, but we couldn't waste our time. I knew someone would eventually find Cepheus and probably bury him again. That thought made me feel a bit better.

The barren trees seemed to want to close in around me as the strong wind bent down their branches. We were right in the middle of the crossroads again when Aquila gave a piercing shriek. We all stopped abruptly.

Perseus slowly walked out from behind one of the obelisks. He stopped in the middle of the path, blocking our exit, then took a few steps closer to us.

CHAPTER 17

I STOOD VERY STILL as Perseus stopped again thirty yards away. His piercing dark eyes shone like two black suns. He still wore those black leather gloves, which gave him a more sinister look. Slowly, the Pleiades came out from their hiding places behind tombs, statues, and obelisks. They looked beautiful, of course, which didn't help boost my morale.

Virgo inhaled sharply. On the path ahead of us, behind Perseus, Corvus and Lupus walked towards us side by side.

"Don't look at the Wolf's eyes," I said as I focused on Corvus instead. He kept his gaze fixed on Virgo and Draco, but I couldn't discern any particular emotion on his face.

Pollux put a hand on my shoulder and pulled me back. Taurus was walking towards us from the path on the right, and Pegasus stood on the left. I immediately wished that Argo could fly and just take us out of there. But of course, my life just couldn't be easy. Corvus stopped next to Perseus, flanked by the Pleiades on the other side. Lupus was behind them, and I avoided looking at his paralyzing silver gaze. Tears glistened in Virgo's eyes as she looked at Corvus, who finally pulled his gaze away from her and glanced at his shoes instead.

Tension crackled around us like electricity.

"Hello again," Perseus said, his gaze trained on me.

"I noticed you took some of our gingerbread cookies on your way out." Rose crossed her arms as she stood close to the Bull. "I hope you enjoyed them."

"They were very tasty," I said.

There was another moment of silence—only the wind dared to howl.

"Give us the Crown," Perseus said.

No matter what you do, in the end it will lead us all into the future I have planned for. He had known I would find the Crown and had planned to steal it from me all along. It was hard for me to admit it, but Perseus was a lot smarter than I had thought. There had to be a way to surprise him. The Prophecies couldn't possibly detail every single event that would happen.

"Give me the Crown," Perseus repeated as he extended his hand to me.

"How about you leave before I kick your ass?" I said.

Perseus smiled. "Your odds are not very favorable here." He cocked his head to one side. "We don't need to fight. No one needs to get hurt. You just need to give me the Crown."

I clenched my teeth. We were slightly outnumbered, but I had no doubt that we could put up a good fight and escape with the Crown and the pack.

Aster shook her head, her eyes flashing with a warning. I quickly looked away from her before the other Pleiades noticed.

"It would be a shame to kick your ass, Orion," Rose said as she flashed a smile. "I grew quite fond of it."

Anger burned in my veins. Maia snickered, and Electra barely held back a chuckle. The other girls just smiled, except Aster. At least the Twins didn't laugh. I looked back at Perseus's dark expression. I had received the message from Aster's gaze quite clearly—this fight was not intended to end well for us.

My scars burned as I sensed Argo, who had moved closer to us. If we ran less than a mile straight ahead of us, it would be waiting for us at the river.

"Like I told you before, Orion," Perseus said as he stepped forward, "I don't want to hurt any of you, but I won't let you stand in my way."

"Neither will I," I said.

Leo jumped from behind me with a roar. His left paw hit Perseus square on the chest. The Lion pushed Perseus flat to the ground with his full weight. He roared again, making the air tremble. A few yards behind them, Lupus growled as he lunged at Leo. But the Lion used his other paw to push the Wolf out of the way as if he was a plush toy. Lupus flew from the ground and landed ten yards away from Leo with a crash that sent dirt springing up around him.

The white bull mooed but was hit on the side by a bolt of lightning that sent him sprawling to the side, crashing against an obelisk that tumbled over him. My ears rang as another bolt of lightning smashed on the left path, making the winged horse jump backwards as it flapped its wings. Aquila shrieked above us. White-purple light ignited in Electra's hands. She raised her hand and electricity snaked towards the clouds, trying to shoot down Aquila. White ice formed underneath Maia and Rose as they stood at either side of Leo. They extended their arms forward and shot ice shards at the Lion, but they didn't even scratch him. Leo opened his jaws to swallow Perseus's head.

"Leo. You want to freeze!" Corvus shouted.

The Lion's jaw remained open inches above Perseus's head, revealing a deadly row of sharp white teeth and a coarse pink tongue. The Lion trembled, trying to break away from the lie.

The rest of the Pleiades—Rose, Tay, Cela, and Merope—made their way around Leo and raced towards us. Ice slid over the ground around them. Draco stepped forward to stand before us. The Pleiades extended their arms at the same time Draco breathed out. Fire met ice as the snow shot by the Pleiades turned to smoke after touching Draco's flames. The smoke dispersed around us, making it seem as if white fog had suddenly descended on us. The mist blocked Leo from sight. I didn't know how much fire Draco could exhale, but knew he probably wouldn't last much longer.

Virgo must have thought the same. She looked up at me, her eyes wide with terror, and I nodded. Virgo pulled up her sleeves and kneeled on the ground. She pressed her palms to the dirt and screamed. The ground began to tremble, but it wasn't like the earthquake in Rome. It felt as if the earth itself could feel Virgo's anger and was letting it out, shaking with rage. I bent my knees to keep my balance. The trees shuddered around us, as if they had suddenly come alive, their branches swaying up and down and to the sides.

Draco stopped breathing fire. Before him, the Pleiades had fallen to the ground, surrounded by snow. The smoke cleared around us, and my attention turned back to Leo, who still stood frozen with his jaw open. Corvus had somehow convinced the Lion to let go of Perseus, who slowly rose to his feet again. His face went paler than Cepheus's when he turned to look at Virgo. Tree roots sprang from the ground right in front of her. Pegasus whinnied in terror as dark tree roots wrapped around his body, smearing his white fur with dirt as they pulled him down. The Horse flapped his wings wildly, making a current of air flow around me. Taurus mooed as roots took hold of his horns and legs. More roots shot up from the ground before me and wrapped around the Pleiades, Perseus, and Corvus. One thin root wrapped around Corvus's mouth, gagging him. Another tree root wrapped around Lupus's snout, pulling his head down. Perseus shouted as he squirmed to free himself from the roots, but they quickly wrapped around his arms and legs.

Aquila shrieked as he flew towards the river. Virgo swayed next to me and I pulled her up into my arms before sprinting forward. We raced around our enemies, running fast as we followed Aquila. My scars burned as I sensed Argo closer to us.

"I'm fine," Virgo said as her head rested against my shoulder.

Bare trees, marble tombs, slabs of stones, and colorful flowers blurred at my sides as we ran. When I dared to look back, relief washed over me as Sirius, Leo, and Maera kept pace behind us. Cancer had also managed to keep up.

The stone wall became visible ahead, and I ran even faster. I was ten yards away from it when Sirius raced ahead of me and jumped over the wall. He scraped his belly and back legs a bit but seemed fine as he let out a bark on the other side. Leo jumped after the Dog, flying above the wall and disappearing on the other side. The Twins jumped towards the wall and pulled themselves up as they clawed at the rough stone. I stopped before the wall, my heart beating furiously. I pushed Virgo up. She grabbed the edge of the wall and with my help managed to climb on top of it. The Twins helped her climb down on the other side. Draco climbed the wall carrying Maera, and the Crab desperately poked at the wall with his legs as he pulled himself up.

Draco sat at the edge of the wall and handed Maera to someone below. I was about to pull myself over the wall too when a force pulled me backwards. I was in the air, staring at the churning sea of grey clouds above me before I crashed on my back. Air fled from my lungs. I couldn't even grunt in pain. I rolled to my side and pushed myself up to my feet, facing back the way I had come from. Standing five in front of me was a tall woman wearing a black, long-sleeved dress. Whatever air had managed to get back inside of my lungs pushed out of me again.

Arianna.

Her midnight-black hair was so curly it resembled small twisting snakes. Her face shone like the moon. Her eyes were inhumanly blue, so intense and colorful that they looked like lanterns. Arianna was as tall as me, and even though she looked as delicate as glass I knew she was one of the most powerful beings in the Universe. She seemed different than on Palatine Hill. Her dress was subtly shifting, as if it was made of Night. It fit her loosely and flowed all the way to the ground, right above her bare feet.

Darkness spread around Ariana's dress and settled around her like ink from an octopus. Darkness had a sound, I realized. I sensed it more than I heard it—it was a chaotic heartbeat pulsing around me, making my bones reverberate to its turbulent rhythm.

Before I could react, a tendril of Darkness shot forward. It wrapped around my ankles and pulled forward. I fell hard on my back again, growling in frustration.

Ahead of me, Arianna turned and slid towards the trees on the right as if she were skating on ice. The rope of Darkness around my legs pulled me forward, and I was dragged over the rough ground after her.

"Orion!" Draco shouted behind me.

Arianna pulled me away from the wall, towards the bare willow trees. My surroundings blurred like shadows as I tried to pull my feet apart and break my ankles free. When that didn't work, I spread my arms around me, trying to get hold of anything. My hands scraped against slabs of stone and tree trunks, but I was moving so fast I barely touched them before they were out of my grasp.

Arianna stopped. The rope of Darkness disintegrated. I immediately shot to my feet. The ground swayed slightly below me as my vision blurred.

"Orion," Arianna's voice was like the wind's whisper.

She was nowhere to be seen. The bare trees were clustered so tightly their branches choked out the sky. Graves surrounded me on all sides like the jagged teeth of a beast. A few feet to my left stood another marble obelisk—its pattern resembled dark red veins bleeding on pink skin. Next to it was a tomb with the statue of an angel at the top, its horn blaring to the clouds. Dry and twisted vines curled greedily around all of the tombstones and graves, as if the earth wanted to pull the tombs down to eat them.

There was no sign of the wall that led to the river, and I couldn't even spot a path cutting through the ground that could lead me there. My scars burned as if I had poured alcohol on an open wound. Argo was far behind me, to the right.

I placed a hand on my back and realized that my jacket was almost in tatters and my jeans were worn down too. But at least my butt wasn't bare, which would have been embarrassing. Although I was sure that would have delighted the Pleiades.

"Orion," Arianna chanted with a sweet voice.

Darkness rose out of the earth like black mist evaporating from the ground. I held my ground, clenching my teeth and balling my fists. I wouldn't give Arianna the pleasure of scaring me. The black mist rose higher, like poisonous fumes trying to reach up towards the branches. It loosely created the shape of a woman. Very slowly, the mist began to liquefy and her pale flesh began to take shape as if Arianna was stepping out of a lake's surface. She finally broke through, her form solidifying. She opened her brilliant blue eyes.

She flashed her teeth with a smile. "I'm pleased that you're here, Hunter. I had been waiting a long time to see you again."

Chapter XV, Verse III

Fooled by his own pride, and wounded by his honor,
The Hunter shall be led into his ruin.
The Crown he shall keep away from the Prince,
But a curse will be laid upon him.
Or the Crown to lose into the hands of those he scorns,
And his power to remain uncorrupted from their dark touch.
The Prince once again will lead the Hunter astray.

CHAPTER 18

"YOU'RE NOT SUPPOSED TO BE HERE," I said.

Arianna's teeth shone like pearls as she smiled. "I have enough flesh now."

I didn't fully understand what that meant but knew it couldn't be good.

Arianna slowly cocked her head to the side. "She gave me part of her flesh too." Her voice resonated all around me, echoing in different tones as if the dead were speaking from their graves. "When she saved your life." Arianna's eyes became brighter, sizzling with electricity. "I would have killed you—but she drank from me to have enough strength to free you."

The ground seemed to sway beneath me. Had Andromeda *literally* exchanged her flesh, or part of her being, for Darkness?

"Where do you think that burst of Light came from? She took a part of me so she could shine brighter."

"No."

Andromeda couldn't have been reckless enough to let Darkness pour inside of her just to save me. But Andromeda was impulsive and bold. Her power had been magnified by a thousandfold just to save me—but it had come at a cost.

Arianna stepped closer to me. She held my chin, forcing me to face her. "Handsome as always, my dear Hunter," Arianna whispered.

Rage flowed through my body like poison. I grabbed Arianna's arm and twisted it away from my face, then kicked her in the stomach. It felt as if I had kicked a metal wall, and my foot burst with pain. Arianna pushed me backwards. I flew off my feet and landed on my side with a grunt, the Crown in my pocket painfully digging into my flesh. I struggled back to my feet.

A cold drop of water fell on my cheek, then another splattered on my forehead. Rain began to drizzle from the sky. The rain turned black on top of the stone-grey tombs, sliding down like dark blood oozing from cuts. Aquila cried out in the distance. Arianna lunged forward, elbowing me in the chest, and I tumbled onto my back. A sharp piece of rock stabbed into my lower back, and I knew it would leave a nasty bruise. I pushed myself to my feet again, my body aching.

"Don't hurt yourself, Orion," Arianna said as she brushed my cheek with her cold fingers.

"What do you want?" I growled.

"Andromeda is already mine. Now I want *you*."

Something burst inside of me. Andromeda would never be hers. I didn't care how much Darkness Andromeda had inside her, or how much Arianna had taken away from her. I knew Andromeda—she would never give in to that power. She wouldn't let herself be enslaved by Darkness. Ever. I screamed in rage as an overpowering strength fill me. I was Orion. I was the Hunter, and everything and everyone else was my prey.

I smashed into Arianna as if I were trying to crash open a door. I knocked her down, but the momentum made me lose my balance and I stumbled forward, my hands stopping my fall. I shot to my feet. Arianna had spread into a black cloud again. The rain fell harder now, the rhythmic sound filling my surroundings. Arianna's laugh cut through the air like a knife. The dark cloud materialized into a woman again. Arianna smiled gently at me, as if she were playing with a child.

Darkness shot out of her dress like tentacles and collided with my chest, knocking me backwards. My feet left the ground for only a second before my back crashed against a tree and I stumbled onto the grass. I growled in pain as I scrambled to my feet once more. My entire body throbbed, and I tried to ignore it. Arianna dissolved into dark fog once more and enveloped me, wrapping me in an embrace.

Everything around me was pure black, but cold drops of water still broke through the Darkness, splattering onto my face. Darkness pushed me against a tree, making my back burst with another shot of pain.

Thunder rumbled. A roar cut through the air like a lance, followed by a howl. Someone screamed. Darkness was sucked into Arianna's form, revealing the trees and tombs around me again. Arianna grabbed my wrists and pinned them to the tree behind me. My muscles strained as I tried to break free, but I couldn't match her strength. Arianna looked at my scraped, bleeding palm. She licked the blood away with her cold tongue. She pulled me forward, away from the tree, and threw me to the right as if I were a doll. I landed on top of a stone tomb. My cheek brushed against the cold, wet surface of the tomb before I pushed myself up again.

The rain fell more heavily now. Cold drops splattered on my bare back where my jacket had torn, making my skin sting.

"Andromeda will give in at some point," Arianna said. "She'll give in just as Perseus has. They are both tied together in Darkness."

"No."

"You'll give in too." Her voice was like a song. "All of you will give in." Arianna smiled gently. "You are the Children of the Stars, Orion."

The rain soaked my hair and face, but I didn't bother wiping it away.

"Your power is to manipulate Light, to materialize it into reality." Even though she had feet, she didn't use them as she glided around the tomb. "Light cannot shine without Darkness. At some point, you will run out of Light unless you seek the Dark."

Wings flapped above me, and for a moment my heart jumped at the thought of Perseus riding Pegasus. The branches broke with a loud snap as two pairs of wings crashed down. Those dark wings definitely didn't belong to the Horse. It was one of the Pleiades. They had *wings* too? I sighed. I should have stayed single.

Tay stood straight, her wings spread around her. They were a dark golden-brown like a giant eagle. Tay's skin gleamed with a subtle yet noticeable golden aura. Her jewel-like copper eyes fixed on me.

Another gust of wind ruffled my hair as another pair of wings flapped above me. The trees on my left shuddered as a pair of black wings broke through the branches. Cela landed next to Tay, the two of them at Arianna's side. Cela smiled at me, her silver eyes sparkling.

A twig snapped behind me, and my scars burned out of instinct but only found a void. I whirled around. Perseus slowly walked towards me. He was calm, as if he were strolling through a park. He startled when he noticed Arianna, who was still standing at the other side of the tomb. He stopped.

"Arianna," he said.

"Hello, Perseus," Arianna chanted with her sweet voice. She looked back at me. "It seemed like you needed some help."

"We could have used some help with Cetus," Perseus said. His voice was neutral, but I could see the anger blazing in his black eyes. I remained quiet. It was interesting to see Perseus angry at Arianna. He was bold when he talked to her, which indicated a level of familiarity.

"I had other things to do," Arianna's voice was all around me. "He needed Darkness after waking up to become strong again, and I needed more flesh."

Perseus's eyes widened. Tay and Cela exchanged a glance. I wasn't sure who *he* was, but with my luck I would meet him soon. Perseus turned towards me.

"Just give me the Crown, Orion," Perseus said. "We'll let you leave if you do."

"No."

"Stars, you're a stubborn man."

"The Crown?" Arianna asked. "Which one?"

"Corona Australis," Cela said, her wings pulling backwards.

Arianna's gaze turned towards me, her eyes sparkling. That only reinforced my determination to keep the Crown away from them.

"Give us the Crown, Orion." Cela said. Her eyes were cold, as if she were speaking to a stranger.

"He lost his chance," Arianna whispered.

Perseus exchanged a glance with the Pleiades. Tay shrugged, then shot her arms forward. I took cover behind the tomb as a wave of cold sliced above me. I brushed some frost from my hair. Why were the girls still insistent in turning me into a popsicle?

The earth underneath me trembled, and the vines twisted angrily over the ground. Virgo appeared running from behind the trees at my side. I jumped to my feet and hurried to her side. Virgo and I stood side by side, facing Perseus, Arianna, Tay, and Cela.

Virgo glanced at Arianna, her lips pressed into a thin line.

"Hello, Virgo," Arianna said, her voice bleak as ice. "It has been such a long time."

Virgo's hands trembled as she balled them into fists.

Arianna's eyes bore into Perseus. "I did tell you she would fight against you someday."

Perseus's jaw twitched. "I don't regret saving her." His eyes never left Virgo.

Virgo remained silent, but the earth spoke for her. A thick tree root rose from the ground, standing almost as tall as Perseus. The tree root pointed its sharp end at his chest.

Darkness spread around Arianna's feet like fog, but vanished a second later. Perseus's eyes shone black. I clenched my fists, bracing myself for whatever came next. The tree root shot forward, but Perseus grabbed it before it pierced his chest. That's when I realized he wasn't wearing his gloves anymore. The tree root went limp in his bare hand, and Virgo inhaled sharply. The tree root turned from dark brown into grey, the color spreading from the tip downwards like an infection. The root cracked as the grey slowly took over it, and seconds later it crumbled to the ground.

Arianna smiled proudly, but Perseus's gaze was so dark I felt dizzy just looking into his eyes.

"I thought you didn't want to lose control of Algol," Virgo said.

How had I not made that connection before? Algol, the Demon Star in Perseus's Constellation, represented Medusa's head, which could turn any living being into stone.

A raindrop fell onto Perseus's cheek, sliding down his face like a tear.

"It's too late now," Perseus said.

CHAPTER 19

A SPEAR FLEW ABOVE MY HEAD. Perseus jumped to his side, and the spear pierced the tree behind him. He seemed shocked for only a second before he turned to glare at someone behind me.

"Almost had him!" Castor shouted as he walked up to my side with a smile. Castor's smile dropped as his eyes settled on Arianna.

Perseus grabbed the spear. As soon as he touched it, the spear turned dark grey and cracked to pieces, falling to the ground. Perseus swayed and leaned against a tree. Grey spread from Perseus's hand onto the tree, making it crack. Virgo gasped, as if she could feel the tree solidifying into stone. Cela took a step forward, then stopped, as if afraid that if she tried to help Perseus, she would also turn to stone.

"Oh boy," Castor said, quite unhelpfully.

"We don't need the Twins," Arianna whispered.

Castor took another step back, hiding behind me as if I could shield him from Perseus and Arianna. Tay flapped her wings softly. She and Cela exchanged another glance with Perseus, who nodded.

Perseus pulled his hand away from the tree. He lunged forward at the same time Virgo shot her hands downwards, causing dozens of tree roots to rise in between us and Perseus like a twisted net. Perseus grabbed a root with each hand. They immediately stopped moving and cracked into stone. Darkness began flowing in between the roots like a gushing river. I jumped backwards and pulled Virgo away from the dark mist. Castor pulled two swords from his back as he stood at my side. A tentacle of Darkness shot towards us, aimed at my chest, but Castor cut it with his sword. I didn't expect anything to happen to the dark mist, but as soon as the bone sword came into contact with the Darkness, it vanished. Arianna howled, the sound booming everywhere around me.

"Orion!" someone shouted behind me.

Pollux stood next to a white obelisk fifteen feet behind me. He threw a sword. I extended my arm and caught the hilt. A tail of Darkness was about to stab Castor on the side. I swung the sword forward and cut it right before it touched Castor. It vanished immediately. Pollux cut another thin ribbon of Darkness before it wrapped around Virgo's waist.

Arianna howled in rage. I couldn't see her human form as Darkness kept pooling around us. Darkness surged forward, surrounding us completely. The four of us formed a tight circle as Darkness shifted around us, making me feel as if I was in the eye of a hurricane. It was a churning ocean made of black mist, forming strange shapes that seemed to want to break free of it—a clawed hand, a screaming face, a three-eyed horse, a bird with four wings. The forms came in and out of existence, shifting, drowning, dying. Virgo took a step forward, holding a knife, and stabbed the wall of Darkness. It pulled back before the knife touched it. Virgo slashed again, cutting a horizontal line through the velvet Dark. For a second, the statue of an angel became visible on the other side, as if we had opened a window. It gazed at us with its hands pressed together in prayer, then the Darkness closed again as if it had been stitched together.

Pollux let out a war cry and waved his axe wildly in front of him, creating large cuts through the Darkness. I gripped my sword tighter and stepped forward. A misty black head broke through the Darkness, gazing at me with swirling eyes. I slashed the sword before me, splitting it in half. I was so busy cutting at the Darkness that I didn't notice the dark tail that wrapped around my ankles until it was too late. It pulled me forward, and I fell hard on my back with a grunt. My head hit someone's shoe and yellow stars danced in my vision. I didn't let go of the sword as I was pulled forward, away from the others. My back began to burn as it scraped against the rough ground. I was forced to face upwards, at the twisted dark branches and the thundering dark clouds above them. The Darkness vanished from my ankles. I groaned and stumbled back to my feet, my head spinning wildly.

A pair of hands grabbed each of my arms. I clenched my fists, then realized I wasn't holding the sword anymore. I was pulled off the ground and growled in desperation. My legs dangled wildly in the air as we broke through the trees and flew higher. "Let me go!" I shouted at the Pleiades, then realized that probably wasn't a good idea.

Cela grabbed my left arm, and Tay held my right arm and hugged my chest with her legs. Two more Pleiades appeared around me. One wrapped her arms around my chest, but I couldn't see her face. Aster grabbed my legs and pulled them up.

I remembered, during our last date, that she had told me she wished she could fly and I had found that a bit silly. I couldn't miss the twist of irony that slapped me across the face.

A shriek erupted above me. Aquila, Electra, and Pegasus flew past us, heading towards the clouds. Aquila was at the front, flying high above the other two with his golden wings outstretched and his beak pointed upwards. Bright purple electricity sizzled in Electra's hands as she followed him. Below her, Pegasus beat his massive wings with such force that it sounded like a helicopter.

The three disappeared inside the clouds. Around us boomed a moan in the form of a howling blast of wind. The clouds exploded with a crackling net of thunder and lightning that spread out as far as I could see. My ears rang as blinding light twisted above me.

The Pleiades glided lower, skimming over the treetops. Thunder continued to rumble powerfully in the clouds. A few seconds later, Electra and Pegasus emerged from the clouds. A dozen forks of lightning sizzled down, following the Horse and Pleiad. Pegasus swerved to the side, flying downwards as he avoided a bolt of lightning that struck a tree. Electra caught two of the lightning bolts in her hands. She screamed as the twisting white light wrapped around her and turned violet. She flew upwards again. White and violet bolts clashed and melded together in booming rumbles of thunder.

I looked below me again, and my heart gave a leap. We flew over a large circular clearing. On one end, Leo stood among a sea of tombstones that protruded from the grass like shark fins. Taurus and Lupus stood at the other end, fifty yards away. Lupus howled. The sound made my muscles contract. Leo bared his teeth with a growl. Lupus raced towards the Lion. Leo jumped forward to meet the Wolf, flying over at least ten tombstones. He crushed a tombstone with his left paw as he landed and swung his right paw forward. Leo's claws buried in the Wolf's side and sent him sprawling away, knocking over more tombstones.

The white Bull sprinted forward. Leo rose onto his hind legs and used his front paws to stand on the Bull's horns. Leo roared in rage as he pushed down on the Bull's head. Fire erupted from the Bull's nose, but it didn't seem to bother Leo in the slightest as the flames licked his belly. The Bull pushed Leo backwards, making the Lion's back paws slide over the dirt, leaving parallel lines on the ground. Lupus stood up and shook himself, then howled again.

I wasn't able to see more as we flew over trees again. A shriek echoed in the clouds above me. Light blinded me for a second, followed by a crack that made my ears vibrate with pain. One of the girls screamed, and all of us went down in a spiral towards the ground. I closed my eyes as the ringing in my ears and hysterical screaming washed over me. My legs scraped against branches, and a second later the bones in my legs shuddered as my feet touched the ground. I crumpled to my knees as the air was knocked out of my lungs.

The world spun around me. I buried my fingers in the mud and dragged myself to the side. The girls' voices echoed distortedly somewhere behind me. I dragged myself further away from the sound. My vision swam in stars, and a piercing ring bounced through my head. After about a minute, the ringing subsided and my vision cleared. I stood up, feeling as if my legs had melted like wax. I quickly took in my new surroundings. A tall statue of a young woman was next to me. She had her hands at her side, clutching her flowing dress. Her eyes were cast up, eternally looking at the sky. Gravestones, tombs, and crosses crowded the space between the trees around me. I couldn't see or hear the girls anywhere near me, but I knew I couldn't have gotten very far away from them.

My inner compass spun and I let out a grunt as my scars burned. Draco was near—somewhere ahead of me. I ran towards him. It had stopped raining, but the ground and tombstones were wet and slippery. I passed by a pair of white tombs with a strange design on the lid that depicted the outline of a body, as if there was someone sleeping beneath a very thin blanket of marble. I hated cemeteries, I decided as I kept running. If I ever died, I would prefer to be cremated and have my ashes thrown into the ocean.

I arrived at Draco's location panting with exhaustion. Draco sat on Corvus's back as Corvus lay face down. He had taped Corvus's mouth shut and bound his wrists together with duct tape. I wondered where he had found the tape. Sirius licked Corvus's cheek as he whined, as if begging Corvus to remember him. Maera wagged his tail excitedly as he stared at Corvus's feet.

"Come on," Draco said, his reptilian red-orange eyes narrowed at Corvus. "We've been friends for over a year. Don't you remember that?" Corvus's dark skin was smeared with mud. His brown eyes stared at Draco with a mix of fear and curiosity. "It was me, you, and Virgo, remember?" Draco pulled out something from his pocket and put it in front of Corvus's face—a picture. Corvus's eyes widened. "Don't you remember the movie premieres with Sirius? When we met all those famous actors? The time the three of us ate so much ice cream in Rome that we were sick the next day? Or when Leo pooped on our neighbor's front door because he was rude to us?"

I accidentally stepped on a branch as I walked closer to them, and Draco's eyes bore into me like knives. His gaze softened a second later. Draco rose to his feet and pulled Corvus up.

"We're taking him," Draco motioned at Corvus.

"They'll come after us for that," I said.

Draco shrugged. "They'll follow us anyway."

Corvus avoided my gaze when I looked at him.

"Where's Virgo?" Draco asked.

"Last time I saw her she and the Twins were fighting with Arianna and Perseus."

Draco went pale as a cadaver.

My scars burned as if Aquila had electrocuted me. "They're somewhere over there." I pointed to the right.

Draco nodded and pulled Corvus along. The dogs followed behind us as we ran. Thankfully, Corvus kept pace with us and didn't try to escape. Thunder rumbled in the clouds and a second later lightning crashed behind us, making the ground tremble.

We came out of the trees and into a clearing. Broken slabs of stone lay strewn across the grass. Random patches of grass were blackened and smoking, and I spotted the two parallel lines that Leo had made when Taurus pushed him backwards. I couldn't hear any roaring, howling, or mooing, and the clouds had also gone strangely silent.

"Come on," Draco said.

We quickly trotted through the clearing. We were halfway through when Draco suddenly collapsed on the ground, letting go of Corvus. Sirius started barking madly. Corvus stood still, staring at Draco and the Dog with a confused frown. Maera whimpered as he looked at Sirius barking like a rabid dog.

"Draco!" I kneeled next to him. He was shaking badly, as if he were having a convulsion. "Draco, what's wrong?"

Draco screamed in pain and held his head in his hands. I looked up at Corvus, who stood immobile and looking quite frightened. Sirius howled at the sky. Somewhere in the distance, Leo roared.

"I can't—" Draco choked on his own words. "MAKE IT STOP!"

"Make *what* stop?" I asked, which probably didn't help.

Draco's head cracked loudly, and he screamed even louder. Two gashes cut through his skin at the very top of his forehead. A black spike grew out of each gash. I stumbled backwards, my heart slamming against my ribs. Draco screamed in agony. The twisted spikes grew out of Draco's head like tree roots pushing out of the earth. Corvus took a step back, but tripped on a slab of stone and fell on his side with a grunt.

I turned to the Dog and my heart dropped into my stomach. Sirius had another head growing on his neck. His normal head was contorted in pain as foam and spittle flew from his snout. The other head was pure pink flesh, but slowly began to grow brown, black, and white hair. It took a few seconds for the hair to fully coat the raw skin. The new head barked madly in pain and squirmed, as if trying to break free from Sirius.

I turned back to Draco, who had stopped screaming. He breathed raggedly as he kneeled on the ground, his head cast down as the two gleaming black horns protruded from his head like a dark crown.

A monstrous shriek exploded around us. It sounded like a thousand goats being sacrificed to the Devil. The clouds parted as a monster broke out of them. It landed in the cemetery fifty yards in front of me, crushing tombstones to dust. It was the most horrible monster I had ever seen. The creature was twenty feet tall, its head towering above the trees. It had the head of a man, but hundreds of black snakes twisted out of his head and neck like hair. Instead of hissing, the heads emitted different animal sounds. They mooed, roared, growled, howled, squawked, shrieked, hummed, bleated, and meowed. The creature's eyes glowed with red fire.

The upper half of his body had the torso of a very buff man, with several pairs of wings growing out of his back. The largest pair was black, like a bat's, extending at his sides like a curtain of dripping darkness. But he also had other smaller wings of birds and insects that grew from his back in random places and looked like deformed scales.

The monster's lower body was made of snake tails. There were so many it was difficult to count them. The snake tails were thick as tree roots and of different colors. Together, they seemed to be enough to support the creature's weight.

The monster looked down at me and smiled. I knew exactly who it was.

Typhon—the Father of all Monsters.

Chapter LI, Verse III

The harbinger of Chaos he will become,
After the hearts of the loyal he has made treacherous.
The Lion will be made a monstrous foe,
And the Eagle an enemy to watch from above.
The Dog with many heads to the Underworld will journey,
Until the Hunter and Weaver from Death return.
And the Dragon into the most dangerous monster will transform.

CHAPTER 20

THE MONSTER EMITTED A HISS from his human
head. His eyes shone like two red suns and his gaze drilled into
Sirius. The Dog now had two other fully formed heads coming
out of its neck. My heart sank when all three pairs of eyes began
glowing red. The monster then turned to look at Draco, whose
eyes burned the color of blood. Long black claws had grown out
of his fingers, and his teeth had turned sharp as tiny daggers.

"My children," Typhon whispered, making my heart shoot
backwards.

A shriek broke through the air before Aquila landed on top
of a stone gravestone a few yards in front of me. The Eagle had
grown double in size. He easily reached a wingspan of fifteen feet.
His beak shone like a gleaming knife, and his eyes pulsed like two
rubies. A low growl behind me made a chill slide down my spine.
Leo slowly stepped out of the line of trees. The Lion was taller
than me now, its eyes like a dying sun.

Leo, Aquila, Draco, and Sirius looked intently at Typhon,
their gazes glued to the monster. Corvus moaned as he crawled
further away from Draco. The monster ignored him.

"My children," the monster repeated.

"Draco," I said tentatively.

He didn't even turn to look at me, his eyes bleeding with light.

"The Hunter," Typhon hissed at me. The snake tails below his torso moved in unison to slither closer to me. I took a few steps back.

This was the monster that Cepheus had trapped before dying. The monster Zia had planned to kill. The monster that would help Perseus rise to full power—a monster we had no chance at defeating.

"They say you can hunt down anything and kill any creature," Typhon hissed. "Let's see how good a hunter you are."

The monster grinned, revealing several rows of pointed black teeth. He set his eyes on Draco, then cocked his head to one side. Draco's head snapped to me, his red eyes blazing.

"Draco," I said gently.

Draco lunged at me. His clawed hands wrapped around my arms, tearing my jacket but not slashing my skin. He pushed me downwards. My legs gave under his force, and we both fell. I had never fought Draco, and he was a lot stronger than I had imagined. My head missed the edge of a tombstone by mere inches before it hit the grass. Draco pinned my arms to my sides. The cold from the ground seeped onto my bare skin, and the Crown in my pocket stabbed at my ribs.

I pulled my legs towards my chest and kicked Draco in the stomach. His grip on my arms loosened. I kicked him in the chest and he stumbled backwards, tripping on a piece of tombstone and tumbling on his side.

I scrambled to my feet at the same time he did. A beastly shriek tore from Draco's mouth.

I turned to my right and jumped behind a large stone tomb. It shook as a wave of heat exploded behind me. Draco's fire had been red and orange, but this time it was pure white as it licked the grass and stone into ashes. The fire extinguished after a few seconds. Sweat trickled down my forehead as I counted to ten. When no more fire shot towards me, I slowly stood up, peeking behind the tomb. Draco stood motionless, looking at me with those fierce yet distant eyes. His fire had burned through most of the tomb, searing it to ash. Whoever had been inside had received a free cremation. Hopefully I wouldn't get one myself.

"Draco, stop!" I said.

Draco inhaled again. My feet propelled me to the left and I threw myself behind another, smaller tomb. The stone heated behind me as if I were crouching inside an oven. The fire stopped, and I risked a glance behind the newly cremated tomb.

Draco hadn't moved from where he had been standing. His column of fire had traveled fifteen yards and left a smoking black path of grass. Typhon hissed, although I wasn't sure if that meant he was having fun watching me, or if he was annoyed I wasn't dead yet.

Three-headed Sirius, Aquila, and Leo watched in utter silence as they stood close to Typhon on the other side of the clearing. Corvus had made his way towards the line of trees on the right, but instead of running away he stood staring at me with eyes wide in terror.

"Draco, it's me!" I said, quite uselessly. His red eyes were like two pits of fire—alien, distant, sinister. There had to be a way to wake him up from whatever trance he was in. At least I hoped he was in a trance, and not in a permanent condition.

Someone screamed behind me. I turned just as the Twins broke out of the trees, running past Corvus and towards me at full speed. After running for about three seconds, they stopped dead in their tracks when they noticed Typhon. The monster cocked his head curiously as he looked at the Twins. I raced towards them, away from Draco, who remained still.

A thin line of blood slid down Castor's forehead, but otherwise both Twins seemed unharmed. Pollux still had his axe, but Castor had lost one of his swords.

"Who the hell is that ugly bastard?" Castor asked when I stopped next to them.

"Typhon," I said, my lungs constricting as if I had run a marathon. "He's controlling their minds." I motioned towards the others.

"That is *not* good," Pollux breathed out.

Castor glanced behind him. "Perseus is chasing us." He turned back to Typhon. "Our fight has become a very dangerous game of tag. If Perseus tags us, we're dead as stone."

I wasn't sure what was worse, Perseus being able to turn people to stone with a touch, or Typhon controlling half of our group. Probably the latter.

"Draco!" Pollux said. "Wake up, friend."

Pollux picked up a stone the size of his fist and threw it at Draco. Draco caught it with his clawed hand and crushed the stone to dust.

"Hmmm," Pollux said.

"What the hell was that?" I asked him.

He shrugged. "Throwing a stone seemed better than throwing my sword."

Typhon's snakes began emitting their strange sounds again—meowing, mooing, barking like rabid animals being slaughtered in a farmhouse. Castor whirled around, his sword ready, just before Perseus stepped out of the trees. He startled when he looked at the giant monster.

"Typhon," Perseus said. He didn't sound particularly excited about the monster's presence.

Corvus gagged loudly on the right, making Perseus turn to him.

"Corvus!" Perseus shouted as he ran towards Corvus. Perseus quickly untied and ungagged Corvus. Corvus stood behind Perseus as they both looked up at the monster.

"The Prince," Typhon hissed. "I didn't think it was possible for someone to have more Darkness than me."

My breath caught. That must have been the reason why Arianna had such a physical form now. She had given her Darkness to Typhon, whom I was sure had more than enough flesh to give her in return.

Perseus looked at Draco, Leo, Aquila, and Sirius, then back at Typhon.

"They are my children," the monster hissed at Perseus. "Monsters who have tried so hard to be human." The animal noises died down, as if they didn't want to interrupt Typhon. "This is their true nature—a nature they cannot escape."

My inner compass spun, and my scars burned. Virgo was back at Cepheus's tomb. Had Arianna forced her to go back there to look for something else?

"We are *so* doomed," Pollux whispered.

I didn't have a good argument to contradict him. We could have probably escaped the Pleiades, Perseus, Corvus, Arianna, and their animal allies. But how would we escape Typhon, who now fully controlled half of our group?

Typhon's head snapped back to us. He grinned again, his teeth flashing black. "The Hunter," he hissed. "Unable to hunt the monsters around him." His grin widened even further, his lips cutting through his face like a curved blade. "You'll be my prey."

Rage burned through me so hotly that my cheeks blazed with fire. I hadn't read any of my Prophecies, but I knew with absolute certainty that my future was tied to Typhon's. I would find a way to kill him, and wouldn't stop until he was dead. Perseus stepped closer to us, pulling my attention back to him. He raised his chin and extended his hand to me.

"Just give us the . . ." he trailed off. Perseus looked confused, as if he had forgotten what he was about to say. He turned to Corvus, who shrugged. Perseus looked back towards me, his face red in frustration. "Give me whatever I asked for before!"

Pollux pulled a chocolate bar from his back pocket. "You mean this!" He threw it at Perseus. I didn't know why he had brought a chocolate bar to a cemetery, but I didn't ask. Perseus caught the chocolate and looked at it confusedly, as if he wasn't sure if he had been asking for a snack all along. He probably realized that he hadn't come all this way for chocolate and threw it away.

"No!" Perseus shouted. "Give me the . . ."

I turned to Typhon. His gaze seemed distant as he stared at the broken slabs of stone. The light in the eyes of Draco, Leo, Sirius, and Aquila had nearly vanished, although their eyes were still red. Something brushed against my leg and I realized it was

Maera, who was whimpering silently. I turned to the Twins, and they both gave me a short nod. I picked up the black poodle and we all sprinted away towards the trees.

"Wait . . ." Perseus said, but his voice trailed off, as if he couldn't remember why he wanted us to wait. I didn't dare look back as trees, tombstones, and tombs blurred around me. I caught a flash of movement next to me as Cancer ran at our side, his large eyes bulging out. Two months ago, getting saved by a giant crab would have been the most ridiculous thing I had ever experienced, but now I was deeply thankful. Maera's head bumped up and down as I ran, the claws in his tiny front paws embedded in my jacket.

I risked a glance back but there was no movement among the trees and graves. I didn't know how long Cancer could distract the others, but I assumed we didn't have a lot of time before they caught up.

My scars stung with flames. Virgo was still at Cepheus's tomb. I raced a few feet ahead of the others and let my compass guide me in that direction as I sprinted between graves. "We need to get Virgo and run back to Argo."

"What about the others?" Pollux asked.

I opened my mouth, then shut it. I didn't know how to break them free from Typhon's influence. I wanted to help them, but I knew it was much more likely that they would end up killing us if we tried. I clenched my teeth so hard that my jaw ached. We burst out of the trees—we were back at the crossroads. I stopped running abruptly and nearly fell forward. The Twins and the Crab stopped behind me. Cancer clasped his claws desperately. Maera whimpered in my arms.

Arianna stood in the middle of the crossroads, her hands clasped behind her. "Leaving so soon?" she sang.

Leo roared behind us. His eyes blazed red, his teeth bared at us. Draco came running behind him and stopped next to the Lion, his face expressionless. Aquila shrieked above us as he flew in circles. Sirius barked as he came up next to Leo, his three dog heads dripping white foam from their snouts.

Perseus and Corvus wisely walked around the others at a safe distance, then stood in front of a stone tomb at the edge of the crossroads. Corvus breathed hard as he rested his back against the tomb, but Perseus didn't seem to have tired from the fight. Next to me, the Twins stood back to back with their weapons, Castor facing Perseus and Pollux glaring at Arianna. Typhon, in a considerably smaller size, slithered out of the trees. He was only a couple of heads taller than me now, but that didn't make him any less terrifying. He looked at his mythological children with excitement. I knew the monster didn't care about them—they were only weapons to him. I bit my tongue in frustration.

"Give us the Crown," Perseus said as he took a step forward. "Let's avoid more fighting."

"The Crown," Typhon hissed like rocks sliding against each other. His eyes shone so bright they made my head throb painfully. "Or I'll have your friends rip you to shreds."

"Maybe giving them the Crown is not such a bad idea," Castor whispered.

My inner compass swirled like a whirlwind, and I almost let out a gasp. What had Virgo done? I reached out my hand to Castor's sword, my gaze never breaking away from Typhon. Castor hesitated, but gave me the sword. In exchange, I handed him the poodle. He reluctantly accepted the dog. I took a step back and extended my other hand to Pollux. He raised a brow but gave me his axe without question. Perseus's red eyebrows shot together as his gaze narrowed in suspicion.

My inner compass spun even faster, making me feel like my organs were swirling inside a blender. I softly nudged at the Crab's leg with my foot. He probably didn't know what was about to happen, but I trusted the crustacean was smart enough to figure it out. I held both weapons tightly, my knuckles turning as white as the swords.

My inner compass pointed towards the path on the right. Typhon screeched, Perseus paled, and even Arianna gasped behind me as Cepheus walked towards us.

CHAPTER 21

CEPHEUS WALKED completely naked, his skin bluish-white. The hole that cut through his stomach was one foot in diameter, with black veins around it. His skeleton seemed to be intact, so his lower spine was visible through the hole. Cepheus slowly walked towards Typhon, his milky-white eyes trained on the monster. Typhon hissed loudly, red eyes widening into large orbs. The snake heads dragged the monster backwards, knocking down tombstones and statues.

I pulled my right arm back and threw the sword forward. It landed right in Typhon's chest, below his left breast, and sank about a foot into his skin. Black blood gushed out of the wound. Typhon emitted a shriek that sounded like a car colliding with a wall. I whipped around and threw the axe at Arianna. She slid out of the way, but the axe still sank into her right shoulder. She screamed.

Above us, Aquila shrieked as he swirled down. Leo roared, his eyes golden once again. Draco shook his head, as if trying to knock the horns out of his forehead. Virgo rushed to his side and Draco opened his eyes. We exchanged a quick glance and Draco nodded. I sprinted forward once more, towards Argo. Everyone else followed behind.

"Wait!" Perseus shouted. Lightning crashed behind us, and I heard nothing more from him. Typhon growled and I risked a glance back. The monster used one of his snake tails to pierce Cepheus through the chest. Cepheus didn't even blink.

I turned around again and ran even faster. We arrived at the wall, and this time I was determined to get everyone over it, including myself. Behind me, Draco was pulling Virgo along as she stared at his horns. We were yards away from the wall. Leo was the first to leap over it, followed by Sirius. The Twins pulled themselves up quickly, still carrying Maera, and fell on the other side. Draco helped Virgo up and then climbed after her. The Crab scrambled over the stones. I wasted no time as I pulled myself up and swung myself to the other side, landing on my feet.

Argo was waiting right in front of us in the form of a submarine. Everyone except Draco, Virgo, and Cancer had already gone inside. The Crab, being completely selfish, clasped his claws menacingly at us and dropped first. Draco and Virgo stepped on the sleek surface next. I was about to do the same when a wave of cold knocked me to the side, sending me sprawling away from the submarine. The Crown dug painfully into my ribs. I sat up and was about to get back on my feet when Rose lunged at me and landed on my chest. Air rushed out of my lungs as my back hit the ground.

"I'm sorry," Rose said, her eyes flashing with honest regret. "I'm so sorry."

She pressed her hands over my face before I could push her away. The pain that shot through my skull was unlike anything I had ever felt. My nose, eyes, mouth, and teeth all throbbed in agony as if acid was melting my face. I knew I was screaming, but the pain drowned out every single noise. My whole body trembled as if I were being electrocuted. My head felt as if it was being hammered repeatedly.

My vision turned dark, drowning me in a black ocean of agony.

I sat at a café in New York, alone. The cup of coffee had gone cold long ago. I wasn't sure why I had ordered it, or how I had made it to that café. I couldn't even remember how long I had been staring into the dark liquid.

It wasn't the first time I'd had a blackout. It tended to happen after being with Zia. I took in deep breaths and closed my eyes, the smell of coffee wafting into my nose.

I opened my eyes again and stared at a small bubble that had formed on the coffee's surface. It popped a couple of seconds later. A shiver ran down my spine as a wave of cold swept over me, even though it was the middle of summer. Maybe that's why I had ordered the coffee, to warm myself. I didn't feel any warmer than I did before though. The cold had become part of me—like a void in my chest that radiated ice.

The bell in the front door rang as someone came inside. The smell of lavender hit me like a hammer to the nose as a woman walked next to me. The chair fell backwards as I shot to my feet. My vision blurred, but I was able to see the bathroom sign and the blue door right next to it. Someone shouted at me as I barged across the room and pushed the door open. The white ceiling, walls, and floor blended together as the smell of lavender clung to me. I opened a stall and fell to my knees. I didn't even have time to close the door before I threw up. My throat burned as if I had drunk lava. I coughed, and was glad when the stench of vomit finally drowned out the lavender. I stayed kneeling for a while—it could have been a few minutes or half an hour—staring at the white wall in front of me.

After some time, I flushed the toilet, washed my hands, and walked out. I chewed on a mint as I crossed the crowded street. I didn't even care where I was going. The noise around me seemed louder than usual, and I only caught fragments of conversations.

"I need those papers signed tomorrow . . ." said a man in a sharp blue suit as I walked by him.

"The weather app says it will rain . . ." A woman in a floral dress looked down at her phone as she talked to a female friend next to her.

"I need a new pair of shorts," complained a young teenager to his mother.

The light from the sun glinted brightly from the high-rise buildings, making my eyes sting. A rumble echoed behind me, and I moved closer to a store window as a guy with large headphones rode his skateboard past me. I wiped a trickle of sweat from my forehead. The heat of the pavement burned my feet through the soles. But the cold inside my chest persisted, as if Zia had crystalized my heart into ice.

I walked past a feeble man who sat in front of a designer boutique. He wore a ragged tank top and had no shoes. His white beard had only a few wisps of color left. He held out a broken Styrofoam cup. I pulled out a five-dollar bill from my back pocket and let it drop in the cup as I passed. The man smiled at me, flashing yellow teeth. I smiled back.

I stopped under the shade of a tree, relief flooding through me as the scorching heat diminished somewhat. My hands still felt numb, and even though I was taking deep breaths I felt as if air was leaking out of my lungs. From the corner of my eye, I noticed a girl, around eighteen, taking a picture of me. I let out a sigh as I pushed away from the tree and kept walking quickly, pointedly avoiding looking at her. It wasn't the first time a teenage girl took a random picture of me, and even though it was annoying I had learned to ignore it.

I passed by a group of tourists who were taking pictures of a random building on the side. I wondered why everyone was so enamored of New York. There was nothing special about the city— it smelled bad, had a lot of taxicabs but no greenery, and a lot of weirdos dressed up in ridiculous outfits.

I passed by a group of girls holding so many shopping bags that they were almost sagging under the weight. They pushed their way into a jewelry store and disappeared inside. I wiped the sweat off my brow again and accidentally kicked a plastic bottle. It skidded away towards the edge of the sidewalk, where a large dog sniffed it eagerly.

After a while I arrived at Central Park. Even though it was a popular tourist spot, there were many quiet spaces where I could just be alone for some time. The trees cast a welcoming shade over me as they rustled with the soft breeze. Small birds chirped and jumped from one branch to the next. I spotted an empty bench but didn't feel like sitting there, so I continued walking until I found an interesting pair of large boulders. One was curved inwards as if someone had tried to carve it into a giant bowl, while the other was flat like a makeshift table. I brushed the leaves from the latter one, but stopped when I noticed movement on one of the leaves. The bright red ladybug froze when I picked up the leaf where it stood. I gently placed it down inside the curved rock, being careful not to harm the ladybug. Then

I sat on the edge of the flat rock, letting my feet dangle a few inches above the ground.

I took a deep breath. Zia wouldn't find me here. Maybe I should just start sleeping in the park. But eventually I would have to go back, because at some point, Andromeda would escape again. My stomach constricted. Zia mostly left me on my own, but whenever Andromeda went missing, she always knew where to find me. I wondered how she could do that. I knew Zia couldn't track people like I could— she always asked me to find specific people—but she somehow always knew where I was. I briefly wondered if she had implanted a tracking device on me.

I glanced at the ladybug again. It had climbed down from the leaf and now crawled over the rock, heading opposite to me. Didn't Andromeda know how much her little escapes cost me? How much I dreaded them because I would be forced to see Zia again? She didn't know, and probably never would. I had to shield her from the truth— it was my only way to protect her. Zia had nearly killed Andromeda only because both of us had rebelled against her. I couldn't let that happen again.

Andromeda didn't care about following Zia's rules. So I had to be the obedient one, letting Zia do whatever she wanted to me so she wouldn't let out her full rage on Andromeda. We couldn't escape Zia—she had made that very clear. So this was the best we could do to avoid the worst of her anger. As long as Zia felt she had control over me, and that in some way I had control over Andromeda, she wouldn't try to kill us again.

I snapped out of my thoughts when a white blur moved at the edge of my vision. It was a girl—a very beautiful one. She slowly walked past a tree fifteen yards away from me. Her hair was the same color as her skin—white as the moon. She glanced at me, and even from a distance I noticed her eyes were a dazzling electric purple. She seemed tall, but I would have to get closer to her to estimate her full height. The girl glanced away, blushing, and kept walking.

I stood from the rock and slowly followed after her. I didn't want to be creepy and scare her, but the girl had intrigued me, and I wanted to know her name. She walked between the trees, her steps light as if she were sliding over the ground. She looked eighteen, around my age. The girl stopped and turned around sharply when she noticed me following. I smiled, trying to appear nonthreatening as I slowly approached her—although with my towering height and strong physique it was always hard to appear amiable. Her eyes narrowed curiously at me.

"It's a nice day for a walk," I said, which had probably sounded like something stupid to say.

The girl smiled. "It is," she said. Her voice was as electric as her eyes. "Although you don't seem to be enjoying it."

"Why makes you say that?" I walked closer to her. Her head nearly reached my mouth. She must have been at least six feet tall.

"You were brooding on a rock," she said with a chuckle. Her eyes were so beautiful—I had never known that shade of purple could exist in someone's eyes.

"I was just thinking," I said.

We began to walk side by side.

"What were you thinking about?" she asked as she looked straight into my eyes.

I shrugged. "Life." We were silent for an awkward moment. "What's your name?" I asked.

"Elena. Yours?"

"I'm Orion."

Her eyes widened. "I'd never met anyone with that name before."

"Neither have I."

She laughed, but her curiosity seemed to have spiked. People always liked my name—it was too unique to forget. The trees rustled as the wind picked up.

"Do you live in the city or are you just visiting?" I asked.

"I live close to the park." She smiled. "Sometimes I come here to get away from my family."

I chuckled. "Me too. They wouldn't come looking for me here."

Elena smiled. "You have a weird accent. Where are you from?"

"I was born in Germany but lived in Britain for a long time." That was not entirely a lie. I didn't know where I had been born, but my earliest memories were from Germany, and I had indeed lived in Britain for a long time with Zia and Andromeda. We had also been in Austria, Switzerland, and Italy before moving to America.

Elena and I stopped at a small restaurant and I bought her lunch. If she was surprised to see me eat five hotdogs, she didn't show it. I hadn't felt so hungry in a long time. We talked for a long while after eating, and I learned she liked playing the piano and the violin, that she sometimes danced ballet, and that she liked to write poems. I didn't have much to say about myself, so I didn't mind letting her talk.

We had been together for a couple of hours when Elena's phone rang.

"Hey," she said, then listened attentively as someone talked on the other end. The voice sounded male, but I couldn't be sure.

"I'll be right there," she said. She turned to me again. "I'm sorry, I think something happened to my brother. I have to go."

"Oh," I said. "Is there anything I can do to help?"

But she was already rushing away from the me. I watched her go, her white hair flowing like rippling waves. My scars burned, and I tracked her as she hurried out of the park. I sighed, suddenly very aware of the void inside me, of that cold that wormed its way through my chest.

I left the park as evening fell and walked aimlessly through the city. The hole in my chest expanded again, but I tried to ignore it as I thought of Elena. There was something special about her. I had memorized how she looked, and it was easy for me to track her. I assumed she lived somewhere in Lenox Hill, since that's where I had sensed her since she had left the park. I knew it would look creepy if I went there to find her again. I could always track her down and arrange a completely "random" encounter. Content with that idea, I walked back to my apartment, took a shower, and went straight to bed. I was surprised that I was able to fall asleep quickly that night, thinking about Elena's electric violet eyes.

The next day I returned to the rocks at the same time as the day before. I was curious to know if Elena would come back too. My scars burned with such an intense pain that I gripped the rock. Elena was a couple of blocks away. After some time, she began walking towards Central Park. My heart sped up, and the pulsing ache of my scars beat in tune with it. Elena was walking straight to my location.

I stopped sensing her right as she passed by the lake. My vision blurred as my scars burst with pain. I nearly tumbled off the rock and had to grip it even tighter. I breathed deeply, feeling the strain of the muscles in my back. I usually used my power only for a few seconds, never during the span of entire minutes. I looked down at the lush green grass underneath my feet as the pain melted away. I closed my eyes for a moment, letting the breeze ruffle my hair.

"Thinking about life again?" Her voice came from behind.

I opened my eyes and turned around. Elena slowly stepped towards me with a smile. She wore shorts and a violet blouse that matched the color of her eyes.

"Maybe," I said as she sat right next to me, her bare shoulder brushing my arm. "Is your family all right?"

"Oh, yeah," she said, looking towards the trees, as if scared her family would appear here at any moment. "My brothers are very reckless. They do silly things sometimes, and me and my sisters always have to fix it."

"I understand how that feels," I said with a sigh.

"Do you have siblings?" Elena fixed her curious gaze on me again.

"Just a younger sister," I said.

"What's her name?" Elena asked, looking at a bird that perched on a branch above us.

"Andromeda," I said. "She's absolutely reckless, and I'm always the one picking up the mess she makes."

Elena laughed. "I feel you."

She met my gaze again, and I was transfixed by the purple thunderstorm in her eyes. She leaned closer to me. Elena's hair softly brushed my cheek, and then her lips were on mine. My body automatically froze. Her lips were soft and tasted like honey. Then the warmth from her lips spread to mine, and it traveled down my neck and into my chest.

Elena abruptly pulled back. "Sorry," she said when I just sat still. "I didn't mean to—"

I pulled her closer and kissed her back, the taste of honey making my stomach flutter. Warmth spread inside my chest. Elena's palm settled on my cheek. I flinched slightly, but didn't pull away. I let the heat flow through me—it had been so long since I had felt anything but the cold. I liked how she traced my jaw with her fingers, and I enjoyed the quick pulse of her heart throbbing against my skin as I brushed my fingers over her neck. It made me forget about Andromeda and Zia. The warmth melted the ice that had frozen up inside me. At some point, Elena pulled away and smiled at me.

"Do you want to get some lunch?" she asked.

"Sure."

I felt famished, as if I hadn't eaten anything in a month. Elena held my hand as we walked. I pulled out my phone.

"Could you give me your number?"

"Of course," Elena said as she took the phone from me and added her number to my contacts.

I sent her a text, and was thrilled when I heard a ping come from her pocket. I would definitely call her after today, maybe take her to the movies, or on walks around the city. Maybe I would invite her to my apartment.

No. I couldn't do that. I didn't know what Zia would do if she saw her there, but knew it wouldn't be good for any of us. I needed to be very careful with this, and make sure Zia didn't find out. My scars burned as I sensed her. She was somewhere in the East Village. I let out a sigh. I would have to keep better track of her now.

I spent the rest of the day with Elena, but as soon as she left, that coldness crept back inside of me. I was determined to make the cold disappear—I would see Elena the next day and her warmth would heat up my chest again.

I really wished Andromeda lasted longer with this foster family, because I wanted to have some time to enjoy myself before I had to *suffer seeing Zia again. The cold crept in as soon as I thought of Zia, but I pushed it away. Now I knew how to make the cold disappear. I would find a way to keep that warmth inside of my chest, to keep myself from drifting off into a void—if it wasn't Elena who gave me warmth, then I would find someone else.*

I knew I had been dreaming, feeling weightless, but as soon as I regained some level of consciousness, I forgot what I had dreamt about.

"Orion," Virgo's voice was firm, pulling me back to my senses.

"Virgo?" My throat felt like I had swallowed a ball of fire.

"He's back!" one of the Twins shouted.

I lay on a soft mattress with a plush pillow under my head. I tried to open my eyes, but only saw darkness. Maybe I was dreaming again.

"Orion?" Draco asked.

"I'm still dreaming," I said in a hoarse voice that made my throat sting with pain. That felt too real to be a dream.

"Orion." Virgo's voice was more urgent. "Rose hurt you very badly."

The memories of the fight in the cemetery rushed back into my mind. The last thing I remembered was Rose pressing her hands to my face and then the agonizing pain. I sat up, my heartbeat shooting into a sprint. My hands immediately went up to my face. I let out a relieved breath. The skin in my face was still smooth except for the stubble growing on my cheeks and chin.

"What did she do?" I asked. I couldn't find anything wrong on my face. My body felt bruised, which I had expected from the fight, but I didn't seem to have any fatal injuries. I needed to open my eyes to assess the full damage, but the impenetrable darkness persisted.

"Orion," Virgo's voice cut through the darkness like a knife. "Rose blinded you."

Chapter XXXVII, Verse I

Of the purest gold the Crown has been fashioned,
Everyone except the King it will dazzle.
After the King's death only the Prince will be able to use its power,
To talk to the ones who from this realm in blood have departed.
The Crown shall remain with the Weaving One,
Until by the treacherous it is stolen,
To take the Prince to his rightful throne full of Darkness.

CHAPTER 22

"WHAT?!"

I looked around me, but nothing except infinite darkness surrounded me. No. I couldn't be *blind.* No, no, no, *no.*

"It means that you can't see," one of the Twins said.

I stumbled out of the bed and shot to my feet, the floor swaying underneath me. Someone grabbed my left arm but I pulled away. My legs crumpled as if they were made of paper, and I fell to my knees.

"No," I said. "This can't be right."

My eyeballs throbbed with every beat of my heart. I looked right and left, but could only see black. My eyelids still opened and closed, but that made no difference.

"No, no, *no,*" I said as I placed my hands over my face.

"The good news is," one of the Twins said, "that your eyes are still as beautiful as always."

"How could she—? How did this happen?" My heart was beating so furiously that my ribcage ached.

"The Pleiades have an association with blindness," Virgo said.

I was blind. I couldn't see. My mind couldn't process that.

"How can I fix this?" I asked, the desperation climbing up my sore throat like bile.

"Well," Virgo said. "In mythology, Orion did become blind and was healed."

"How?"

Virgo hesitated for a moment. "Orion fell in love with the youngest Pleiad, Merope, but when she rejected him, he hurt her, and—"

"That never happened in real life!" I said. My moral values may not have been great, but I had never hurt any of my girlfriends.

"I know," Virgo said gently. "This is just what happened in mythology. So, after he hurt her, Merope's father poked Orion's eyes out. The god Hephaestus took pity on Orion and helped him consult an oracle. The oracle advised the Hunter to look east towards the sunrise, and that miraculously restored his eyesight."

"What time is it?" I immediately asked.

"I don't think looking at the sunrise will work," Draco said somewhere to my left, then quickly added. "But we could try."

Desperation clawed at my heart, ripping it out with sharp talons. I couldn't see *anything* except that darkness around me. I had the sudden urge to just punch a wall, or punch someone. I needed to do *something*.

"Orion," Virgo said softly. "It will be all right. We'll find a way to restore your eyesight."

My chest caved in. Ragged breaths tore through my mouth. Someone pulled me up and helped me sit at the edge of a bed. My inner compass spiraled inside me. Draco was the one holding my arm on the left. Virgo stood a few feet to my right, and the Twins were five yards in front of me, but I couldn't tell them apart.

My mind spun round and round like a flaming carrousel. If I couldn't see, then how would I be able to track down new objects or people? Panic hollowed out my heart. Rose had crippled my power.

My scars burned like flaming rivers rushing down my spine. I grunted at the pain, but felt a small sliver of relief crawl into me as I sensed Andromeda. She was not in Switzerland anymore. She had moved to Denmark, close to the eastern coast. I sensed her moving in slow circles inside a small space.

No matter what you do, in the end it will lead us all into the future I have planned for.

Perseus's voice pierced my skull like a lance. *He* had planned to make me blind and had convinced Rose to do it. He could have done it when I was chained in his basement, but he had waited until we had found the Crown.

"Where's Corona Australis?" I asked, nearly choking on my own saliva.

"We escaped with it," Virgo said.

I sighed in relief. So, in the end, Perseus hadn't gotten what he had so desperately wanted. That gave me a small sliver of satisfaction.

I scratched my cheek, the thick stubble raspy under my fingers. "How long have I been out?" I asked.

"Five days," one of the Twins said.

"*Five days?*"

"Yeah," said Draco. "We haven't really done much aside from taking care of you, but if we want to stop Perseus before his next rising, we need to come up with a new plan."

"Which will be in less than three weeks," one of the Twins added, just in case I had forgotten our tight deadline.

"We have no chance against Perseus," I said as despair wrapped around me. Having stolen the Crown from Perseus now felt like a minor victory. "He has Arianna, who is essentially invincible. And Typhon will make us kill each other. And I'm *blind*."

The darkness tightened its grip, squeezing my chest.

"We need Andromeda's help to defeat Perseus," Virgo said.

"No." Knowing how powerful Perseus had become—that he could turn anyone into stone with a touch—made me want to send Andromeda to another planet.

"We *need* her," Draco said after a minute of silence.

I sighed, clenching my fists in frustration. Maybe the best way I could protect her was by being at her side. Andromeda wouldn't stand a chance on her own.

"Do you know where she is now?" Virgo asked.

My compass twirled inside my chest. "She's in Denmark."

"Where in Denmark?" one of the Twins asked.

The frustration inside my chest swelled like a hot-air balloon. "On the eastern coast. But since I can't see a map, I can't show you where." I had studied maps for many years, and even though I knew much about geography, I hadn't memorized all the cities and towns.

My heart twisted painfully. I wouldn't be able to see Andromeda. Last time I had seen her she had been covered in bruises and cuts. The fingers in her left hand had been swollen and purple, and the bandage tied messily around her head had been stained with blood where Perseus had hit her with a rock. That image was seared inside my memories. I wouldn't see how she had healed, how her hair had grown, how her light blue eyes sparkled like the clear sky.

I would have traded my pinkie finger for one last memory of Andromeda where she looked healthy and lively. When I had said goodbye to her in that forest, I hadn't known it would be the last time I would look at her. No, that wouldn't be the last time. I would regain my eyesight.

"We can find Andromeda after we visit Ophiuchus, like we had planned," Draco said. "We need to recover that asteroid metal to defeat Typhon."

"And," Virgo added, "in mythology, Ophiuchus was the most skilled healer. He was powerful enough to raise the dead. If there's anyone who can heal your eyesight, it would be him."

I nodded. The despair I had felt moments ago dispersed like smoke. A thread of hope dangled before me, and I desperately clung to it.

"I just hope he doesn't try to kill me again," I muttered.

"Do you know where he is?" one of the Twins asked.

I nodded, my inner compass spinning. "He's in Northern Ireland."

"Once we get closer, we'll need you to guide us to a more specific location," the Twin said.

I nodded. "I'll try my best."

A second of silence ticked in the room.

"Do we still have the pack that Zia left at the grave?" I asked as my heartbeat became louder in my ears. I had forgotten about that too.

"Yeah," Virgo said. "We left it in the living room."

I remained sitting as the others shuffled around me.

"Oh, right," said one of the Twins.

Someone grabbed my right arm, making me flinch. My inner compass indicated it was one of the Twins. "I'll help."

"Who is *I*?" I asked.

"Pollux, the handsomest Twin."

I reluctantly stood up again. I hated being touched by people but didn't have an option.

"Okay," Pollux said. "So, we are walking out of the room, and into the hallway."

Presumably, as narrated, we walked out of the room and into the hallway. The darkness around me was solid black, making me feel that I was walking inside a void. I had the urge to extend my hands and feel what was around me, but that would look stupid. Our footsteps were muffled by a thick carpet, and the faint smell of metal and detergent brushed against my nose. I became more aware of the pain that plagued my body. My head ached, my back felt like my skin had been flayed off, and the muscles in my arms and legs were completely sore. I took one unsteady step after the next as Pollux guided me forward.

"To your right and left, there is a wall," Pollux said.

A bark echoed ahead of me.

"Sirius is in front of us. Now he's walking at your other side."

The Dog's snout brushed against my leg, smelling it loudly as if trying to suck my scent like a vacuum. At the same time, a wet lick slid across my ankle.

"Does Sirius still have the three heads?" I asked.

"Unfortunately," Pollux said. "Draco still has the horns too, and Aquila and Leo remained in their much larger sizes."

"Why does Sirius even *have* three heads?" I asked.

"It's one of Sirius's myths," said Virgo somewhere ahead of me. "The Constellation of the Dog also represents Cerberus, who was the three-headed dog who guarded the gates of the Underworld in Greek mythology."

That didn't sound very fun. I definitely liked the one-headed boxer dog better. "Now we will turn left in the hallway." Pollux pushed me to the left, and I turned. Ahead of us, I could sense Draco and Virgo a few yards away, and behind us was Castor. "At our sides, there are more walls."

"Thanks for the detail," I said. "Wouldn't have known that without your guidance."

The smell of roasted chicken wafted towards me.

"Anytime," Pollux answered, and I could imagine him smiling. "To the right is the kitchen, where Draco and Virgo will grab us some early breakfast. To the right is a painting of—"

My foot stepped on lower ground and I was thrown off balance. I slipped out of Pollux's grasp and fell forward. My hands thankfully stopped the fall. They burned with pain, and I remembered that I had scraped them a couple of times.

"Oops, sorry," Pollux said. "I didn't see the step."

I swallowed my angry complaints and pushed myself to my feet again, feeling dizzy.

"Pollux!" Virgo shouted behind me.

"I said sorry!" he repeated.

Virgo gave a frustrated huff. She gently took my right arm. "I'll guide you. Pollux, help Draco with the food."

"Thanks," I muttered.

Virgo guided me forward, thankfully without giving me a tour of the walls and paintings. She was patient when we walked down the stairs, letting me know how many steps I had to descend so I could count them. I felt dizzy, and it took me a few moments to realize that maybe the floor *was* moving underneath me.

"Is Argo still a submarine?" I asked.

"No," Virgo responded. "It turned into a boat."

Virgo helped me sit down on a plush couch and sat next to me. A few minutes later, the Twins and Draco arrived with food. One of the Twins handed me a plate, and the smell of roasted chicken intensified.

"It's roasted chicken," the Twin confirmed.

He handed me a fork and I accepted it. My stomach growled. I used the fork and poked down on the plate, but missed the chicken and poked an empty spot of plate instead. The fork clanked loudly on the ceramic plate. I gritted my teeth, poking down the fork several times before it found the chicken. It seemed as if the roasted chicken was purposefully moving around the plate, hiding from me.

"Do you want me to feed you?" Virgo asked after a while.

"No, it's fine."

It took me longer to find the chicken than to eat it, but I managed. I knew the others were looking curiously at me, but I couldn't blame them. The chicken left me hungry, but Pollux promised me he would make us some tacos later.

"Can someone pass me Zia's package?" I asked. There was a moment of silence. "You guys already opened it, didn't you?"

"Guilty," one of the Twins said.

After some shuffling, I sensed Draco standing up from the couch a few feet in front of me. He picked up the package and walked closer to me. He sat at my other side.

"She left a note," Draco said. "For you."

My heart knotted in pain. Zia had known I would find Cepheus's tomb. That meant she *had* intended to leave that key in the freezer. She had led me into one last hunt. My throat contracted painfully.

"What does it say?" I could barely push those words out.

Draco cleared his throat. "It says: *The Northern Crown for the Princess and the Arrow for the Hunter. I once used to own these weapons and left them hidden for when they would be needed again. Find them to defeat Perseus, Orion, and don't let him take the Southern Crown . . .* That's it."

"What?" I asked. "There has to be something else. She must have left some other message to me or Andromeda."

Silence.

Rage flared up inside me. I had expected Zia's letter to explain the past she had hidden from us. Or maybe just a message to me and Andromeda saying . . . saying what? That she apologized for everything she had done? That even though she had abused us she still loved us? That last thought sent a wave of pain emanating from my chest.

I shouldn't have expected anything else from Zia—she had left us clues to find two weapons that she had believed would destroy Perseus. That's exactly what I had been looking for. Zia must have been afraid that something would happen to her and she prepared for that outcome so we would be able to protect ourselves. She *had* cared and loved us in her own way.

"Was there anything else in the package?" I asked.

"Yes," Virgo said. "Zia left drawings of an Arrow and a Crown. These are very detailed drawings—good enough to almost look like a picture. I'm assuming the Crown is Corona Borealis, and the Arrow is Sagitta." She paused. "I think she expected you to see the drawings so you could track these weapons."

I bit my tongue. Frustration pounced at my chest like a wild orangutan. I took a couple of calming breaths. We were on our way to Ophiuchus, and if he didn't heal me willingly, I would force him to do it. Then I would be able to see again and track down those weapons. Everything would turn out just fine.

"Was there anything else?" I asked.

"No," Virgo said. "That's all."

As I exhaled slowly, the weight of our new mission pressed heavily upon me. *The Crown for the Princess. The Arrow for the Hunter.* It was a glimmer of hope amidst the looming darkness, the promise of Zia's hidden weapons offering our only chance against Perseus. They would have to be enough.

CHAPTER 23

 "Are you okay?"

I realized I had been quiet for too long. "I'm fine," I said.

Anger pooled in my chest as I thought of Perseus again. He had blinded me to prevent me from finding the weapons that could destroy him. Had he read about that in the Prophecies? I took another calming breath as bile rose up my throat. Ophiuchus would help me. I would thwart Perseus's plans and grind him to dust.

"Cassiopeia hid Corona Borealis, Corona Australis, and Sagitta," Draco said, pulling me out of my thoughts. "Could she and Cepheus have hidden Crater too?"

"I hadn't thought of that before," Virgo said. "We never really did find out who hid Crater in that cavern, but it could have been them." She paused.

Draco cleared his throat. I assumed it was Draco because it sounded like he was trying to swallow a fireball. "But didn't the tour guide say that the newest inscriptions, the Prophecy lines, dated a few centuries into the Common Era? That would mean Cassiopeia and Cepheus hid Crater thousands of years ago."

"If Cepheus and Zia are the ones who hid Crater in that temple," one of the Twins said, "then did they trap Hydra there too to guard the Cup?"

"Could be," said Virgo.

A moment of long silence followed. My heartbeat seemed too loud inside my ears.

"Could they have found, and hidden, Libra and Lyra too?" Draco finally asked. "I don't think anyone has ever found them."

"We haven't heard about them either," one of the Twins said.

"Maybe," Virgo said. "Maybe Cassiopeia and Cepheus found all the Star Objects and hid them long ago."

"That would explain why Perseus is so obsessed about Zia's past," I said.

"But every Star Child can only possess a single Star Object," one of the Twins said. "So Cassiopeia and Cepheus couldn't have been able to use the power of all of those Star Objects at once."

"That's true," Virgo said. "Maybe they wanted to keep the Objects away from others and decided to only own the most powerful ones." That certainly seemed like something Zia would do. "But I've begun to think that some Star Children are tied to certain Star Objects," Virgo said. "We know Corvus owns Crater. Both objects belong to the same myth, so maybe Corvus is the only one who can use the Cup. The Ship Argo is related to the myth of the Argonauts, where Castor, Pollux, and Hercules traveled, so maybe you three are the only ones who can own the Ship. Sagitta is a magical arrow, and it's tied to the mythologies of Hercules and Orion, so it's possible that only you two can use it."

I considered that.

"But that would mean that Cassiopeia and Cepheus couldn't own Argo," one of the Twins said. "But Orion found a picture of Cassiopeia with it."

"I'm not saying this theory has to be true," Virgo said. "I was only trying to find an explanation for why neither Draco nor I could bond to Corona Australis."

"You tried to bond with the Crown?" I asked.

"We *tried*," Draco said. "But the Crown didn't respond. I can see the light coming out of it—it's certainly a Star Object, but it refused to interact with Virgo and me."

"I was thinking that the Crowns may be tied to the royals in the Constellations," Virgo said. "The royal family is Cepheus, Cassiopeia, Andromeda, and Perseus." I could see where she was going, and I wasn't liking it. "Cepheus and Cassiopeia owned the Crowns before, but now that the King and Queen are dead, the Crowns would be inherited by the Prince and Princess."

Another long silence made my breaths sound more ragged.

"Maybe Orion should try," one of the Twins suggested.

"I guess I could," I said. I extended my hand, my heart thumping against my chest. The metal dug against my aching palms. It was unnaturally cold, as if I were holding ice. A few seconds ticked by. Then a few more. Someone coughed. More silence. I could feel everyone's eyes on me and the Crown like burning lasers.

"What exactly is supposed to happen?" I asked.

"If a Star Object bonds it will speak to you," one of the Twins said.

"Well, I'm not hearing anything so I don't think I can bond it either," I said. I placed the Crown next to me on the couch.

"The best thing we can do is to keep it away from Perseus, who might be the only person who can bond with the Crown."

"We'll keep it hidden then," one of the Twins said.

"Does anyone know what Sagitta and Corona Borealis can do?" I asked.

"Sagitta has several myths," Virgo said. "It's Hercules's poisoned arrow, or Cupid's arrow that makes people fall in love. And it's also the god Apollo's arrow, which he used to kill the Cyclops after they murdered his son Asclepius, who is represented by Ophiuchus in the Constellations. In another myth Orion uses the arrow to hunt down wild beasts."

That jumble of myths didn't give me any definitive indication of what the Arrow's power was.

"What about the Crowns?" I asked.

"Those myths are more obscure," Virgo said hesitantly. "In Greek myths they are both associated with the god Dionysus. Corona Australis is the Crown he gave to his mother after he retrieved her from the Underworld and Corona Borealis is the Crown the god gave to his wife, Ariadne of Crete." The cushion moved as Virgo shifted. "The problem is that we've mostly focused on Greek myths to explain the power of the Constellations." Virgo said. "But after what happened in Egypt, I believe that the power of our Constellations may include different myths across various cultures."

I let that thought sink in for a few seconds. "So even if Greek myths don't explain what the Crowns or Arrow do, we could read other mythologies to know their powers?" I asked.

"Maybe," Virgo said. "Most ancient cultures had myths of the Constellations—the Greeks, Egyptians, Mayans, Mesopotamians,

Celts, Norse, Hindus, Aztecs. While some Constellation myths are similar across cultures, others are very different."

I hadn't thought of that before, but Virgo was right. Greek myths tended to predominate over others, but that didn't mean they held the absolute truth. My thoughts traveled again to Zia. I had never seen her do anything out of the ordinary—I had never even seen any of her scars shining. In the Greek myths Cassiopeia was just a vain Queen, but what if she was something else in other mythologies?

"The problem is that Constellation myths from other cultures are harder to find," Draco said, his voice raspier than normal. "The easiest thing we can do is observe our own powers."

"We *have* seen some of our powers change based on geographical locations," Virgo said.

"Like what?" I asked.

"Like Sirius," Draco said. "Normally that Star gives the Dog fame, honors, and riches, because that's what Sirius represented to the Greeks." Draco cleared his throat again, as if he was trying to gulp down lava. "But in Egypt, Sirius accidentally flooded the Nile River because that's what the Egyptians observed from the Star."

"Yeah," said Virgo. "We know that the Light from the Stars in each Constellation are what give them their distinctive powers. And I believe that the Light from the Stars doesn't travel uniformly and affects the world in different ways."

"That's interesting," one of the Twins said. "Castor and I do feel more powerful in certain regions of the sea, usually in the Mediterranean, which is where the original myth of Castor and Pollux comes from."

"I've traveled a lot around the world," I said. "But I haven't felt different. But that doesn't mean you're wrong, Virgo. Maybe the Constellations that have drastically different myths in different locations change more."

"These are all just theories," Virgo said, and I imagined her shrugging. "I'm just trying to figure out what the Crowns can do, and since Greek myths don't explain their powers, maybe we have to look at other mythologies."

"We'll definitely have to investigate more about that," one of the Twins said.

Another long silence stretched in the room, and the darkness somehow felt *darker* around me. I couldn't see people's faces and try to guess what they might be thinking or feeling. My hands clenched instinctively.

"Orion," one of the Twins said after a while, "are you sure you can't find these objects unless you see them? I mean, if we gave you a description of the object, would that work?"

"I don't think so," I said.

Draco sighed. "Then we have to hope that Ophiuchus will heal your eyesight so we can find these objects after we find Andromeda."

The mention of Andromeda made my heart skip a beat. She would be furious when I found her—she had made me promise not to chase after her. But maybe the best way we could protect her was by being close to her.

"Hopefully these Star Objects give us an advantage over Perseus," one of the Twins said. "I'd rather not get turned to stone."

"I didn't even know Perseus could do that," the other Twin said.

"He has Algol's power," Virgo said. "Which is technically Medusa's power. And that power is getting stronger."

"Then we have to get stronger too," one of the Twins said.

He made it sound so easy. As if we could all just go to the gym and buff up to stand a chance at defeating Perseus.

"Oh," Virgo said, "dawn is almost here."

"So?" I asked. Then I remembered Orion's myth.

"It might be worth a try," one of the Twins said.

I stood up and waited for someone to help me. I was glad when Virgo grasped my arm gently and led me outside. A wave of cold washed over me, making me inhale sharply. Virgo stopped, and I did too.

My scars burned as if they were pouring fire. The sun was to my left, and I turned in that direction. I had never tried to sense the sun before—it had always just been there. Footsteps echoed behind me. The others must have come to watch.

The cold wind blew at my hair, and the ocean waves sloshed loudly at the sides of the ship. I didn't hear any birds, which meant we were far from any coast.

The first rays of heat grazed my skin. I had never paid much attention to how the sun felt, but it was a distinctive experience, as if a very thin veil had wrapped around my skin, giving me a gentle caress. That feeling spread through me, and my chest warmed up.

The warmth intensified, but the darkness prevailed, and my chest tightened. I could only hope that Ophiuchus would help me see the light again.

Chapter XX, Verse III

The slumber now ends, after in a deep dream it fell.
From fire and from death the bones of the dead shall repent.
Flames rise higher as the screams of the living mourn the loss,
Of the one who was never supposed to be born.
The man and the beast only one will live to walk away,
From the day when the sun hid behind the night,
And the Demon Prince rose to full power.

CHAPTER 24

I LAY ON MY BED, the darkness around me an endless black ocean. The pair of rings rested heavily on my chest, digging into my flesh. The others had decided to get some rest before we arrived in Ireland in a few hours. I'd wanted to go back to sleep too—to just close my eyes and forget about everything for a moment. The simple pleasure of just closing my eyes was gone, because open or closed the darkness was the same. It felt strange—as if I lived within an infinite dark vault but was confined in a small box at the same time.

I tried to focus on my breathing, hoping it would lull me into sleep, yet my body remained awake. At some point, I wondered what time it was, but I couldn't see clocks anymore. Time was another thing that became abstract as I lay alone.

A growl to my left broke through the darkness. I sat bolt upright with a thundering heart, my scars burning. The growl came again, softer this time, almost as a purr.

"Oh, hey Leo," I had no idea how the giant Lion had walked inside the room. Maybe Argo, being a magical ship, had opened the door for him.

The Lion remained silent, and I lay back down. Maybe the Lion just wanted to give me some company. I took a deep breath, trying to focus on my heartbeat. The rhythmic thump of my heart made me feel more at ease—I was alive, at least.

If Ophiuchus didn't want to help me, then we would force him. But what if he couldn't heal me? No. I pushed that thought away. Ophiuchus was basically the god of medicine. He would find a solution. I held on to that thought as the darkness wrapped tighter around me. I knew Arianna didn't control the darkness around me but fear still prickled my heart. What if Arianna's face suddenly materialized out of that darkness?

"Orion."

I jumped to my feet, my heart slamming against my chest so hard I felt it had fractured my ribcage. My muscles complained at the sudden action, but I ignored them. My scars burst with fire as my inner compass spun, but I only sensed Leo in the room.

"Who said that?" I asked. The voice had been masculine and very deep, completely opposite to Arianna's. It wasn't a voice I had ever heard before. "Who spoke?"

Leo growled.

That couldn't be. Lions didn't speak, and I was sure someone would have figured out by now if Leo was capable of it. Maybe the blindness was slowly driving me into madness.

". . . Listen . . ."

The voice was loud enough that I couldn't have imagined it, but I didn't know if I was hearing it with my ears or if it was coming from inside of my mind. Leo gave another growl.

"See . . . st"

The voice cut out as if I was trying to listen to someone with a terrible cellular connection.

Leo roared.

"How are you doing that, Leo?" I asked.

Leo remained silent, and I didn't hear the voice again. I took a couple of steps back until my legs bumped against the edge of the bed. I sat down and brushed away the sweat trickling from my forehead.

"Leo?" I asked, but the Lion didn't even growl.

I sat crossed-legged on the bed, my muscles sore and burning. Leo moved closer and lay down on the floor. Somehow, I sensed his tail as he wagged it left and right. I had never been able to sense with that much detail before. Maybe I hadn't realized I could do that since I could generally see those subtle movements.

Why was I able to hear Leo's voice inside my head? How did Leo even have a voice? Was I listening to his thoughts somehow? Or had Leo tried to get inside of my mind? I rubbed my forehead as a headache threatened to take over me. Leo's tail abruptly stopped swinging. I tensed.

Someone knocked on the door, but I couldn't tell if the door had been left open or closed. My inner compass spun.

"Yeah?" I asked.

The handle clanked and the door creaked open. I had no idea how Leo had managed to close a door, and wondered again if Argo had done that.

"Hey," Draco said.

Leo's paws scraped against the floor as he stood. The Lion slowly exited the room. Draco gently closed the door. The bed swayed a bit, and I could tell Draco sat at the edge of it.

"What's up?" I asked.

I tried to imagine Draco as he had been before—his sandy blond hair, pale skin, and orange-red eyes. I decided not to imagine the horns and the claws.

"It's just . . ." Draco sighed. "I was sure we would find a way to defeat Perseus, even if he had the Prophecies. But now Typhon has changed everything, and I don't know if we'll survive Algol's next rising."

"We'll find a way." My voice sounded a hundred times more determined than I felt. We were ridiculously outnumbered and outpowered against Perseus, and I was very literally blind against him. But I held on to the hope that the weapons Zia left behind would give us an edge.

"I just don't know if I'll be able to survive seeing Typhon again," Draco said. "His power is unlike anything I've ever felt." He paused. "I've always known that the Dragon still lives inside of me, dormant. But Typhon made the Dragon stir from its slumber."

Draco sounded a bit like Perseus with Algol. Maybe the Dragon was a monstrous aspect of him that he couldn't control.

"I couldn't break away from Typhon." Draco's voice was almost a whisper. "And the Dragon began to awaken as soon as Typhon's power flooded inside of me. It's as if Typhon *wanted* the Dragon to come out." Draco paused. "I'm afraid that if I see Typhon again, I will lose control and hurt you, or worse—I'm afraid that next time I see Typhon, he will make the Dragon fully awaken."

"We'll find a way to defeat Typhon," I said. Somehow.

"I could've hurt Virgo," Draco whispered, so low I barely heard him. "I smelled her. She smelled good." Something began clicking loudly. Could those be Draco's claws tapping against the wall?

"Does Virgo have any thoughts on this?" I asked.

"I haven't told her about the Dragon," Draco said slowly.

"Why?" I asked.

There was a long pause.

"She has her secrets, and I have mine," Draco said cuttingly.

"Fair enough," I said.

Draco exhaled.

"Is the Dragon a separate being from you?" I asked.

"Yes. The Dragon was awake long before I came into existence," Draco said. "*I* was the one who awoke only a few years ago and tamed the Dragon."

"How?" I asked.

"I'm not sure," Draco said. "I just know that my consciousness awoke inside the Dragon a few years ago, and I was just . . . awake. I don't really know how to explain it."

"It sounds hard to explain," I admitted.

"The point is that I became more powerful and took over the Dragon, or maybe the Dragon just weakened considerably. In any case, I turned myself human. The Dragon tried to fight back, but in the end, it fell into a slumber."

"But now Typhon has made the Dragon stir," I said as fear curled down my spine. "Can you fight it? Can you keep it asleep?"

"For now," Draco said. "Typhon didn't awaken the Dragon completely, and as soon as I broke free from Typhon's power the Dragon went to sleep again. But it's not in that deep-sleep state anymore, it's more of a light sleep now. And next time I encounter Typhon . . ."

He didn't need to end the sentence for me to know what would happen.

"I'm going to need your help, Orion," Draco said. "That's why I came to talk to you."

"What do you want me to do?" I asked.

Draco exhaled. "When I lose control of the Dragon, I want you to kill me."

"DON'T BE DRAMATIC, Draco! I'm not going to kill you."

I couldn't see Draco's face, but he sounded dead serious.

"You've killed before, haven't you?" Draco asked, his tone matter of fact. Then his voice softened. "You're the only one who *can* kill me."

"Did Orion kill Draco in mythology?" I asked.

"No, it was Hercules, but—"

"Then go ask Hercules to kill you." I shook my head. "We'll find a way to keep that Dragon sleeping, Draco, but I refuse to kill you."

"When we see Typhon again the Dragon *will* awaken. And when that happens, I'm not sure I'll be strong enough to fight it. The Dragon is a wild and dangerous creature. It will kill you, and Andromeda, and the Twins, and Leo, Sirius, Maera, Aquila, and Virgo."

"We'll find a way to overpower the Dragon and keep *you* in control," I said. "We'll kill Typhon before he can control your mind again."

"I don't know if we'll be able to do that, and I won't let the Dragon hurt or kill any of you," Draco said. "I want you to kill me when I lose control."

"No."

"Orion, please."

"No."

"But—"

Someone knocked on the door.

"Come in!" I said immediately.

It was one of the Twins. "It's Pollux," he announced. "We're an hour away from Northern Ireland, just wanted to let you know." There was a short pause. "Virgo is asking if you can help her make some lunch before we disembark."

I assumed he was talking to Draco. "Sure," he answered hesitantly. The bed shifted again as Draco stood up from the edge. "We'll talk later, Orion."

I didn't answer as Draco and Pollux left the room. The abrupt silence after that tense discussion made my skin crawl with anxiety. I wouldn't kill Draco. Killing him would be another victory for Perseus, and I wasn't going to let him have that. Besides, Draco seemed like a good guy, and he was a powerful ally. I refused to lose anyone from our team to Typhon. I would find a way to destroy that monster.

I took a deep breath, then slowly stood up from the bed, feeling my way around the room. I walked forward as I let my hand slide along the cold wall. I stopped when I grasped empty air. I stepped into what I knew was the bathroom. One hour was enough time for me to attempt to take a shower. I walked forward, slowly, my hands before me. I moved my arms to my sides and stretched my hands, but still felt nothing. I moved them in front of me again as I took another step forward. My fingers finally brushed against smooth glass. I pushed, but it didn't budge. I pressed my palms on the glass walls and stepped to the sides until I found the door and pushed it inside.

That wasn't so bad.

I walked inside the shower, trailing my hand along the tiled walls until my fingers brushed the cold metal handles. I tried to remember which one was for hot water. I moved my hands along the wall again until I found a little metal tray secured to the wall. Thankfully, there was a nice-smelling soap there. That was all I needed.

I took my clothes off and left them outside the shower, then found the handles again and turned the one on the right. Freezing cold water rained over me. I gritted my teeth. I turned that handle off and turned on the other one. Warm water splattered over my sore skin. I slid my hands along the walls again and accidentally bumped into the metal tray with my elbow. Something hard fell on my foot and I groaned. Stupid soap. I crouched down, my hands brushing the soaked floor, but couldn't find the soap. I frantically swept my hands as water splattered around me, and it took me the better part of a minute to find the soap. I stood again, then took one step forward to get closer to the water. My head burst in pain as I crashed into something hard instead.

"AHH!" I yelled in frustration.

I clenched my fists instinctively and the soap slid out of my hand and fell down again, splattering water on my left leg. I stood still for a few seconds, anger seething inside of me.

"Everything okay?" one of the Twins asked in a muffled voice as he spoke through the door. "Do you need help?"

"No!" I answered quickly. "I'm fine!"

The reply came a few seconds later. "Okay. Let us know if you need anything."

The water felt hotter on my skin, like drops of fire raining over me. I didn't need their pity. I didn't need their help. I was capable enough to take a shower. I sighed, then crouched down again and searched for the soap as the water kept pouring over me.

"Okay," one of the Twins said. "How about this one?"

"That's the most horrible hat I've seen," Draco responded.

"It's not that bad," Virgo said.

For the last ten minutes, Draco and the Twins had been try-ing to find a hat that could cover Draco's horns, without much luck, while Virgo and I sat hearing their arguments.

"Oh, come on," one of the Twins said. "Try it."

Fabric rustled as Draco presumably put on the hat. After a few seconds a loud tear ripped through the air.

"What's happening?" I asked.

"Draco tried on a cowboy hat," Virgo explained.

"It didn't work out," said Draco. I really wished I could have seen that.

"I mean . . ." one of the Twins said, "maybe we can just say it's a costume. The cowboy hat and the horns make a good combination."

"Maybe if it were Halloween we could pull it off," Virgo said.

There was more tearing fabric and grunting as Draco pre-sumably took off the cowboy hat.

"How about this one?" one of the Twins asked.

"That's a leprechaun hat," Draco said.

"What's that?" I asked.

"It's one of those tall green hats that people wear on St. Patrick's Day," one of the Twins responded.

More shuffling, and again the tearing of fabric.

"You look like a very cute demon-leprechaun," one of the Twins said, most likely Pollux, before both Twins burst out laughing.

"This isn't funny!" Draco said. "How will I hide these horns?"

"Hmmm," one of the Twins said. "I have an idea."

His footsteps echoed away, then became louder as he came back.

"You've got to be kidding me," Draco said.

"Nope," the Twin said.

More shuffling.

"It hides the horns perfectly!" one of the Twins shouted.

"What hat is it?" I asked.

"It's not a hat," Virgo said with a chuckle.

"It's a really big, recyclable cloth bag with happy-faced fruits," Draco said.

"We got it for free at the supermarket!" one of the Twins exclaimed. "I knew it would be useful someday!"

"I'm not going to walk in public with a cloth bag over my head!" said Draco.

"It looks weird," Virgo admitted. "But it's the only thing that fully hides the horns."

Draco sighed. "What do we do with my claws?"

"Ooh, I have something for that," one of the Twins said.

"Come on!" Draco said. "You want me to wear that?"

"What is it?" I asked.

"Cooking mittens!" one of the Twins said excitedly.

More shuffling as Draco tried them on.

"We also have to hide your sharp teeth," Virgo said.

"Well," one of the Twins said, "we do have this very nice scarf."

"Why does it have bleeding snowmen on it?" Draco asked.

I wasn't sure what he meant by "bleeding snowmen." Did snowmen bleed blood, or water? I was afraid to ask.

More shuffling.

"There!" one of the Twins said. "It's perfect!"

I tried to imagine Draco wearing a "bleeding snowmen" scarf, cooking mittens, and a cloth bag over his head decorated with smiling fruits. My imagination failed me.

Draco grunted in frustration.

"We'll have to leave Leo, Cancer, and Sirius behind," Virgo said, her voice strained. "They'll attract unwanted attention."

"Hopefully it won't take long to find Ophiuchus, get Orion healed, and return," Draco said, his voice muffled by the scarf.

"All right then," Virgo said. "We should get going."

Even though we didn't expect Perseus to know we were in Ireland, dread still gnawed at my chest. My scars ached as I instinctively tried to track Perseus. I sighed. We could worry about him later.

We promptly disembarked from the Ship. As soon as I stepped out of Argo a blast of cold air whipped past, ruffling my hair. Seagulls cried somewhere above me, and the ocean waves roared as they crashed against the shore. The salty air was thick as a dense cloud hovering around me.

"Just point where you sense Ophiuchus," Virgo said.

As we walked away from Argo, my inner compass spun again. I pointed to the right. "He's about five miles inland."

"Walking all the way there will take too long," one of the Twins said. "Let's get past the docks and try to find a cab, or maybe a train."

We set forth in the direction I had pointed. Virgo held my arm lightly as we walked. The salty air became thinner, replaced by a cold wind that made my nose hurt just breathing it. After a few minutes, the sound of crashing waves became drowned by people's voices, but I couldn't make out what they were saying. A man on our right spoke hurriedly. He could have been angry, or excited. Laughs erupted somewhere ahead, and a few seconds later a woman began talking as the laughter died down. A high-pitched bark made me startle. A chorus of loud bells rang ahead. The wind picked up again, slamming the scents of wet dog, raw fish, sausages, and frying oil into my nose. I gripped Virgo's arm tighter as I started breathing through my mouth instead, but the stale taste of fish still found its way to the tip of my tongue.

The ground began to sway underneath me as the blaring voices turned into dissonant sound waves. My body throbbed in pain as all my wounds decided to make their presence known. My back burned and my hands pulsed with biting aches.

"Are you all right?" Virgo stopped walking.

I shook my head, knowing that if I spoke, I would throw up. I took deep breaths as my scars flared up in pain, trying to make sense of my surroundings. Virgo was to my right, Pollux and Castor had stopped walking a few feet ahead of me, and

Draco stood behind me. But everything else was just darkness—a blackness penetrated only by the cacophony of noises and smells.

"Would you be able to drive us a few blocks in that direction?" one of the Twins said.

The reply came as a grunt.

Virgo pulled me forward. "Watch your head."

I slowly climbed into a car, which smelled like someone had spilled some very sugary lemonade inside of it. Virgo helped me put on my seatbelt as Draco and one of the Twins climbed in at my sides. The other Twin was in the passenger's seat in front. Virgo must have been sitting on Draco's lap.

"Could you take us a few miles east?" the Twin ahead of me said. "We'll tell you when to stop."

The driver grunted and the engines roared to life. If the man found anything strange about us, he didn't say a word about it. We drove in silence, and I tried to focus only on Ophiuchus. My heart sped up as we got closer. I wasn't sure what to expect from Ophiuchus. He had tried to kill me, but now he was my only hope at recovering my vision. I told myself that no matter what Ophiuchus wanted to do, we would find a way to make him help me. About ten minutes after we had climbed inside the car, I sensed Ophiuchus close enough to walk to his location.

"We can stop here," I said.

We slowed to a stop as I felt the car veering to the right. There was shuffling ahead of me.

"Is this enough?" the Twin in front of me asked.

"Ya," the driver answered in a hoarse voice.

Virgo unbuckled my seatbelt, and we all exited the car. The cold air blasted me in the face again. The humid smell of wet stones drifted around me, and I wondered if it had rained recently.

My heart sped into a race as my scars flared up.

"He's about fifty yards ahead of us," I said as I pointed in front of me. "Is there a building? I sense Ophiuchus a few floors up."

"That's interesting," Draco said in a muffled voice. "That's a hospital."

"Ophiuchus is a healer," Virgo said at my side. "It makes sense that he's a doctor or something."

"We should still be careful," I said. "He attacked me last time we saw each other."

We quickly walked towards the hospital, and Virgo guided me inside. The sharp tang of disinfectant burned into my nose.

"We should go ask," Virgo said as she pulled me along. We came to a stop a few seconds later. "Hello," Virgo said. "We're looking for Dr. Asclepius."

I wasn't sure why she had said Asclepius instead of Ophiuchus but decided to trust her.

"Ah yes," a man said in a very heavy accent. "Do you have an appointment with him?"

There was an uncomfortable silence. This would have been so much easier if Corvus were here.

"I have an appointment," I said. "I got bit by a snake a few days ago and Dr. Asclepius told me to come back so he could check the wound."

That sounded like a very reasonable explanation. I refrained from saying it had been the magical king cobra that Dr. Asclepius himself had instructed to bite me.

"I do not see your appointment on the list," the man said.

"Well that's strange," I said. "I'm sure I made one."

"It's all right, sir," the man said, although I wasn't sure I looked old enough to be called "sir." "You can write your name on the list here. Let me check the system and try to log you in for an appointment today."

"I'll write your name," one of the Twins said.

Virgo guided me towards a pair of couches while we waited. I nervously tapped my foot on the floor, unable to sit still. My heart pulsed so strongly it strained, and the roaring of rushing blood inside my ears drowned out the mundane conversation the others were having.

Everything would be all right.

Ophiuchus would cure me.

We would defeat Perseus.

I would keep Andromeda safe.

Virgo gripped my arm, pulling my attention out of my head.

Someone cleared their throat. "Mr. Onion, Dr. Asclepius will see you now."

The Twins snickered at the name *Onion,* and I didn't doubt that they had purposefully miswritten my name.

I stood again, and Virgo led me down the hallway.

The man cleared his throat. "Only the patient is allowed to come in."

"I'm blind," I said, the words slicing through my throat as I spoke them. "So I'll need at least one of my friends to take me there."

The man was silent for a very long moment. "I can guide you to his office while your friends wait here."

"I'm coming with him," Virgo said firmly.

A long silence stretched around us.

"Very well then," the man finally said with a sigh. "But the rest of you wait out here."

I wasn't happy that only Virgo and I would be meeting with Ophiuchus, but we didn't have much of a choice. One of the Twins mumbled something behind me. Virgo held my arm tighter as we walked forward again. I tried to calm my battering heart with a few deep breaths, but that only made the tang of disinfectant stronger. We walked for a while until Virgo pulled me to a hard stop. My heart hammered against my chest as I prepared myself for some unseen danger.

"You almost crashed into the elevator," she said.

"Oh."

The elevator beeped and Virgo pulled me forward as we entered it. Classical music drifted from the speakers as we rode up. There was another beep, and the doors pulled apart with a slight screech.

"This way," the man said.

Virgo gently pulled me forward as we walked through numerous hallways. Was this a hospital or a maze? My scars blared to life with an intense pain. Ophiuchus was only a few yards ahead now. My heart pounced so loudly inside my ears that I was sure Virgo could hear it. We stopped, and a couple of seconds later a door creaked open. I instinctively balled my palms into fists.

"Ah," Ophiuchus said in a flat tone. "I'm happy to see you came to your follow-up appointment, Orion."

Chapter XLIV, Verse I

The curse shall befall the King after he has been betrayed,
By the Queen he once loved the best.
Until much later he will discover the truth she hid.
Then the Healer he will seek before his death,
To find a cure to end the one in a deathless slumber.
The Celestial metal shall hold the key,
For a poison to finally end the eternal dream.

CHAPTER 26

DR. ASCLEPIUS'S OFFICE was thick with an oily scent. Virgo and I sat on a pair of chairs as Ophiuchus closed the door. My scars stung. The doctor walked behind me, then around what I assumed was a table, before sitting down to face us.

"Does the wound still feel painful or bothersome?" he asked.

"We need your help," I said, trying to hide the desperation from my voice.

"How about the nausea? Are you still dizzy?"

I stood bolt upright, and was glad when I sensed him startle.

"We. Need. Your. Help," I repeated. He remained quiet this time, and I could feel those lightning-grey eyes boring into me. "The Pleiades blinded me. I need you to help me restore my eyesight."

There was a clicking noise, which sounded like a pen. My scars flared up as something slid over the floor. Virgo gasped as the snake that had bit me slithered towards Ophiuchus.

"Serpens," Virgo said. The snake hissed in response as it curled on top of the table. I half-expected the snake to lunge at me, and my muscles tensed in anticipation.

Ophiuchus shuffled and the chair screeched against the floor as he presumably pushed it back to stand. "Let me check your eyes," he said. The doctor grabbed my arm and pulled me to the side. I was stunned for a second, then let him pull me along.

"Sit," he instructed.

I slowly sat down on what felt like a leather chair. There was more shuffling around the room before Ophiuchus stood in front of me again. I reeled back when his cold palm settled on my cheek.

"I can't check your eyes if you don't let me," he said.

I clenched my teeth and leaned closer to him. Ophiuchus grabbed my chin gently to hold my head in place. Something cold and hard dug into my skin right below my right eye, then below the left one. *Click, click, click.*

"Do you feel anything different in your eyes?" he asked after a minute.

"No."

"How about now?"

"No."

"Hmmm." His breath felt hot against my face as he leaned closer. "Your iris is responding normally, and there is no physical damage to your cornea or lens." He paused. "There seems to be no damage in your optic nerve either. That is certainly strange." There was a soft drumming, and I sensed Ophiuchus tapping his foot on the floor. "How exactly did you lose your eyesight?"

"The Pleiades," I repeated. "Rose, I mean Alcyone, touched my face and I felt a very intense pain. I passed out and woke up without my eyesight."

Ophiuchus stopped tapping his foot. "Hmmm."

"Can you help me?" I asked again.

"Lean back on the chair," he instructed.

I did as he said. I flinched again as Ophiuchus held my head between his hands.

"What are you—?" Virgo began to ask.

Searing pain shot through my head. It drowned the darkness in pure white light that burned through every single cell in my body. I screamed. Then the light shattered into a million pieces, sharp and painful as glass exploding inside my head.

"Orion!" the voice was distant, as if coming from the end of a dark tunnel. "What did you do?" Virgo demanded.

"Orion," the doctor asked calmly as my senses returned. "Can you see anything?"

"No." My tongue tasted like iron.

Virgo gripped my right arm. "What did you do?" she asked again.

"I tried to heal him," the doctor said, and I noted the hint of disbelief in his voice. "This shouldn't be possible. No Star Child is powerful enough to counter my full power unless . . ."

"Are you okay?" Virgo tightened her grip on my arm as if I might slip from existence.

"Yeah," I said.

"I can't help you." His voice was cold.

"What?" I stood up again, the floor spinning below me.

"But you're the most powerful healer in the world," Virgo said.

"I can't cure wounds created by Darkness," he responded.

A whirlwind of emotions raged inside me, and if it hadn't been for Virgo's strong grip I would have crumpled to my knees.

"But—" Virgo protested.

"Whatever the Pleiades did to blind him is beyond my power," Ophiuchus said. "I would need to do more research to find a cure. Come back in a year and I may have something."

Terror razed through my chest. If I couldn't see then I wouldn't be able to find the Star Objects Zia had left behind. I wouldn't be able to defeat Typhon and he would destroy us. I wouldn't be able to fight against Perseus and protect Andromeda.

"There has to be *something* that you can do," I said firmly.

"There is always a cure," Virgo said.

"There is," Ophiuchus agreed. "But none that I know of. It will take me time to find one. Assuming I *do* find a cure."

"Isn't there anything else you can do?" Virgo asked.

The doctor walked away from me. He sat on his chair again. Serpens slithered closer to Ophiuchus with a hiss. "I can prescribe you something for the snake bite, just to make sure your body gets rid of all the poison."

He loudly typed on a keyboard. Fury boiled inside of me, and I contained the urge to strangle the doctor.

"If I don't recover my eyesight *now*, then we're all as good as dead because Typhon, Perseus, and Algol will kill us all." My voice was almost a roar.

Ophiuchus stopped typing. "Typhon has returned?"

"Yes!" I said angrily. "He tried to kill us a few days ago."

"Cepheus had captured Typhon inside an asteroid metal, but Perseus freed him a couple of weeks ago," Virgo explained.

I had been so focused on my blindness that I had completely forgotten about the asteroid metal. My inner compass burned—it was somewhere to the left. "Why did you steal that metal from me?" I asked.

Click, click, click.

"It has a few medical applications I was interested in researching," he said.

I knew he was lying. He had nearly killed me to get that metal, and I had seen that mad look in his eyes—there was something more he wanted from it.

"And how did you know it was in that building?" I asked.

Ophiuchus didn't respond.

"You knew Zia, didn't you?"

"Yes," the doctor said in a cold tone.

"How? When?" I asked.

Ophiuchus exhaled loudly. "We met long before she met you." From his cutting tone I doubted he would say more on that matter. He walked to one side of the room. Metal clanked as if two knives were grinding against stone. "I have taken enough samples from the metal." Another loud clank resonated across the room, possibly from a slamming cabinet or drawer. "You can have it back. I don't need it any longer."

I sensed how Virgo quickly took the metal from the doctor and held it close to her. "Do you know how we can use it to imprison Typhon again?" Virgo asked.

"If you carve the metal into a knife and use it to stab the monster through its heart it could be possible to imprison the monster, but . . ." Ophiuchus trailed off as he headed back to his chair.

"But?" I asked.

"Cepheus already imprisoned him once," the doctor said. "I don't believe the monster can be imprisoned again, at least not with that piece. The one Cepheus had before was nearly five times as big." He paused. "At most you could wound Typhon and incapacitate him for a few minutes."

I breathed deeply, trying to calm the roar of my heartbeat as hope began to slip from me like water oozing out of a cracked glass.

"You're the one who told Cepheus how to capture Typhon," Virgo said with an edge to her tone.

The doctor ignored her. He scribbled on something. Another drawer squealed open, then slammed closed few seconds later. "Take this medicine twice a day, when you wake up and just before going to sleep. It should help purge the last of the snake venom from your system. As for your eyes . . . come back in a year and I may have a cure for you."

I ground my teeth together so hard that my jaw ached.

"Why can't you just use your powers to heal that snake bite?" Virgo asked.

"Serpens's poison is immune to my power," the doctor said. The snake hissed loudly in agreement.

"There has to be something else you can do to help," Virgo said. "Perseus and his allies *will* kill us all if Algol rises to full power with Arianna's help."

Ophiuchus sighed. "This is your battle. Not mine. I have fought my own wars and ended them."

"You do realize that *all of us* includes you too, right?" I asked.

I tensed as my senses sharpened when Ophiuchus leaned closer to Virgo. "Make sure he takes these medications. Has your appetite been normal, Orion?"

"So you're just going to wait here until Perseus comes to kill you?" I asked.

"Perseus is your problem, not mine."

I almost growled in anger. How could he not care? The sound of scribbling was so loud that I wanted to pull that pen out of his hand and plunge it into his neck.

"He *will* become your problem," I said. "He killed Zia, threw a knife that pierced straight through her heart." The scribbling faltered for a second, so briefly that it would have been easy to miss if I hadn't been listening carefully. "What makes you think he won't do the same to you? The only reason he didn't kill Cepheus was because Typhon took care of that for him."

Ophiuchus stopped writing, and I could feel his eyes boring into me with thunderous fury.

"They chose that," he said, his tone so cold the temperature in the room seemed to drop. "They chose to step back into the fight. I won't. I'm done fighting. I've been done with it for centuries. I won't go back in because some big-headed Star Child thinks he can rebel against the power of the Stars."

There was a moment of pure silence, only interrupted by voices outside of the room that faded a couple of seconds later.

"You were part of that generation," Virgo's voice was small compared to his. "Those of you who were born hundreds, maybe thousands of years ago."

"Yes," he said. More shuffling, as if he were ordering some papers, maybe flipping through pages of a book or notebook. "I fought Darkness when it came and defeated it. We knew it would eventually come back, but now it's your turn to fight it. I'm done."

"Why?" Virgo asked. "We're all in danger. You can't just walk away from this."

Serpens hissed in a way that sounded like a sigh. "The war will never end," Ophiuchus said slowly. "Light, Darkness—they have fought since the beginning of time and will fight until the end of it. This is merely another battle, just one more fight in an interminable cycle of Chaos. Even if you defeat Perseus, a new enemy will rise eventually. If Arianna is defeated now, Darkness will come back in another form someday." His words slashed through the air like blades sharp with bitterness. "We fought the Children of Shadows for millennia. What good did that do? We banished one form of Darkness for another one to come barely two thousand years later." *Click, click, click.* "You're young, you're fresh, you haven't seen entire empires disappear under the sand and new ones rise from the ocean. At some point you will walk away from the war too." He gave a low chuckle. "You can't fight against the very nature of this Universe."

"Then why do you work at a hospital?" I asked as anger ignited in my veins. "Sickness will never disappear. Death will always claim the living—that's the nature of the Universe. But you still keep healing. Why?"

Silence filled the room.

"You should leave. I have given you what I can. If I find a way to cure your eyes, I will contact you," his voice sounded hollow.

Virgo held onto my arm and began guiding me towards the door.

"You're just a coward," I said. "If you really believed that you couldn't fight against the nature of this Universe, you would have abandoned this profession a long time ago."

Virgo's grip tightened as she pulled me towards the door. I could feel Ophiuchus's furious glare on my back, but I didn't care. Virgo closed the door behind us. We rode the elevator down to meet with the others again. They didn't say anything to us. Maybe they noticed the expressions on our faces and decided not to ask.

As we walked out of the hospital, I felt as if my bones had turned into wet clay. Something twisted painfully inside my heart, as if someone had stabbed me with a jagged blade. My eyesight wasn't healed. We wouldn't be able to find the Star Objects Zia had left behind. Typhon would make us kill each other if we ever encountered him again.

No matter what you do, in the end it will lead us all into the future I have planned for.

Perseus had already won.

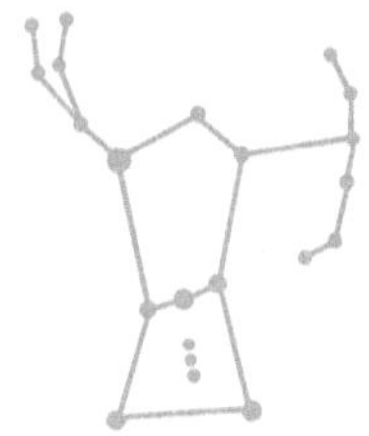

I LAY ON MY BED as Argo swayed slowly. I assumed it had turned into a ship because I usually never felt the submarine move. It would be a few hours before we arrived in Denmark to search for Andromeda and I wasn't sure how to feel about that.

Since we had left the hospital a few hours before, I hadn't felt anything, as if my heart had just gone numb. Even my body had stopped hurting. After undoing my bandages to change them, Virgo had noticed all my wounds from the cemetery battle had disappeared. Ophiuchus must have healed them with his power when he had tried to heal my eyes. But the scars Zia had inflicted were still there, and I had briefly wondered why those hadn't healed too.

The darkness around me was the same as it had been before— just an infinite black ocean. It surged around me, silent, barren, somber. I was submerged miles below the ocean surface, crushed by its immense pressure. I was drowning, floating in an endless expanse full of unknown dangers. I couldn't escape it.

We had about three weeks until Perseus's next rising, and I knew as surely as I knew the sun would rise in the morning that we wouldn't defeat him. How could we? Maybe, if we had found the weapons Zia had left behind, we could have stood a chance. But Perseus had made sure to keep them out of our grasp.

At least if he killed us all, I would die with Andromeda. I couldn't protect her. I had tried so hard to keep her safe from Zia, and had mostly succeeded, but I was completely defenseless against Perseus.

Someone knocked on the door.

"Come in," I said. My scars flared as Draco and Virgo walked in.

"Hey," Draco said.

"Hey," I responded.

"We just wanted to check on you," Virgo said. "How are you feeling?"

"Terrible."

Virgo sighed, then sat at the end of the bed. Draco stood at her side.

"I'm useless now," I said.

"You're not useless," Virgo said.

"There's nothing I can do anymore," I said.

"Yes there is," Draco said. "You don't give up. Because the moment you do, you let Perseus win."

"We have time before Perseus's rising," Virgo said. "I'm sure we can come up with a plan to at least survive what comes next. And just because you lost your sight doesn't make you anything less than the rest of us. We're all in this together and we'll get through it together." I could imagine her giving me a gentle smile. "You're very strong, Orion. You'll get through this."

"Okay," I responded, but didn't feel any more motivated.

Draco and Virgo were silent for a few seconds.

"We'll leave you to rest," Draco said. "But let us know if you need anything."

"Thanks," I said.

Virgo stood from the bed, and they both walked out of the room, leaving me alone in the darkness once again. I appreciated their encouragement, but there was nothing they could do to help me feel better. We were doomed, and there was nothing we could do as we waited for the end.

My inner compass spun and I sat up just as Leo walked into my room. His large paws scraped against the floor as he walked closer to me.

The Lion's meaty breath slapped against my face.

"Hey, Leo." The Lion emitted a low growl. "I'm not in the mood for interpreting growls right now so—"

"*Orion!*" The powerful voice rattled my bones. "*I need . . . listen.*" His voice cut out.

"How am I listening to you, Leo?" I asked.

I wasn't even sure I wanted an answer to that. What difference would it make if I could talk to a Lion?

"*LISTEN.*" His tone was urgent.

"Listen to what?" I asked. I didn't want to listen. I wanted to *see.*

Silence settled around me, and again I wondered if I was imagining Leo's voice. I wouldn't have been surprised if I was going mad, slowly spiraling into insanity in the dark prison of my mind.

"*Listen . . . ears . . . heart.*"

I wasn't sure what that meant. "Listen with ears my heart?"

Leo gave a frustrated growl, as if it was *my* fault that I couldn't understand him.

"Listen to my ears with my heart?"

Leo roared, making the air tremble.

"Listen . . . heart."

"Listen to my heart?" I asked.

"Yes!"

"Why? Last time I listened to my heart it led me to the Pleiades, and we all know how *that* turned out."

Leo growled deeply. *"LISTEN WITH . . . ART."*

"Fine!" I said, just so the Lion would stop bothering me.

I didn't know how to listen with my heart, but didn't want to ignore the Lion. I could feel his golden gaze on me. Leo was so close that the heat from his body drifted to me as if I were standing next to a heater. I focused on hearing my heartbeat—I didn't know what else to do. I put my attention on the slow thumping of my heart against my chest as it pumped blood through my body.

What would Andromeda think about my blindness? What would she think of the whole situation with Perseus? Leo growled, as if he had somehow sensed my attention slipping away from my heart. I pushed my thoughts away. *Thump thump, thump thump, thump thump.*

Despair swam with me in the darkness. I wouldn't be able to see Andromeda. I might never get to see her again before we all died. I would die in that absolute blackness. What would Death look like? Would I be reborn again, as many mythologies claimed? Or would I go straight to Hell? I already knew I wouldn't get a spot in Heaven. What if Death was just as dark and empty as the darkness that surrounded me now?

Leo growled again.

Thump, thump.

The thought of being alone in the darkness sent spikes of fear through me. I would have rather been surrounded by rivers of fire in purgatory.

Leo emitted another growl, and I groaned in response. It was hard to keep my mind quiet. I took a deep breath and felt every beat inside my chest. The steady rhythm made me feel calmer. Part of me just wanted to disappear inside the darkness and vanish into oblivion. Maybe it would be better if Death just ended my soul and put a stop to my suffering.

"Can you listen?" His voice sliced through the darkness like a sword of light, clear and sharp. It was louder than before, and there was no mistaking it for madness anymore.

"Yes," I said as my heart raced across my ribcage.

I didn't hear any replies, and after a few seconds Leo let out a frustrated growl.

"Broke . . . on."

"I broke the connection?" I guessed.

Leo roared again.

I hadn't even known I had *made* a connection. I exhaled as the darkness closed in on me again.

"Leo, I really don't feel like doing this."

I startled when a heavy weight settled on my leg. It took me a second to realize it was his paw. I let out an exasperated sigh.

"Fine," I said through clenched teeth.

Leo removed his paw.

I focused on my heart once again. *Thump thump, thump thump.* I had once heard that the heart was the most powerful muscle in the body, and in that moment I truly felt it.

"Can you listen?" The voice was still powerful, but this time I was careful not to lose my focus.

"I can."

"Good." Leo said, sounding pleased. *"If you want to protect your friends, and if you want to defeat Perseus, you will have to listen to me."*

I shuddered as his voice rang through my blood. Something broke inside of me, and I immediately knew I had lost my connection with Leo again. My head felt lighter, as if it was about to float off my shoulders. I was suddenly very weak, as if a vacuum had sucked out whatever strength I had left.

"What the hell was that, Leo?" I asked.

The Lion didn't answer, and I didn't feel strong enough to forge another connection. I wasn't even sure how I had managed to momentarily connect to Leo's mind—I'd never been able to do that before. The Lion let out a soft growl, then walked away from me and back towards the door. His claws scraped the floor loudly as he exited the room.

I lay stunned in my bed for a few moments. Leo's speech had sounded human. I had known that the Star Animals had enough intelligence to understand everything we said, but this was something else. Leo was more than just a big, powerful, smart Lion. I wondered what the Lion could possibly know to give us an advantage over our enemies. I needed to tell the others about this, but didn't feel like it, not when we were just about to find Andromeda.

I exhaled and rolled to the side. I closed my eyes, but the darkness was the same—absolute black. It might have been my imagination, but it seemed to be swirling around me, forming a face that had become too familiar. The face smiled, waiting to see how much longer I could stay afloat in the darkness before it consumed me whole.

●————●————●

It was already midnight as Zia, Andromeda, and I drove through the empty highway back to New York to drop off Andromeda at her new foster home. I had turned eighteen two months ago, so Zia and the government couldn't force me to be with a family anymore. I had chosen to live alone. Surprisingly, Zia hadn't argued against that and had even gifted me a credit card.

Andromeda sat next to me in the back seat, her head turned away from me as she looked out the window. Drops of rain splattered against the clear glass with a loud clatter. Andromeda's braid had come loose, and her black hair curled down her neck and into her jacket. She hadn't talked to me during the whole ride. I knew she was furious I had told Zia that she had gone to the airport with a fake passport to escape the country.

I didn't know why Andromeda was so intent on escaping. She was fifteen years old—she couldn't have survived on her own for long. But Andromeda rarely thought into the future. How would she earn money? Where would she live? How would she afford food? What would she do with the rest of her life? She couldn't keep running forever.

In front of me, Zia drove in complete silence. Her hands were tight around the wheel. I knew how badly she wanted to beat Andromeda, but she wasn't going to risk it this time. Andromeda had tried many times to tell her families, and even the police, that Zia was physically abusive. But we had no pictures or any other sort of evidence that we had lived with Zia most of our lives. No one had ever believed Andromeda. Zia had made everyone think Andromeda was simply a mentally ill girl..

After an hour of driving, we finally arrived at Andromeda's new foster house. Zia climbed out of the car after shutting off the engine. Andromeda sighed, then unbuckled her seatbelt and opened the door.

"I'll see you later," I said.

Andromeda climbed out and banged the door shut, making the car sway. I waited inside, staring out the window. Andromeda pulled up the hood of her jacket as the rain pelted down on her. She hesitantly stepped forward, her hands buried inside her pockets. She slowly made her way up the stone steps towards the red-bricked house, Zia close at her side. They stopped before the white wooden door and Zia knocked. Andromeda's shoulders sagged in defeat, and she cast her gaze down to the wet ground. The door opened, and a tall man stepped out. He seemed very thin inside the loose sweater he wore. His dark hair had white wisps at the side, and even from a distance I could make out his small eyes behind a pair of rectangular glasses. The man smiled gently at Andromeda. She looked up from the ground, and the man waved at her to walk inside.

I looked away and focused my gaze on the opposite window, watching the drops of rain slide down the glass. They reflected the golden light from the streetlamp next to the car, making it seem as if each drop encompassed a diminutive sun of its own. After a few minutes, Zia came back to the car. We silently drove away from the house. Every few minutes my scars would flare up in flames as I sensed Andromeda at her new house. She probably wouldn't try to escape tonight, but I still instinctively searched for her.

Forty minutes later we were back in Manhattan. I had assumed that Zia would drop me off at my apartment, so I was surprised when instead we drove into the parking lot of her building. Zia shut off the engine and motioned at me to get out of the car. I did as was told and shut the door close behind me.

"Any reason you want me here?" I asked as we arrived at the elevators.

Zia shrugged. "You're eighteen now, I thought we could share some drinks."

The elevator beeped and the metal doors slid open.

"But the legal age to drink in the United States is twenty-one."

Zia laughed. "In Europe it's eighteen."

I didn't argue against her logic as I followed her into the elevator. I had only drunk alcohol once before with some of my high school pals. The alcohol hadn't tasted bad, but it had numbed my powers, as if my inner compass had interference from a magnetic field and didn't know which way was north anymore. I'd never gotten drunk after that, and I had also kept that a secret from Andromeda and Zia. They didn't need to know alcohol made me vulnerable in more than one way.

The elevator stopped when we arrived at Zia's floor. The smell of lavender wafted into my nose as I walked into her apartment. I sneezed. I didn't understand why Zia liked to light scented candles everywhere. I couldn't spot any of the candles, but knew they must have been around somewhere. Zia took off her coat and let it drop on the couch. I sat on the metal chair, letting my elbows rest on the kitchen counter. I didn't take my jacket off—I didn't imagine I would be there for long.

I watched Zia as she moved through the kitchen at the other side of the counter. Zia pulled out a bottle of wine from a cabinet above the sink and poured us some drinks. She let out a sigh as she sat on my left, pulling down her hair tie and letting her blonde hair spill out of the ponytail.

I drank a small sip.

"So," Zia said. "Now that you're eighteen and living alone, what are your plans for the future?"

I shrugged.

"You could go to college," Zia said. "Start working and get a job."

"And then what?" I didn't want to go to college. High school had been bad enough. I had a gift—a power that no one else possessed. I knew that I had to take advantage of it, but I wasn't sure how I could do that. When I turned back to look at Zia, she was staring intently at me as if trying to solve a puzzle on my face.

I took another sip of wine as an excuse to look away from her. My scars burned—Andromeda was still in her new foster house. She was in the upper floor, pacing slowly as if already plotting her escape.

I turned back to Zia. She chugged down the wine as if it were water.

"I'll be right back," she said as she stood up and walked towards her bedroom.

As soon as she was out of sight I hurried to the kitchen and spilled half of my wine into the sink, then rinsed the remains away. I walked back to the counter and sat down again, taking another sip of wine as Zia came back. She seemed content as she glanced at my cup. As soon as she sat down again, she poured herself more wine. I had never seen Zia get drunk, but I assumed I was about to.

"You could become a spy," Zia said, her accent thicker than normal. "A private detective maybe. People go missing all of the time. You could find them."

Was that what I wanted to do with my life?

"Maybe," I finally said.

Zia set her cup down—it was halfway empty again. She chuckled, then licked her lips, her tongue bright red.

"Maybe," she repeated slowly. She looked at me again. Her eyes were distant as a small smile appeared on her lips. It was as if she was looking straight through me at someone standing behind me. Zia traced the rim of the glass with her index finger, the dark wine staining her skin as if she were bleeding. Zia slowly stood up. She was the same height as me while I remained sitting. Her pale golden hair spilled around her shoulders. Zia placed her right palm on my cheek—it was cold as ice.

Zia leaned down and kissed me.

Ice spread from my cheek to the rest of my body, paralyzing me. I couldn't move as Zia's cold lips pressed against mine. She pulled back after a couple of seconds, and I let out a breath that had become trapped in my chest. Zia smiled again. My chest hollowed in as if she had hit me with a hammer.

"Orion," Zia whispered. "The demigod son of Poseidon, the mightiest hunter, and the handsomest man alive." Her smile widened. "I knew you would grow up to be just that."

Her words crossed straight through my head as if she was speaking in ancient Greek. Zia leaned down and kissed me again, harder this time. I was glued to the chair, and even though my mind blared in alarm, I still couldn't move. Zia's frigid fingers cut through my hair as her cool lips pressed against mine.

I could have pushed Zia away and run out of the apartment— but I couldn't. I was powerless, and I didn't know why. I felt so small and weak—so utterly defenseless. Zia pulled back again. Her bare hands touched my waist, and my breath caught painfully. Zia slowly slid her hands along my back, tracing my scars with her fingers. I inhaled sharply, my vision blurring as if oxygen had been sucked out of the room.

"I wish you hadn't made me hurt you," Zia whispered into my ear. "I've never liked beating you. It hurts me as much as it hurts you." Zia pulled my shirt further up. She placed her crisp hand on my chest, right over my heart, making it solidify into ice.

Whatever happened after that was a blur. I simply wasn't there anymore. I was floating somewhere above, far, far away. Alone. At some point, I came back to myself. I stood outside in the drizzling rain. The dim streetlamps barely illuminated my surroundings. I realized I was barefoot when I nearly slipped on the cold, wet ground.

I wasn't sure how I had gotten there, or how I had left Zia's apartment. Thankfully, I was wearing my jacket. The drops of rain splattered down gently over my head, as if wanting to soothe me. I walked through the street with a blank mind, my surroundings fragmented—a black car racing past, a tall tree with branches spilling down on me, lightning reflecting off a window. I stepped on a sharp pebble, my right foot bursting with pain. The sound of laughter echoed somewhere behind me.

My feet stopped, and my inner compass flared up. I realized I was standing outside Andromeda's new foster home. The dark windows revealed everyone was asleep. I walked up the stone steps, towards the door. I needed to tell Andromeda what had happened. She would be furious at Zia, mad with rage, and then . . .

My hand hovered an inch away from the white door. Thunder crashed behind me, making my ears ring slightly. I let my hand drop *to my side. Then I walked away. I didn't know where I was heading, but I just put one foot in front of the other.*

I could never tell Andromeda the truth. Ever. If she knew what Zia had done, Andromeda would go mad. She would definitely try to kill Zia, just like she had tried to do months ago. And just like last time, I knew she wouldn't be able to. Zia had nearly killed Andromeda, and if Andromeda ever threatened her life again . . . I didn't think Andromeda would walk out of that fight alive. Zia wouldn't let her. Once again, it would be my fault that Zia hurt Andromeda.

My pace quickened almost to a jog as I hurried away from the house. Why had Zia done that? I love you. Her words cut through my heart like broken glass. Was that love? No, that was . . . I kept walking in the rain, faster. Maybe Zia had been too drunk and had just gotten out of control. Maybe I had imagined that. Maybe she hadn't meant to do anything. Maybe, maybe, maybe.

I stepped on another sharp pebble and cursed under my breath. I couldn't tell Andromeda. I had to protect her, no matter the cost. I kept walking away, my feet scraping the rough ground. We were trapped. Even if we both escaped, Zia would search for us until the ends of the world to find us. Zia had already shown us she would.

What if I—? No.

How could I even consider killing Zia? She had given us a home, food, clothing, and she had raised us. Without Zia, Andromeda and I would never have had anything. We owed her. And just thinking about harming her made my heart contract. I had disobeyed her orders and she had punished me—that was my fault.

The drops of rain felt heavier as they splashed on my head and dripped from my hair. My teeth clattered as the cold seeped into my bones. I shuddered as the rain slid down my neck and back.

I would have to find a way to stay as far away from Zia as possible. That would be hard though—every time Andromeda escaped, Zia always found me and asked me to hunt down Andromeda. That thought made my stomach twist painfully.

But Andromeda would be all right, I reminded myself. I knew she hated foster homes, but she was safe there. Even if Zia got angry with her after she escaped, she wouldn't beat Andromeda to death— even though Andromeda might get a lash or two. Instead, Zia would let out most of her anger on me. *I was fine with that, I told myself. I could deal with whatever she did. I was strong enough to bear it. Zia would be content knowing she had me under control, so she would focus less on Andromeda.*

I kept walking without a sense of direction. I didn't want to go back to my apartment because I knew Zia would be able to find me there if she wanted. I would just keep walking.

My chest felt as if it had been frozen solid, but the cold wasn't coming from the rain—it was coming from somewhere deep inside of me. Andromeda will be safe as long as you obey Zia, *I told myself. I could bear the weight of Zia's wrath—I had to.* She'll be safe. *I repeated that inside my head over and over again.* Andromeda will be safe. *That was all that mattered.*

The rain poured down on me as I kept walking.

Chapter XLI, Verse II

The Dog shall retain her Queenly shape once again,
But only in the poisoned nightmare that has been spun out of his head.
The deathless dreamer imprisoned in the Silver Castle,
Will remember the Dog's origins and its true power.
The curse of Love shall only be broken,
If the Hunter can see the door invisible to everyone else.
Her power she shall regain only if the sacrifice has been reversed.

CHAPTER 28

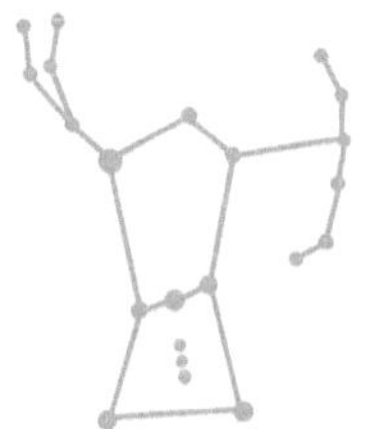

VIRGO LED ME as we disembarked from Argo. The wind was so rough I felt like it wanted to scrape my skin off. It howled loudly, as if lamenting something it had lost. The ocean behind us met the rocks with rhythmic pounds—almost like a heartbeat. The fresh air smelled like pine and freshly cut grass.

To avoid unwanted attention, we had decided to leave our animal friends behind for the moment, except Aquila. I still hadn't told the others about my strange experience with Leo, but planned to do it soon.

"Where to?" one of the Twins asked as we walked away from the Ship.

Darkness stretched around me in all directions—an interminable void that threatened to suffocate me. Andromeda's signal came through it like a beacon of light. I could sense her as strong as I ever had, without the strange interference that blocked her from me sometimes.

"Orion," one of the Twins said.

"Ummm." My inner compass spun. I pointed my finger right ahead of me. "She's around four miles inland. Are there any cabs around here?"

"I don't see any," Virgo said.

"There aren't many signs of habitation here," Draco said in a muffled voice as he presumably spoke through his "bleeding snowmen" scarf. "Just a dirt road, some little houses over there, and I'm not sure what that building is."

"Guess we'll have to walk," one of the Twins said.

I knew that the others still weren't used to my blindness, but I would have appreciated more details from Draco. We began walking in the exact direction that I had pointed. The ground sloped up a bit as if we were climbing up a hill. Maybe we were. Draco walked in front of me, and the Twins were ahead of us. Aquila flew above our heads as he surveyed the land.

Of course Andromeda would have tried to find the most desolate place she could, where others would leave her alone and she could have as little social interaction as possible. But how was she feeding herself? Had she stolen some money? It was unlikely that she had earned money through a job. It was surprising, even a bit impressive, that she had managed to survive all this time on her own.

"Look!" one of the Twins shouted. "It's a goat!"

"Hmmm," I answered.

"You're not missing out on much," Virgo said. "It's just a goat in a pen. Have you guys never seen a goat?"

"We have," one of the Twins answered defensively. "That's just a cute goat."

As we continued forward, Virgo tried to describe the landscape as vividly as she could, which I appreciated, even if I was still mostly disoriented.

"I think Argo may be able to sail through that river as a small boat," she said. "The river is about forty yards wide, but I don't know how deep. On our right there's a couple of small houses. A few of them have pens with animals. There are a few trees around us, although I wouldn't call this a forest. It looks more like a fishing village."

I tried to imagine what Virgo was describing, and while it made me feel a bit better, I still missed seeing the little details. What color were the houses? What kind of animals, asides from goats, were in the pens? Was there light coming out of the houses? I didn't even know what time of the day it was. Were we in a grassy meadow? Or was the ground barren? Did any mountains or hills dominate the landscape?

Some time later, my inner compass flared up. I stopped abruptly and Virgo pulled on my arm before she came to a stop.

"Sorry," I said. "I sense Andromeda a bit to the left." I tried to point exactly where I sensed her—she was still about two miles away. "Is there anything in that direction?"

"There's a forest," one of the Twins said.

We began walking towards it, and even without seeing I felt the difference when we entered. The wind stopped blowing on my face, and the howling became muffled as if trapped by the branches. The scent of pine grew stronger, and the ground beneath my feet became uneven. Instead of walking straight, as we had done before, Virgo constantly pulled me left and right, presumably to avoid crashing against trees. Faint cracks echoed around me as the others stepped on fallen branches and leaves.

"What does the forest look like?" I asked Virgo.

"The trees are tall," Virgo said. "I don't know what type of trees they are but they all look like really big Christmas trees."

"Except they're not decorated," one of the Twins added.

We continued walking in silence. My heart beat louder in my ears as I sensed Andromeda closer. It had been over a month since I had last seen her, but it felt as if I had said goodbye to her an eternity ago.

I abruptly stopped walking again as my scars flared with pain, making Virgo stumble. "Sorry," I said again. "I sense Andromeda there." I pointed in the direction my inner compass pointed. She was close enough for the others to be able to see her.

"There's a small house there," Virgo said in almost a whisper, as if Andromeda would hear us.

"I wouldn't call that a house," one of the Twins said.

"I've seen sheds bigger than that," said the other Twin.

My heartbeat rushed inside of my ears.

"Umm, guys," I said. "Would you mind waiting out here while I talk to her? Just for a bit."

I didn't know how Andromeda would react to seeing me again after I had promised I wouldn't track her down. I didn't want to make things worse if she saw I hadn't come alone.

"Sure," Virgo said, although she sounded reluctant. "I'll lead you to the front door." We walked slowly, my heartbeat furious. My scars ignited with fire as I sensed Andromeda closer and closer.

"Three steps up," Virgo whispered. One. Two. Three. "The door is right in front of you."

Virgo let go of my arm and walked away. The others were a few yards on the side, maybe hidden behind some trees. Aquila had also stopped flying, and now seemed to be perched on some tall branch a few yards to my left.

I tried to calm my breaths. I could sense Andromeda inside

the house. She was moving slowly. I pressed my ear closer to the door, and after a few seconds I heard a muffled scraping. Was she sweeping the floor? I pulled back again and took another deep breath.

I knocked on the door.

CHAPTER 29

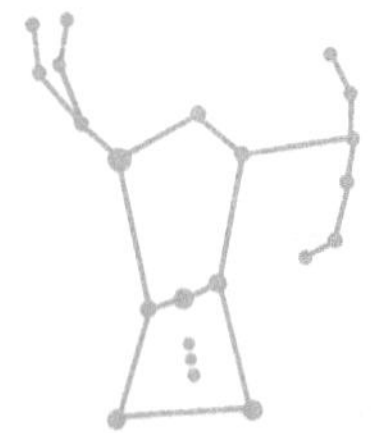

ANDROMEDA WENT VERY STILL. I knocked again, but she didn't move. Maybe she thought that whoever was knocking would go away if she didn't answer. I knocked a third time and waited.

After a few seconds, Andromeda walked to the door. Something clicked, and the door creaked as it slowly opened inwards. Silence stretched, taut as a wire, as we stood three feet away from each other. I expected her to say something, but she didn't.

"Andromeda—" A sharp pain slashed across my face as a slap echoed around me. The sound was so loud I knew the others had probably heard it.

The door banged close. I rubbed my cheek to ease the pain of the slap. I sighed as Andromeda moved away from the door. I hadn't heard her lock it. I extended my hands forward until I touched the cold wooden door. I slid my hands over it, grinding my teeth as splinters dug into my fingers, until I found the handle and pushed the door inside.

"I didn't say you could come in!" Andromeda shouted. I closed the door behind me. I could feel her glare on me like two lasers trying to burn through my chest. Andromeda stepped closer to me, and I could feel her breath on my neck as she presumably looked up at my face. "You *promised* you wouldn't come find me! I asked for one thing, just one. I want to be *alone*."

I didn't answer. I sensed the others moving closer to the house, maybe curious to hear our argument.

"What are you even staring at?" Andromeda asked.

My inner compass spun as I tried to locate Andromeda better. She was five feet in front of me, and a bit to the right. I turned in that direction, but I could have been staring at her stomach, her face, or at somewhere right above her head.

"What the hell is wrong with you?"

"Perseus blinded me." My heart twisted in pain. "He and his allies attacked us and—" My voice caught. I didn't know how to explain the whole situation. "We need to make a plan."

The others were right outside the cottage. Andromeda walked away from me, towards the right. Something solid hit me in the stomach, and I doubled over in pain.

"Ouch! What the hell was that?" I asked.

"A sack of flour."

"Why did you throw a sack of flour?"

The sack had fallen to the floor, but I couldn't tell where it was now, and hoped I didn't trip on it.

"You really can't see?" Her tone was flat.

"That's what *blind* means," I said.

"I know what it means!"

I sensed her walk closer to me, then stop. I looked down, longing to see her face. I wished I could see her eyes and tried to imagine them—a clear blue like a cloudless sky.

"You shouldn't have come." The floor creaked as she took a few steps back. "I told you I wanted nothing more to do with Perseus and this whole mess."

"We can't escape what's coming, Andromeda. Trust me, I would like to, but we can't run away from our futures."

"*We?*"

"Yes," one of the Twins said behind me. "*We.*"

I ground my teeth so hard it was a miracle they didn't crush into dust. "I told you to wait outside!"

"It started snowing," the Twin said. "And I heard there was a sack of flour here—oh, there it is! We should bake some cookies. I should have brought Argo's cookbook."

"Sorry," Virgo said she stepped into the house. "I tried to keep them outside."

"Virgo!" Andromeda said. Anger flared through me, and I bit on my tongue. Andromeda had never been excited to see me.

"You're still wearing the sweater," Virgo said cheerfully.

"Yeah. Draco," Andromeda snickered, "what are you wearing?"

There was some shuffling behind me as Draco presumably removed his fashionable accessories.

"You're a bit late for Halloween, Draco," Andromeda said after a second.

One of the Twins laughed.

"And who are *you* two?"

"We're the Gemini Twins," they both said simultaneously.

"Where's Corvus?" Andromeda asked.

For a few seconds, silence settled in the room like a blanket of snow.

"He's with Perseus," Virgo finally said.

Andromeda sighed. I knew that she didn't want anything to do with any of the Star Children, but we had no choice anymore. Perseus would come find Andromeda anyway, and we would need all the help we could get to fight him. Or at least if he defeated us we would go down together.

"It looks like I missed out on a lot," Andromeda said.

"You have," Virgo said. Her tone was gentle as always, but there was an edge to it. Maybe she wondered if things would have turned out differently if Andromeda and I hadn't left them.

Andromeda shuffled around.

"What are you doing?" Draco asked.

"I'm guessing this is a very long story," Andromeda said. "So we might as well bake some cookies while you tell me what happened."

"Yes!" one of the Twins said. "I'll help."

I was surprised that she had learned how to bake cookies. Maybe her time alone had been good for her. Virgo guided me to a chair and I settled down comfortably. Virgo and Draco explained what had happened after the battle in Palatine Hill, with the Twins intervening every now and then with a comment. Andromeda never interrupted. After Draco and Virgo were done describing the battle against Cetus, I told Andromeda what had happened in the last few weeks. Part of me was reluctant to do it. After all, I had been furious that she had been so stupid to trust Perseus. She would be beyond furious that I had been stupid enough to trust the Pleiades. Then we all explained what had happened at the cemetery. I had expected her to say something, at the very least comment about how much she hated Perseus, or insult my romantic failures.

"What a mess," she simply said.

"Which is why we need your help," Virgo said.

"I can't," she said. "Sorry."

I balled my fists. "Why can't you?"

"I will not be a part of this war," she said. "I won't follow my Prophecies and fight Perseus. And I refuse to search for anything Zia left behind."

"She left those weapons for *us*," I said. "So we could protect and defend ourselves. Why wouldn't you want to find them?"

"I don't owe Zia anything," Andromeda snapped. "I'm not about to go on a quest to retrieve a Crown that once belonged to her. I'm done following Zia's orders. I was done with her a long time ago."

My jaw ached as I clenched my teeth again. "This is not following Zia's orders," I said. "We're trying to track down powerful weapons that could help us defeat Perseus."

"This *is* following Zia's orders." Andromeda's tone rose. "Even after she's dead she expects us to follow her instructions. I'm done with her, and I don't ever want to hear about Zia again. But of course, you're not done with Zia. Like always, you're willing to do exactly what she tells you to do like the obedient dog she turned you into."

I felt that like another slap in the face, and anger boiled so hotly inside of me that it burned my cheeks. Andromeda's rage and resentment towards Zia were clouding her judgment. The others, wisely, remained silent. Even the Twins knew this was a conversation they shouldn't get into.

"Andromeda," I said. "Could we speak in private, please?"

Andromeda didn't answer and simply stormed away. I stood up, and Virgo guided me by the arm towards Andromeda. The door shut behind me as Virgo exited the room.

"You shouldn't have come," Andromeda said in a low voice, as if the thin walls might betray our conversation to everyone else.

"I wouldn't have unless it was absolutely necessary," I said. Her reluctance to help us seemed too exaggerated. This wasn't just about her hate for Zia, or her hate for Perseus. I knew it was something else, and in that moment, standing in the dark, I realized what it was.

"You're afraid of the Darkness Arianna gave you."

I sensed Andromeda startle. She didn't respond.

"Don't even try to lie to me about it. She told me the truth."

"Hopefully she didn't kick your ass too hard."

I sighed. Why was talking to Andromeda always such a challenge? "You took that Darkness from Arianna to save my life."

I wished I could have at least stared at her face to read her expression.

"Even after her death, you're still following Zia," Andromeda finally whispered.

"Don't change the subject."

"This is a much more important subject," she said. "You're still Zia's dog, blindly following her around, and the blind part has become literal now."

"I'm not her dog!" I spat out.

The others would probably be able to hear most of our conversation. I didn't really care at that point.

"Yes, you are," Andromeda said, her tone angry. "You're sniffing around to find the scent she left behind."

"What she left behind may be the best weapons we have to fight Perseus, Typhon, and Arianna!" I hated how Andromeda twisted things in the wrong direction.

"Zia doesn't deserve that," Andromeda hissed. "We shouldn't have to fulfill her dying wish and find those cursed objects."

"This isn't about Zia!" My cheeks burned with rage. "I don't give a damn about her! I give a damn about *you*! Perseus is Prophesized to kill you, and if there is anything that can protect you from that future, I'll find it!" I was sure that even Argo had heard that from miles away.

"Don't lie to me!" Andromeda shouted back. "We both know that this *is* about Zia. Even after her death you try to win her approval, hunting down the clues she left behind."

"This. Is. Not. About. Zia."

"It has *always* been about her!" Something smacked on the floor.

The sugary smell of cookies began drifting into my nose, and I hoped that someone pulled them out of the oven before they caught on fire.

"No, *you're* the one that always makes it about Zia!"

Andromeda started laughing hysterically. So much time alone must have damaged her mental health, which had already been broken.

"*I'm* the one who always makes it about Zia?" Andromeda said slowly. "*You're* the one she abused, and she left you so scarred you can't break away from her."

So that's what she was getting at. Before she died, Zia must have told Andromeda something about what she had done to me, but I didn't know how much Andromeda knew.

"That has nothing to do with this," I said. "This is about surviving Perseus's next rising and defeating him before he kills us, not about what Zia did while she was alive."

"You're still scared of her." Andromeda poked my chest with her finger. "Zia still drives you like a—"

"Why would you even care?" I asked. "You never cared about what Zia did to me before! Why would you care now?"

Andromeda was silent for the better part of a minute while my heart beat wildly. "I do care about you," she said in almost a whisper.

"You just care about being right," I spat back. "You just want me to admit that Zia was a horrible monster who deserved to die."

"She *was* a monster," Andromeda said. "She hurt you so badly you can't even see that. You won't be free from her until you can admit it."

I laughed bitterly. "Says the girl who traveled halfway around the world so she could be 'free.' Tell me, have you truly felt 'free' this last month? You say I'm the one still trapped by Zia, yet you're the one who can't stop thinking about Zia for a second and focus on helping others." My chest heated up with rage, as if it were a knot of fire getting tangled up with my heart.

"At least I'm doing something for myself," Andromeda huffed. "I have a life after Zia. Tell me, what was the first thing you did after returning from Rome?" She paused, but before I could say anything she continued. "If you weren't looking for Zia's secrets, then what would you be doing with your life?"

"I . . ." I tried to come up with an answer.

"You see," Andromeda said. "Without Zia, you're no one."

I took a deep breath. Arguing with Andromeda would get me nowhere. "You were right, I shouldn't have come. I should have known that you were still the same selfish person you've always been, who just cares about being 'free.' Well, have fun with your three weeks of freedom before Perseus kills us all."

I stormed towards the door, fumbled with it until I found the handle, and burst out. I didn't know how far away the front door was but I walked forward anyway. I didn't care if I crashed through a window, I just wanted to leave.

"Orion," Virgo said tentatively.

"I'm leaving," I said firmly.

I stretched my hands out in front of me until I touched a solid surface.

"A bit to the right," one of the Twins said. "And a bit down."

I found the handle and opened the door. A blast of cold air whipped at me. I stepped outside, then remembered there were three steps, and somehow managed to climb down without tripping and falling on my face. I walked to the right, just because I felt like it. Three seconds later, my left shoulder burst with pain as I crashed against something and fell forward on the cold snow. I pushed myself to my feet again and continued forward a bit more slowly, then stopped.

I lowered myself to my knees, my breaths ragged as if I had just run a marathon. The pain in my heart burst like a dam overflowing with water. It drained out of my chest and into the dark ocean around me—like sewage contaminating the sea. The snow melted underneath me and soaked through my clothes, but I didn't care. I stayed kneeling on the snow for what seemed like an eternity, letting the pain drift out of me as the cold oozed into my heart.

Chapter XIII, Verse IV

Her cruel heart many sorrows has caused,
And many more lives out of spite she has ended.
An evil deed committed to the one she used to love,
After blinded by her own power she has become.
Her curse will remain in a deathless slumber inside the Castle,
Until the Hunter puts an end to the slaughter.
Her deeds will neither be forgiven nor forgotten.

CHAPTER 30

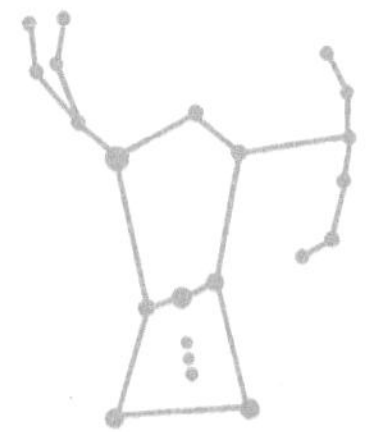

I LAY ON MY BED inside of Argo. It was a much smaller bed since Argo had shrunk down to a boat to fit inside the river. Andromeda was less than a mile away, but after leaving her the night before we hadn't gone to visit again. The others hadn't asked me anything since we had returned, but it was obvious that Andromeda didn't want to help us.

Without Zia, you're no one.

Her words had stung, more than I cared to admit. I did have a life without Zia—this was not about her. It was about Perseus. Because unless we managed to defeat him, none of us would have a life. But if, by some miracle, we managed to defeat Perseus, then what would I do next? I had no idea.

My scars burned, pulling me out of my thoughts. Leo's claws scraped against the floor as the giant Lion walked into my room. He stopped right next to my bed.

"Not now Leo," I said.

Leo roared and pressed his paw on my leg. I didn't move for fear that his claws would rip through my skin if I tried to pull my leg away.

"Walk . . . out." His voice rang inside my head.

"You want me to walk out of my room?"

Leo roared again.

"And go where?"

Leo roared.

I heaved a sigh, but didn't sit up. I really wasn't in any mood to leave the bed. Leo pressed his paw on my leg with more force. Pain throbbed in my thigh. I clenched my teeth but didn't move. Hot air blew across my face, and something prickly and humid struck my face.

"Argh!" I sat bolt upright, then fell from the bed in a tangle. "Leo!"

I wiped his saliva from my face as I stood up again, the floor swaying under my feet.

"What happened?" Virgo asked as she walked into the room.

"Leo licked my face," I said.

"Why would you do that, Leo?" she asked.

"Because he wants me to go outside with him," I said, but didn't explain how I knew that.

Virgo seemed to consider that for a moment. "I think that may be good for you." She paused. "You haven't left that bed for hours."

"I don't want to go outside," I said.

But Virgo didn't listen to me. She shuffled around the room, and then walked back to me and fitted me into a thick coat.

"Fine! But just for a few minutes," I said.

Virgo helped me get into a pair of boots and guided me outside of Argo.

As soon as I stepped out, warmth embraced me. It must have been a sunny day. Somewhere to my left, the water rolled through the river in a loud rush. The scent of pines lingered faintly, and the crisp air was cold enough to make my nose sting a bit whenever I inhaled it. I sensed Leo behind me as Virgo led me forward. She stopped a couple of minutes later.

"Here's a nice rock next to the river where you can sit for a while," she said.

I slowly sat down on the rough, cold, and uneven rock. I sensed Virgo walk back towards Argo, which was about a hundred yards away. Leo stepped closer to me, and I could feel the intensity of his golden eyes.

"Now what?" I asked the Lion.

"*Listen . . . Heart.*"

I rubbed my chin, the growing beard prickling my fingers. I would have to ask someone to help me shave. "How is that going to help?" I asked. "We're doomed, Leo. I know you want to help but I don't think there's anything we can do to defeat Perseus."

"*Tr-y.*" His voice was distant, as if he were whispering to me across a field.

"Fine."

I put my attention in my heart like last time. *Thump, thump, thump.* The rush of the river soon faded into the background. After a while, I began to feel how my heartbeat pulsed through every inch of me. I also became aware of my breathing as I slowly inhaled and exhaled. The rhythms of my heart and lungs were different—one was fast and powerful, the other slow and steady. I focused on that for what felt like a long time. Then I began feeling something else. It was a different rhythm—I could tell that immediately. The new rhythm was much slower than both my heartbeat and my breathing, coming from somewhere in the center of my chest. I tried to focus more on it, but as soon as I did, the new rhythm disappeared, and my breath caught. I coughed, feeling as if I had tried to breath underwater.

Leo gave a soft growl. "*Again.*" This time his voice was clearer inside my mind—it felt more real, more physical.

I took a deep breath, the darkness around me completely motionless. I focused on my heart again, feeling its rhythm. After a few minutes, my heartbeat seemed to intensify, and the new rhythm began to pulse slowly inside of me. It was like a circular wave expanding out of my chest, then collapsing inwards again. It felt like an ocean tide, surging forward, then ebbing back towards its origin. The wave flooded to my extremities, then retreated into my chest. After another minute, the wave flowed a few inches out of my body, then drew back in. With each beat the wave expanded further out.

The wave brushed against Leo. A surge of strength filled my veins, as if someone had injected me with adrenaline. I inhaled sharply, but didn't break my focus.

"*Good.*" Leo's voice was firm.

"What is this, Leo?" I asked.

Leo let out a deep growl. "*If you want to protect your friends, you will have to learn how to use your full power. I can teach you what you need to know to be strong enough to face Perseus, Typhon, and all of the others.*"

"What do I need to learn? How is it possible that I can communicate with you? What is this strange rhythm I feel inside of me?"

"*Do you know what the Constellation of Orion means?*" Leo asked.

"I am the Hunter," I said.

"*In some mythologies, yes. But not in all of them,*" Leo answered. "*You are not just a Hunter, Orion. You are the Eye. You are the Portal.*" Before I could say that I had no idea what that meant, Leo continued. "*In some myths, Orion is represented as a hand with the fingers pointed downwards. The hand has an open Eye in its palm that symbolizes a Portal. In other mythologies, Orion brings souls into the Afterlife. You are the Portal that can access realms outside of our own. You can create a Connection between this world and what lies beyond.*"

"I . . ." I didn't know what to say.

"*Do you remember what Virgo was talking about the other day?*" Leo asked. "*About the power of Constellations changing based on location?*"

"Yes," I said.

"*She was right,*" Leo sounded proud. "*Just as the myths and powers of each Constellation change across the world and across different times, so does our own power.*" He paused. "*Stars evolve—they are born and they die, and in between they change in their brightness, magnitude, and color. Stars are not static, and neither are the Constellations they create. That means our powers are not static either. You must learn to use your different powers, to go beyond the Hunter and learn to become the Portal.*"

"Why haven't I discovered this power before?" I asked.

"*Since you can't rely on your two eyes anymore, another Eye had to open.*"

"So you're saying that if I hadn't become blind, I wouldn't have known about this?" I asked.

Leo took a few seconds to answer. "*If you still had your sight, you probably wouldn't have focused on sensing what was beyond, on seeing in a different way. Maybe you would have eventually discovered this power, but it would have been too late for you to learn how to use it against Perseus."*

"How *can* I use this to fight him?" I asked. "I can only talk to you. And how is talking to you connected to my Portal power or whatever this is?"

"You have discovered the Portal in your heart that allows you to connect to different levels of reality," Leo explained. *"The Portal connects you to me and allows you to listen, and if you let me teach you, it will allow you to sense things beyond your body."*

"But how will this defeat Perseus?" I asked.

"You can use the Portal to find the Star Objects you seek," Leo said. *"And if you learn how to fully use your power, you will be able to sense everything around you."*

As soon as Leo mentioned the Star Objects, my heart sped into a race. "So I can find Corona Borealis and Sagitta even if I don't have my vision?"

"Yes."

"Teach me then," I said.

Maybe we weren't completely doomed.

"Patience," Leo said. *"It will take some time. You will have to train, hard."*

"Then I'll train," I said. "But we don't have much time, Leo. Perseus's second rising will be in less than three weeks."

"I know," the Lion said. *"We will start training very soon, but first I need you to talk to the others. You need to tell them what I have said."*

"Will you train them too?" I asked.

"We don't have enough time, sadly. We need to find the weapons Cassiopeia left behind. Those will be powerful enough to protect us

from Typhon and help us kill Perseus, so I will only have time to train you."

I nodded, my chest warming up with hope.

"How do you know all this, Leo?" I asked.

"I've lived a long life."

"You knew Zia."

The Lion was silent for a few seconds. *"Yes."* I could sense some pain in his tone. *"I knew Cassiopeia, and Cepheus. We fought together for many centuries, and were together for millennia."*

"You fought the Children of the Shadows?" I asked.

"How do you know about them?" His tone darkened.

"Ophiuchus told me."

The Lion sighed. *"We all used to fight together, long ago. Cepheus, Cassiopeia, Sirius, Aquila, Centaurus, Ophiuchus, Ursa, Capricornus, Cygnus, Aries, Lupus—we were the Generation of Old."*

That revelation took a couple of seconds to fully settle inside my mind. Zia had been thousands of years old. Even though we had already guessed that, it felt different to have Leo confirm it. Sirius and Aquila were also ancient, and I wondered if they knew as much as Leo did. The world of the Star Children was much more complicated than I had thought before—a lot more extraordinary than I could have ever imagined.

"So you knew Lupus before too?" I asked.

"We used to be friends," the Lion said sadly. *"We were all friends, and even when we had our fights and disagreements, we always protected each other."*

"What happened?" I asked, truly curious. Barely a month ago, Leo and Lupus had brutally fought each other.

Leo was silent for so long I thought he wouldn't answer. *"Once the War of Shadows ended, we realized our goals and ambitions didn't align anymore."*

He didn't elaborate, but I knew what he meant—the Star Children had conflicting ideas about Destiny, Fate and Prophecy, which had led them to choose different sides in this battle.

"Why are you helping us, Leo?" I asked. "Ophiuchus said he was tired of the fight. I haven't met half of the Star Children that were part of the Old Generation so I assume most of them retired. But you're still here. Why?"

"I have always fought for what I believe in," Leo said. *"And I have never been able to turn my back on those who need protection."*

"What about Sirius and Aquila?" I asked.

"Aquila is just like me; he's never backed down from any fight. And Sirius . . ." Leo paused. *"Her soul is too noble to turn away from this war."*

"She?" I asked.

I had been pretty sure Sirius was a male dog.

Leo laughed inside of my head. It sounded human. *"This is the same as I explained before. Constellations are not static. They shift with time as they evolve. That means that the Light of the Stars three and four thousand years ago was very different from the Light they have now."*

"Okay," I said, still a bit confused.

"Most of us from the Old Generation were very different back then than we are now," Leo said. *"Sirius was not a dog. She was a beautiful woman. But the Light of her Stars changed, and her Constellation changed too. In ancient Egypt Sirius used to be a*

Goddess, but thousands of years later with the Greeks the Constellation became a Dog. Time changes us."

"Were you different before too?" I asked.

"I had a human form once."

I felt a jolt inside of me, maybe shock. How was it possible that Sirius and Leo had gone from human-looking into a Dog and a Lion?

"I used to be a King, one that history has now forgotten." Leo exhaled. *"That's a story for another day. Now, go talk to the others. We need to start planning what to do next, and I need to train you to use your power so you can find Sagitta and Corona Borealis—those will help us defeat Perseus in his next rising."*

"What can Sagitta and Corona Borealis actually do?" I asked Leo. "Have you seen them before?"

"Yes," Leo said. *"Sagitta kills any creature it wounds. It can kill Typhon even if the Arrow only grazes his skin. And Corona Borealis can create a Silver Shield—a protective Circle—that can keep us safe from Typhon's influence as long as we stand within it. With those objects, we will be able to kill Typhon and Perseus. Now go talk to the others and tell them this."*

Relief swept through me. Finding those weapons would change the tide against Perseus.

"What about Corona Australis?" I asked.

"I'm glad you managed to keep that away from Perseus," Leo said. *"The Southern Crown can summon the dead and command them. Perseus could have created an army with it."*

I shivered at that thought.

"We can't use it, so the best next thing we can do is leave it hidden in Argo and make sure he never gets his hands on it," Leo said.

"Sounds like a good idea," I said.

The Twins had already hidden the Crown, so it would remain out of his grasp. It felt like a minor victory that at least we wouldn't have to be fighting the dead along with the living.

"Let's get back to the others."

I sensed the Lion take a few steps away from me. "Leo?" I asked before our Connection broke.

"Yes?"

"I . . ." I didn't know how to phrase the question, and suddenly felt the heavy pull of the two rings around my neck. "You knew Zia. I—I want to know more about her past. Why did she leave Cepheus? Why did she leave you? Was Zia always so temperamental? Why would she have kept the truth from me and Andromeda for so long?"

Leo didn't answer, and for a moment I thought the Connection might have broken. *"I know you want to know more about her, but you may not like what I tell you. Sometimes the past is better left buried, Orion."*

The Lion walked away and something collapsed within me. I coughed as my heartbeat went into a furious race and my lungs contracted. The rush of the river filled my ears. The darkness was still motionless around me, but it didn't feel threatening anymore. Now I knew there was a new power awaiting me beyond the dark.

CHAPTER 31

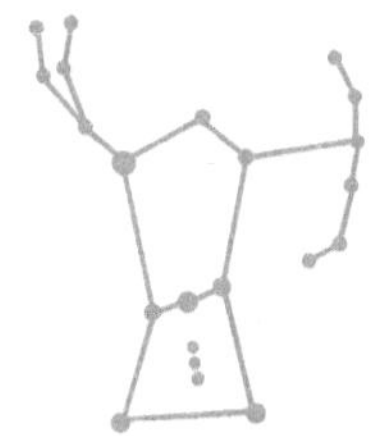

"I HAVE A PLAN," I announced.

Virgo and Draco sat at my sides, and the Twins were right in front of us. Argo always seemed to have a living room, no matter how many times it shifted into different aquatic vehicles. The smell of fried bacon hung in the air and I wondered what the others had cooked that they hadn't shared with me.

"I also have a plan," one of the Twins said. "We could sail to China and eat sushi until we die."

"Sushi is from Japan," said the other Twin.

"Then we should sail to Japan," the first Twin said.

Silence.

"Orion, what did you say your plan was?" Draco asked.

"And does it involve sushi?" one of the Twins asked.

I ignored the Twin and explained what I had just learned from Leo.

"Sirius was a *woman*?" one of the Twins asked.

"Didn't see that one coming," said the other Twin.

"Leo," Virgo said gently. "I'm sorry we never knew any of this. It must have been frustrating that you couldn't communicate with us."

The Lion growled.

"We don't have a lot of time left before Perseus's next rising," I said. "But I'm sure I can train fast enough and learn how to use my power to track down the weapons Zia left behind. Leo said they would be powerful enough to protect us."

"What can those Star Objects do?" Draco asked.

"Leo said that Sagitta can kill anyone it wounds, and that Corona Borealis can protect us from Typhon's influence, so we would be safe from the monster's power," I said.

The cushions moved underneath me as Draco shifted. "It can?" Relief brimmed from his voice. "So Typhon won't be able to control our minds and turn us against you?"

"Leo seemed pretty confident that Typhon wouldn't be able to if we have the Crown, since it creates some sort of shield," I said. "And I can kill the monster with one shot from Sagitta."

"Then we definitely have to find those objects," Virgo said. "With them, we actually have a chance at defeating Perseus."

"But what's the point in going to Perseus's next rising to fight him if Andromeda isn't coming to kill him?" one of the Twins asked.

Then there was that little detail. I didn't know what I could possibly do to convince Andromeda.

"I could try talking to her," Virgo said.

"Good luck with that," I huffed.

"We convinced her to join us the first time," Virgo said. "I'm sure we can convince her again."

There was a pause.

"What will the rest of us do while Orion trains with Leo and Virgo tries to convince Andromeda?" Draco asked.

"I guess we could also train," one of the Twins said. "Perseus won't go down without a fight, and he has very powerful allies to protect him. We should take this time to buff ourselves up."

"If you give me a sword or a lance I could train with that," said Draco.

"Yeah, we'll help you train," one of the Twins said.

"Sounds like a plan," Virgo said cheerfully.

I breathed in, and a wave of determination flooded through me—I would make my new powers work. I didn't let myself think of any other option.

No matter what you do, in the end it will lead us all into the future I have planned for.

Perseus couldn't have planned for this to happen. He had made a mistake—I would use it to destroy him.

———

I crashed against a tree, my shoulder bursting in pain. I nearly tumbled down but regained my balance, biting down a curse. Leo wasn't close enough to talk to me, but I could still feel his gaze on my back.

I took a few deep breaths, trying to temper my growing frustration. I didn't know why I had thought this would be easy—Leo had said it would take some time. Yet I had been hoping my new power would feel natural to learn. But the rhythm flowing through me sometimes felt like an alien organism living within me.

My skin tingled as snow fell over me. It was a still day, the faint scent of moss hanging in the air like an aftertaste. At least everyone else was far away so they couldn't see me make a fool of myself. I instinctively sensed for Andromeda, and my scars only ached mildly. She was close to Virgo, and I imagined they were in her cottage. Only then did I realize that my scars hadn't hurt as much as they should have.

Leo finally stepped closer to me, and his voice flowed smoothly towards me. *"Try again."*

"This isn't working, Leo," I said.

I had crashed into five trees so far, even though Leo had insisted that I should be able to *sense* them.

"How do you normally find people or objects?" Leo asked.

"I just do." I had never thought too much about it. "Once I see something, and then visualize the object or person again, I *know* where it is."

"What you really *do is form a Connection with those objects or people,"* Leo explained. *"You are the Hunter, so that Connection allows you to track down what you seek after you have seen it. But your power goes deeper than that, and that's what you must learn. So far you have only used that Connection when you see something with your two eyes, but now you must learn to find things with a power beyond your body using the Portal."*

"I'm trying," I said through gritted teeth.

"Walk," he said.

"But—" I complained.

"Walk."

I began walking to my right, very slowly. The wave that flowed out of me, and the circular field it formed, moved with me. I kept walking, my hands held in front of me. Leo trotted to my side and pushed my arms downwards with his paw.

"If I don't have my hands in front of me I'll keep smashing my face into these trees," I said.

"You need to learn to sense without feeling. Put your hands down."

Leo stepped back again, and I hesitantly lowered my arms. I took one small step forward, then another, and another. The darkness around me moved like a churning ocean, but there was no lighthouse to warn me about any impending dangers. My body instinctively tensed, preparing for the inevitable impact. The circular field remained flowing in and out of me, but it was hard to focus on it when I was moving.

Pain erupted from my right arm. I immediately stepped to the left, but my foot slipped on the snow and I stumbled backwards. The field around me collapsed right before my back hit the cold ground. I lay there for a couple of seconds, recovering my breath, then pushed myself to my feet again. The darkness around me whirled in a dizzying spin.

"This is not working," I said after Leo walked into the field.

"Why do you believe it is not working?" Leo asked in a gentle tone.

"I don't know," I said. "I barely know what I'm doing."

I sensed the Lion swish its tail from side to side. *"Why did you stretch your hands out?"*

"Because there are trees around me and I can't see them." That seemed glaringly obvious to me.

"Why did you tense your body?" He asked.

"Because I knew I would eventually crash into a tree."

"The reason you are not able to sense is because you still rely on feeling. You stretch your hands to feel the trees. You tense your body

to feel the impact. You will never be able to sense what's on the other side that way."

"Then what do I do?" I asked.

"Stop feeling."

The Lion stepped back again.

I let out a huff. That was easier said than done—Leo wasn't the one getting knocked down by the forest. My body was trained to fight, to tense when it sensed danger coming, to be ready to sprint into action. That wasn't something I could just shut down.

I took a deep breath. This was going to be a lot more painful than I had imagined, but I was determined to make it work. If there was even the slightest chance that we might defeat Perseus, then I was taking it.

I expanded the field three feet away from my body and began walking forward very slowly, feeling the field's vibration. My muscles had instinctively tensed when I took the first step, and I had to relax them again. I took another step forward and stumbled face-first into another tree. I fell backwards again with a grunt, my forehead pounding with pain as the field shattered around me.

I stood up again and opened the Portal. I stepped to the left. It took about fifteen seconds for me to smash into another tree and fall back down again. I stood up, made the field, took a few steps, and then crashed again. It became an unending loop of pain and frustration. I banged my head, scraped my hands, and bruised almost every inch of my body.

The darkness was impenetrable, an endless expanse full of dangerous obstacles. No matter how hard I tried to break through it, I still couldn't sense anything beyond it. At some point, after what felt like hours, I sat on the cold snow. My body was so bruised and sore I felt I'd just walked out of a fight. Leo came back to me and I expanded the field once again to listen to him.

"This isn't working, Leo," I said dismally.

"Then get up and do it again." His tone was gentle, yet commanding.

I would have rather sailed to Japan to eat sushi, but I couldn't give up. I took another deep breath and stood up again despite the throbbing pain. I created the Portal, then began walking. At that point I didn't care if I crashed into every tree in the forest—let the trees beat me to pulp.

My feet crunched as I stepped on the snow. The Portal around me continued to pulse with its usual rhythm. I focused on that rhythm instead of thinking about the trees, letting myself get completely immersed inside of it, like taking a deep breath before letting myself sink into a pool.

Then I sensed something beyond me—a new rhythm that beckoned me to follow it.

Chapter XLIII, Verse II

The Eagle much has seen in his life,
But to silence he has been consigned.
After the battle of the Shadows has ended,
He will fly over the land laid to waste with bones and ash.
With one last breath the Great Bear a secret will share,
Before at last she rests in despair.
The Eagle will be the key to find the Path of the Stars.

CHAPTER 32

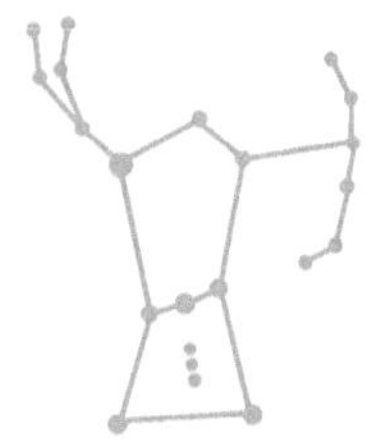

I ABRUPTLY STOPPED walking. It was as if I were standing at the edge of the beach and the ocean waves were washing over my toes and pulling back again. Except that the wave had a rhythm, a different one than the rhythm that rolled out of my chest. The new rhythm was faster, like a drum. It made my skin vibrate in tune with it. The rhythm pulsed stronger when I focused on it, as if that simple recognition drew me closer to it. Could the rhythm have been coming from a tree?

Very slowly, I began expanding the Portal four, five, six feet around me. The Portal remained steady as more rhythms poured through me in tune with the one I had sensed before. It felt as if different drums were beating to the same song. Each of them originated from a different direction. Were all those rhythms coming from the trees? It was as if all the trees were connected to the same beating heart. I kept expanding the Portal until I sensed a new rhythm. It was slower, but sharper—like sticks beating against stone. It was somewhere in front of me, but I couldn't tell what it was.

Leo stepped closer. I inhaled sharply as his rhythm poured into me. Leo's rhythm was powerful, almost drowning out the others, like a marching army preparing to go into war. It rose and fell as a soldier's steps would, never faltering. The Lion didn't talk as he stood a couple of feet behind me. I tried to walk forward, but couldn't. My feet were rooted into the ground. The rhythms faded, but they didn't disappear.

"Why can't I walk?" I asked Leo.

"*You are in the boundary between two worlds now,*" Leo said, his voice reverberating inside of my mind. "*You stand between the physical world and the Connected Realm. It will take practice for you to learn to move in both at the same time. Space is not linear in the Connected Realm, and neither is Time.*"

"I don't understand what that means, Leo," I said.

"*You will,*" he said. "*Just try to sense the world on the other side. Sense its rhythms.* Connect *with that World. You don't have to understand everything right now.*"

I exhaled. My heartbeat slowed. It felt as if I was an antenna and could pick up vibrations that were otherwise undetectable. I focused on Leo's powerful rhythm again, letting it tremble through me. It *was* like a marching army—an army so large that it made the earth shake as it moved into war.

I switched my focus to the rhythms that I believed came from the trees. I let that drumming tune wash over me. This rhythm was livelier than Leo's—more vibrant and less destructive. It was faster too, like cheerful music at a festival.

I tried to stretch my arm to the left so I could touch the tree the rhythm was coming from. It felt as if I were trying to swim against the current of an invisible river. My hand shook as I strained to move it.

"*Don't fight against the current,*" Leo said. "*Follow it.*"

I stopped trying to move my arm, then took a deep breath, feeling a cold gust of wind scrape against my cheeks. What even *was* the current? Was it those rhythms I sensed flowing around me? I thought about a current of water in a running river. If I wanted to follow a river's current all I had to do was let go. I breathed deeply again, clearing my head. I let myself become fully wrapped around the rhythms—let them flow straight through my heart.

Something inside me unlocked, as if I had opened a valve that had only been leaking before. A rush of energy flooded through my chest. I panicked for a moment, feeling like I was about to be swept away into the open ocean. But I didn't fight against it and instead let the current carry me. A chorus of rhythms rang out around me. The trees were the loudest—I simply knew they were trees—with their lively drumming rhythm. The slow and sharp rhythm I had sensed earlier came from a large boulder. I could even sense the rhythm of the snow beneath my feet. It was smooth, as if it were coming from a violin. All the rhythms, even though markedly different, still fit together to form a coherent melody. I couldn't describe it with words, because it wasn't something I heard or felt—it was a song that simply existed beyond the visible world, tying everything together.

I moved my arm to the left, not feeling the pull anymore. My palm touched the rough, cold surface of the tree trunk. It was strange to both feel the tree and sense its rhythm. It was as if I was leaning against someone's chest, feeling their heartbeat. I stayed like that for what seemed like a long while, letting the music flow through my chest.

After some time, I pushed away from the tree. I focused on my own heartbeat again. It drowned out the other rhythms, making them fade into the background, until finally they disappeared. I let out a breath.

"You did well," Leo said inside of my mind. Only then did I realize that the Portal around me hadn't collapsed. *"You did much better than I expected."* He sounded genuinely surprised.

I smiled. I had to tell Andromeda what I had learned. Only a second later I remembered that Andromeda didn't want to talk to me, and she would probably slap me in the face again if I came too close. Pain twisted in my heart, but I quickly pushed it away.

"When will I be able to use this power to track down the objects Zia left behind?" I asked.

"Maybe in a few days," Leo said. My stomach tangled into a knot. I felt the weight of time pressing upon me. We didn't have a few days. *"Don't be hard on yourself,"* Leo said. *"We'll have just enough time to do everything we need to do before we fight Perseus and his allies again."*

I nodded.

"Let's go back to the others."

For a second, I simply stood there. Then I followed Leo as he moved away from me. I couldn't sense his rhythm anymore, but I could sense him as I had been able to sense things before. I walked right next to the Lion, my shoulder and arm brushing his fur. If Leo had retained his bigger size after meeting Typhon, then I assumed that he was at least a head taller than me now. A shiver curled down my spine as I remembered his eyes pulsing with red light. I pushed that thought away—I had to focus on training so I could find the Crown and Arrow that would defeat Typhon.

"I'm not sure I understand what just happened," I admitted.

Leo let out a growl. *"Reality has many layers, Orion. It is made of several different Veils that overlap. Humans are used to only experiencing the physical world, but there is so much more beyond it. There exist so many Veils that connect separate worlds, but in the Connected Realm everything is part of the same fabric of reality."* Leo let out another growl. *"Reality doesn't have a single definition, it doesn't have a single form—it has many, and you have just started to discover some of the elements that make up the Universe we live in."*

I tried to let that settle inside my mind. "What is the Connected Realm?"

"How do you think that all the layers of reality stay together? How do you think that they coexist in the same Universe, but simply in different levels?"

"I don't know," I admitted. My head spun as I tried to find an answer.

"They have to be Connected somehow, right?"

"I guess."

"That is the world you have begun to experience," Leo said. *"The Connected Realm. It Weaves all the worlds together—every single particle, every atom, everything is connected there."* He paused. *"Your power allows you to sense each one of those Connections, but you don't need to see to sense them. Those Connections already exist, whether you have observed an object or not. You need to learn to sense the Connection itself, not the object or person."*

"Is that what I was sensing?" I asked. "Those rhythms are Connections?"

"Yes," Leo answered. *"Those are the rhythms of the Connected Realm. Just as every human heart beats to a rhythm, every Soul and*

Spirit has its own as well. Every tree, every rock, every leaf, every drop of rain has its own rhythm. You are able to sense those rhythms through the threads that connect us all."

"I . . ." I sighed. "Sorry, this is just hard to understand."

"I know," Leo said. *"The most important thing you must know is that everything is connected. And there are different ways to sense those Connections."*

"Can you sense those Connections too, Leo?" I asked.

"Only a bit," he answered. *"All Star Children can access the Connections, but some of us have a stronger bond to them and can access them more easily."* He paused again. *"As I said, your Constellation represents the open Eye—a Portal. You are very intimately Connected with other planes. Through your heart you can open a door that allows you to fully sense these Connections and experience those rhythms. Your Constellation is profoundly united with the Connected Realm and the threads that Weave reality together."*

I nodded. My scars flared in pain and I winced—Virgo and Andromeda were close, about two hundred yards ahead of us.

"Why don't my scars burn when I sense the rhythms?" I asked.

"You shouldn't feel pain in your scars," Leo said. *"That means you are consuming your own Light, your own Essence to use your power. Didn't—"* Leo paused abruptly. *"You have never been trained to use the Connected Realm to fuel your powers, but if we want to defeat Perseus you will need to learn how to do it. The others should learn it too."* Leo sighed. *"I wish I could have been able to communicate with you earlier. I would have had more time to train all of you. But tracking down those weapons is our priority, so I won't have time to teach everyone."*

The scent of roasting meat drifted into my nose, and I wondered if we were having a barbeque. My scars burned again—Draco and the Twins stood about twenty yards to my right. Andromeda and Virgo were thirty yards behind them. I stopped walking, and Leo stopped with me.

I opened the door in my heart again, letting the rhythms flood through me. I sensed the Gemini Twins first—their rhythm felt like sharp waves beating against a cliff. Like a sea storm in the middle of the ocean. The Twins were a fierce tempest that would wreck any ship and drown any man who messed with them. For the first time since becoming blind, I was able to tell Castor and Pollux apart. Their rhythms were very similar, but Pollux's rhythm was more rapid than his brother's.

I focused on Draco's rhythm next. Two rhythms beat out of him. I assumed one rhythm belonged to Draco and the other to the Dragon—two souls in the same body fighting for dominance. The first rhythm felt like dancing flames. It was a candle lit at midnight to write a love letter, the flame used to melt wax to seal a promise. Draco was a protective fire that crackled like logs in a sacred hearth.

The other rhythm was something else entirely. It was a comet raging through space, a forest fire ready to devour everything in its path. It was a torch lit at a forbidden temple to call upon gods who didn't belong to this world. Yet those flames had been doused with water, and only the smoking logs remained. But something still burned in that rhythm. A single spark would bring that raging fire back to life. The Dragon was still sleeping, but it wouldn't take much to awaken it.

I inhaled sharply as the rhythms beat through me, conveying flashes of images that tried to tell me a story about their origins.

It felt a bit like listening to music and letting my mind wander into a daydream. Yet I couldn't fully control what I imagined. The rhythms led me through the broken narrative they shared with me.

"Are you all right, Orion?" Draco asked, making the rhythms dim into the background as he pulled me out of my thoughts.

"Yeah," I said. "I came back for dinner."

"I think Andromeda might have cooked something," Pollux said.

I immediately sought out Andromeda's rhythm and a couple of seconds later it flowed through my chest in a torrent. Her rhythm had no pattern. It was a dissonant cacophony of deaf musicians who all played different instruments out of sync. My hands instinctively clenched into fists. Had Darkness jumbled Andromeda's rhythm when she had consumed it?

"She took too much from Arianna," Leo said next to me, his tone pitiful.

"How can we fix it?"

Leo began walking away from me. *"We can't."*

My chest caved in with pain, and the Portal around me finally collapsed. Darkness poured around me like a flood, and I suddenly felt lonely. With the rhythms the darkness had vanished. It hadn't completely disappeared, but the rhythms had given me something else to focus on, letting me travel to a world beyond the dark. Now the black void engulfed me again, and I felt it pressing on me like violent waves trying to drown me beneath the surface.

It had been my fault that Andromeda had drunk that Darkness. If I hadn't been stupid enough to get captured by

Perseus, she would never have had to come rescue me. If I had managed to escape him, Andromeda would never have gone to Palatine Hill. I could have tried harder to escape, to fight him.

The pain in my heart twisted like a jagged blade. I regretted everything I had told Andromeda the day before. She wasn't selfish—she was the only one who truly cared about me. She was the only girl who hadn't used me, the only person in the world who had been willing to die to save me. My knees nearly gave away, but I managed to remain standing.

I hadn't been able to protect Andromeda from Perseus in the last battle. She had risked her life to save me, sacrificed part of herself to keep me alive—now it was my turn. I would do anything to protect her, no matter what it cost me.

CHAPTER 33

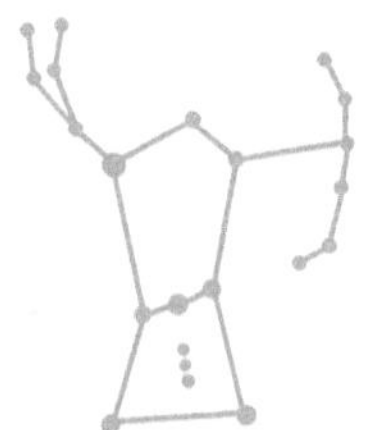

PAIN ERUPTED FROM the back of my neck.

"Argh!" I complained as I spun around.

Pollux's stormy rhythm beat a few feet in front me. I barely had time to sense the smooth rhythm of the snowball in his hand before he threw it at me. I moved to the side but it still slammed into my left arm.

Pollux exhaled loudly. "You need to do better."

"I know," I said, frustrated.

It had been two days since I had started training with Leo. I had also tried talking to Sirius and Aquila, but Aquila's words were too jumbled and his sentences made little sense. The Eagle never had a human form, so maybe human speech was difficult for him. And even though Sirius could have been able to talk to me, since she'd once had a human form like Leo, the Dog had remained silent. When I had asked Leo about it, he had been slightly confused as well, but I wouldn't pressure the Dog to talk. Sirius would talk to me if he felt like it.

But beyond what I had learned that first day, my skills hadn't improved since then. It had become easier for me to open the Portal in my chest and sense the rhythms around me. I could

345

do that in less than a minute now, but even though I sensed the rhythms, it was hard to use them. The Twins had been delighted when Leo suggested throwing snowballs at me so I could train. The Lion wanted me to become better at sensing fast-moving objects—like knives, spears, or swords that Perseus and his allies might throw at me, but it wasn't easy to use the rhythms for that.

Even though I could sense where a rhythm was coming from, I couldn't sense the exact dimensions of an object. I could generally avoid stumbling face first into a tree, but I sometimes miscalculated the thickness of a trunk and ended up grazing or bumping my arm against one.

"Rhythms are just waves of energy," Leo had explained. *"Everything in the Universe is energy. Even matter is made out of energy, but matter is the densest form of energy. You have to learn how to translate those rhythms, those waves of energy, into matter."*

"Okay," I had said. "And how will this help me track down Sagitta and Corona Borealis?"

"You must sense their energies to find their material forms through the Connection you have with them."

It almost felt as if Leo wanted me to accomplish two things at once. He wanted me to sense the material world around me, but he also wanted me to sense the Connection between me and objects that were miles away.

"We should take a break," Pollux suggested.

Leo roared.

"I'm hungry!" Pollux complained. "I'll go get a sandwich or something and then I'll be back."

Pollux walked away from me, his rhythm fading into the dark. I sighed, kneeling on the snow as exhaustion swept through me. Leo moved closer, but he didn't say anything. I knew Leo expected more from me, but I just didn't know how to improve on skills I barely understood. The weight of time pressed heavier on my shoulders. Perseus and his allies must have been training too, and they must have been managing a lot more progress than we were—or at least a lot more progress than I was.

When not throwing snowballs at me, the Twins had been training intensely. Castor was an excellent swordsman, and Pollux was deadly with spears, knives, and axes. They'd taken the initiative to train the others too. Draco was becoming a master spearman, or so I had heard. And Virgo's sword fighting skills were improving. I had been surprised to hear that Andromeda had joined the training. She still hadn't agreed to come with us and had explicitly stated she wanted nothing to do with Perseus. But I knew Andromeda—her actions were more important than her words.

I hadn't talked to her at all, not even when we all sat down at her table to eat. I knew that eventually I would have to apologize for what I had said to her, but I didn't feel ready for that conversation. I had other, more immediate problems to fix. If my new powers didn't improve, then we wouldn't be able to look for Sagitta and Corona Borealis, and until we found those, we wouldn't be safe from Typhon and be able to defeat Perseus.

"You should also have lunch," Leo said, pulling me out of my thoughts.

"I'm not very hungry," I said.

"Still," Leo said. *"You should—"*

Leo cut off at the same time Virgo's rhythm vibrated through me. Out of all the rhythms I had sensed, hers was the strangest. It felt like cherry blossoms blooming in spring, but those flowers had been brought into a funeral. It was the birds and insects that chirped in a forest during a sunny day, but the graves dug into the earth among the trees and the slabs of stone no bird dared to perch on released an eerie silence that felt abandoned.

Virgo slowly approached us, and I stood up from the ground. My scars burned as she stopped a few feet in front of me, her rhythm beating steadily.

"Hey, Virgo," I said.

"Hey," she said.

"She seems nervous," Leo told me.

"Is everything all right?" I asked.

"I think I can help you," Virgo blurted out.

"This should be interesting."

"I—" I imagined Virgo clutching her knitted sweater. "I should have tried to help you earlier. I thought you would figure it out, but you haven't." Virgo exhaled loudly.

"It's okay, Virgo," I said.

"I've been scared of my power for too long," she said in such a low voice that I almost didn't hear her. The memory of Cepheus's dead body at the cemetery flashed through my mind. No one had mentioned the incident—maybe because they were also afraid of what Virgo was truly capable of.

"What *did* you do to Cepheus?" I asked.

Virgo took a couple of seconds to respond. "I don't know," she finally whispered. "I heard Death calling."

A shudder trailed down my back.

"Death has always followed me, but in the cemetery, with my powers restored, Death opened a door." She paused. "But I didn't come here to talk about Death. I'm here to help you."

"I would appreciate your help," I said.

"Do you remember what we talked about in Argo before going to the cemetery?" Virgo asked.

"Yes."

"So you remember I told you about the men who kidnapped me, and how Corvus and Perseus helped me escape?"

"I remember."

"I used my power to kill the men who had hurt me. But I nearly killed myself." Her voice was almost a whisper, as if she didn't want the trees to know about her dark past. "Perseus and Corvus decided to save me, so they threw me into Eridanus."

"Isn't that another Constellation?" I asked. I was sure I had heard that name, but I didn't remember which Constellation it represented.

"Yeah," Virgo said. "Eridanus is the Celestial River."

"Where is it?" I asked.

"You can summon Eridanus to any river on this planet," Virgo said.

"Hmmm," Leo commented.

"Eridanus is the only Star Child that flows through the Universe," Virgo said. "It is the Celestial River that connects all planes." She paused again, and Leo remained silent. "When Corvus and Perseus threw me into Eridanus, I traveled through the river to go to another world."

"Which one?" I asked, my heart beating with anticipation.

"Eridanus took me to the bottom of the Three Wells where the River ends," Virgo said. "The home of the Three Weavers."

"Remind me who the Weavers are," I said.

"The Weavers are the beings who assign Fates to all living beings so they can arrive at their Destiny."

"Okay."

Virgo paused for what seemed like a long time.

"I lived with the Weavers for some time," Virgo said. "I don't remember most of it though. I was barely alive. It took me a long time to recover." She paused again. "But once I did recover, the Weavers taught me some things." Snow crunched under Virgo's shoes as she stepped a bit closer. "They taught me to weave. That's how they tie Fate into Destiny; they weave it together. That's how the entire Universe is made—it's all just a woven net of energy."

"Everything is connected," I said, remembering what Leo had repeated to me several times.

"Yes," Virgo said softly. "Every living thing, including Planets and Stars, are woven into the fabric of reality."

"Ask her if the Weavers taught her to sense those Connections," Leo said.

"Can you sense those Connections?" I asked.

"No," Virgo responded. "But I can see them."

"This may help you," Leo said, although he didn't sound too convinced. *"Maybe if you can see the Connections, it will be easier for you to sense them."* The Lion paused. *"I don't like you to rely on seeing if I'm training you to sense, but given we don't have enough time, this could make tracking Sagitta and Corona Borealis much easier."*

"Could you teach me how to see it?" I asked.

"I'm not sure if I can teach you," Virgo said. "It took me a long time to learn to see through planes, time we don't have right now. But I can show you how it looks."

"That should help," I said.

"This would probably have been useful to know since you started training but I was just scared." Virgo's voice wavered. "My power nearly killed me last time. I'm scared that I'll lose control."

"You won't," I assured her. "You were too young when that happened; you barely knew how your power worked and what your limit was. Now you've grown and you've learned. You won't lose control again."

"I hope you're right," she said. She took a deep breath. "All right then, we should start."

"Be careful," the Lion warned.

I nodded.

"So how do you actually see into another world?" I asked.

"I don't think there's a natural way to do it. It's just—I'm not sure I can explain that with words." She paused. "I'm going to grab your hand," Virgo said hesitantly.

"Sure," I said as I slowly extended my right hand towards her.

Virgo's warm hand wrapped around mine. "It may feel weird, but I'm going to pull you into the other side with me."

"Okay."

I took in a deep breath. Virgo's grip tightened around mine. For a long time, we stood with our hands linked together. I could still sense the rhythms around me, but I couldn't see anything except for the impenetrable darkness. It flowed smoothly, entrapping me in its silken web. The wind stopped, holding its breath.

Then everything exploded with light.

Chapter XVI, Verse III

The Weaving One her full power has discovered,
But fearful she remains of the true face of Death.
Sky, Earth, Air, and Fire she will command,
Only when she has found peace from her past.
Until then her power in the shadows shall remain,
Unbridled and raging with regret,
Unless the truth she discovers about the White Flame.

CHAPTER 34

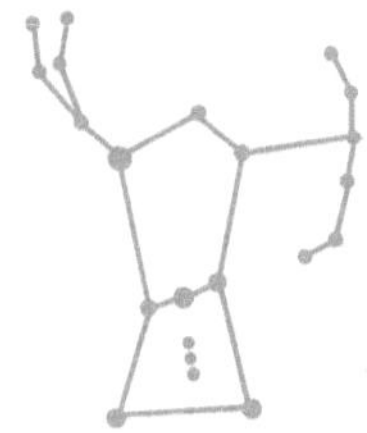

A BURST OF COLORS exploded beyond me like a chaotic fireworks display. I held on to Virgo's hand as I plummeted into a brilliant void, my body turning itself inside out.

Everything stopped.

A burst of joy shot through me when I realized I could *see*. Knots of light hovered around me. It felt as if I were looking at a knitted sweater through a microscope. Most of the colored knots shone a deep emerald green. Their light pulsed like twinkling Stars. Right next to me hovered a large knot that shone bright gold—that had to be Leo. Below my feet lay tiny light-blue knots—the snow? These also pulsed, but in a rhythm different from the trees and from Leo. Were those the rhythms I had sensed earlier? The knots were like beating hearts suspended over a vast expanse.

I couldn't make out the color of the background beyond the knots—it could have been black or white or both. It simply had no color. I turned to my right and was met by a lime-green light. Virgo? I looked down, but I couldn't see myself—I couldn't even see a knot of energy below me, as if only my mind existed in this world but not my body.

I tried to call out Virgo's name, but no sound came out of my mouth. Did I *have* a mouth here? I focused on the forest of green knots, and only then saw the thread connecting them. The line was so thin that it was almost transparent. It only became visible once I focused on it. The thread shone with pure silver light. More threads became visible as I placed my attention on them—they were everywhere. Each tree was connected to every other tree, and they were all connected to me, and Virgo, and Leo. Even the tiny knots on the ground, every particle of snow, were connected to everything around them. This world was a three-dimensional web—a network of silver threads intertwined to form colorful knots.

Next to me, the golden knot of energy moved closer to me. The silver lines attached to it moved as Leo did, making the fabric around me shift. The Universe was a fluid web of energy and light. Leo had tried to explain it to me—reality was a living fabric. Every knot pulsed to a specific rhythm that was then transmitted through the silver threads, as if every knot was a beating heart that was pumping blood into infinitely many arteries.

I glanced up and was shocked at the sight—above me floated a sea of color. A giant orange knot dominated the sky, beating slowly and steadily. Around it was an infinite number of knots, each of a different color—blue, yellow, green, white, red, purple, orange, and every single combination of those. It was an ocean of jewels. Some knots changed color—from purple to red, from green to white, and they all beat to different rhythms. It was the most beautiful sight I had ever experienced. All of those knots, all of those Stars, each pulsed with life and color. The Stars seemed so close to me that I had the urge to raise my hand and graze them with my fingertips, except I didn't have a physical arm in that world. Yet they were so distant I knew no spaceship would ever reach them. Silver threads came out of every single Star, connecting them to everything I could see around me.

I focused again on the threads surrounding me. Were those the Connections Leo wanted me to sense? At the thought of Leo, one of the threads around me thickened like a bulging vein with bright silver light. It was the thread that connected me to him. The pulsing silver line combined both our rhythms.

Andromeda's image flashed through my mind—her bright blue eyes, raven-black hair, small nose, and big ears. Another thread burst with light, swelling to become thicker than the rest, and disappeared somewhere to my right. The thread moved slightly to the side, and I wondered if Andromeda was walking in that direction.

Then all the color and light disappeared. My body turned itself inside out again as darkness enclosed me. A wave of cold washed over me, and my body began to throb with pain. I fell to my knees as Virgo let go of my hand.

"Sorry," Virgo said. "I tried to stay there for as long as I could."

"It's all right," I said.

Virgo helped me get to my feet. Leo roared behind me, and it took me a few moments to create the Portal around me to listen to the Lion.

"Did you see the Connections?" Leo asked.

"Yeah," I said. "I saw the Connections." I paused. "That was beautiful. Thank you, Virgo."

"I'm sorry we couldn't stay there longer," Virgo said. "Could we try this again tomorrow? If you give me some time to rest, I can take us back there so you can look for Sagitta and Corona Borealis."

"Yeah," I said, breathless. "I know this must have been hard for you, but I really appreciate you taking me there."

"Of course," she said. "That's what friends are for."

I smiled.

Virgo took a step to the side, as if she intended to walk away, but hesitated.

"What's wrong?" I asked.

"It's just . . ." Virgo sighed. "It's not my place to intervene in your issues with Andromeda, and I'm not trying to, but I thought someone should say something."

"About what?" I asked, tensing.

"About what she said about you not being anyone without Zia," Virgo said. I hadn't thought about Andromeda's words in a while, but the wound still stung as if it were fresh. "I didn't mean to eavesdrop, but you were both being very loud." Virgo quickly added. "I don't know if my words mean anything to you. But . . ." She hesitated again. "I dealt with a similar problem for a long time. I didn't know who I was without the pain I had dealt with in my early life." Virgo took a step closer to me. "And for an even longer time I felt worthless because I had lost my power. But we're more than our power, and we're more than the people who hurt us. It might take a while, but you'll find out who you really want to be. I'm still figuring that out too, but I think we will someday be able to move beyond our past."

"Thank you, Virgo," I said as my throat constricted and tears threatened to drop from my eyes. "Your words mean a lot."

"I should go back to the cottage to eat something." Her footsteps began to echo away.

"Wait," Leo said.

"Wait," I repeated.

"What?" Virgo asked.

Leo exhaled. *"I've never had the chance to talk to Virgo."*

"Leo wants to talk to you," I said.

Virgo didn't respond.

Leo was silent for an uncomfortable few seconds. *"You're much stronger than you realize, Virgo. So much stronger."*

I repeated Leo's message.

"You know I'm broken," Virgo whispered.

Leo stepped closer to her. *"My dear, we're all broken. Being strong is not about being whole; it's about how we rebuild ourselves after we have lived through something that should have made us shatter to dust."* Leo purred. *"Don't let your fear hold you back. Don't let your past be a roadblock to the future. And always know that no matter what happens, I'll be here to watch your back."*

"Thank you, Leo." Virgo stepped closer to Leo, and I imagined her hugging the Lion.

"I'm very proud of you," Leo said. *"Of how much you have grown, and how you have shown kindness to others even when they didn't deserve it."*

"He deserved it," Virgo said. "He saved my life once."

Leo growled softly. *"You forget how cruel he was to others, how cold and merciless. But you changed him, you helped him become a better version of himself."*

"Not that it matters anymore." Virgo's tone was resentful. "He forgot everything." Her voice cracked. "Just to save me. He shouldn't have."

"He knew how special you are," Leo said.

Virgo didn't answer.

"Everyone can see that except you, Virgo," Leo said. *"You're so much more than your scars. Don't let them hold you back."*

Leo's words hit home. I knew they weren't directed at me, but they still made my throat knot.

"Thank you, Leo," Virgo said. "I love you."

I heard a kiss and couldn't help but smile.

"I love you too, my dear girl."

Virgo sniffled. "All right, I'm heading out to get lunch now." And with that she walked away.

I sat on the snow as Leo stepped closer to me.

"Thank you, Orion," Leo said.

"Anytime."

Leo breathed out. *"Now do you understand how your power works? If you can focus on the Connections Virgo showed you, you will be able to find anything you seek,"* Leo said.

"I understand that now," I said.

"What I also want you to understand is that Virgo doesn't have to show you those Connections for you to use them." Leo's tone was gentle, but I could feel his frustration. *"You rely too much on visual detail, and in the long run that may not be helpful. For now, since we're pressed for time, Virgo's help will be useful, but afterwards you should try to only* sense *those Connections."*

I nodded, but disappointment rolled through me. I wanted to *see.* I wanted to look at those beautiful knots of energy and silver threads that created reality. I was tired of the darkness.

"Isn't there a way I could learn to see what Virgo just showed me?" I asked.

"You're learning things that normally take years. We don't have time to teach you everything. Maybe one day you will see them."

"But you said that my Constellation was an eye, right? Shouldn't I be able to see that world too?"

"Not necessarily," Leo said. *"The Eye can see without seeing. Learn to see without eyes and without colors."*

I gritted my teeth. I wanted my eyes and colors back. With just one look at Zia's drawings, I would have been able to track down those weapons. Sensing them was exponentially harder. I breathed out and imagined mist coming out of my mouth.

"I know this isn't easy," Leo said. *"But you need to be patient with yourself as you learn. You will realize how powerful this new gift is."*

"I don't have time for patience."

The Lion roared. *"You're so stubborn sometimes."* He huffed. *"Let's get lunch. We're done for today."*

The Lion started walking back to the cottage and I followed at his side.

"Okay, but first thing tomorrow I'll go back into that Connected Realm with Virgo and track down Sagitta and Corona Borealis."

"All right then," Leo said. *"But I would suggest we focus on tracking down one object first, finding it, and then tracking down the other one. If your focus is solely on one object the Connection will be stronger, instead of being divided in two."*

I nodded.

Leo sighed. *"Now that you have seen the Connections, you can understand how Perseus intends to destroy Fate, Destiny, and Prophecy. The threads that connect the Stars to every single being are what drive Destiny. The Weavers weave those threads, and they make sure to thicken or thin the futures they want us to experience."*

"What do you mean by thicken or thin?" I asked.

"The thicker a thread is, the more connected you are to it," Leo explained. *"The thicker threads Connect you to the people and places you know. So you would have a thick thread connecting you to me, and Virgo and Andromeda and the others. But you would have a very thin thread with someone you have never met."*

"I did see the threads swell and become brighter when I thought of someone," I remembered.

"Exactly," Leo said. *"The Weavers work with those threads. When they thicken a Connection between two people, that ensures that they will meet somehow, but when they thin a Connection, they make sure it is something that you never encounter."* Leo paused. *"That is how they manipulate Fate, how they make sure that those Connections get you to the Destiny you need to find. The Stars are the beings that create the energy necessary for those Connections to stay alive and lead you to Destiny."*

I sensed a tree on my right and pressed closer to Leo, his warmth seeping through my jacket. "So what does Perseus actually want to do?"

"I believe that he wants to cut the Connections between the Stars and every living being on the planet, and he wants to destroy the power of the Weavers so they cannot manipulate the threads of Fate."

"But wouldn't that be dangerous?" I asked. "If the Stars and the Weavers don't direct the Connections—if they don't lead us to our Fates and Destinies—then what happens?"

"Chaos," the Lion roared. *"What Perseus is trying to do has never been attempted before, at least not during my long lifetime. If the Stars and the Weavers don't order Fate and Destiny, then Chaos will take over. The Connected Realm would be a fabric of disorder, tangled and twisted. Perseus believes that he's giving us freedom, but he will only bring disaster upon the world."*

"Perseus must be able to see the Connected Realm then," I realized.

"Yes," Leo said. *"Arianna must be training him to see that dimension. I don't know how Perseus would actually manage to cut those Connections, but that must be something that Arianna certainly knows how to do."* Leo paused. *"Arianna is waiting for Algol to reach the apex of its power so Perseus can use it to fully sever the Connections."*

I exhaled. How would the Connected Realm function if those threads weren't there anymore? It wouldn't. Perseus would literally rip the Universe to pieces knot by knot. My gut clenched.

"We'll find a way to stop him," I said.

"I hope we do," Leo said. *"And having seen that world, you can also understand how our power works. We can influence those threads too, materializing our thoughts and intentions into reality."*

"What are you able to materialize, Leo?" I asked. "I mean, I know you're a lion, but what's your power? How do you influence those Connections?"

Leo was silent for a long while. *"I was able to do many things once, but I lost much of my power. I used the Connections to lend other Star Children strength, both physical and mental."* He paused, and I could sense the grief in his tone. *"I made the mistake of being loyal to people who weren't loyal in return."* He paused again. *"They took my strength and didn't give it back when I needed it the most, so I didn't have enough power to keep myself in human form. I—that's why I became a lion, fully, instead of being able to alternate between forms as I should have been able to do."* Leo growled. *"I knew the risks of lending my strength, of making such a strong Connection to others, but I did it anyway because I wanted to protect my family. But in the end, most of them kept my strength, so I became . . . this."*

His words came out in a torrent, his usual confident tone replaced by a tide of sadness. My heart twisted, as if Leo was also able to transmit his pain to me.

"I can understand why Ophiuchus decided to stay behind," Leo said. *"Light and Darkness are in an eternal conflict, and they will be until the end of Time. And when the Universe dies and is reborn, the war will start again."* Leo slowed down his pace. *"There will never be peace between Light and Darkness; that's just how the Universe works. But it is from that eternal fight that Life emerges. With absolute Light or absolute Darkness there would be no Life, for Life needs both."*

We continued walking in silence until a new question popped into my head, one I hadn't considered before. It felt like a small betrayal to Draco, but I needed to know more about his past to be able to help him.

"Leo," I said hesitantly. "Did you know Draco before? I mean, when he was the Dragon."

"Yes," Leo immediately answered. *"How do you know about the Dragon?"*

Guilt clawed at my chest. I stopped walking, and Leo did too. My scars burned as my inner compass indicated Draco was half a mile away.

"Draco told me," I said. "He told me that Typhon made the Dragon stir inside of him." A knot formed in my throat. "And he asked me to kill him before the Dragon resurfaced again."

Leo became very still as he stood next to me. *"I care very much about Draco, and I would do anything to protect him."* He paused. *"But I do believe that the best way we can protect Draco is to kill him before the Dragon resurfaces."*

"You can't be serious," I blurted out. "I *won't* kill Draco."

"You may not have a choice."

"I don't even understand how the Dragon and he are in the same body," I said.

"I don't know either," Leo admitted. *"For some reason, he evolved differently than the rest of us did. I became a Lion, but I still retained my consciousness and mind. I am the Lion. Sirius became a dog, but it is still her Soul and Spirit inside of that dog. They are one and the same, but Draco—"* Leo growled. *"At some point, two different beings, two minds, emerged. Draco became the dominant mind and he took over the body of the Dragon to become what he is now. I don't know how that happened, but the Draco we know is not the Dragon. The Dragon is possibly the most dangerous monster in the Constellations if we don't count Typhon. It fought against Hercules millennia ago and tried to destroy humanity. If the Dragon awakens, it will become our enemy."*

"I won't kill Draco," I repeated. "I won't kill you either if Typhon turns you against me again."

"You may have to, Orion," he said. *"Even though I don't have another entity to take over me, my mind still corrodes when Typhon is*

near." Leo let out a deep growl. *"If he takes control over me again, he will make me kill you, and I won't be able to stop myself."*

"I'll find Corona Borealis to keep you safe from Typhon's influence, and Sagitta to kill the monster," I said determinedly.

Leo sighed. *"Good, then let's focus on your training. We'll worry about death later."*

CHAPTER 35

I SAT ON A LARGE ROCK next to the river, listening to the flowing water, sensing its lively rhythm. It flowed smoothly in rapid beats.

I had promised Leo that I wouldn't train more today and rest to prepare for tomorrow, but I still wanted to sense the rhythms so I wouldn't have to feel entrapped in blackness. Now I knew something existed beyond the dark, a world full of color and light. My heart beat faster at the thought of going back there.

An erratic rhythm began to pulse behind me, gaining strength with every second. My muscles tensed in anticipation as Andromeda walked closer to me. I didn't know how much Virgo and the others had told her about my new powers, and wondered what she thought about it.

Andromeda stood behind me but I didn't dare turn around. Something crunched softly as she stepped closer to sit next to me. For a long while neither of us said anything. I wished I could see her, knowing I would have been able to read something from her expression.

"I'm sorry," I finally said. "I was an asshole for saying that you are selfish. You're not. You're more selfless than I've ever been. You saved me when no one else would have." I paused. "I'm just—I'm sorry, Andromeda."

Andromeda didn't answer. Her chaotic rhythm made my skin crawl as it pulsed through me. It simply felt *wrong*. Did Andromeda know how much Darkness had affected her? Did she know that Darkness had eaten all the way into her soul? The wind howled around us, making the trees rustle. Did the trees still have leaves, or was I hearing the swishing branches?

"You've never apologized before," Andromeda finally said.

"Of course I have," I said.

"Name one time when you did."

I bit my tongue. Off the top of my head I couldn't remember, but surely I had done so at some point of our lives, hadn't I?

"I *am* sorry," I said.

"I know," Andromeda responded coldly. She shifted next to me, her shoulder grazing my arm. "I don't want to see Perseus again. I don't want to fight him. I—" Andromeda made a strange choking sound. "I don't want to be tempted by Darkness again. Remember the time Zia left us without food for a few days and only gave us water?"

"Yeah."

"It feels like that," she said. "Like I'm living off of water and only Darkness can give me the food I really need. There's no way back. I know I'll never get rid of it. All I can do is make sure I don't take any more. But if I see Perseus again, if I fight him, and if Arianna is there, I will get tempted to take more to fill this hunger."

"You're strong enough, Andromeda," I said. "I know you are."

My tongue numbed after saying those words. Was she really strong enough? I had no doubt that if she kept training with the Twins, she would find a way to kill Perseus. She wouldn't hesitate to kill him, not again. But was she strong enough not to take any more Darkness? Andromeda had always been reckless and impulsive. If that Darkness gave her the power she needed to destroy Perseus, would she take it? I knew she would, even if it ended up destroying her too.

"I wish we'd just run away," Andromeda whispered. "Before any of this started, before we even knew what we were." My heart throbbed with pain, as if Andromeda had squeezed it in her hand. "I wish we'd just packed our bags and left Zia behind."

How many times had Andromeda tried to escape? How many times had I brought her back? If I had let her escape, if I had escaped with her, would our lives have turned out differently? Or would Prophecy have caught up to us eventually? But we both knew, deep down, that Zia would never have let us be free from her. The only time we tried, she had nearly killed us both.

"We can't escape our future, Andromeda," I said. "We can't stop what's coming."

"We could try."

I chuckled. "You still think you can run away from those Prophecies?"

Andromeda's shoulder pulled away from my arm.

"You've always found a way to escape, but I don't think there's a way out from this."

The wind howled around us, pulling at my hair.

"Do you really think we need the Arrow and Crown to defeat Perseus and Arianna?" Andromeda asked.

I exhaled. "We barely made it out of that cemetery alive," I said. "We didn't know what we were truly facing, but we do now. And we'll need both weapons to win this battle."

Andromeda was silent again as the river rushed by. A beat blasted above me with an electrifying pulse and thundering rhythm—Aquila. The giant eagle circled around us a couple of times, then flew to the left. His rhythm faded away.

"When did Zia start?" Andromeda asked. I clenched my jaw. Why did every conversation always had to pivot back to Zia? "It must have been after she put us into foster care. You weren't like that before."

"I wasn't like *what* before?" I asked.

"Like *this*," she said. Something cold brushed my cheek and I instinctively reeled away.

Anger burned inside my chest. "Haven't I always been like that?" I asked. "I don't remember any time I have liked you putting your hand on my face."

"You didn't seem to mind when we were at the lake." I opened my mouth to reply, but the words died on my lips. I hadn't thought about that day in a very long time. "You were still *you* that day, and then you changed."

I still didn't know what *change* she was talking about. Andromeda had never noticed anything between me and Zia until Zia had explicitly told her.

"Did you ever see her scars shining?" Andromeda asked.

"No, I never did." If she was a Star Child, and had lived for so long, then surely she must have had some scars. Had I been so disconnected from myself that I had just never noticed? I was sure I had never seen any *shining* scars on Zia, but maybe I had just never noticed any of her normal scars?

"I don't remember seeing any of her scars either." Andromeda's voice was tight. "Isn't that weird?"

"Yeah. She must have had scars. At least *one*." My mind itched.

Memories flooded through my mind—the three of us sleeping in the same room on a small bed and couch. Zia glancing out a window at night. Zia scrambling on the floor to look for the flashlight when the light went out. How had Zia hidden her scars?

Andromeda stood up abruptly, pulling me out of my thoughts. "I'll go with you to find Sagitta and Corona Borealis." My heartbeat roared in my ears. "But you have to promise that you'll stop tracking the crumbs that Zia left behind."

"What does that even mean?" I asked.

Andromeda huffed. "What have you been doing since we left Rome? What is the first thing you did when you went back to New York? You went to Zia's apartment to look for clues about her past. You've spent the last month being obsessed with Zia."

"That's not—"

"She's dead, Orion," Andromeda said flatly. "I know you won't admit it to yourself, but you just can't let her go. You can't admit that she did what she did because she was sick and absolutely insane. Instead, you hunt for whatever scraps she left behind, trying to justify her actions. You just can't let her die."

"It's not about that," I growled.

"Then what is it about?" Andromeda asked.

"I wanted to find the truth."

"The truth about what?"

"About the Star Children and Perseus so I could learn how to defeat him to protect you. And I guess, yeah, I wanted to know more about Zia. Who was she, really? Why did she want to destroy Perseus too? Why did she hide the truth about what we were? Why didn't she ever tell us anything!"

The Portal collapsed and darkness flooded inside me, making me gasp for air. Andromeda placed her hand on my shoulder and squeezed.

"Please," she pleaded. "Just let Zia die."

My throat tightened. The weight of the two rings hanging from my neck pulled down, digging into my flesh. "I . . ." Something hot burned down my cheek. "She left us those Star Weapons because she cared about us and wanted us to survive Perseus's risings."

Andromeda was silent for a moment. "And once we find those weapons, will you finally stop looking for clues? Or will you keep searching for her past?"

I was about to say that I wouldn't keep digging into her past, but could I really walk away from her? She had left so many unanswered questions—a long life full of secrets. But did I really need to know those secrets? Assuming we managed to defeat Perseus, what good would it do to keep uncovering Zia's past? Would I live the rest of my life chasing down a ghost?

Virgo's words found me again. I *could* be more than the person Zia had made me. I wanted to be. But I had no idea who that was. If I wasn't a hunter and killer, then what was I? Draco had come directly to me to ask me to kill him, and even though I hadn't given much thought to that specifically, it now stung that he might have seen me as nothing more than a killer. But I could change that. I *would*—assuming we managed to survive Perseus.

"I'll stop." My throat tightened painfully, and I forced myself to take a deep breath. "I'll stop hunting for Zia, *if* you stop running away."

Andromeda pulled her hand back, as if I had electrocuted her.

"You only run because you feel you can finally rebel against Zia, even after she's dead. You run from her, from me, from Perseus, from the other Star Children, and from everything else you can run from, just to make a point." I paused. "Stop running from Zia and I'll let her die."

Andromeda was silent for such a long moment that I wondered if she was still breathing.

"Fine," she finally whispered.

Andromeda walked away from me, leaving me sitting alone on the rock. I didn't feel strong enough to open the Portal around me again and try to find my way back to Argo. So I just stayed there, hearing the river flowing by, feeling the current of darkness slowly squeezing my life out.

●———————●———————●

Andromeda and I sat on the edge of a lake. The scathing hot sun and dense humidity made me feel I was being boiled alive. Sweat covered me from head to toe, making my clothes cling to my body. The lake before us reflected the bright blue sky like a rippling mirror, edged by hills covered in dark trees. We had parked the black car under the shade of a tree. We should have been on our way back home but had decided to take a break from driving and enjoy the scenery. It was also one of the last few moments Andromeda and I would have together.

In a week, we would both start living with foster families. That had been an abrupt and shocking decision by Zia. A couple of months before, Andromeda had tried to kill Zia, and that had pushed Zia over the edge. That was your fault, I said to myself. Andromeda had only tried to kill Zia because Zia had left me unconscious after she beat me. If I had never agreed to run away with Andromeda, then Zia would never have beaten me, and Andromeda wouldn't have tried to kill her. My memories of that day were as painful as a purple bruise on my heart. Zia had beaten Andromeda so brutally for trying to kill her that I had worried Andromeda might die. She had eventually recovered though, and I had too.

Part of me was glad that we would be in the foster care system—Zia wouldn't be able to beat us if we didn't live under her roof, but I knew she would find other ways to keep us in line. I wondered what she would tell the foster care system—that she had found us abandoned on the streets? I knew she would pretend she had never met us before. Maybe that would be better.

I wondered what my foster family would be like. I had never lived with anyone who wasn't Andromeda and Zia. Would they force me to go to public school? That didn't sound exciting.

I exhaled and tried not to think about all that mess. I would have plenty of time to worry about my new life in the coming weeks. For now, I would enjoy the nice lake. A flock of birds flew above us like a black cloud. They screeched as they sped away, then disappeared into the distance.

I stood up. Not bearing the heat any longer, I took off my shirt and pants, only keeping my underwear.

"I'm going in," I said.

Andromeda didn't answer as I left my clothes bunched up next to her. The long grass tickled my feet as I stepped towards the edge of the lake. I bent my knees, then jumped. I was in the air for a second before the cold water wrapped around me. I kicked my feet and swam upwards until my head broke through the surface. I breathed deeply. The sun was as bright as it had been seconds ago, but it didn't bother me anymore. I glanced back at the edge of the river, where Andromeda sat staring at me. I smiled at her, and she looked away from my gaze.

"Aren't you coming?" I asked.

Andromeda was sweating heavily too, and she didn't look too comfortable on the hot grass.

"Zia said we better be back by nightfall," she said. "She won't be happy we stopped here."

"And since when do you care about what makes Zia happy?" I asked. Most likely Andromeda was afraid of another beating, even though she would never admit it. Andromeda looked up, her eyes as bright as the sky. Then she glanced back at the car as if to make sure it was still under the shade of the oak tree.

"Zia doesn't have to know we're here. We'll tell her we got stuck in traffic," I said.

Andromeda ignored me. She closed her eyes as the faint breeze swept at her long black hair, which fell all the way to her elbows. Andromeda looked so calm just sitting on the grass, her eyes closed as if she were meditating. I quietly swam closer to the edge of the lake, the water rippling around me. I placed my palms against the warm grass and pulled myself out of the water. I stepped closer to Andromeda. As soon as my shadow blocked the heat of the sun from her face, her eyes shot open.

I grinned.

"Oh, no you—"

I didn't let her finish as I pulled her up and hauled her over my shoulder. She was so light. She struggled against my grip, trying to squirm away, but her strength didn't match mine. I walked back to the edge of the lake.

"Wait!" Andromeda squirmed even harder, like a dying fish flopping in my arms.

"One," I said.

"Don't you dare!"

"Two."

"I'm serious, Orion."

"Three."

"I'm going to—"

I threw Andromeda into the lake and jumped in after her, laughing. The water felt warm as I swam back up. Andromeda was already there, glaring at me, her eyes like two blue lasers. I laughed. Her black hair extended around her like tentacles, which I found funny.

"You're the worst," Andromeda gasped.

"I know."

Andromeda pushed her hair out of her face and glared harder at me, as if her eyes could cut the smile out of my face.

"What are you going to do?" I asked. "Drown me?"

"I'll try."

Andromeda began swimming towards me as her blouse inflated around her like a balloon. She was a terribly slow swimmer. I swam backwards and circled her, staying out of reach. After a minute, I ducked beneath the surface. I opened my eyes, my vision perfectly clear. The light from the sun created flowing patterns over the green algae that covered the ground like patches of grass. I had always been *able to see perfectly underwater, and I could hold my breath for min-utes. I simply didn't feel the need to breathe.*

I looked up as Andromeda kicked her legs to stay afloat. I swam upwards again. Andromeda's scowl greeted me as she floated a few feet in front of me. I submerged myself again, a few feet beneath the surface. Andromeda followed after me. She opened her eyes, blink-ing rapidly. Her blurry vision still found me floating on her left. Andromeda lurched towards me before I could move. She wrapped her arms around my torso and pulled me further down. I hugged her back and was embraced by the heat of her body. We remained floating for a few seconds, until Andromeda kicked her legs to swim upwards. I didn't let her escape my arms as we both reached the surface. I took a deep breath as soon as my head was in the air again.

"I don't think that's how you drown people," I said.

Andromeda didn't pull away from me, and I kept my arms around her. Our gazes met, and her blue eyes darkened as if a cloud had passed over them.

"Are you mad at me?" Andromeda asked.

"I was never mad at you," I said. I had never blamed Andromeda for what had happened. "I know you were only trying to do what was best for us both but—"

I didn't know what else to say. Andromeda had always been braver than me when it came to Zia. She had fought to defend us both from Zia's beatings, but she had taken it too far and Zia had retali-ated. It wasn't Andromeda's fault though—Zia's violence had simply driven her to the same level.

"But . . ." Andromeda prompted.

I sighed. "But now, because of what you did to Zia . . ." My throat tightened as I swallowed. "She'll never let us live with her again. And she's made it clear she doesn't want us to live together either."

It was the second part that worried me the most. I wouldn't have minded being away from Zia, but I couldn't imagine what my life would be like without Andromeda. We teased each other mercilessly and argued on a regular basis, but we had never made each other feel threatened. Andromeda had always been part of my life, and I felt a hole inside my chest when I thought of her absence. Even if we didn't want to, I knew we would grow more distant from each other.

"I'm sorry," Andromeda whispered.

I knew she didn't regret what she had done, but she did regret that we would be apart now. I still didn't blame her. She didn't need to apologize to me. If anything, I was the one who needed to apologize for not being strong enough to protect us both. I felt sheepish when I thought of that. I was older, and stronger, but I didn't have the strength to face Zia.

"I don't like this, Andromeda," I said. "We'll have to be more careful to keep our secrets." It wouldn't be hard for someone to notice our scars in the dark. We would always have to wear long sleeves as a precaution, and lock our rooms at night. Hopefully I wouldn't be sharing a room with anyone. Zia had taught us never to trust anyone. People wouldn't understand that Andromeda and I were different, and what people didn't understand, they feared, and what they feared they sought to destroy.

I turned back to face Andromeda. "I won't be able to make your life miserable now," I said.

"Neither will I," Andromeda said.

A bird chirped in the distance. The trees rustled with a sudden gust of wind that made the water ripple. For a moment I felt that the world had gone still around us as I stared into Andromeda's blue eyes. Then her soft lips were on mine. Heat spread from the center of my chest to the rest of my body, making my stomach flutter. I held Andromeda's delicate face with my palm. At least Zia had never touched that. With my fingers, I traced her nose and her smooth cheeks as we kept kissing.

Part of me knew that this was wrong. Andromeda and I had been brought up as siblings. But another part of me told me that we weren't actually related, and that this couldn't be wrong if we both wanted it. Andromeda's hands moved to my bare back. She slowly traced my scars, her fingers gently following the ragged lines that cut through my skin. She had seen my scars many times, but it was as if her curious hands were exploring unknown territory.

I brushed Andromeda's neck—her heartbeat pulsed strong and fast. Then I traced my hands down to her back. She had so many scars that I couldn't tell where one began and another ended. Fury swam inside of me. A lot of those scars had been my fault. Andromeda had tried to escape Zia, and I had helped her run away. If I had stopped her instead of escaping with her then she wouldn't have been beaten until she nearly bled out. I could feel the pain in all of them. Andromeda might have acted like she didn't care, like she would rather get beaten a hundred times than obey Zia. If she couldn't care for herself then I would have to do it—no matter the cost. Even if she ended up hating me.

I kissed Andromeda more fiercely. She kissed me back harder, her hands still at my back. At some point the water got cold around us as the sun sank lower in the sky. We kept kissing even after the sun disappeared below the horizon. I wasn't sure how much time had passed, and didn't care either. In the dark, our twinkling scars shone underwater. They dimly illuminated Andromeda's face, making the shadows ripple with every pulse. Sometime later, when the stars blinked above us, we both stopped kissing, breathless. I looked into Andromeda's eyes. They shone like melted ice as they reflected the white light. I kissed her one last time, and her hands buried in my hair to pull me closer.

We didn't talk as we got out of the water, dripping wet. Thankfully, we had brought a change of clothes. Zia couldn't know what had happened, so we dried our hair with a blanket and left our wet clothes under the tree.

We drove back home in complete silence. There wasn't anything to talk about anymore, but as I drove guilt tore at my chest. We shouldn't have done that, but there was no way to undo it now.

This is wrong, *a voice inside of me repeated. She was supposed to be my sister, not anything more. But Andromeda was the only person I had ever been close to.*

As I kept driving through the night, I realized that it didn't matter whether the kiss had been right or wrong—I had lost the meaning of those words a long time ago.

Chapter X, Verse I

A victim of Death he nearly became,
Until by Love he was wounded beyond repair.
At night he shall find the one he was cursed to desire,
And a new Child of Light shall be born.
His heart poisoned and driven by maddening grief,
He will seek to restore the one who was unjustly deceived.
The murder shall remain a secret until it is confessed in his dream.

CHAPTER 36

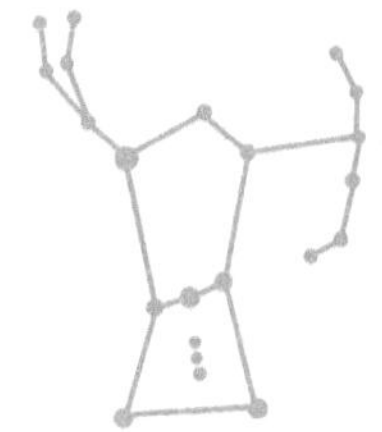

"YOU NEED TO FOCUS," Leo said. *"Every time you think about an object, a place, or a person, you are thinking about the Connection you have with them. Everything is connected, so even if you haven't seen an object, or haven't visited a place, or haven't met a person, you are connected to it."*

"But how do I sense the Connection from something I've never seen?" I asked Leo. "There are an infinite number of Connections tying us all together, how do I know which is the right one?"

"You know Sagitta and Corona Borealis exist," Leo said. *"You don't need to have a mental picture of them; you only need to know that the Arrow and Crown are connected to you. Focus on that."*

"Fine," I said, still struggling to understand what I had to do.

Footsteps crunched over the snow behind me as Virgo walked over to us.

"Are you ready to go back?" she asked.

"Yeah," I said.

"How much time will you need?" Virgo asked.

"I don't know," I admitted. "How long can you keep us there?"

"I don't know."

I exhaled. "I guess we'll find out."

Virgo's hand wrapped around mine, and I squeezed back. I took in a deep breath, my heart battering against my chest in anticipation. For a long moment, nothing happened. Then my skin felt as if it was turning itself inside out. I was falling through an endless void, but I had no mouth to shout. Darkness pulled me further into that absolute blackness until fireworks exploded around me. They vibrated through me with color and light. The world opened up in front of me, and I was back again in that strange realm with beating colors. Knots of emerald green surrounded the clearing where I stood. Leo's golden knot beat steadily on the left as the Lion stood still. Virgo's lime-green light pulsed brightly at my side, tangled into a tight knot.

Above me the bright sea of shifting colors twinkled like a collection of jewels. I glanced down again. Even though I couldn't see my body I could still see the Connections coming out of me. The silver threads became visible only after I noticed their trans-parent gleam. They shone like silver rivers. Those were the threads that connected me to everything—to every tree, every Star, every particle of snow. My surroundings became an interwoven fabric of Light.

After another few moments of admiring my surroundings, I put my attention back on the mission. I thought of Sagitta first, the Arrow Zia had left for *me*. I imagined Sagitta based on the description of the drawing the others had given me—a wooden shaft with a golden tip. As soon as I thought of that, I felt a pull inside of me, yanking me in different directions. Most threads around me became transparent, but thousands of them remained glowing. I imagined the Arrow again, Virgo's description of it flowing through my mind. *A smooth wooden shaft, a sharp golden point, and a fletching of gleaming black feathers.* More Connections dimmed out, but the ones that didn't became thicker and more brilliant. The pull inside of me strengthened, but I was being pulled in so many directions that I couldn't go to all of them at once.

Frustration gnawed at my chest. This would have been so easy if I could have just *looked* at the drawing. I would have immediately known where Sagitta was. This felt like finding a needle in a haystack.

I took a deep breath. I didn't know how long Virgo would be able to keep us here. I needed something more to find Sagitta. It was not like every other arrow connected to me—it was the *only* Arrow in the world that was made of Light. Like me, Sagitta was born from the Stars.

More threads dimmed until only one was left shining. The silver thread was as thick as my thumb and extended from my chest into the far distance on my left. I focused on that Connection, sensing the rhythm that traveled through it—it was a tune of sharp vibrations that cut through its surroundings, but it didn't bring me closer to the Arrow.

I needed Sagitta to kill Typhon and destroy Perseus's allies. The pull grew stronger, as if I had a rope tied around my waist and someone was reeling me into the horizon.

I was the Hunter—that Arrow belonged to *me*.

Where are you?

My heart dropped to my stomach as I was pulled to the left. For a moment I was flying, gliding over the ground. Colors blurred past me like bright slashes of paint, as if I was traveling on a bullet train through an underground tunnel full of graffiti. Then it stopped and the colors, silver threads, and knots were gone. I was once again engulfed in pure darkness. Terror dug into my chest as the unmovable darkness seemed to squeeze the air from my lungs.

Then I sensed something beyond me. It was a rhythm that felt forgotten, a sound like sorrow and death, flowing like poisoned blood. It was ancient too, coming from a place that had long ago been left in ruins, buried deep beneath the earth. The rhythm didn't belong to Sagitta, but to the place where the Arrow had been hidden. The rhythm was like bones beating against each other, like skeletons fighting to the death.

I pushed away from that rhythm to find something beyond it. If I wanted to lead the others to Sagitta, I would need a location we could find on a map. I imagined Sagitta again, felt it pulling me towards it. If I was connected to the Arrow, then I was also connected to the place where it was hidden, and to whatever was above the underground ruins. I needed to find *that*.

Where are you? I asked the Arrow. *Give me a location.* A new rhythm pulsed around me, faint but present. It was coming from above. I followed the rhythm, gliding towards it until it vibrated through me. The new rhythm was dry, flowing around me like sand.

Sand.

I needed something more specific than sand, so I focused on the rhythm more closely. It pulsed slowly, as if the musician felt tired and dizzy and could barely get the notes out. But I couldn't glean any more information from it. I took a deep breath and pushed away the frustration.

The dying rhythm of the underground ruins blared strongly, but I ignored it. I focused only on Sagitta and its rhythm—it was swift like air, vigorous and vibrating. If I could have compared it to an instrument, I would have said that it was like a flute. It whistled sharply as it cut through the air. Yet something intense thrummed through it too, but I couldn't explain exactly what it was—it was an eternal song, yet finite within that eternity. It was the beginning of an end and the end of a beginning.

I imagined the silver thread that connected us, strengthening our bond—we were both part of the same fabric of reality, tied together by that thread, bound together by Prophecy.

A rush of energy flooded through my body, and the location simply appeared in my mind. The rhythms around me collapsed, and my body felt like it was disintegrating one atom at a time. Fireworks burst around me, then the darkness returned like a punch in the stomach.

I groaned in pain as I fell onto the wet, snowy ground.

"Orion!" Virgo shouted.

Leo roared.

"I'm fine," I said. My head felt light, as if I had inflated it with helium. But my bones were so heavy that I couldn't lift them. "I'm okay."

Virgo managed to pull me into a sitting position.

"What happened?" Virgo gripped my shoulders tightly. "You were right next to me and then your light was gone."

I breathed out. "I know where Sagitta is."

CHAPTER 37

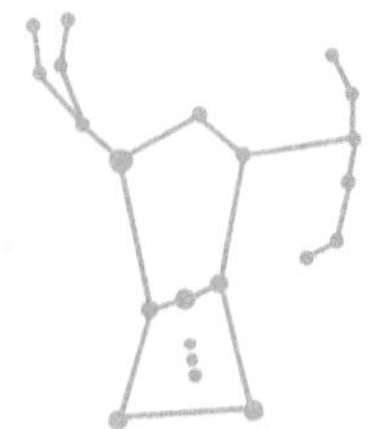

WE ALL SAT in Argo's living room. It was the first time Andromeda had decided to set foot on the Ship. She sat right next to me on a plush couch. The Twins were on my left, Leo on my right, and Virgo and Draco a few feet in front of me.

Part of me was frustrated that I hadn't been able to find Corona Borealis before the Portal collapsed. But finding Sagitta had left me weak and I didn't feel strong enough even to open a portal to talk to Leo. The Crown would have to wait. Leo had suggested that we could go find the Arrow while I recovered my strength, and that once we had Sagitta I could search for the Crown.

"So," one of the Twins asked, "where's the Arrow?"

"It's in Iran," I said. "In the Great Salt Desert." I was thankful that Zia had made me memorize maps and important locations in every country. "I sensed it somewhere underground."

"I don't know where that is," one Twin said. "Let me look at the atlas."

There was some shuffling as one of the Twins stood up, and a few seconds later the sound of flipping pages filled the air.

"So you just have an atlas lying around?" Andromeda asked. "If Argo is a magical ship, shouldn't it have a GPS or something?"

"You would assume so," one of the Twins responded. "But Argo is a bit old school."

I really hoped the Ship didn't feel offended by that.

"It must be somewhere—*aha!*—here it is."

Andromeda stood up and moved closer to the Twins. Virgo and Draco did the same.

One of the Twins whistled. "That's very far inland."

"Yeah, that might be a problem," the other Twin said. "I'm not even sure what route to take."

"Going around Africa and then back up to the Arabian Sea will take too long," Virgo said.

"Argo!" one of the Twins shouted. "Take us on the fastest route to Iran. If you can get us to the Caspian Sea, that would be better."

I conjured a mental image of a world map. I had no idea how Argo would get us from the North Sea, to the Atlantic, through the Mediterranean, across the Baltic Sea, and somehow into the Caspian Sea.

"Is that even possible?" Andromeda asked. "The Caspian Sea doesn't seem to be connected to the rest of the ocean."

"Argo will know how to get there," one of the Twins said. "One time he took us from the Pacific Ocean to the Dead Sea."

"How?" I asked.

"Through the Underground," the Twin responded, as if I should have known what that was. "Don't worry. Argo will get us there."

"The problem is what we'll have to do once we get to Iran," the other Twin said. "Argo can't go inland."

"We can steal a truck," Andromeda suggested. "One big enough for Leo and the others. We can drive it from the coast to the desert."

"Do you know how to steal trucks?" one of the Twins asked.

"I do," Andromeda said. "I can open locks with my power, and I know how to hotwire cars, so it shouldn't be a problem."

"I guess that works," Draco said. "Orion, once we're at the desert you'll have to guide us to a more specific location."

"Sure."

"Great!" one of the Twins shouted. "We have a plan now!"

Leo roared, making me jump.

Even though I was sagging with fatigue, I forced myself to open the Portal in my chest.

"What is it?" I asked.

"I know that location," Leo said, and I translated it to the others.

"You've been to that desert before?" Virgo asked.

"Last time I was there, it wasn't a desert," Leo said. *"It was a large city."*

"A lost city under the sand? That's so cool!" one of the Twins said excitedly, although Leo's dark tone seemed to indicate it had been anything but cool.

"That must have been the ruins I sensed," I said, remembering the macabre rhythm.

"The city was already in ruins when I last visited."

"How long ago where you there?" Virgo asked.

Leo didn't answer immediately. *"Three, maybe five thousand years ago?"*

I had known Leo was old, but the fact that he had been alive for at least five thousand years made me feel lightheaded.

"Wait," Andromeda said. "I'm not an expert in history, but I'm not sure I ever heard of a large city in the desert that was *that* old."

"It was a city of Giants, not humans," Leo explained. *"But they were already long gone by the time I went there."* My head spun. I really hoped those Giants were dead—we already had enough problems to deal with. *"Cepheus discovered the city. It was one of the lands that had been invaded by the Children of the Shadows."*

"And who are those?" asked one of the Twins, alarmed.

"They're all dead," Leo said. *"The city should be empty. At least, it was empty when I left it."* That wasn't very encouraging. *"The city is a place that no human can enter, and it is so vast that trying to find the Arrow there would be impossible unless one had a specific location."*

"I can guide us to the Arrow. We just need to get into the city," I said.

"But how will we actually get in?" Draco asked. "Even if Orion knows the specific location, the city is buried under the desert."

"I remember an entrance," Leo said. *"I could try to guide us to that location and see if it's still there, and if not we'll have to find another way in."*

"You must have a great memory, Leo," Andromeda said. "I sometimes forget what I ate for breakfast."

Leo, wisely, didn't answer.

"Can you tell us more about the Arrow?" Virgo asked.

"Like I said before, it can kill anyone and anything. It has a poisoned tip and even a scrape is lethal. I don't know much else—I didn't get along very well with its last owner."

"Who was the last owner?" I asked.

"Centaurus used to own it. But if Cassiopeia and Cepheus hid it, then Centaurus must have broken his Connection to the Arrow at some point before that."

Someone tapped their foot on the floor.

"Leo," Draco said. "Do you know why Cepheus and Cassiopeia hid these Star Objects? Do you think they hid Crater too?"

"I do not know," Leo admitted. *"I didn't even know Hydra was guarding Crater. I thought the snake was dead—we used its bones to fashion most of our weapons."*

"So *that's* where all of the weapons in Argo come from!" one of the Twins exclaimed.

"They must have had a specific reason for going through all this trouble," Virgo said.

"I don't know them as well as you think I do." Bitterness tinted Leo's voice, and I remembered what he had said earlier—about how his family had taken his strength when he needed it to keep his human form. Could he have been referring to Zia and Cepheus? *"I don't even know how they found one of the Prophecies or why they wrote it on the temple wall."*

I leaned back on the couch. The fact that Leo didn't know why Cepheus and Zia had hidden the Star Objects bothered me. That meant the two of them had a secret agenda they hadn't shared with anyone else.

"I'm worried about this," Virgo said. "Let's not forget Perseus has our Prophecies. What if he knows we're still looking for these Star Objects? I'm afraid that we're playing a part of his game and heading exactly where he wants us to go."

My stomach knotted at Virgo's words, and Perseus's threats echoed inside of my head.

"I think we're giving Perseus too much power with those Prophecies," I said. "He wouldn't have blinded me if he had known that this would reveal additional powers to me, right?" I paused for a moment. "His plan must have been to blind me so I *wouldn't* be able to find Sagitta and Corona Borealis."

"That's the problem," Virgo said. "We don't actually know what his plan is. Maybe he *did* want you to discover your new powers."

"And how would that give him an advantage?" I asked.

"I don't know," Virgo responded.

"I don't think Perseus knows what we're up to," one of the Twins said. "But we should still be ready for anything. Our plans never go as planned."

A long silence stretched in the room.

"Maybe, for once, everything will work out fine," Draco said.

I really hoped that was true.

Chapter XX, Verse IV

The Dragon defeated by he who claims to be the Hero,
But only death and sorrow he will bring upon the land.
The White Flame he will seek to regain,
After one life awakens and another one falls into slumber.
The power of Prophecy will remain in his hands,
Until the Prince of Darkness a new secret discovers,
Before the Dragon and man fight to the death.

CHAPTER 38

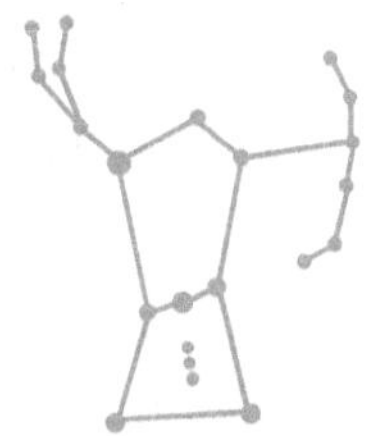

I SAT ON THE PASSENGER'S SEAT of the large truck we had stolen as Draco drove down the road. I couldn't hear the others in the trailer hitched behind us, but sensed them close at my back. Everyone had come on our quest for Sagitta except Argo. The Ship had gotten to the Caspian Sea without any trouble, and it would be waiting for us there when we returned from our quest.

It would take about twelve hours to get from northern Iran, where we had docked, to the desert. I wished we could have arrived faster, but there was no other mode of transport we could use. We made several stops at gasoline stations to fill up the tank and buy some food. We didn't know how long we would be in the city, so we bought enough food for a few days. We also bought water bottles, toilet paper, and flashlights. Before leaving Argo, we had armed ourselves with Star Weapons—just in case.

The engines roared loudly as we drove, the darkness silently oppressive. I wished I could have looked out the window to see the desert.

"Orion," Draco said at some point.

"Yeah?"

Draco was silent for a second, but I knew exactly what he wanted to talk about. "I can feel the Dragon stirring."

I didn't respond.

"If we don't find Corona Borealis and Sagitta, or if something goes wrong while we're fighting with Perseus, I need you to kill me."

"No. Corona Borealis will protect you while I kill Typhon with Sagitta."

"But if something goes wrong, I need to know that you can help me," Draco said. "The Dragon *will* try to kill you. I'll die before I let that happen. Even if . . . this isn't an easy decision for me either. But if there is anything I *can* do, it's protect the people I care about."

"We'll find a way, Draco," I said. "Leo seems pretty confident you will be safe with these Star Objects."

"Shoot me straight through the heart," Draco said. "Unless you pierce the heart, the Dragon won't die."

"I'm not going to shoot your heart," I said determinedly.

"Please," Draco begged. "The Dragon will trap me inside of it. You're not killing *me*, Orion. If the Dragon awakens, I will likely be dead by that point."

I gritted my teeth.

"Please, Orion," Draco said. "I don't trust the Twins with this, and I can't ask Virgo to do this. I need *you* to kill me if something goes wrong. You're the only one strong enough."

His unspoken words still rang through me. *You're the best killer among us.* My lungs felt as if someone had squeezed the air out of them.

Draco's voice was almost a whisper. "If you won't do it for me, do it for Virgo, for the Twins, for Andromeda. Do it to protect them."

I really didn't want to kill Draco, not after how hard we had fought to survive. He deserved something better—we all did. And I refused to give Perseus the satisfaction of letting him turn us against each other.

But if the Dragon awoke and killed Draco anyway . . . was I willing to risk letting it kill the rest of us?

"Fine." The word slashed through my throat as if I had spat out glass. "*If* something goes wrong, I'll do it. But we'll find Corona Borealis to protect you, and I'll use Sagitta to kill Typhon before he can even try to hurt you."

Draco exhaled in relief, but I didn't share the same feeling. I scratched my cheek, where the beard continued to grow since I hadn't asked anyone to help me shave. I let out a long breath, but Draco didn't say anything else. The possibility of killing him troubled me, leaving a pulsing pain in my chest. Killing someone who had fought by my side, someone who had done nothing wrong to deserve death, made my chest tighten.

But had any of the people Zia asked me to kill deserved it? I hadn't known them, so it hadn't mattered. She had turned me into a killer, and I had stepped into those shoes without questioning it, feeling like I had no other choice but to obey her.

I can be better. I reminded myself. But I couldn't completely let go of the killer inside of me—I would murder Typhon and do whatever it took to destroy Perseus. I would kill to protect the people I cared about. Did that make me any better than before, though? I didn't know.

After some immeasurable amount of time, my scars burned. I groaned. It had been a while since they had hurt.

"The Arrow is that way," I pointed to the right.

"There's no road leading there. We would have to drive over the sand and I'm not sure if a truck this heavy can do that," Draco said.

Draco slowed to a stop. With his help, I got down from the truck and we opened the back doors to talk to the others. We quickly explained the situation.

"How far away is Sagitta?" Virgo asked.

"I don't know," I admitted. "Several miles to the right."

"I don't love the idea of crossing a desert at night but I don't think we have another choice," one of the Twins said.

Leo roared.

"All right then," Virgo said with a sigh. "Let's get going."

It took us a few minutes to make sure we had all the supplies we needed and exit the truck. I followed Sagitta's pull into the desert, leading the others. One moment I was stepping on solid ground, then my feet sank. I stumbled forward, but a steady grip on my arm prevented me from falling.

"It would be embarrassing to see you fall on your face," Andromeda said.

I smiled. "I trust you won't let me fall then."

"I'll try my best," she responded.

As we walked, I opened the Portal inside my chest. The rhythm of the desert immediately flowed through me—dry, humming, and lazy. It was the same rhythm I had sensed when I had tracked down Sagitta the day before. We were in the right place.

"I know what we forgot!" one of the Twins shouted. "We left Cancer behind!"

I almost burst out laughing. I had completely forgotten about the Crab until then.

"Who's Cancer?" Andromeda asked.

"Long story," I muttered.

"Hopefully we won't need him," Virgo said.

After that, we walked mostly in silence. The night was bleak, the cold seeping into my bones through the jacket. My feet sank into the sand with every step, slowing down our trek, but thankfully the boots kept it out. Andromeda's grip was tight on my arm, keeping me steady. The darkness around me seemed to be an interminable desert of its own with neither the moon nor the Stars to guide me.

Every time I thought of Sagitta, my chest stirred with its rhythm—we were closer to the Arrow, but it was very far beneath us. What civilization had inhabited the ruins now lost under the sand? Leo had mentioned the Giants, but I didn't know who those were. At that thought, the darkness around me seemed to expand into a vast unknown—there was so much I didn't know, so many secrets hidden in that blackness.

After what seemed like hours, Andromeda pulled me to a stop.

"The entrance used to be here," Leo said, and I translated.

"Are you sure?" Castor asked. "This sand dune looks exactly like all the other sand dunes around us."

"No, it is here," Leo insisted.

"So what do we do?" Pollux asked. "Dig?"

"We didn't bring any shovels, again," Castor said.

"I think I can do it," Virgo said hesitantly.

"How?" Andromeda asked.

Virgo didn't answer. "I think—I think I can move the sand."

She didn't sound very confident, but I knew that Virgo was just starting to experiment with her powers and needed more practice.

Aquila landed next to us. The Eagle shrieked a second later.

"You should all come closer to me," Virgo said.

We formed a tight circle around her. Everyone's rhythms overlapped, forming a powerful song that flowed around me like a booming orchestra. The ground shifted, as if a snake was slithering right beneath my feet. The rhythm of the sand changed—it was the first time I sensed any rhythm changing like that. Its beat sped up, rippling like a storm.

Andromeda gasped. Leo roared. I had never felt claustrophobic before but I suddenly felt as if I were being buried alive.

"What's happening?" I asked.

"We're descending into the sand as if we were in an elevator," Andromeda whispered. "The sand is moving below us, caving inwards, creating a sort of tunnel."

I could sense it, the sand standing like walls at my sides, ready to crumble at any second. We descended for what seemed like interminable minutes, until my feet touched the hard ground.

"The entrance should be here somewhere," Leo said.

"I can't see," Andromeda said. I heard a click on my right. Maybe someone had turned on a flashlight. A few seconds passed in silence. "Is that what we're looking for?"

"Hmmm," Pollux said. "That doesn't really look like an entrance."

Leo growled.

"Okay, well I guess it *is* an entrance."

"Can you open that?" Virgo asked.

"I think so," Andromeda responded.

I had no idea what they were talking about, but I didn't want to interrupt. Andromeda let go of my arm and I sensed her lower onto the ground. Tense silence thrummed in the air around us. Rocks ground against each other, then a loud crash echoed somewhere beneath me.

"I don't see a ladder," Castor said a few seconds later.

"Maybe I can make one," Virgo said.

The earth rumbled for a minute.

"I guess that works," one of the Twins muttered.

The others shuffled around me, and I assumed we were getting ready to descend. I sensed the Twins go down first.

"Can you see anything below you?" Draco asked.

"Just a big creepy room," Pollux said, his voice echoing back to us.

"Orion," Virgo said. "You should go next."

"I'll help you," Andromeda immediately said.

I hesitated. "Okay."

Andromeda took me by the arm and pulled me forward a couple of steps, then pulled me to a stop. My stomach made a small leap as I neared the hole. I didn't know how big it was, but I could just *sense* a void right in front of me.

Andromeda pulled me down. I crouched.

"Ummm," she said. "The hole is right in front of you." She grabbed my hand and pressed it to the cold ground, then guided it a few inches forward until my fingers brushed the edge. "The stairs are on this side, so you have to turn around." I did as she instructed, the gaping hole right at my back. "I'm going to step in first and then I'll guide you."

"Okay," I said, blood rushing in my ears.

I closed the Portal in my chest—I didn't want the rhythms distracting me. Andromeda shuffled next to me. She descended a few feet below me. I sensed movement in front of me and felt Draco grab my left arm.

"Just in case," he said.

"The first step is about four feet below the edge," Andromeda said, her voice echoing below me. I tightly gripped the edge of the hole and lowered one leg. "A bit lower . . . just a few more inches."

My foot touched solid rock, and I breathed out in relief. Draco kept his grip on my arm as I lowered the other leg, and then he let go.

"From here, every step is about two feet below the other one," Andromeda said.

I nodded. Slowly, and with Andromeda's help, we both climbed down. My hands ached as I gripped the rough stone ladder, but I ignored the pain. As we descended further, a rotten smell drifted into my nose—like blood and sweat mixed with poison.

"Just one more step," Andromeda announced.

I lowered my left foot and felt the coarse ground under my boot. I let out an exhausted breath as I pulled away from the ladder. Andromeda led me away from the wall, a few feet deeper into the room where the Twins stood together.

"Wait," one of the Twin's voices echoed around me, "is Leo just going to—"

A loud crack made the ground tremble.

"Oh, wow, he just dropped through," The Twin said.

Leo growled in acknowledgment. Aquila shrieked as he flew in.

"Come on, boy, I'll carry you," Draco said in the distance. Sirius barked. I wasn't sure how Draco was going to descend the steps while carrying the massive dog, but he somehow made it work. Virgo descended last, and a few minutes later we all stood together in the room.

"What do we do about the hole?" Draco asked. "The sand will spill in and we can't close the hatch because Andromeda broke it."

"I didn't break anything," she snapped. "It just dropped."

"I can just close the rock," Virgo said.

After some rough scraping, two rocks seemed to slam loudly into each other. I felt we had been sealed into a tomb. Clicks echoed around me as the others presumably turned on their flashlights.

"So where to now?" one of the Twins asked.

"Give me a minute," I said before opening the Portal in my heart.

I immediately sensed the rhythm—like bones beating on drums made of flayed skin. Death played a ghastly song as the beats of loss and sorrow drummed together. The rhythm intensified, as if trying to warn me away. I breathed deeply. I didn't care how many dangers awaited us—we wouldn't leave without the Arrow.

CHAPTER 39

I FOCUSED ON SAGITTA, and the Arrow's swift rhythm found me like a gust of wind. "It's ahead," I said. "In that direction." I pointed my arm a bit towards the left.

Leo walked ahead of me before I could say anything else. Andromeda grabbed my arm and pulled me forward, following Leo. Our footsteps echoed for a few seconds, and then the echo died down behind us. I stopped sensing the walls, as if they had suddenly disappeared. I imagined we must have been entering a much larger cavern. The dense, rotting smell disappeared, replaced by a damp, moldy odor. My nose itched at the aroma of dust stirred up from the ages of neglect.

Someone next to me let out a gasp, and Andromeda pulled me to a stop.

"Can someone please tell me what we're seeing?" I asked.

"Well," Pollux said, "it's just *wow*."

"That was a great description," I said. "Thank you."

"It's like we're within a giant building that has other buildings inside of it," Virgo said.

"You mean like a city inside of a dome or something?" I asked.

"Something like that," Andromeda said. "We're standing on a balcony overlooking what looks like a city, but as Virgo said the whole city is enclosed in what seems to be something else, but it's not a dome. It's like . . . another giant building."

"The architecture is so strange," Virgo said. "This place is so big, and the shapes of the buildings are so unnatural."

Frustration tore at me. Why was everybody so bad with descriptions?

"Let's keep going," I said. I pointed again to where I sensed Sagitta. "What's in that direction?"

"It looks like you're pointing at one of the buildings on the far side of the city," Draco said. "The tall and pointy one."

"I think that used to be a temple," Leo said, and I immediately translated. *"But I never entered it, so I don't know what's inside."*

"Let's get going," Andromeda said. "This place makes me feel nervous. The faster we find Sagitta, the better." She pulled me towards the left. "There's some stairs leading down to the street."

As we slowly descended the stone stairs, Sagitta's rhythm was replaced by the city's—it was the pulse of a dead, rotten heart trying desperately to hold on to life. I tried to ignore it, but couldn't. It blared around me as if a speaker was blasting music next to my ear. My skin vibrated to the rhythm, making my heart shrink inside of my chest. As we descended further, the rhythm became violent and murderous, like the clash of a mob fighting against each other. It was as if the rhythm was trying to tell me what had happened in the city, but it was a language that I barely understood. I thought about closing the Portal in my chest, but part of me was reluctant to do it. Maybe my power would warn us of any danger if I sensed a new rhythm around us. I also didn't want to lose contact with Leo.

"We're two steps away from the street," Andromeda whispered into my ear.

The street felt uneven under my feet. Maybe the ground had cracked with age. Leo's paws scraped loudly as he walked at the front of the group. A boom echoed in the distance and I immediately stopped. I didn't sense any new rhythms.

"You said the people who used to be here are dead now, right Leo?" Pollux asked.

"They should be," the Lion answered.

Hesitantly, Andromeda pulled me forward again. The city's rhythm became more sorrowful—grief strung around me like a vibrating moan, then took on a higher pitch like a resonating scream.

"That statue looks weird," Draco said in a very low voice behind me.

"Yeah," Virgo whispered.

We continued forward. Leo was silent, and I wondered what he might be thinking. He had been here before, millennia ago—it must have been strange to be back.

Andromeda held my arm tighter.

"What is it?" I whispered.

"It's just . . ." Andromeda sighed. "This place doesn't feel right."

It definitely didn't. The rhythms agreed—a forbidden melody indicated it was a city that shouldn't have existed, and the rise and fall of its chorus told me it had been forgotten and rediscovered several times, yet the sorrowful strings of that song indicated that this city had always led its people to ruin and death.

As we kept walking forward, the rhythm of Sagitta intensi-fied again, flowing swiftly like a spring breeze. But the Arrow was still miles away, beckoning me like a distant lighthouse. In the city, the darkness around me was restless, and in my mind, dark figures twisted about.

After what seemed like a long time, Leo stopped ahead of me. Andromeda pulled me to a stop. The rhythm of Sagitta was stronger than before, somewhere below us but still a good dis-tance away.

"We have to climb some broken steps," Andromeda said.

We slowly ascended the steps, but to me it felt like we were climbing the side of a rocky mountain instead. Once at the top, Andromeda pulled me forward. A few seconds later our footsteps echoed loudly around me.

"Where are we now?" I asked.

"It's just a strange room," Castor said unhelpfully.

"It's circular," Virgo explained. "And divided into four sec-tions. It looks like the sections might have been divided by water that flowed down the walls and dropped down a circular hole in the middle of the room."

"The Arrow is somewhere below us in the direction I'm pointing," I said.

"Below us?" Andromeda asked.

"I don't see any steps leading down," Draco said. "And this is the last building inside of the city. I don't think there's anything beyond this."

Andromeda pulled me a couple of steps forward.

"*Wait!*" Leo let out a dangerous growl.

"What is it?" I asked.

"Someone else is here."

My body tensed. Was Perseus here? How had he dug through so much sand? I didn't sense any new rhythms around me, but that didn't mean Leo was wrong.

"Look at the marks on the floor . . . I've seen those before."

"Is it just me?" Castor asked. "Or do those look like a horse's hoofprints?"

"CENTAURUS!" Leo roared.

"Didn't you say Centaurus was Sagitta's last owner?" I asked.

"Yes."

"The hoofprints lead to the back of the room," one of the Twins said. "Yeah look, there's a hole there."

Shuffling and rapid footsteps echoed across the room.

"We need to jump to the other section," Andromeda said. "They're separated by a line cut into the rock that is three feet wide. I'll tell you when to jump." Andromeda pulled me forward before I could say anything, and my feet immediately responded, running with her. "Jump!"

I bent my knees and shot forward. My stomach knotted for a second before my feet touched solid ground again. Andromeda kept tugging me forward, then stopped abruptly.

"What were you doing here?" Leo said in a distant tone.

I could sense something below us—a twisted and broken form bent at odd angles. I was surprised that I was able to sense it with that much detail and assumed that my new power was evolving. I couldn't sense the form's rhythm, though.

"Is that Centaurus?" Virgo asked, her voice almost a whisper.

"It was," Leo said, sorrow sharp in his voice. *"What was he doing here?"*

"Is he dead?" I asked hesitantly.

"He is," Andromeda said. "It looks like he was stabbed through the chest."

"I'm not a doctor," Pollux said. "But that wound doesn't look natural. It's rotting yellow and blue."

"He has so many cuts . . ." Virgo said. "And a lot of his bones are broken."

"This smells recent," Draco said. "And the body hasn't decomposed that much."

Andromeda's grip tightened on my arm, and my own muscles tensed.

"Centaurus must have been here to recover Sagitta," Leo said. *"And someone killed him before he could find the Arrow."*

My heart sped up as I clenched my fists. The rhythm of death strengthened around me, crying like a moaning violin, urging me away.

"The Arrow is below us, in that direction," I pointed to the right.

"Look, there's an opening next to Centaurus," Virgo said.

I gritted my teeth, but couldn't blame my friends for forgetting that I couldn't *look*.

"I'm not liking this," Pollux said. "I'm not liking this one bit."

"We don't have a choice," I said.

"We're going to have to jump down," Andromeda said. "It's about a six-foot drop."

I took a deep breath, then nodded. Andromeda pulled me forward, and we both jumped down. The stench of death hit me like a hammer to the nose. I gagged at the smell of decomposed meat. The others dropped down too, coughing and cursing. Leo let out a mournful roar as he stood next to the broken figure.

"Why were you here for the Arrow, Chiron?" Leo asked his dead friend. I was sure I had heard the name Chiron somewhere in the myths, and assumed that must have been Centaurus's other name. *"Who killed you?"*

Deadly silence filled the air around us.

"Orion," Castor said next to me. Something smooth and cold brushed against my fingers. "It's a sword. Take it, just in case."

I gripped the hilt. I wasn't sure how I would fight with a sword if I couldn't see anything, but I felt safer having it with me. I pointed the sword down until it touched the ground—it was nearly the same length as my leg.

"Let's move," Leo said.

Andromeda guided me to the right. The rhythm of the city changed as we walked forward, becoming somehow more . . . chaotic. It wasn't the same type of Chaos as Andromeda's rhythm. It felt more as if short pieces of different songs had been stitched together and the rough transitions sent jarring jolts through me.

"In the name of the Stars," Leo cursed. *"Not this place again."*

"What?" I asked as my heart hammered against my chest.

"I only see a long hallway ahead of us," Andromeda said. "It's huge, about fifty feet wide and about a hundred feet tall. It must be beyond the city because it wasn't visible before."

"It branches off in several different directions," Virgo added.

"Cepheus must have chosen this location to hide Sagitta," Leo's voice was bitter and resentful.

"What is this place, Leo?" I asked again.

"The Maze."

"That sounds exciting," Castor said.

"Is there anything particularly worrying about the Maze?" Virgo asked.

"It's gigantic," Leo said. *"Last time I was here, I was lost for ten days."*

"I'm not sure the toilet paper will last that long," Andromeda said.

"Maybe we could leave a toilet paper trail to find our way back," Pollux suggested.

"I won't waste my toilet paper on that," Andromeda said.

"Well, I don't suppose anyone brought any breadcrumbs?" Castor asked. "Or maybe a thread?"

"I'm more worried about our food rations," Virgo said. "They definitely won't last ten days."

"We don't have ten days to waste here," I muttered.

"I don't think it will take us ten days to find Sagitta," Leo said. *"Last time I was stuck here only because the Shadows prevented our retreat."* He paused. *"I imagine Sagitta must be hidden at the center of the Maze. Getting there might only take us a couple of days."*

"A couple of days doesn't sound too bad." Draco didn't sound very convinced.

"Maybe I can move the rocks and . . ." Virgo trailed off. "Wait, I can't. The rock doesn't respond to me here, as if it's dead."

"This place is corrupted," Leo said. I wasn't sure what that meant, but it didn't sound like good news for us. *"That must be why Cepheus chose this place. He knew there is no way to cut across the Maze."*

"Do you remember how to get to the center, Leo?" I asked.

"No."

"I'm not liking this," Pollux said.

"We'll make it through," Leo said determinedly, although my voice didn't transmit that same confidence. *"We'll have to be very alert, because whoever killed Centaurus could be hiding in the Maze."*

My muscles strained with anticipation.

"All right then." Andromeda squeezed my hand. "Let's get going."

Chapter XIII, Verse V

Once a beautiful Queen beloved by many,
An appropriate end she met, her blood spilled in the forest.
Not for long she shall remain buried under the earth,
Because a new form will be hers to take shape.
The White Throne the Princess shall await,
To give her enough power to defeat the Prince she hates.
Only after a promise to the Silver Crown has been made.

CHAPTER 40

PAIN PULSED IN TUNE with my heart, plaguing every inch of my body. Fragments of my memory returned to me in a broken mosaic.

"Please," Andromeda said. "She's not the same Zia she was before . . . We need to leave before she . . ."

Another stab of pain tore through me. I wanted to scream, but my mouth wouldn't move.

"She'll be furious if we try to escape," I whispered back.

Andromeda pleaded with her eyes. "Do you know how many scars you have on your back?"

I opened my mouth to respond, then shut it.

"Or has she beaten us so much that you've lost count?"

I looked away from her.

"Please, Orion," Andromeda said. "We can't keep living like this. How many more times are we going to let her beat us?"

Agony burned through me, like a slow fire devouring me from the inside.

I drove through the highway, looking at the rearview mirror every couple of seconds. Was leaving Zia the right decision? She had given us everything we had, but Andromeda was right—she wasn't *the same as she had been before. She had become more violent and brutal.*

"She'll kill us," Andromeda had said.

Would she? All I knew for sure is that I didn't want to find out. My scars burned.

"Zia's following us," I said.

"What?" Andromeda swiveled around on her seat to look behind us. "How?"

"I don't know."

She shouldn't have known where we were. We had escaped the house in the middle of the night, and had stolen several cars to make it harder to track us. I knew Zia had left the house a few hours after we did, but I hadn't expected her to catch up so fast—as if she could sense exactly where we were.

My back pulsed with agony, as if I lay on a bed of knives.

Zia's headlights flashed in the rearview mirror as she smashed her car into ours. We spun, then stopped abruptly as we hit something else. My vision darkened, fractured images flashing before my eyes as I battled to stay awake. Yells echoed around me. Two strong arms dragged me out of the car. Pain stung my eyes as I stared at the headlights.

"How dare you abandon me!" Zia hissed.

My vision came back into focus. My head throbbed, my surroundings a haze of smoke as I sat in the back seat of her car. Dark fog pulled me into its depths, then evaporated when my head hit something hard. I opened my eyes, staring dumbly at the wooden floor. Dim light filtered through the thin curtains at my side. I groaned. We were back at the house.

Zia kicked me hard in the ribs. Red stars danced in my vision, exploding like fireworks. I struggled to breathe.

"Stop!" Andromeda shouted.

I groaned as my shoulder imploded with agony.

"You ungrateful brats would leave me after everything I have given you," Zia said as one of my ribs cracked, sending a blast of pain through my torso. "You can't escape." She whispered in my ear. "You'll always be mine."

"No!" Andromeda shouted.

Screams meshed together with the pain in a net of agony. The stars continued to explode in my vision, like shards of blood erupting in all directions. The red intensified, flowing around me like ribbons.

My scars flared like rivers of fire, and my vision came into sharp focus once more. Andromeda stood in front of me, holding a knife in her hand—my knife. It glinted with the silver light of the moon.

"Don't," I managed.

Andromeda startled and turned to look at me. She narrowed her eyes. "She'll break us, Orion," she whispered. "She'll beat us until we die."

"She didn't mean to hurt me." She had only reacted that way because we had tried to abandon her. "We should never have tried to leave."

Andromeda's voice turned cold as ice. "Look at you. You can't even stand up. What happens next time she gets angry?" I wanted to say that we could just avoid making Zia angry by doing whatever she asked, but Andromeda continued. "Zia said next time she would beat you worse than this. She's become a monster."

The nauseating pain made my vision blur. We should never have tried to escape. Zia would never let us—she had made that clear. She shouldn't have been able to find us so quickly, but she had—like a wolf hunting its prey. No matter where we ran, she would always find us.

Andromeda gripped the knife tighter, her knuckles turning white.

"Please don't," I said. "She does care about us."

We were her children, after all. Andromeda's gaze darkened. She stormed out of the room. I wanted to go after her, but as soon as I tried to move my body erupted in pain all over again, and the red ribbons wrapped tightly around me, choking the air out of my lungs.

Andromeda screamed. Zia shouted. I tried to get up. I needed to help Andromeda. I pushed through the pain and stood from the bed. I managed one step before I crumpled to the ground like a heap of dust. I groaned as torturing pain cut through me like blades.

"Andromeda." I wasn't even sure I had spoken.

The ribbons spun even faster, dizzyingly twisting and turning. Then it was all dark, and just for a moment everything went still. I breathed out, my vision coming back into focus. I was staring at the white wall. I groaned as I pulled myself to my feet. My entire body felt broken, but I ignored the pain as I hobbled out of my room and into the hallway. My heart shrank as I entered the living room.

She's dead, I thought. Blood pooled around Andromeda, her body so bruised and cut it looked like she had been trampled. I dropped to my knees next to her. Andromeda's face was swollen and bloodied, her hair plastered to her side. Andromeda slightly turned her head to look at me, and I let out a relieved breath. I carefully wrapped her in my arms and planted a soft kiss on her forehead.

I pulled her closer to me. Our eyes met.

She's broken.

There was no escape—Zia would rather have us dead than free, but I couldn't let Zia ever do this to her again. I knew Andromeda would try to run away again. There was nothing that could keep her bound—it was her nature. But how could I ensure that Zia didn't leave her like a corpse again?

I gently pulled Andromeda's hair out of her face. I would have to clean the wounds to make sure they didn't get infected.

If Andromeda was going to play the rebel, then I had to be the obedient one. Zia was all about control, and as long as she had one of us on a leash, she would be mostly content. She knew I would find Andromeda if she tried to escape, so her violent rage would be contained. That was the best thing I could do to protect Andromeda. I knew I couldn't save us from all the beatings, but at least it wouldn't come to this again.

"It's okay," I whispered to Andromeda through my own pain. "I'll keep you safe." But was I truly keeping her safe? "I'll keep you alive." That seemed more appropriate.

I planted another kiss on Andromeda's forehead, sealing my promise.

●————●————●

The Maze was silent except for our footsteps. Andromeda didn't let go of my arm as we moved through interminable corridors. The darkness surrounding me made the journey even more frustrating. To me, the Maze was just a cryptic shadow.

Sagitta's rhythm was strong, but still far, and I tried to guide the others towards the Arrow as best as I could. But we hit dead ends at least once every ten minutes and had to turn back. We didn't have anything to leave as a trail, but Draco used his claws to make spiraled scratches on the walls we had already passed. I didn't think that would be enough to guide us back, but at least we would know if we had already been in a specific place.

The cold seemed to intensify as we moved further inwards, making my hands feel numb. The place also had a distinctive smell—like ash and blood mixed with oil. I kept the Portal inside my chest open, hearing the familiar rhythms of my friends and the foreboding rhythm of the city.

Leo always walked at the front of the group, followed by Draco and Virgo, then by me and Andromeda. Behind us were the Twins, Sirius, and Aquila. The Eagle couldn't fly far in the enclosed space, but the flap of his wings echoed off the walls every now and then. I stayed alert as we moved forward, gripping the sword tightly. Someone or some*thing* was here, and I didn't doubt that whatever had killed Centaurus would try to kill us too.

As we walked in silence, I couldn't help thinking about Zia. The rings that hung around my neck were a constant reminder of her mysterious past. She had gone through a lot of trouble to hide the Star Objects. Why? Who was she hiding them from? And why had she decided to leave this secret to me? In her own way, I knew she had cared about me and Andromeda, enough to leave us with the key to finding these weapons so we could survive. But understanding Zia's past was as complicated as traversing through the Maze—I always seemed to hit a dead end whenever I thought I had answers. I let out a long sigh. I had promised Andromeda I would let go of Zia's secrets, but they still hovered around me like specters.

We took a couple of breaks to eat and go to the bathroom, which felt awkward to do in a giant Maze, but we had no choice. Even though Pollux had a watch and tried to monitor our progress, I lost all sense of time.

"Should we stop to sleep?" Virgo asked at some point.

It had probably been at least twelve hours since we had taken turns to nap in the truck.

"That sounds like a good idea," Andromeda said. She pulled me to the side and then let go of my arm. For a second, I wasn't sure of what to do, then slowly lowered myself to the ground, placing the sword next to me.

"Someone should keep watch," one of the Twins said.

"I can take the first watch," I said.

"Me too," Leo said.

The Lion moved closer to me, sitting at my side. Warmth radiated out of him in waves. I slid closer to him, hoping he wouldn't mind.

The others settled around us.

"Andromeda," Castor said, "can I use one of your toilet paper rolls as a pillow?"

"No," she immediately replied.

"Then where am I supposed to sleep?" Castor complained.

"Your brother's butt looks cushioned enough," Andromeda responded.

I bit back a burst of laughter and nearly choked on my own saliva. Snickers and chuckles erupted around me.

"Just use your backpack as a pillow," Virgo suggested.

After a few more complaints, the others settled to sleep. Andromeda lay on my right, with her backpack right next to my leg. I sat with the frigid wall at my back and Leo on my other side. For the first few minutes, there was a lot of shuffling, but eventually silence filled the space around me.

"Orion," Leo said.

"Yes?" I whispered.

"Have you been able to sense your surroundings better?" he asked. *"To sense the material world instead of sensing the frequencies and rhythms?"*

"Only a few times, I think," I whispered. "But it's hard."

"Try to practice more."

"I'm trying, Leo," I whispered. "I really am."

"I know." Leo's voice was gentle.

I sighed, then let my head rest against the wall behind me. After that, Leo remained silent. I tried practicing going beyond the rhythms, but couldn't. It was like listening to music and trying to find an object that represented each song. Frustration clawed at my chest like a caged beast. I wanted to *see* the world around me, not sense it. I wanted to see colors and shapes, not sense rhythms and beats. I couldn't bring myself to let go of the hope that I would see again one day.

When it was my turn to sleep, I thought that I wouldn't be able to do it. I was so anxious and tense that I didn't think my mind would simply slip away into sleep. I let my head rest on a backpack and I closed my eyes, the darkness unchanging around me. It seemed like only minutes passed before Andromeda nudged me awake.

"Hmmm," I said.

"We need to keep moving," Andromeda said.

"How long was I asleep?" I asked, a bit confused.

"Like five hours."

I felt more groggy and tired than before, and my body was sore from sleeping on the hard floor. It was as if the Maze had sucked the energy out of me through my dreamless sleep. "Come on." Andromeda grabbed my arm and pulled me up. Reluctantly, I pushed myself back to my feet with a groan, then retrieved my sword from the ground.

"Let's keep moving," Draco said. "I want to be out of this place as soon as possible."

We kept moving towards Sagitta, through an interminable number of twisting corridors. I sensed we were closer to the Arrow, but it was still a few miles away.

I opened the Portal in my chest to sense the rhythms around me. I wanted to go further, to truly sense the physical objects around me, but the instructions Leo had given me were too vague. I focused on the beat of the Maze, even though I hated it. Death pulsed around me like a bleeding heart. As we kept walking, I immersed myself completely in that rhythm, as if nothing else existed around me. My bones shuddered, and my heart beat more furiously. Ruin and despair rippled around me like a wave, like the dead pounding on their coffins to be set free again.

The Portal in my chest closed abruptly, and I stumbled forward. Andromeda gripped my arm tighter, pulling me back, and another strong hand caught my other arm.

"Whoa," one of the Twins said. "Are you all right?"

"Yeah," I breathed out.

The Twin let go of me and we continued forward. Andromeda didn't loosen her grip on me. If she noticed I wasn't all right, she didn't say it. I gritted my teeth in frustration—there had to be a way to go past those rhythms. Andromeda pulled me to a sudden stop as we rounded a corner, her grip tightening.

"What?" I whispered, holding my sword tighter.

"There's a big splatter of blood on the wall," Andromeda whispered.

My hand ached as I tightened my grip on the sword.

"Could that be Centaurus's blood?" Virgo asked behind me.

"I don't know," Andromeda answered.

"Let's keep moving and stay alert," one of the Twins said.

Hesitantly, Andromeda pulled me forward again. I knew we were passing by the splatter because Andromeda dug her nails into my jacket.

Before rounding each corner, we stopped, and one of the Twins peeked into the next corridor to make sure it was empty. My heart pounded hard against my chest, my muscles tense and ready to fight at any moment.

Reluctantly, I opened the Portal in my chest again. The ghastly rhythm came back once again. It seemed the same as it had been before, with no clues as to what lay ahead. The darkness around me didn't reveal anything either—it was just a sea of black churning like a storm. The Arrow's swift rhythm punctured through it, and my heart gave a leap of joy. We were so close now—a bit over a mile away. Then something else broke through the darkness.

I stopped.

"What?" Andromeda demanded.

The distant rhythm vibrated like claws raking against a blackboard. I shivered. It gained strength each second—like metal grinding against stone, like blood dripping into an endless ocean.

"There's something ahead," I said.

Leo emitted a deep growl. *"I hear it too."*

The sharp rhythm intensified as I tightened my grip on the sword. It felt stronger on the left. And then I *heard* it—a rhythmic clank like giant needles stabbing at the stone ground. The raucous rhythm moved closer and closer as we stood waiting.

Andromeda seemed to have stopped breathing as she crushed my arm with her grip. The clanking stopped, and I knew the creature was right ahead of us. Silence shivered around us for a second.

Then Leo roared. *"RUN!"*

CHAPTER 41

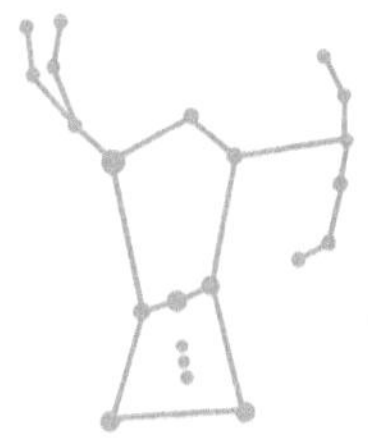

I RAN.

My bones shuddered with the shriek that echoed across the Maze. The creature's rhythm remained behind us as we raced forward. Andromeda abruptly pulled me to the left, and I almost stumbled to my knees. She pulled me to the right, then right again. The rhythm dimmed a bit, but I could still sense it like a crying wail behind us. We ran through so many corridors I quickly became disoriented.

We stopped, the others breathing heavily around me.

"What was that?" I asked.

"*Scorpio!*" Leo said. "*It's supposed to be dead. Cassiopeia killed it millennia ago . . . Or maybe she didn't.*"

"You mean *the* Scorpio of the Constellations?" Virgo asked.

Leo growled.

"Why do Cepheus and Cassiopeia have the ugliest Star Monsters guarding the Star Objects?" Pollux asked. "How did they even get the Scorpion inside the Maze?"

"*We will have to split up,*" Leo said.

"That's a terrible idea," Andromeda said. "That's how everyone always dies in horror movies."

"*Scorpio is outnumbered, that's our only advantage,*" Leo said.

"That's not such a terrible plan," Castor said. "I mean, at this point all of our plans are terrible, so whatever."

"I'll go with Orion," Andromeda said.

"*The rest of us have to distract Scorpio,*" Leo said. "*It must be guarding Sagitta, so we will need to draw it away from the Arrow so Orion can take it.*"

"How do we even fight that thing?" Pollux asked.

"*Pierce its head or its heart,*" Leo said.

"Easy peasy lemon squeezy." Pollux huffed. "We just have to stab its head without letting it cut us in half with its claws or letting it slice us with its stinger."

"That sounds more lemon squeezy than easy peasy," Castor said.

"How will we find each other again?" Virgo asked.

"I'll find you," I said.

"But we're in a Maze," Virgo said. "Even if you can sense us, how will you know the right path to get back to us?"

An earsplitting shriek erupted somewhere behind us, and the metallic rhythm intensified.

"I'll find a way," I said.

"*Stay away from the Scorpion's stinger,*" Leo hurriedly said. "*Its poison is lethal and will kill you with a scratch.*"

"Got it," one of the Twins said.

"*Go!*"

Before I could say anything else, Andromeda pulled me forward. My heart gave a painful beat. The others would be all right—they had fought other monsters before. They were probably better prepared to fight Scorpius than Andromeda and I were.

"If the Scorpion is here, that means Sagitta must close," Andromeda said. "Where do you sense the Arrow?"

The Arrow's rhythm flowed around me as soon as I thought about it, pulling me towards it. "It's to the right. I'm not sure how far away, but about a mile?"

"I'll try to take us in that direction," Andromeda said.

We ran side by side. I was thankful for all the rigorous training Zia had made us go through. Is this what she had been preparing us for?

"Come get me, you hideous thing!" Castor shouted. "You're even *uglier* than Cetus and Hydra!"

Andromeda pulled me to a stop as a shriek erupted ahead of us. A swoosh cut through the air as someone presumably swung their sword. The Scorpion shrieked louder.

"Back!" Andromeda hissed. We turned around and kept running. "Where is Sagitta?" Andromeda asked after we had made about three different turns in random directions.

"It's somewhere ahead of us," I said.

We continued forward. There was something thrilling about running at her side, as we'd done so many times before. For a very brief moment I could forget that we were Star Children, chased by a giant Scorpion and looking for a magical object. It was just her and me again.

Turn right. Run to the end of the corridor. Turn left. Turn left again. Dead end. Go back. Keep running. Our hurried footsteps became the only noise in the Maze. Andromeda pulled me to a stop, breathing heavily.

"I need a break," she whispered.

"Yeah."

I was tired, and my lungs ached, but the adrenaline kept me alert. I didn't even know how long Andromeda and I had been running. Half an hour? Maybe more?

"I think Zia sent us on a suicide mission," Andromeda said in between ragged breaths. "She could have warned us about the Scorpion, but she didn't."

"Maybe she didn't know it was here," I said.

"You heard the others, Zia and Cepheus also trapped Hydra in a cave to guard Crater," Andromeda said. "They must have trapped Scorpius here so he could guard the Arrow."

"We don't know if they trapped Hydra to guard Crater," I said. We had also just assumed that they had been the ones to hide Crater, but didn't have any solid proof of it.

"Can you stop protecting her?" Andromeda snapped. "Why can't you just admit that maybe Zia wanted us dead? That maybe she hated us, that she was just using us?" She let out a tired breath. "Why do you still want to believe she cared about us?"

I clenched my jaw hard. "Let's keep moving."

We walked fast while she recovered her breath. Sometimes we got closer to the Arrow, but most paths took us further away from Sagitta, as if the Maze never wanted us to reach it. After we had recovered our strength a bit, we began trotting.

Sagitta's swift rhythm eventually became stronger around me—we were getting closer. The Arrow was still a few hundred yards away, but after the lengthy distances we had traveled that was nothing.

A shrill squeal broke through the darkness. I stopped. A second later the creature emitted a shriek. The Scorpion's rhythm blared right in front of me as it moved closer.

"That thing is so ugly I might die just looking at it," Andromeda whispered.

My scars burned as my inner compass instinctively searched for the others. They were all moving, somewhere far on our left. They seemed to be walking further away from Andromeda and me. They were all right, but the Scorpion had managed to get away from them.

"We should run," Andromeda whispered.

"No," I said. "Sagitta is right ahead. The Scorpion knows we're close and it's trying to drive us away."

"How are we supposed to get past the monster?" she asked.

We couldn't play cat and mouse here forever. The Scorpion was a smart creature. It could just keep chasing us until we ran out of supplies and either died or had to leave.

Scorpio's legs clanked on the ground as the creature moved closer. I stood still, defiant. I held my sword in front of me, ready to strike.

"Tall . . . Mmmm . . . Strong . . . Mmmm." There was a loud clasping noise that must have come from the Scorpion's claws. *"Fight me then!"*

"Is that what you want me to do?" I ask. "You want me to fight you?"

The Scorpion backed away.

"You can listen."

"Yes."

The Scorpion clasped its claws again. *"You are the first who can. Yet there is not much I can say."* The rhythm moved a few inches closer to me. *"All I can give you is pain and death."*

"Why are you here?" I asked. "We could help you escape if you let me pass."

The Scorpion's shriek almost sounded like a laugh. *I cannot let you pass, even if I wanted to. The Queen corrupted me, and now I must do her biding.*

I felt that like a punch in the gut. There was only one Queen among the Constellations.

"Cassiopeia corrupted you?" I asked. On my left, Andromeda moved closer to me, her shoulder brushing against mine.

The Scorpion clasped its claws again. *"She corrupts every-thing she touches,"* the Scorpion said, his voice ringing through the darkness.

"What does that mean?" I asked.

The rhythm moved closer, washing over me. I didn't back away.

The Scorpion emitted another laughing shriek. *"She is the Queen of Light and can manipulate it to create illusions and glamours. She made everyone think she had killed me."* The Scorpion inched closer. *"I wish she would have. Instead, she corrupted my heart."*

"Orion!" Andromeda shouted.

I jumped to the side and heard a swoosh as something sliced the air where I had been standing. I turned to face that sound and swung the sword in front of me. It cut through something hard. The creature let out a shriek that made my ears ring in pain.

Andromeda held onto my wrist and pulled me towards the right, launching into a sprint. Sagitta's rhythm faded behind me.

"We have to go back," I said.

Andromeda stopped. The Scorpion's metallic rhythm drummed behind me.

"The Queen instructed me to kill anyone who came in search of the Arrow," Scorpius said behind me. *"It has become my destiny, Hunter. I wish I could help, but no one can escape the dark touch from the Queen."*

"What does that even mean?" I asked again.

"She used to be able to create Light, but she lost the Light, so she began stealing it from others to stay alive."

The Scorpion's words struck me like a lance. Is that what she had done to Leo—stolen his Light so he was forced permanently into a Lion? Is that why Zia had adopted us? Is that why she always wanted to keep us close, because she needed to feed off our Light? Was this the only reason she had ever loved us, just to save herself?

Something broke inside of me, something that had been cracked for a long time. Pain circulated through my blood like poison. I didn't hold back the pain. I couldn't. It had been buried within me for so long, frozen solid into my heart. But now it suddenly melted, pouring rivers of sorrow from it. The pain broke through the rhythms. It was a grieving ache that shattered through the world and let me sense what existed on the other side.

There *was* something beyond the darkness, something that couldn't be seen. It was a world bereft of color, but one full of emotion. Sadness, grief, horror, loss, rage, passion, love, happiness, and joy colored that world. It was a world of seeing, not with the eyes but with the heart. There were no rhythms anymore—those rhythms were part of something bigger. The rhythms were waves of emotion that defined the physical world. They were the language that translated energy into matter, Darkness into Light.

Everything around me took shape within the darkness. The walls stood tall at my sides, separated by a fifty-foot-wide corridor. They were smooth, too smooth. Cracks cut through the ceiling like a crooked spider web. Andromeda stood next to me, her sharp sword held out in front of her. The Scorpion was twenty yards in front of us. A thick, solid carapace covered its skin. Long and twisted legs extended out of it. The stinger, rising more than ten feet above the ground, was sharp as a knife.

"She stole my Light," Scorpius mourned. *"And now I must do her bidding."*

I screamed, letting the pain flood out of me. Rage gushed through my veins, igniting my muscles. I lunged forward. The Scorpion's stinger came down at me. I jumped to the right just in time, turned on my heel, and slashed the sword forward. I sensed how the sharp bone cut through the carapace, how blood spilled from the wound. Andromeda was immediately at my side. Her sword cut one of the Scorpion's legs. The monster jumped, making my heart lurch forward. Scorpius landed on the left wall, shrieking.

I raced forward, Andromeda at my heels. We both ran past the Scorpion, who realized its mistake too late.

"COME BACK!" it shrieked.

The Scorpion scurried across the wall, chasing after us, but we didn't stop. Sagitta was right ahead of me, less than a hundred yards in front of us. The Scorpion jumped from the wall, flying above our heads. Andromeda and I stopped at the same time as Scorpius landed right in front of us. It took me a split second to sense it fully. Its massive claws hovered at my sides, enclosing me. The Scorpion's face twisted inches from my own head. I thrust the sword in front of me, my bones jarring as the tip buried into something hard as metal. Something hit me from the left, and my feet left the ground. I didn't lose my grip on the sword as I crashed onto the ground, feeling a crack in my side.

"Orion!" Andromeda screamed.

My sensing became blurry—surfaces blending into each other. I pushed myself back to my feet, my chest and lungs on fire. Something large and sharp moved behind me. I turned and slashed my sword. Scorpius shrieked. Where was Andromeda? It took me a few seconds to sense her behind the Scorpion.

Scorpio brought its stinger down, aiming at my head. I jumped to the left, nearly stumbling down. I took support from the smooth wall to regain my balance, then pushed myself away. The Scorpion's tail was right in front of me, the tip of the stinger buried a few inches into the solid rock. I swung the sword, the muscles in my arms straining as I sliced through the thick carapace of the monster's tail. I couldn't cut the stinger off but did leave a deep wound.

Scorpius shrieked, then jumped up again, landing on the right wall. I didn't waste a second. I sprinted towards Andromeda, and we ran side by side, faster than before.

"Where do we—?" Andromeda asked.

I didn't let her finish as I made a sharp turn on the corridor to the left, sensing the opening. Andromeda followed me. My feet slid across the floor as we turned right at the end of that corridor. I kept running forward as Sagitta's rhythm beckoned me closer. I didn't sense the Scorpion behind me, which made me nervous. I knew Scorpius wouldn't just let us take the Arrow, but we had to keep going.

The space around me opened up and I stopped. I couldn't sense it fully—it was too big. Sagitta was right in front of me, a few yards away. It had been placed on a table, or at least something that had the shape of a table. I took a step forward.

"Wait!" Andromeda held my arm.

"What?" I asked, my senses sharpening. Twisted figures covered the ground.

"This place is full of skeletons," Andromeda whispered, as if afraid the dead would hear us.

Andromeda let go of my arm and I carefully stepped forward. Part of me was glad I didn't have to see the dead bodies. Had Scorpius killed them all? Or had they already been dead when he arrived?

I stopped walking when I sensed Sagitta right in front of me, lying on a table that reached up to my waist. The Arrow was as long as my arm and thick as my pinky finger. I took a deep breath, then reached down and held the wooden shaft. I had assumed it would be cold, since the Arrow had been here for millennia—but it was blazing hot to my touch. For a moment, nothing happened. Then I was pulled beyond the darkness.

Chapter XL, Verse I

Inside the Maze the Scorpion shall await,
The coming of the ones who seek to pierce its heart.
Many secrets it knows but by a vow he must not share,
The true reason the Arrow was hidden amongst the bones.
The Hunter it shall kill with a single sting,
Or by his sword to perish before the secret has been revealed.
The Scorpion will be born again from the fire in its bones.

CHAPTER 42

EVEN THOUGH THE SUN'S midday rays bore down on me, I didn't feel its heat. The lake was so still it could have been a solid mirror reflecting the bright blue sky above. The yellow grass below my feet had dried but the mountains beyond were dotted with bright green trees. I turned behind me, but the car was not under the oak tree.

"*Who are you?*" a voice whispered. It didn't sound male or female. It was a whisper that seemed to come from another galaxy.

I looked down at my hand and realized I was holding an Arrow.

"Why am I here?" I asked.

"*I do not know,*" the Arrow said.

This must have been a dream, an illusion.

"*There are no illusions,*" Sagitta said. "*Only different realities.*"

"You can hear my thoughts?" I asked.

Sagitta didn't respond. I looked at the Arrow more closely. I wondered if the image truly represented the Arrow. The smooth wooden shaft didn't have a single scratch. The golden tip shone as if it were a piece of the sun. The feathers on the other end were so black they gleamed blue.

"*Who are you?*" Sagitta repeated.

"I'm Orion," I said.

"*Why have you sought me?*"

"I need your power," I said.

"*Why?*"

"To protect the people I care about."

"*What are you protecting them from?*" Sagitta asked.

"From the Star Children who wish to destroy Destiny, Fate, and Prophecy," I said. "I want to protect my friends from Perseus, Typhon, Arianna, and the rest of their allies." I paused. "And I want to defeat them to save the Universe."

"*Hmmm,*" Sagitta said. "*A worthy mission.*"

"Will you help us?" I asked.

"*Yes, but if you want my power you will have to abide by the rules of my Light,*" Sagitta said.

"What are the rules?" I asked.

"*For every shot of Death there must be one for Love.*"

"What?" I asked, confused.

"*I am the Arrow of Death and Love. There must be a balance— for every Death there must be a new Love,*" Sagitta said.

I had known that in some myths Sagitta represented the Arrow of Cupid, but I hadn't expected the Arrow to actually have that power. I wasn't sure how much this would impact us in our battle with Perseus. Death would be useful, but Love wouldn't defeat him. And how did Death and Love balance each other?

"Fine," I said. "I agree to those rules." One fatal Death shot would have to be enough.

The Arrow vibrated in my hand. Darkness burst from the lake like an erupting volcano. It drowned the mountains and the grass, submerging the blue sky under its black waters. The pain returned to me at once, and I struggled to breathe.

"Orion," Andromeda said, alarmed.

I lay on the ground as she gripped my arms, shaking them. It took me another second to remember where I was.

"I'm okay," I groaned. "Let's leave."

Andromeda helped me get back to my feet. Slowly, we walked out of the room full of bones. We had taken one step out of the chamber when I sensed movement to my right.

"Run!" I yelled.

Andromeda and I sprinted forward. Scorpius followed close behind. My sense sharpened once again. Its claws were mere yards behind us and its stinger raised high, ready to impale us.

"You are a fool!" the Scorpion shouted. *"That Arrow will bring your doom, just as it brought down the Queen from her Throne."*

Sagitta vibrated in my hand. I didn't have a bow to notch the Arrow, but I was sure that I could still use it to stab the Scorpion. But then that meant that my next shot would have to be for Love. I wasn't sure I wanted to waste my Death shot on the Scorpion when we needed it for Typhon.

I stopped, my feet sliding over the ground, and spun around. I screamed as I swung the sword in a semicircle in front of me, and heard the wet slice as it cut through the Scorpion's face.

The monster shrieked.

I was thrown off my feet and landed on my back a second later. Air rushed out of my lungs, and my lower back exploded with a wave of pain that made black stars dance in my mind. I clenched my fist, but the Arrow was gone from my grasp.

Scorpius cried out, making my ears throb. My senses took a second to sharpen again. I pushed myself to my feet. Andromeda stood in front of me. Beyond her was the Scorpion, who had latched itself to the wall again. My senses crawled over the ground until I found Sagitta lying right below the Scorpion. Scorpius went still as he stood on the wall, but its face still twisted.

"Do you know why the Queen hid the Arrow?" the Scorpion asked. The question burned my chest. The Scorpion tensed on the wall, bending its legs as if it intended to jump. *"Do you know why she instructed me to kill anyone who might come for it?"*

I gripped the sword tight. Scorpius jumped off the wall. I sprinted forward. Seconds stretched into infinity as the Scorpion sailed through the air, its legs like sharpened spears. I tried to follow the trajectory of the Scorpion's fall as best as I could. Then I dropped to the floor, falling on my back. I thrust the sword upwards. Gravity did the rest of the work. The Scorpion landed right on top of me, and it took all of my strength to keep the sword raised high. The weight of the Scorpion pushed down on me, and for a split second I worried that the hilt of the sword would impale me. But my arms held the weight, straining with effort. Something hot dropped on my stomach—the Scorpion's blood.

Scorpius let out a piercing shriek as the sword dug deeper into its flesh. Its legs frantically clanked against the ground. Then the Scorpion raced forward, towards Andromeda. I kept hold of the sword as the Scorpion dragged me over the ground. I pulled the sword with the remaining strength I had. Scorpius stumbled forward, landing on its back. The Scorpion's legs jerked wildly at his sides.

"Get Sagitta!" Andromeda shouted.

I pushed myself to my feet again. My chest felt as if I had inhaled gasoline and set it on fire. I pushed the pain away and focused on Sagitta. I raced forward. Behind me, the Scorpion shrieked in rage, racing towards me. How was that thing still alive? I crouched down and grabbed the wooden shaft of the Arrow, then stood up again. Scorpius continued to rush towards me. I ran. My rapid footsteps echoed through the Maze as the Scorpion chased me. Scorpius ran slower than before, but the monster was relentless.

Andromeda was somewhere behind Scorpius, but she was far away, moving slowly. My heart nearly fell to my stomach. Had the Scorpion hurt her? I was sure he hadn't stung her, or else she would have been dead, but she could have been wounded. I turned to the left when I sensed an opening, trying to make my way back to her. The Scorpion ran at my heels, its face twitching madly as it emitted a long shriek. I turned to the left again but stopped before I crashed into a wall right in front of me. I spun, but it was too late; the Scorpion had already rounded the corner, blocking my only exit. Scorpius slowed down.

"She stole your Light too, didn't she?" Scorpius asked.

Rage and sorrow burned through me. The Scorpion advanced closer. I bent my knees and jumped, launching myself into the air. I landed on the Scorpion's carapace, falling to my knees. I managed to keep my balance as I kept hold of both the sword and the Arrow. I was about to plunge the Arrow down on the Scorpion but hesitated—I couldn't waste my shot for Death.

I summoned whatever strength I had left and pushed myself to my feet on the back of the Scorpion. I raised the sword and spun, then brought it down on the creature's head. A crack split the air as the sword sank deep into the monster's skull. Scorpius's face stopped twitching.

"Orion!" Andromeda screamed behind me.

Pain stabbed the base of my neck. Agony seared my skin. The Scorpion twisted, throwing me off its back. I landed on the ground, shaking uncontrollably as a torturing throb spread from the base of my neck to the rest of my back. It felt as if I had been injected with lava that was slowly burning its way through my veins.

A roar cut through the air.

"Orion!" Andromeda cried.

My throat was closing up, tightening. My lungs strained for air. The darkness caged around me, pressing into me, wrapping me so fiercely that I couldn't breathe. Shouts, roars, screams, and shrieks erupted in the air. Then it all disappeared.

●——————●——————●

My hand trembled slightly as I drank more water. The clear glass felt warm, or maybe I was just too cold. The snow had settled in a thick blanket outside. It covered our small backyard completely, and earlier that day I'd had to shovel it from the driveway. Andromeda sat next to me, pushing rice around her plate with a fork. We both startled when a muffled scream erupted downstairs. The neighbors wouldn't hear, though; no one ever heard what happened in the basement—no one had ever heard our screams when Zia beat us. My last set of scars felt itchy with the sweater I wore, but at least they weren't painful anymore. I already had five lashes on my back.

Another scream echoed back to my ears. I set the glass down. Andromeda and I didn't know why Zia had decided to bring the man home—she never took captives. She had instructed us to steal some files from his house, and we had. But in the spur of the moment something had made Zia change her mind and she had taken the man too.

Andromeda pushed her plate to the side, brushing her black hair from her face. She looked out the window, her eyes bright as they reflected the white snow. Another scream came, this one louder, but neither of us flinched. We just kept looking out the window. After a few minutes, snow started drizzling again. Andromeda leaned forward as the snowflakes stuck to the window. She pulled up the sleeves from her blue sweater, burying her hands inside the soft wool.

"This one is pretty," she said, pointing at a tiny white flake.

I leaned forward to stare at it. I counted twelve curved spikes. They were formed in perfect symmetry, which amazed me. There must have been millions of snowflakes raining from the sky, and all of them would have different yet perfectly symmetrical designs. How did nature know how to form them? Was there a superior intelligent being, as some religions claimed, that simply knew how to make such things?

The door burst open behind us. I jumped to my feet, instinctively grabbing the fork next to my plate. Zia stood at the door, her expression cold.

"I need you to help me, Orion," she said before disappearing down the stairs again.

A moan climbed up from the basement. I hesitantly put the fork back on the table. Andromeda gave me a pitying look, but we both knew better than to disobey Zia. I took a deep breath and slowly descended the stairs, my hands shaking slightly as they held on to the rail. I stopped at the bottom, my heartbeat rushing into my ears. Zia stood at the opposite end of the room with her arms crossed, looking at the man who lay on the floor in the middle of the room.

His hands were bound behind his back, his legs tied together. A black cloth bag covered his head—it seemed tied a bit too tightly around his neck. The man moaned, and I wondered if he was gagged. He had been wearing a suit, but was now stripped down to his underwear and a white shirt smeared with blood.

I turned to Zia, who stared intently at me. My muscles tensed instinctively. Zia pulled a gun from her back. It had a long silencer at the tip. Zia had once made me and Andromeda watch how she killed a man who had almost stabbed her, and I guessed she was about to do the same. I wondered why had only asked me to see this. Zia stepped slowly towards me, the gun pointed at the floor. She stretched the gun towards me, her gaze challenging. My mind went numb, and then I hesitantly took the gun. The cold metal dug into my skin as if I was holding a block of ice. My hands were strangely steady.

"Shoot him in the head," Zia said.

"What?" I blurted out.

Zia took a step closer to me. She grabbed my arm gently and pushed it down so the gun pointed at the floor. She placed her other hand on my shoulder.

"He won't be the first person you'll have to kill to survive, and I want you to get used to it." Zia's cold hand gently grabbed my chin, forcing me to keep my gaze on her. For a moment, her eyes didn't seem human. They were so light blue they were almost white, like ice—ice that had been frozen for thousands of years and had never melted. "You will have to fight, and you will have to kill."

"No." That word simply fell from my lips.

"No?" Zia's voice was like a knife. She buried her fingers in my hair. "The day will come when you won't have a choice, and I don't want you to hesitate then." Her eyes were like two white holes boring into her skull.

Zia stepped behind me, my back brushing her chest as she climbed the first step. She placed her hands on each of my shoulders.

"Do it."

The man whimpered, and my head felt light enough to float away. Zia squeezed my shoulder, but I simply couldn't move.

"Do it," Zia hissed into my ear.

My arm levitated upwards. I aimed with deadly precision. A click echoed inside my head, bouncing through me like a pinball. Darkness wrapped around me. Then I was crawling up the stairs towards an opening of light. Andromeda was there, speaking, but I couldn't hear her. She dragged me across the floor when my legs refused to move. I closed my eyes, and when I opened them again, I was staring at the empty fireplace. Ashes from the night before lay scattered in a heap.

"Orion," Andromeda said at my side, her voice trembling. "You killed him."

I had held the gun, but I didn't remember pulling the trigger.

You need to become stronger. Zia's voice stabbed at me. The day will come when you won't have a choice. She hadn't given me a choice either. Andromeda hugged me, her arms tight around my chest.

"I killed him," I blurted out, and felt so sick my stomach nearly turned itself inside out.

"I know," Andromeda said. She didn't sound scared, but her voice was distant. "I know."

I didn't even remember his face. I had seen him when Zia gave us the file, and when I dragged him onto the trunk. But his face was gone now, as if my brain had gone into override and deleted it. Andromeda held me as I sat staring at the ashes for a long time—they seemed like dead snowflakes.

I had killed a man.

The time will come when you won't have a choice.

CHAPTER 43

DARKNESS HAD A FORM. It wasn't Arianna's form though. It was a form that I couldn't describe. Did fire have a form? Did water? They did, yet at the same time they didn't. Like fire and water, Darkness had its own shape.

I slid into the Darkness, letting myself flow deeper and deeper inside of it. The thought crossed my mind that I might be dead, and I strangely didn't feel sad at that idea. My weightless spirit floated within dark waters, but I felt nothing except peace.

Then there was Light. Stars floated all around me, shimmering like rays of sunlight glinting on the ocean surface. Maybe I was dead, but I would never stop existing. Everything would always remain Connected. There was no pain, or hurt, no emotions or thoughts crossing through my head. There was only the Connection, and that made me feel whole.

Virgo had once told me that Stars were alive. I hadn't understood what she meant. How could balls of fire have life? Now I understood. The sea of Stars around me was alive, beating, breathing. Their Light pulsed with life, with emotion, with intelligence. They were aware of *everything*. Stars listened, sensed, and saw. They directed everything into motion, using Light to create reality. I tried to listen to them, but they spoke in a language that I didn't comprehend. They sounded like crystals, that was the best way I could describe it—like crystals gently clanking against each other.

There wasn't a single spot of Darkness or empty space; the Stars covered the Universe with their beautiful light. All the colors I could imagine were around me, shifting and glowing with life.

The twinkling crystals became more urgent, but I still couldn't understand their tongue. I felt I should have been able to—I was a Star Child after all.

"Go back." The crystalline voice was weak, but the words broke clearly through the soft clanking. *"We need you to fight for us."*

Why would they need *me* to fight? The Stars were much more powerful than I was. They were ancient beings—beings that could control the Destiny of every single being in the Universe. If they were so grand and powerful, why couldn't they end Perseus and his allies themselves?

"Go back," another crystalline voice said.

But I didn't want to go back. I had no pain, no worries, no traumas here. I existed in a place without time, where eternity felt like a second. I felt warm and Connected here. I was whole, made of pure Light. Back in the physical world I had the burden of matter, trapped within a broken body. Why would I want to return to that?

Andromeda's image flashed through my mind, my name bursting from her lips as the Scorpion stabbed me with its stinger.

"Go back."

All the Stars disappeared, and I felt like I was dropping through an endless void. Only Darkness filled that void with its shapeless form. I kept falling until I crashed into something. Pain flooded back into my body. Muffled noises drifted around me. I moaned. I wanted to go back to the Stars, to see that colorful light again. I didn't want this pain. I didn't want this Darkness.

Then there was Light—pure, white, blinding Light. It burned through my body like searing flames. I screamed and was surprised I could hear my own voice. The Light vanished at the same time the pain stopped. Darkness closed in on me again, but this time it finally let me rest.

I startled awake inside of the darkness, breathing heavily. I coughed, then sat up. Only then did I notice I lay somewhere soft.

"Orion!" Andromeda exclaimed. "You idiot! You nearly died!"

Her arms wrapped gently around me. I couldn't help but smile. The base of my neck, closer to my right shoulder, ached as if I had been stabbed. My memories came back to me in a rush.

"I got stung," I said, my tongue and lips numb.

"Yes," Andromeda said, pulling back. "Virgo's sweater protected you from getting stabbed right through the chest, but the Scorpion's stinger still stabbed you below the neck."

"I should have died," I said. "Leo said the poison would kill us."

"It should have," Andromeda said.

"Then why didn't it kill me?" I asked.

Andromeda was silent.

"The venom wasn't as lethal for you as it would have been to anyone else." Ophiuchus's voice made me startle. My heart immediately sped up.

"What are you doing here?" I demanded. My throat was so raw and dry that my voice sounded like I was choking on sand.

"Serpens's venom saved you from Scorpio's," the doctor said. The snake hissed somewhere on my left. "Snake venom can make you immune to other types of venom if you survive it. Having that immunity bought you enough time for me to get the Scorpion's poison out of your system before it killed you."

I was silent for a few seconds. "Thank you, I guess." I paused. "How did you even find us? Where are we now? Did someone bring Sagitta?"

"I brought Sagitta," Andromeda said. "And we're back at Argo."

"How long was I out?" I asked.

"Only three days," Ophiuchus replied.

"THREE DAYS?" My head spun with pain.

We had lost three more days because of me. Now we had about two weeks until Perseus's next rising, and we still had to find Corona Borealis.

"Carrying you back here was not easy," Andromeda said. She cleared her throat. "I'm going to get you some food." She hesitated. "And leave you here to talk to the doctor."

Her footsteps echoed away from me. A door opened and closed.

"Why did you come find us?" I asked.

"There are many snakes in the desert," Ophiuchus said. "One of them spotted you and reported back to Serpens."

"Why did you decide to come help us?" I asked again.

Ophiuchus was silent.

Pain pounded in my back as the numbness went away. I couldn't contain a groan. Ophiuchus was immediately at my side, peeling away something from my shoulder. Only then did I realize I was shirtless, and that the doctor was uncovering the sting wound from the bandages.

Ophiuchus went still once my wound was exposed. He muttered something to himself and walked away. Then his hands were on my back again. He pressed something onto the wound. Blaring pain shot through my shoulder, and I let out a scream. The doctor rubbed a cold and slimy paste onto my skin and quickly bandaged me again. The pain subsided somewhat.

"It may take a while for you to recover your full strength," Ophiuchus said. "My power only goes so far in healing wounds inflicted by other Star Children, and a bit of the poison remained inside your bloodstream."

That's when I realized that the rest of my body didn't hurt. My lungs were no longer on fire, and my ribs didn't even ache. Ophiuchus must have healed my normal wounds.

"Why did you come find us?" I asked again as sweat trickled down my back.

"Let me check your eyes again." I flinched as his cold hand settled on my cheek. I ground my jaw as Ophiuchus grabbed me by the chin and pulled me closer. I didn't know what he was doing, but after a minute he turned my head to the other side, then let go of me. "Your eyes haven't deteriorated, which is good. Structurally they are intact, but functionally still not working. Hmmm . . . I will have to keep looking for remedies."

"*Why* are you here?" I asked.

Ophiuchus scribbled something, the pen swishing sharply on paper. I doubted that the doctor had experienced a change of heart and had decided to help us and selflessly save my life.

"You wouldn't understand," Ophiuchus finally said. He scribbled so loudly I was sure the pen would snap.

"Try me," I said.

Ophiuchus kept writing.

I breathed out, then lay back on the bed. My back exploded with pain, so I shifted to my left side. "Scorpius said Zia had corrupted him," I said. The scribbling stopped. "He said that she had lost her Light so she needed to steal it from others to survive."

"Yes," he said coldly. "Cassiopeia lost her Light long ago, so she began to feed off of us."

"She must have fed from Andromeda and me," I said. I paused, afraid to ask the next question, but I quickly gulped down my fear. "Are there any consequences or side effects from that?"

"It depends," Ophiuchus said. "If she had completely drank your Light, you would have become her puppet, too corrupted to have free will." He paused. "Both you and Andromeda seem well, so I don't suppose she took too much from you. How long were you with her?"

"Over ten years," I said.

Ophiuchus was silent, and even though I couldn't see or sense him, I knew he had gone very still. "She must have drunk enough to keep herself alive, but not too much to extinguish your Light." He was silent for another few seconds. "Time should replenish the Light you lost. I wouldn't worry too much about it."

My heart throbbed in pain. Is that all we had been to Zia—a convenient Light supply to keep her alive? Was that why she couldn't stay away from us for long, not even when she sent us into foster care? And why hadn't she warned us about Scorpius if she had left him there to guard Sagitta? Had this been a suicide mission? Or had Zia been confident that even without her warning we would be able to defeat Scorpio?

I let out a deep breath; those questions were too painful for me to consider now. If Ophiuchus said I shouldn't worry too much about it, then I wouldn't. I had other things to think about. We needed to find Corona Borealis now and didn't have a lot of time left.

"The snake bite is completely healed, by the way," Ophiuchus said after a minute. "It scarred nicely."

"Good to hear."

Ophiuchus started clicking his pen again. "Be careful with Sagitta."

"I already know it's dangerous."

Click, click, click.

"I owned it once," Ophiuchus said.

That took me completely by surprise. "I thought Centaurus had owned it."

"I owned it after him," Ophiuchus said. "The fool probably went to the city to retrieve the Arrow and died." He sighed. "That Arrow is very dangerous. You can't use it as a normal weapon, and need to be very cautious about whom you shoot. You need to be especially careful when choosing whom to give Death and Love to."

I huffed. "The Arrow of Love and Death. That sounds like a terrible rock song."

Ophiuchus didn't laugh at my bad joke. "I'm serious, Orion. You can't just shoot the Arrow at anyone who crosses your way. Be careful."

"I will," I assured him. "Although I'm not sure how I would use the Love part unless it was Valentine's Day."

Ophiuchus laughed—it was a cold, bitter sound that sent a shiver down my spine. "You're too young to understand, and I don't blame you for that."

"Too young to understand what?"

"Love can be deadlier than Death." His voice was like a snake's whisper. "Take it from someone who has lived over four thousand years. Death is swift, and eventually it comes for all of us. It brings an end so a new beginning can emerge." He paused. "But Love has brought down empires, made even the wisest become blind and consumed by it. Love is more poisonous to the hearts of men than that of any creature." A chair screeched as Ophiuchus stood. I listened silently as he shuffled next to me, maybe grabbing his things. "Be very careful about whom you use that Arrow with, and be especially careful about whom you choose to give Love to. I can tell you this: Love brought more destruction to my enemies than Death ever did." Ophiuchus's footsteps echoed away. "Just keep that in mind."

Chapter XXI, Verse I

Love and Death at opposite ends of the shaft remain,
One of them will bring destruction, and the other only an end.
In equal balance they shall be used to pierce only flesh,
To bring down kings and empires when blood is shed.
No one shall escape its swift strike shot with a graceful hand.
But only One will be able to use the full power of the Arrow,
To combine Love and Death in one last embrace.

CHAPTER 44

TWO DAYS PASSED. I had wanted to immediately go find Corona Borealis but after much insistence from the others, I had rested. Scorpio's poison left me weak, nauseous, and with fever. Ophiuchus seemed confident that I would feel better in a couple of days, but I still felt like I would arrive to Perseus's rising worn out and exhausted. As much as I hated doing it, I did need some rest.

At least the others had been more productive than I was. The Twins had kept training Andromeda to fight with a sword, and they were happy to report she had improved. She probably wouldn't be as good as Perseus—none of us would ever be— but she would be better prepared to face him. Virgo and Draco had also been training with their weapons, but I hadn't heard much else about them. Draco hadn't talked to me in the last few days, but I knew that as the battle with Perseus drew closer, he was thinking about the Dragon. I wondered if he had asked Ophiuchus for help. Could there be a cure to get rid of the Dragon?

Ophiuchus had spent the last couple of days in Argo doing "research," although he hadn't specified what he was working on. He insisted that he, and Serpens, were trying to find a cure for my blindness. And while he may have been putting some thought into that, I didn't believe that was all he was researching. We still didn't know why Ophiuchus was here to help us, and I wouldn't trust him as long as he kept that a secret.

After those two days had passed and I had recovered somewhat, I finally got up from my bed to look for Corona Borealis. Leo had guided Virgo and me to a large empty room where we now stood. I would still need Virgo's help to see the Connections—it would make my search easier, even if Leo insisted I should just sense it.

"Are you sure you feel strong enough?" Leo asked, concerned.

"Yes." The wound from the Scorpion's sting still throbbed with sharp pulses of pain sometimes, but I could ignore it.

"All right then," Virgo took my hand and held it tightly. "Ready?"

"Ready."

My body was pulled inside out, and I felt I was dropping through a bottomless hole. The feeling stopped abruptly, and the pain disappeared. The first thing I saw was Leo's golden knot of energy, pulsing brightly in front of me. Virgo's green loop hovered directly on my left. All around us were tiny knots of sapphire that I assumed must have belonged to Argo. They formed a large circular chamber with a flat roof. Transparent silver threads connected every knot of energy into a tapestry of light.

I focused my attention on Corona Borealis. There were many crowns in the world, but only one of them was the Northern Crown from the Stars. Only one Crown was powerful enough to protect us from Typhon's influence. I immediately sensed the

Connection, and a thread thickened in front of me, glowing brighter.

I focused on that thread, on the rhythm with which it pulsed. The thread disappeared somewhere outside of Argo, into a place across the vast ocean. The Northern Crown would protect us from Typhon, and it would keep us safe from Perseus. It had once belonged to Zia, but now that she was dead it belonged to Andromeda. Something pulled inside of my chest, and my surroundings blurred into swift lines of color. I stopped, and darkness overtook me once more.

All was still for a moment.

Then the music began to play—a full orchestra that created a majestic classical song fit for a royal ball. It reached out a gloved hand to me, inviting me to a dance. The rhythm was adorned with colorful velvet strings and jeweled beats. I almost joined in, yet something held me back. Something didn't feel right about the song. It played too loudly, as if it were trying to hide a wailing cry in another room.

Corona Borealis didn't have one rhythm—it had two.

I moved deeper into the hidden rhythm, yet it felt as tricky as trying to navigate the Maze. I was lost inside an infinite castle trying to find a secret room. The new rhythm played softly, pleading with me to listen. I held on to it, and let it reel me deeper into it.

Something was wrong with that rhythm.

It belonged to something that existed beyond death. It was immortal, but dying. It beat inside an endless sleep full of poisonous dreams. Inside the royal ball was a masked guest who hid a deadly secret. Was that rhythm screaming to get my help, or was it trying to lure me into a trap? The rhythm pulled away from me, as if it could sense I had discovered its deceit. The orchestra came back at full volume, pulling me into its dance floor.

Where are you? I asked the Crown, trying to ignore its blaring rhythm. I imagined that shining silver thread. I let myself feel that Connection, that thread that united me with the Crown. We were one and the same, just two knots in the vast fabric of reality that had been woven together since the beginning of time.

The pull inside of my chest became so strong that I felt I was flying. I traveled through the Connection, as if the thread were a highway I could glide through. It took me exactly to where the Crown had been hidden, to the mound where it had been buried.

Pain wrapped around me like a blanket of needles as I was shot back to the physical plane. I doubled over, coughing. Leo roared in concern.

"I'm fine," I said. "I know where Corona Borealis is."

Virgo pulled me back to my feet, and with her help I walked to our usual meeting spot in the living room. The others arrived only a couple of minutes later.

"Corona Borealis is in northern Scotland," I announced. "Near the coast. Once we get closer, I can guide Argo to a more exact location."

Someone exhaled loudly. "It would have been easier to search for Corona before Sagitta. We were basically right next to it!" one of the Twins said.

"But whatever," the other Twin said. "Argo! Take us to northern Scotland!"

"I wonder why it's in Scotland," Draco said. "Leo, is there anything there?"

We all knew what the real question was: was there another lost city in Scotland? Might there be a monster guarding the Crown? Was Scotland a place Leo had visited before with Cepheus and Cassiopeia?

"Not that I know of," Leo responded.

"I sensed something in the Crown," I said. "It had two rhythms instead of one. It was weird. One of the rhythms was hidden. Trapped. It felt like it had a secret to hide."

"Hmmm," was Leo's only response.

"If Corona Borealis is in Scotland, it must be under Druid influence," Ophiuchus said.

"Which means what exactly?" one of the Twins asked.

"In Celtic myths Corona Borealis does not represent a Crown," Ophiuchus said.

"Then what is it?" Andromeda asked.

"A Castle," Ophiuchus said.

"A Castle?" one of the Twins asked.

"Corona Borealis was seen as the Castle of Arianrhod, Goddess of the Moon, Reincarnation, Magic, and Fertility," Ophiuchus explained. "But it also represented the Silver Circle or Crown, which is a shield of protection."

"Yes, the Silver Crown creates the Silver Circle of protection, which is what can keep us safe from Typhon," Leo confirmed. *"But I never saw the Castle and I don't know why Cassiopeia would have kept it in that form."*

Ophiuchus chuckled bitterly. "Cassiopeia never told you, did she, Leo?"

"She didn't even tell us her real name," Andromeda muttered.

"What didn't she tell me?" Leo asked.

Ophiuchus didn't respond, but by the growl Leo emitted the Lion must have read something from his expression.

"Why do you think I was so intent to get the asteroid metal?" Ophiuchus asked.

Leo did not respond, but another growl rumbled from his chest.

"I made a cure using a piece of the asteroid Cassiopeia left in New York," Ophiuchus said. "We tried to stab her with it without any luck, but we never had her drink it. I found a way to turn the metal into a poison that will destroy her."

"Destroy who?" Virgo asked, alarmed.

Leo went very still.

"They locked her in the Castle, didn't they?" Sirius asked. It was the first time I had heard the Dog, who had a melodious feminine voice. It shocked me so much that it took me a few seconds to translate to the others.

"Yes," Ophiuchus responded. "But Cassiopeia never told me where she hid the Castle. I've been looking for it for millennia so I can put an end to what I started."

"Oh my Stars," Leo said slowly. *"I thought she was dead. Permanently dead."*

"No," Ophiuchus said. "They couldn't kill her so they just locked her away somewhere she would never be able to escape."

Leo roared. Even though he didn't speak, his grief shattered through the darkness.

"What the hell are you all talking about?" Andromeda said.

"Cassiopeia and Cepheus had a child, a girl, very long ago," Sirius said slowly.

Shock washed over me like a cold wave.

"Then what happened?" one of the Twins asked.

"Their daughter was killed during one of the battles against the Shadows," Ophiuchus said slowly. "I tried to save her. I tried to bring her back to life . . ."

"But . . . ?" one of the Twins asked.

"I made her a monster instead," Ophiuchus said.

The other rhythm inside Corona Borealis was Zia's daughter. That slowly registered inside my mind.

"It wasn't your fault, Ophiuchus," Leo immediately said, sorrow punctuating every word. *"You did your best to save her."*

"I don't want your pity, Leo," Ophiuchus snapped. "I made her the most dangerous monster any of us had ever faced."

"You only tried to save her," Sirius said.

"She tried to kill us all," Ophiuchus's tone was bleak. "But none of us were strong enough to kill her."

Leo let out a guttural roar. *"Cassiopeia never told me she had trapped the girl in the Castle. I just assumed they had found a way to destroy her."*

Ophiuchus chuckled again. "How convenient of you to forget she existed, Leo."

"I didn't forget her," Leo said with another growl. *"Cassiopeia lied to me."*

"Welcome to the club," Andromeda muttered.

"You don't understand what this means," Leo snapped. *"The only way for Andromeda to take possession of Corona Borealis is if that child is dead."*

Stunned silence filled the room.

"Being Cassiopeia's blood daughter, she technically owns the power of Corona Borealis, even if she is imprisoned inside of it. Unless

we kill her, Andromeda won't be able to inherit that power. And if Andromeda can't use the Crown, then we won't be able to have the shield that can keep us safe from Typhon's influence."

A whirlwind of emotions blasted through me, but I didn't have time to focus on them. Footsteps marched on my right as Andromeda stormed out of the room. I stood from the couch and immediately followed after her. My senses weren't as sharp as they had been at the Maze, but I managed to grab Andromeda's arm and let her guide me away from the room. She stopped after a minute and we entered a new room.

"Didn't know Argo had a mug collection," Andromeda muttered as she closed the door.

"What do we do?" I asked. "We need Corona Borealis to protect Draco, Sirius, Aquila, and Leo. Without it, Typhon will make them kill us."

"I know," Andromeda said in a flat tone, but I knew a storm was brewing inside of her. She let out a long breath, emptying her lungs. "Even after her death, Zia is still trying to manipulate us, to make us do her dirty work. Can you see that now?"

"I . . . yeah."

"She wasn't able to kill her zombie daughter so now she wants *us* to do it." Andromeda sounded as if she was about to grab one of Argo's mugs and smash it on the floor. But I guessed she didn't want to make the Ship angry. "I hate her!" Andromeda shouted. "She's just as monstrous as her zombie child!"

"That must have been why she was a bit violent with us," I said. "She must have been emotionally scarred, and those wounds never healed."

"Don't try to justify her actions!" Andromeda said. "Just because she was hurt and traumatized doesn't mean she had to do the same to us. Zia was a monster because she let that trauma turn her into something despicable, and she used her pain to hurt us."

"She wasn't despicable," I said. "She was just hurt, and didn't know how to deal with it."

"Then tell me what she did to you these last couple of years," Andromeda said. "Tell me that wasn't despicable. Tell me she was just trying to do her best."

The pain from Scorpius's sting seemed to expand further down my back, and my bones suddenly felt like dough. Scorpio's words flowed back into my mind. Zia had trapped the Scorpion in the Maze and bound him to kill anyone who might come in search of the Arrow. And then she had sent us to retrieve it without warning us he was there. She had trapped her own daughter in a magical castle and lied to Leo about it—lied to us about her past. She had only adopted us to feed off our Light and remain alive. I couldn't ignore the truth anymore, the pain of it crystalizing into broken shards that pierced my chest.

Ice swept across my body and made my heart freeze. Formless faces appeared and vanished, dark and twisted. I tried to make them disappear, and the darkness settled into a black pool once again.

"Did you listen to what I just said?" Andromeda asked. "You can't justify what Zia did to us by digging up her past and trying to find the causes. There is no justification. She took the conscious decision to become a violent and abusive person."

It hurt. The truth twisted inside my heart like a jagged dagger. Maybe a very deep part of me wanted to believe that Zia had been a good person. I wasn't even sure why I *wanted* her to be good. Maybe I just wanted to believe that she had actually cared about us, that she had truly loved us. Did it matter if she never had?

I didn't feel the tears on my cheek until Andromeda wiped them away. Then she hugged me. After a stunned second, I hugged her back. Her solid shape against my chest kept me upright or else I would have crumbled to my knees.

It hurt.

It hurt so much.

Zia had chosen to do what she did to us, and I couldn't blame anyone or anything for the person she had become. The pain didn't sharpen my senses, I didn't let it. For once I just wanted to feel the pain and let it pour out of my heart.

"Come on," Andromeda said after some time. "Let's go to your room."

Andromeda led me through Argo, and thankfully we didn't encounter anyone else. I was glad when Andromeda closed the door of my room and I collapsed onto the bed. I had been awake for only a couple of hours but I felt so tired, so drained. The bed shifted as Andromeda sat at the edge.

"She broke us," I whispered. "We're so broken."

Grief tore loose inside of me. I was fractured in so many pieces. I'd had multiple girlfriends at once because I couldn't stand being on my own and having to deal with Zia's abuse. I flinched every time someone touched me by surprise. My back was a web of scars. How many more cracks cut within me that I hadn't even noticed?

"Yeah," Andromeda said. "Now it's up to us to pick up those pieces and rebuild ourselves."

"Assuming we live long enough to do that," I said with a huff.

The bed shifted again, and it took me a second to realize Andromeda was standing on the bed. She stepped over me and sat back down on the other side. Then she lay down, and our shoulders brushed. I tensed for only a second, then let myself relax.

"I'm not sure how I feel about fighting Zia's child," I said.

"Me neither," Andromeda admitted.

"I know she's a monster," I said. "But it just doesn't feel right to kill her."

"She's already dead," Andromeda said. "I think we would be doing her a favor."

"Maybe."

We were silent for a while. Andromeda's breathing was out of rhythm with my own breaths. I couldn't remember the last time it had just been the two of us, relaxing. We had so many things we needed to worry about, but at the moment my heart and mind simply couldn't find the space for all of them. I let the grief sink into me. I couldn't fight it, and I couldn't ignore it any longer.

"Hey," I said after some time. Andromeda didn't answer, but I knew she was awake. "Thank you."

"For what?" She asked.

"Just . . ." I sighed. "For always being there for me, and for saving me even when I didn't deserve it. For just accepting me as me. I know I'm terrible, but thank you for still being with me."

Andromeda was silent for a few seconds. "I'm terrible too, so I guess we deserve each other's terribleness."

I laughed. "I mean, you're probably the only person in the world who truly sees me as I am and still accepts me. Thank you."

"You don't need to thank me for that," Andromeda said. "That's barely a favor, and everyone else in this submarine sees you for who you really are. It's not just me."

That was true. The others had become the closest thing I had to friends, even though we hadn't known each other for long. Fighting side by side like that against Perseus and the other monsters we had encountered—that was what friendship was about, right? We had each other's backs and I knew I could count on them to save my life. I hoped they counted on me too to protect them from Typhon and Perseus. Would Zia have given her life to save us?

"Do you think Zia ever loved us?" I asked.

Andromeda took so long to answer I thought she had already fallen asleep. "Maybe, in her own sick and perverse way."

That somehow made bearing the pain a bit easier.

"She stole our Light," I whispered. I had already shared what Scorpio had told me with the others, and it had felt like the person most surprised to hear what Zia had done was me.

Andromeda tensed next to me. "But she didn't extinguish it."

"But what if there *are* some side effects?" I asked.

The rings around my neck slid from my chest to my side.

"Then we'll deal with it," Andromeda said. "It shouldn't even surprise me that she did that. She never did anything for anyone except herself." Her tone was bitter. "But we can be better than her."

"Yeah," I whispered. "We can." A knot bulged in my throat. "I promise I'll be better." How many times had I acted out Zia's orders and brought Andromeda back to her for a beating, even if I was trying to protect her from something worse? How many times had I hurt her even though I was trying to keep her safe?

"I know," Andromeda whispered. Her hand found mine, locking my palm in a loose grip. "I'll try to be better too."

"You have always been the better one out of the two of us," I said.

"Am I?"

"I think so."

"Hmm."

Andromeda squeezed my hand, and I squeezed back. We fell asleep with our hands still intertwined.

CHAPTER 45

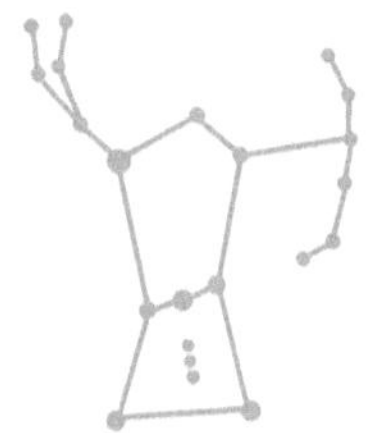

ARGO ARRIVED at the North Sea a bit after I woke up again. I tried to guide the Ship as close to Corona Borealis as possible. The Crown was less than a mile away from the coast, and the others told me that there were no signs of towns or other forms of habitation as far as they could see—only green hills and empty meadows.

The brisk air swept at my hair as we disembarked, bringing a light musky scent with it. Behind me, the waves crashed loudly against the shore, drowning out the howling wind. I didn't hear any seagulls or birds, nor any voices in the distance. Even though the weather was bitingly cold, the sun still gave me some warmth.

I pointed where I sensed Corona Borealis. "It should be in that direction, about a mile away."

"I don't see any castles," Virgo said. "Only small hills."

"Maybe we'll see it once we're closer," Andromeda said.

We began walking forward.

"Andromeda, Orion," Ophiuchus said, walking up to us. "Here's the cure I mentioned. You have to make her drink it and make sure she doesn't spit it out. But be careful it doesn't touch your skin, or else it will act like a corrosive acid and burn through your skin."

"Fun," Andromeda said flatly.

"I made enough for all of us to have one vial," Ophiuchus said.

Andromeda pulled my hand closer to her and placed something cold on my palm. I held the vial tightly. It was about the size of my thumb and heavier than I had expected. I placed the vial in the inner pocket of my coat.

"So what's the plan?" one of the Twins asked. "We just get inside the Castle, find zombie-girl, kill her, and leave?"

"That seems like a sound plan," the other Twin said.

"Be very careful," Ophiuchus warned. "The girl is incredibly strong and fast."

"Good to know," Andromeda said.

We kept walking through the landscape. This time, the others didn't offer any descriptions of my surroundings. All I could see were the curved shapes of darkness as it shifted around me. Shadowy mountains and hills rolled in the distance, stirring under a starless night made of mist.

After a while, I opened the Portal in my chest, sensing the rhythms around me. Most rhythms were familiar now, except two of them.

Ophiuchus's rhythm roared like one giant heart. It drummed with steady beats, yet it had an undertone that broke the pattern—like a baby's first breath before giving a startled cry. A butterfly softly breaking out of a cocoon before taking its flight. A moment in between moments, like the sun right before it broke through the horizon when the world seemed to pause momentarily. The doctor's song was the raw potential of life.

The Serpent's rhythm was markedly different. It had slow, fluid notes followed by rapid strokes—like a snake coiling tightly before springing to attack its prey. But just like the Doctor, the Snake had another instrument adding another dimension to the song. This one flowed thickly like poisoned honey. Too much of it would kill, yet in small doses it could save a life. Serpens was Death and Regeneration.

As we walked further inland, the Crown's rhythm became stronger. It felt as if someone was having a grand royal ball ahead of us, full of dance and laughter, but something still hid beneath it like a knife hidden under a gown.

"It's somewhere right ahead of us." I pointed. "You should be able to see it now."

"There's no castle there," Andromeda said. "Only a small mound."

"Maybe it's not in the form of a Castle," Ophiuchus said. "It could be in any other form, buried somewhere here."

"Maybe the Castle and the Crown exist simultaneously," Leo said.

I was surprised that neither of them knew more about Corona Borealis, but Zia must have kept the Crown's true power a secret from them. We slowly climbed the mound. The rhythm pounded with such force it almost pulled me into it.

"It's buried somewhere here." I pointed at the ground.

"Ha!" Pollux exclaimed. "We did bring shovels this time!"

Andromeda and I stepped back as the Twins did the work. The shovels thudded loudly against the earth in a steady rhythm. After some time, a sharp clang erupted around us.

"Eureka! I think we hit something," Castor said.

"It's an ornate Silver Crown with sharp spikes," Andromeda said, then added. "I could try to stab Perseus with that."

"Leo was right," Ophiuchus said, ignoring her. "The Crown and the Castle must exist simultaneously."

"So how do we get into the Castle if it's a Crown?" Draco asked.

"I think touching it should work," Ophiuchus said. "We can try that first and if it doesn't work, we'll figure something out."

"Then let's hold hands and paws and whatever else we have," Pollux said. "And someone can touch the Crown."

Leo moved closer to me. I wasn't sure I wanted to hold his massive paw, so I touched his soft side instead. Andromeda held my other hand. Virgo stood at Leo's other side, then Draco, the Twins, Sirius, Aquila, Ophiuchus, and Serpens.

"Okay then," Andromeda squeezed my hand tighter. Her heartbeat pulsed against my hand. Andromeda pulled my hand down as she lowered herself to hold the Crown. "Let's see if this works."

My body felt as if it had been sucked by a vacuum. I screamed, gripping Andromeda's hand tighter and digging my nails into Leo's fur. Then the feeling stopped. The darkness around me went completely still. The first thing I felt was the cold—it was a different sort of cold than the one before. There wasn't any wind, but the chilly air around me seemed to be alive, scratching me with sharp metal claws. The ground beneath my feet felt hard and smooth, and a faint metallic scent filled the air.

I opened the Portal in my chest. The Castle's rhythm blared with full force around me, inviting us into a joyous dance. And somewhere deep within the walls of this fortress was that immortal rhythm that floated weightlessly like a venomous dream. I moved beyond the darkness, and willed my senses to sharpen. It surprised me how easily my new power came to me. It was as if I had discovered an invisible limb in my body, and now that I knew of its existence, I could use it without much effort.

My senses weren't as sharp as they had been at the Maze, but they were clear enough for me to know where I was. The impossibly smooth walls at my sides stood twenty feet apart.

Andromeda grabbed my arm and pulled me forward towards a large rectangular hole. The others followed behind us as we passed through. A path in front of me cut through the room like a beam of light piercing through the darkness. Twisted forms stood at its sides, but I couldn't make out what they were. Some were curvy with sharp ends, others were rough like jagged rocks, and still others were smooth like flowing silk.

"This is creepy," Pollux whispered. Even though I didn't have the rhythms anymore I could sense his long hair.

"What?" I asked.

Andromeda leaned closer to me. "We're in an atrium full of weird statues," she whispered.

"We should split up," Ophiuchus whispered.

"That's a terrible idea," Castor said. "Last time we split up in the Maze Orion nearly got killed."

"If we all stay together then we are less likely to find her," Ophiuchus said in a flat tone, but I could sense the urgency in his words.

"But splitting up would make us more vulnerable," Virgo said. "My powers don't feel right here. I don't know how much I'll be able to do."

"Leo?" I asked.

The Lion was silent for a few seconds, probably weighing our options. *"Our only advantage is that she doesn't know that we are here, or how many of us there are. We will not beat her by force or power, but by surprise. If we split up, we are more likely to surprise and defeat her."*

I let out a sigh. Either option was dangerous. We were a big group, and moving together through a giant castle wouldn't be effective, but if we split up, we would be more vulnerable.

"Fine," Andromeda said. "Let's split up."

"Okay then," Ophiuchus immediately said. "Andromeda and Orion can stay together, the Twins make another pair, Leo can go with Virgo and Draco, and—"

"I'll go with Orion and Andromeda," Sirius whinnied.

I wasn't sure why the Dog wanted to come with us, but I didn't complain.

"That's fine," Ophiuchus said. "Aquila can go with the Twins then. I'll be with Serpens."

It seemed strange that the doctor wouldn't want any of us to go with him, and I still felt he was hiding something, but there was little I could do about that. I pressed my hand to my side, feeling the vial pressing into my ribs.

"And you're sure that the cure will kill her, right?" I asked.

"Yes, I'm sure," Ophiuchus said.

"Well then," Pollux said, "good luck everyone."

"Good luck," I muttered.

"We'll see you guys soon," Virgo said.

Andromeda grabbed my arm and pulled me to the right, passing right next to the statues. Sirius followed right behind us.

The walls at my sides pressed closer to me as we walked into a narrow hallway.

"Could you tell me how the Castle looks?" I whispered.

"It's all silver," she whispered back. "I can only see white fog out the windows. It's kind of creepy."

That wasn't the elaborate description I had been hoping for, but it would have to suffice. Our footsteps were silent as we moved forward. Andromeda slowed down before we entered a new room. My senses were disoriented for a second before they sharpened again. An oval surface rose off the ground a few yards in front of me, suspended by a few thin rods at each end. Was that a table?

"We're in a dining room," Andromeda whispered. "There are plates full of food."

The cold pressed into my skin, burrowing inside my bones. Andromeda gripped my arm tighter as she led me around the table. I tried to sense the plates with food, but couldn't—there was only a smooth surface. I did sense the chairs though, or what I assumed were chairs. I counted thirteen of them. Once we were at the other side of the room, we walked through another opening.

"It's a kitchen," Andromeda said. Something jutted from the right wall but I couldn't make out what it was. In front of me stood another rectangular table. "The oven is on, but I can't see what's inside of it. And there's a dead pig on top of the table. It looks like someone is preparing a feast."

"I can't sense the pig," I said. "The table is empty."

"Do you see it too, Sirius?" Andromeda asked.

The Dog let out a low whine, which sounded like a terrified *yes*.

"That's strange," I muttered.

We continued forward, walking past the empty table where Andromeda saw the dead pig.

"We're going up," Andromeda whispered as we neared a narrower opening. I was able to sense the steps clearly enough not to trip on them. Andromeda held my arm tighter. "It's so dark I can barely see."

It took us a few minutes to ascend the spiral staircase until we finally came to another opening at the top—did the Castle have no doors? Several rectangular objects lined the corridor. Bookcases maybe? We walked down that hallway, which split into two directions at the end. Andromeda pulled me to the right. At the end of the corridor, we entered a new room. There was something large and rectangular on the left, but I couldn't sense anything else in the bare room.

"It's a bedroom," Andromeda said. "The floor is full of wooden toys and rag dolls."

I instinctively clenched my fists as I scanned the floor. There was nothing there I could sense. Andromeda, still holding my arm, led me to the right, towards another opening.

"It's a bathroom," she said. Something large and hollow lay ahead of me. "The tub is full of steaming water." Andromeda pulled me closer to it. "The water's warm, look." She grabbed my hand and pulled it down, but I felt no water—only cold, empty air.

"I can't feel the water," I said.

"What do you mean?" Andromeda asked. "Our hands are literally submerged in it. Doesn't your skin feel hot?"

"No."

Andromeda pulled our hands out as if we had touched poison. "I don't like this place," she whispered.

"Me neither."

We walked out of the bathroom and exited the room, then went to the other corridor and passed through another rectangular hole. Sirius silently followed us.

"What do you sense here?" Andromeda whispered.

"I think that's a bed on the right," I said as I pointed. "And maybe a stool in that corner?"

"Do you sense anything on the other side of the room?" Andromeda's grip tightened.

"Just a bare wall. Why?"

"There's a fireplace," Andromeda whispered. "Can't you feel its warmth?"

"No."

Andromeda pressed herself closer to me. "This place is playing tricks on my mind," she hissed. "It probably doesn't work on you because you can't see it."

"The Castle is full of illusions," Sirius said behind me, and I quickly translated to Andromeda.

"Then how do we know what's real?" She asked.

"We don't. Only Orion will be able to tell us," the Dog responded.

We quickly exited the room. "There are no more hallways here," Andromeda said. "We'll have to go back the way we came through."

I nodded.

We descended the stairs and walked into the kitchen again.

"The pig is gone," Andromeda whispered. We quickly exited into the dining room. Andromeda stopped abruptly. "It looks like someone came and ate most of the food."

"It's not real," I whispered. "Let's keep moving."

We made our way back at the atrium where we had started. "Do you sense the statues?" Andromeda asked.

"Yes, I do sense those."

We quickly walked along the path cutting through the statues. Halfway through, Sirius barked and Andromeda pulled me into a run.

"The statues are moving!" she said.

I didn't sense any movement. "They're not."

Andromeda didn't listen, pulling me further along the path as if the statues were chasing after us. We stepped into a narrow corridor.

"Andromeda, stop," I said.

We both pulled to a stop, Andromeda breathing heavily. "They were chasing us. The statues came to life."

"That wasn't real," I said.

"It seemed *very* real," she responded.

"Let's just keep going," I said.

We continued through an interminable number of hallways, corridors, and rooms that led us to dead ends. We climbed up infinitely many stairs, and I lost count of how many floors we had ascended. Andromeda didn't give me any more descriptions, and I was glad for that. I didn't want to rely on what she was seeing, knowing it wasn't real. Even though we walked for hours, we didn't run into any of our friends. I tried to sense where they were, but I couldn't sense their exact locations—we were all just inside Corona Borealis. That made me nervous. How would we find each other again?

As we walked through a hallway, I sensed a very large opening on my left. It was different from the others—curved like an archway instead of rectangular, and a few feet taller than me. Andromeda passed it without a glance. I stopped.

"What?" Andromeda immediately asked, cutting off the circulation in my arm.

"There's an opening on the left," I said. "It feels different than the others."

"I only see a wall," Andromeda whispered.

I backed up a few steps and stood directly in front of the hole. "It's right in front of us." I clearly felt the cut in the wall giving way into another corridor beyond. Andromeda held my arm with both of her hands, and the Dog pressed itself against my leg, one of its heads brushing against my hip while another sniffed my knee.

"Lead us through it then," Andromeda whispered.

I stepped forward. Andromeda tensed, as if she were about to collide with the wall, but I only felt air as we passed through. The new hallway led to a sweeping staircase that ascended to a wide landing.

"Why is there a piano playing itself?" Andromeda asked.

"I don't hear a piano," I said.

"It's next to the stairs," Andromeda whispered. "Playing a classical tune."

I only heard our breaths and my thundering heart. "Let's go up the stairs."

We slowly made our way forward through the corridor. "There's so many paintings on the walls," Andromeda whispered. She didn't elaborate more on them, and I didn't want to know what they showed.

"I don't like the tune the piano is playing," Andromeda whispered, pressing herself even closer to me. We climbed up the steps and stopped at the landing. I could sense another curved archway a few yards in front of me.

"Do you see the opening?" I asked Andromeda.

"Yes," she said in barely a whisper.

We walked forward very slowly, then stopped at the threshold. Andromeda's grip tightened, but she didn't say a single word. Sirius went very still. A large bed stood in front of us with a figure lying on top of it. I could clearly sense the outline of a tall, thin body. But it had no pulse, no movement of the chest to inhale or exhale. I summoned the rhythms and they immediately responded. A cruel beat emanated from the body in thick waves. It mocked Death and scorned Life. But it was neither—an infinite dream of cruel nightmares. I shut off the rhythms again, sharpening my senses once more as my heartbeat spiked into a sprint.

Zia's daughter lay on the bed.

Very slowly, Andromeda let go of my arm. I didn't dare talk in front of the girl, in case she could listen and awoke from whatever slumber she seemed to be in. Andromeda slipped her hand into her jacket and pulled out a small, smooth object. Without saying a word, Andromeda walked to the left and I stepped to the right as we slowly rounded the bed.

My heartbeat was so loud I was sure it would give us away. Andromeda and I stopped at opposite sides of the bed. Below me, the girl lay completely motionless. Andromeda opened the glass vial, then leaned down and held the vial right above the girl's lips.

Her eyes snapped open.

Chapter X, Verse II

The Healer and the King conspire in the Night,
Wishing to kill the one whom they once held in high regard.
A scheme to destroy the one left in a deathless sleep,
Until by the Forgotten One the King is killed in fright.
The Healer alone shall remain of the three who once took faith.
An end to the curse he will finally deliver,
With the help of the Hunter and his new friends.

CHAPTER 46

I REACTED ON INSTINCT, jumping on the bed and pinning the girl's arms at her sides. She let out a scream of pure terror. Sirius barked wildly. The girl pushed me back with such force that I flew off the bed and crashed onto the metal floor. For a moment my senses became disoriented, but they quickly picked out the sharp movements behind me. The girl stood on the bed as Andromeda scrambled to get back up from the floor. I jumped to my feet and lunged at the girl, locking her into an embrace. We both fell side by side on the hard mattress. The girl strained inside of my arms as she tried to break free. Her shrill screams made my ears ring with pain. Andromeda moved closer to us, but the girl kicked her on the stomach. Andromeda's feet left the floor for a second, the vial flying out of her hand. She fell with a loud thud. The vial shattered. Sirius barked madly.

The girl drove her elbow into my stomach, pushing the air out of my lungs. I gasped for breath, weakening my hold on her. She pulled herself away from me, then pushed me onto my back. Something cold pressed against my face. Ice swept across my chest like a snowstorm.

I opened my eyes. White clouds hovered above me. It took me a second to realize those were not clouds but white veils that created a canopy above the bed.

I scrambled back in shock and accidentally fell off the bed. The domed ceiling glittered with golden stars against a marine blue background. I slowly rose from the floor as I took in the rest of my surroundings. The silver walls reflected the misty light coming from the open window at the other end of the room. A red rug that covered most of the floor depicted wolves, owls, deer, and ravens crowding around the base of a large tree. A canopy of white silk flowed over the bed with a soft breeze. The bedsheets and pillows had vines embroidered with golden thread.

Zia appeared before me. I startled back, then realized it was *not* Zia. The girl's eyes were the same color as the walls instead of blue. They gleamed unnaturally bright. Her hair was darker than Zia's had been, like tarnished gold instead of light blonde. Her lips were full and pale, her cheeks sharp, and her eyebrows thin. She wore a peach nightgown that hung loosely from her body.

For a moment the girl and I just stood facing each other. Something was wrong but I couldn't remember what it was. The girl walked closer to me—her head reached up to my chest.

"Who are you?" she asked, her voice sweet as honey.

"Who are *you*?" I asked.

The girl looked me up and down with her electric eyes. "My name is Zia."

I felt like I had been punched in the gut. For a moment, the floor underneath me seemed to sway.

"I'm Orion."

The girl stepped closer. She was so much like Zia, but there was a gentleness to her eyes that Zia never had—a childish tenderness and innocence.

"Have you come to free me from the Castle?" The girl asked.

Is that what I had been doing? "I . . ."

The girl pulled me towards her and kissed me. Her soft lips tasted like actual honey. "I knew someone would eventually come save me," she whispered as she pulled away.

Why had she been trapped? Where was Andromeda? Hadn't I been with her a moment ago?

"What's wrong?" the girl asked. "You look troubled."

"I . . ."

The girl slid her fingers across my jaw, making spikes of ice stab against my skin. Hadn't Zia done that to me once? Then the girl slid her cold fingers down my neck.

"Such a handsome man," the girl said.

"Thanks," I muttered.

She placed her hand over my chest, and my heart felt like it had been dipped into a frozen lake. "You're hurt," the girl whispered. "My mother hurt you. My mother has always been good at hurting people." She wrapped her arms around my neck and pulled me closer to her. She was so cold. *I* was so cold. "Let me help you."

Movement flashed behind the girl, and my eyes darted to the other side of the room. A tall woman stood next to the window. Her flawless dark brown skin gleamed golden and her eyes shone blue. She had a small nose, thin eyebrows, and full lips on a heart-shaped face. The woman's straight hair was like threads of midnight. She wore a white dress that flowed down to the floor, covering her feet.

"Don't listen to her, Orion." Her voice was powerful and commanding.

The girl spun on her heel, facing the woman. "Sirius!" The girl hissed. "Get out of my dream!"

I wasn't sure what stunned me more—the fact that I was inside someone's dream, or that the beautiful woman at the other side of the room was Sirius.

Sirius's piercing blue gaze locked on the girl. "Hello, Zia. It's been a long time."

Zia didn't answer.

Sirius turned to me. "You need to break away from this illusion, now."

Zia lunged forward at Sirius, and the two collided. I closed my eyes. This wasn't real—I couldn't really see. I let the rhythms flood into me as shouts of rage exploded around me. A rhythm of wicked nightmares wrapped around me. I let that rhythm flow through my chest.

Darkness fell over me like a curtain, and pain vibrated through my body. Somewhere behind me, Andromeda screamed. My sensing sharpened instinctively. Andromeda lay on the floor next to Sirius, who barked like a rabid dog. The girl, who had been lying on the floor at my side, jumped to her feet with inhuman speed and raced out of the room. I pushed myself to my feet, ignoring the dizzying sway of the floor, and chased after her.

The girl descended the steps two at a time, then sped forward through the hallway. I tried to keep up as my muscles began to burn. I lost a sense of where I was going—left, right, left, down another flight of stairs. All the corridors seemed the same to me as I sped past them.

I tried not to think of the strange illusion the girl had trapped me in, but it was hard not to. Had Leo, Sirius, and Ophiuchus known the girl was capable of that? They would probably have warned us if they had. And why had Sirius appeared as a woman instead of as a Dog? Was that Sirius's original form? The human form that the girl remembered?

I sensed something running behind me. Sirius. The Dog raced past me and caught up to the girl. Sirius leaped forward, knocking her down. I was barely able to stop myself before tripping over them. The Dog barked. The girl screamed.

I dropped to my knees and held the girl's arms at her sides, but I needed a free hand to grab the vial and make her drink it.

"Please," the girl pleaded.

She threw me to the side and I smashed against the wall. My back burst with pain, and black fireworks shot across my head. Sirius's middle head bit the girl's leg while the other two heads barked. The girl kicked Sirius on the side. The Dog hit the wall with a whine.

"Sirius!" I shouted.

"Go!"

I stumbled to my feet and raced after the girl as she ran away once more. Sirius remained on the floor behind me, whining, but I couldn't turn back now. The Dog would be all right. The girl was right in front of me, barely beyond my grasp.

Sirius barked in warning. I sensed the hole too late and fell right through it. I was in the air for a second before ice-cold water wrapped around me. I kicked my feet upwards, unable to sense the bottom of the pool. The girl was a few feet to my right, swimming away in that direction. I frantically swam after her. The girl pulled herself up at the edge and kept running. I followed right behind her, dripping wet. We raced through an arched opening. The walls and ceiling vanished.

I nearly stumbled as my feet stepped over soft ground. The cold seemed stronger here, more penetrating. Were we outside now? We kept running through a wide expanse for what felt like an eternity. I was two feet behind her when she stopped. I crashed into her and we both tumbled to the ground. I didn't have time to hold her down before she held my face between her palms.

A beautiful garden bloomed around me. Bushes shaped like animals decorated the edge of the path I stood in. The one next to me was a horse running at full speed. The trimming was so detailed I could see the horse's tendons on its leg, make out the hairs on the mane. Next to it were a lion and a tiger. The leaves were of different shades of green to contrast the lion's dark mane and the tiger's stripes.

On the other side of the path a collection of colorful flowers formed a rainbow over the grass. The red roses were the color of blood, their petals delicate and thin. Poppies were next, with bright orange petals like a sunset. Then there were bright yellow daisies, green roses, a dark blue flower I had never seen, and lavender.

The bright colors felt like a breath of fresh air after almost drowning inside the darkness. I looked beyond the flowers, into the distance, and almost gasped at the sight. The most magnificent castle I had seen stood atop a mountain. Statues, elaborate carvings, and large arched windows decorated every inch of it. The silver gleamed with light, as if it were reflecting the rays of a white sun above it. The structure was about a hundred stories tall, and I craned my neck to see the tips of its massive towers disappearing into the mist. A path led from the entrance towards the garden where we now stood. Beyond us stretched a curtain of white mist that hid the rest of the world, as if the Silver Castle hid among the clouds.

The girl walked closer to me, pulling my attention back to her. She trembled as her nightgown dripped with water. Her eyes shone with terror. What if Zia had tricked us into killing her but she was innocent?

"Please help me escape this place," she whispered. "Do you know how long I have been here?"

"No."

"Neither do I. There are no days and nights here." Her eyes settled on my chest, and she placed her palm right over my heart. "She hurt you too," she whispered. "I'm sorry."

"You have nothing to be sorry about," I said, then added. "I'm sorry she locked you in here."

"Did she tell you how I died?" the girl asked.

I shook my head. "She never told us about you."

A tear fell from her eye, mingling with the water as it slid down her cheek.

"The others said the Shadows killed you during one of the battles," I said.

The girl looked into my eyes, as if searching for something in my gaze. "The Shadows didn't kill me," the girl said. "My mother did."

CHAPTER 47

MY CHEST CAVED IN as if it had been crushed by a boulder. I looked into the girl's clear grey eyes, at the sorrow and betrayal that raged inside them like a thunderstorm. Zia had been violent, but would she be capable of killing her own daughter?

"Why would she kill you?" I asked.

The girl hesitated. "Because she knew I would tell my father the truth," she whispered. "She knew I would tell Cepheus that I had caught her with Ophiuchus."

"Ophiuchus?" I whispered.

Is this why he had been so desperate for the metal and had come back to find us? To finish her off so whatever secrets he had shared with Zia would be taken to the grave?

"Ophiuchus did something to me after I was killed. I don't remember much, only a white light pulling me back." Her silver eyes met my own. "I tried to tell them what my mother had done, but they wouldn't believe me." Her lower lip trembled. "They thought me insane, a monster, so they tried to kill me. But they failed. My mother imprisoned me in this Castle, and I have been here ever since." She paused. "Did he send you here?"

My silence told her the answer.

"He knew you were strong enough to kill me, didn't he?" she asked. "Tell me, do I look as monstrous as Ophiuchus made me sound?"

She was so beautiful, more beautiful than Zia had ever been. Her face was pale as death, but I could imagine her cheeks being rosy once, soft as the flower petals in this garden.

"I . . ." the words jumbled inside of my mouth. "No."

"I am no more monstrous than you, Orion," she said. "We are both what she made us. Do we deserve to pay the price for that?"

Her words cut through my chest like knives.

"Do you deserve to pay the penalty for all the people she made you kill? For all the other crimes you committed because she gave you no choice?" she continued.

My lungs constricted painfully.

"It's okay," the girl said. She stepped closer to me and wrapped her arms around me, locking me in a loose embrace. "It's okay," she whispered.

I held the girl too, the skinny bones in her back digging into my arms. Zia had been a monster, there was no ignoring that now—but I didn't have to let the pain she had inflicted turn me into something worse than her.

I couldn't kill this girl.

"Orion!" Leo shouted in the distance.

I whirled around. Even though I had expected it, I was still surprised to see Leo in his human form standing a few yards away from us. Leo was tall, at least half a head taller than me. His skin radiated sunshine. Leo's hair was like a mane of gold around his long oval head. He had thick eyebrows, a high-bridged nose, and thin lips. His eyes were still the same—two rings of molten gold. He wore golden armor that molded perfectly to his muscular body.

Leo opened his mouth to say something.

The illusion shattered like a mirror, and I braced myself for the darkness; shadows rose around me, slithering like formless beasts.

Somewhere far in the distance, Leo roared. The girl pulled me to my feet with incredible strength, grabbed my hand, and started running. I stumbled after her.

"Wait," I said.

The girl didn't loosen her grip as she ran faster. I struggled not to trip and have her drag me across the ground. The roar behind me made my bones tremble, but I couldn't sense the Lion. He must have been at least a hundred yards away. My senses sharpened as we entered a narrow hallway.

The girl kept pulling me forward as I got lost inside my own thoughts. Zia had killed her own daughter to keep her affair with Ophiuchus a secret from Cepheus. Zia had always been a monster. It wasn't the death of her own child that had driven her mad. Would she have killed me and Andromeda too at some point?

But why had Ophiuchus tried to revive the girl? That would have exposed his secret. And why had he become so obsessed with finding a way to kill her afterwards?

The girl finally stopped running as we entered a small, circular room. Something lay on the floor against the far wall. It seemed like three rectangular boxes. The girl let go of my hand and walked to the middle box. I stepped closer as the girl opened it and pulled something out.

"What is that?" I asked.

I stepped back as she held a thin, large, and deadly sharp object—a sword.

"This used to be my mother's," the girl whispered into my ear. Even her breath was cold. "It is a Shadow Weapon, made from the Heavenly Metal."

"What do you want me to do with it?" I asked.

The girl's lips brushed against my ear, making a shiver run down my spine. "He turned me into this, trapped me eternally."

"Ophiuchus."

"Yes. I need you to kill him." She cupped my face, softly. "I need you to avenge me for what he and my mother did. She was responsible for killing me, but he gave me this curse."

She moved the sword closer to me. I hesitated for a moment, then gripped the hilt. The metal was so cold it hurt, and it was heavy too. I had gotten used to the Star Weapons being light, but this was a completely different type of weapon—one that could kill even the darkest monsters.

Ophiuchus and Zia must have worked together to find a way to destroy the girl. He was just as bad as Zia. But I wouldn't let him use me like she had. I wasn't Zia's puppet anymore.

The girl held my other hand, and together we walked out of the room.

"I know where he is," the girl said.

We walked down a corridor and descended a staircase to the floor below. My mind was blazing as the girl led me forward. Ophiuchus had tricked me. He had let Zia kill her own daughter to keep their affair a secret. Fury burned inside of my heart, hot as the sun. The girl pulled me to a stop.

"He's in the room right ahead," she whispered.

I walked slowly, the sword held in front of me. The girl let go of my hand and hid behind me. We entered the new room. The smell of dried mint wafted into my nose. The ceiling above me was curved like a barrel cut in half. Thin and twisted lines covered the walls and part of the floor—were those vines? Were we in a greenhouse?

A warning hiss erupted in front of me. I held the sword tighter as Serpens slithered over the dead plants, cutting through my path. Ophiuchus's steps echoed inside the room as he walked closer to us. He stopped a few feet in front of me. I could have sliced him in half with one swing of the sword—would asteroid metal actually kill him?

"Orion," Ophiuchus said in his cold voice. Poisonous hate swirled within me.

"You lied to me," I growled.

"I don't know what she told you," he said carefully. "But I need you to listen to me."

"No. I'm done listening to your lies," I snapped as fury swept through me. "I'm done being manipulated by monsters like you and Zia."

"I didn't lie," he said.

"Zia, I mean Cassiopeia, killed her own daughter to cover up her affair with *you*."

Ophiuchus was silent.

"Did you really try to save her or were you trying to bury your secrets?" I asked.

"She's manipulating you, Orion. I need you to listen to me."

"*You're* the one manipulating me," I said. "Like Zia, like Perseus, and the Pleiades, and Corvus, and everyone else!"

"Orion," Ophiuchus said as Serpens slithered closer to him. "Do you remember what I told you about Sagitta?"

"Don't change the subject," I hissed.

"Centaurus and I were in a fight long ago," he said. "He wounded me with Sagitta."

"You—" I cut off.

Ophiuchus stood still as a statue, but I could feel his brilliant gaze on me, expecting me to put the pieces together. I lowered the sword.

"Death would have been easier to deal with," Ophiuchus said, his voice loaded with bitterness. "But that Love destroyed us."

The truth hit me like a hammer to the face. The girl had bright grey eyes—just like Ophiuchus.

Chapter VII, Verse II

Once worn by the Queen, but never by her daughter,
The Princess will be the one to save the Crown from its horrors.
A promise the Crown will require, one that will bring many sorrows,
Or the Prince of Darkness to rise to full power.
Many secrets the halls of the Castle hide,
Waiting for the right one to find the door of Light.
Only then will the war come to its fateful end.

CHAPTER 48

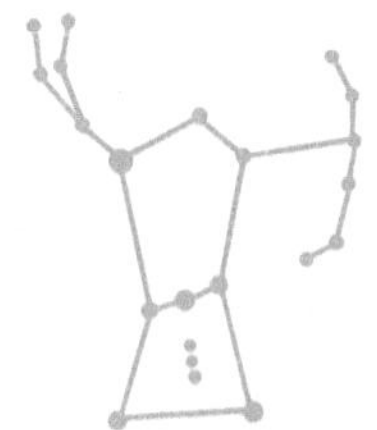

THAT'S WHY OPHIUCHUS had brought her back from Death—he had tried to save his daughter's life.

"Did you know Cassiopeia killed her?" I asked.

Ophiuchus inhaled sharply. "It took me a couple thousand years to figure that out." He paused. "Now do you see how dangerous that Arrow can be?" His voice was like a void. "The Children of the Shadows, our biggest enemy, were never able to break us. Darkness and Death were no match for our Light, but one forbidden Love ruined us all."

The girl went very still as she stood behind me.

The sword trembled in my hand.

"I tried to bring my daughter back and failed." He paused as his voice caught. "But she's gone," he whispered. "I don't know what she's been showing you in her illusions, but the girl standing behind you is a rotting corpse."

I was kicked in the back and nearly impaled myself with the sword as I fell. I let go of the hilt before hitting the floor and the weapon clattered away. I grabbed the sword again and pushed myself to my feet, but the girl had already exited the room. I raced after her. Ophiuchus followed close behind me as we ascended a set of stairs at the end of the hallway.

We came into another corridor. The girl passed through a door on the right. Before I could follow her inside, she came back out with a sword in her hand. I stopped, then jumped back as she swung the sword in front of her. The air sang as the sword nearly cut my head clean off my body.

Ophiuchus backed away. The girl let out a beastly growl as she brought the sword down on my own. My bones trembled with the force of the impact, and the clang of metal echoed painfully in my ears. Pain erupted below my neck, and I bit back a scream. The girl took a step back and kneeled. I jumped back a second before her sword swept over the floor to cut off my legs. I raised my sword and brought it down on the girl. She blocked my strike as another painful clang echoed around us.

The girl moved fast, slashing her sword in front of her as she aimed to cut my side. I blocked her just in time. The girl's attacks were vicious, making me back away into the corridor. I dropped down into a crouch as she swung at my neck again. The metal bit into the wall instead. I staggered to my feet again, raising my sword to avoid her next blow. Another painful clang vibrated through my bones at the force of the blow. I stumbled backwards into an opening, but quickly regained my stance. I couldn't sense the ceiling or walls, and the ground felt cushioned beneath my feet. The girl must have pushed me outside the Castle. She swept her sword in a wide arc aimed at my head. I ducked, then tried to swing my sword to cut her side, but she blocked me again.

"Kill me then, like the monster she made you," the girl growled. "Kill me like my mother did. With a stab to the heart."

The pain in my chest was so strong that for a moment I wondered if the girl had cut me, but I couldn't feel any warm blood sliding from a wound. The pain was coming from a gash very deep inside of me, one that had been bleeding for a long time.

My senses sharpened into focus, much clearer than ever before. I sensed how the girl's hands tightened around the hilt of the sword, the brittle flesh of her fingers cracking. Horror made me stumble backwards at the tattered texture of her rotting skin—smooth bones peeked through ragged holes that dotted her entire body. In the illusions her face had been beautiful, but she had no delicate nose or full lips, only broken teeth bared angrily at me. Her clothing dripped from her body like a mummy with torn bandages, unlike the nightgown I had seen her wear.

The girl slightly bent her knees before she slashed the sword at me again. I sensed the metal as it cut through the air—it wasn't completely sharp as I had thought before. The ragged edges had been eaten up by time. I lurched sideways and the sword came inches away from my body.

I raised my sword and deflected her next blow. The girl screamed in rage. I bent my knees and arched my body backwards as the sword swept right over me, grazing my coat. Then I came up again and swung the sword in front of me, aiming at her side. She quickly swung the sword to her side to block my blow. Our bodies vibrated with the strength of the impact.

I sensed the blades of grass under my feet, my swirling coat as I moved in a deadly dance with the sword, the ornate walls of the Castle behind us, the hollowness of the girl's body. Her organs had decomposed into dust long ago—she was a shell full of rage.

Zia's sword swung to strike me on the head and I pulled backwards. The girl let out another hollering scream as she struck me again and again, but I deflected all of them. The grass, the Castle walls, the swords, the girl—I sensed everything at once like an extension of my own body. I was Connected to everything.

The girl brought her sword up, and I sensed the trajectory of the sword about to hit my shoulder. I spun in a circle, the sword grazing my coat. The girl bent her knees again as she raised the sword and brought it down on my head. I raised my sword to block her strike once more. Serpens slithered slowly over the grass. I could sense his smooth scales, his glassy eyes. The Snake lay immobile on the ground a few feet away as I parried another strike from the girl. My arms ached with the impact, and the sting from the Scorpion pulsed with pain.

Serpens shot forward, wrapping itself around the girl's legs. She screamed, a sound barely human. I grabbed my sword with both hands and hit the weapon out of her grasp. It flew through the air, landing yards away from us. I let my sword drop and lunged forward, knocking the girl down. I fell squarely on top of her, grabbing her coarse, rotting arms and holding her down. The Snake shifted, becoming thicker and longer as it wrapped around her legs.

Ophiuchus rushed towards us, kneeling at my side. He pulled the vial out of his pocket and opened it. The girl screamed again. Ophiuchus didn't hesitate as he poured the liquid down her throat. The girl let out a shrill scream, trying to pull away from my grip. I didn't move, and neither did Serpens. Zia squirmed and screamed and thrashed and cried. It felt like hours passed until she finally went still.

Serpens unwrapped from her legs and slithered behind Ophiuchus. I finally let go and pushed myself away, sitting on the grass. My bones ached, my muscles felt like overstretched rubber bands, and the area beneath my neck burned with pain.

Ophiuchus let out a scream that made me startle. It was a scream of raw sorrow, coming from his very soul. He leaned closer to the girl, taking her into his arms, cradling her like a child. He gently caressed what was left of her hair and cried without constraint.

Too numb to move, I just sat on the grass, my mind blank with shock and pain. The portal inside of my heart closed abruptly, and I didn't try to open it again. The darkness around me seemed to respond to the pain, creating phantom faces that contorted in agony, like ghosts trying to escape from Hell.

It seemed like an eternity passed before the others finally found us. At that point, Ophiuchus had gone silent. Virgo said something, but I didn't understand her. Someone held my hand, and my body felt like it had been sucked by a vacuum.

Warmth fell on my skin, hugging my body, cloaking the pain.

"Should we bury her?" Virgo's voice broke clearly through the darkness.

"No," Ophiuchus immediately said, his voice like cracked ice. "Star Children should be burned, not buried." He paused. "She has been buried long enough."

We lay the girl on the mound where we had found the Crown. I didn't open the Portal in my chest again. For the first time, I welcomed the darkness around me, letting it drown out the sorrows surrounding me.

"I can blow out a bit of fire," Draco said.

It hit me like a wave, wrapping me in intense heat. The fire crackled loudly as it consumed the body. Leo roared in grief. Sirius's three heads howled in anguish. Ophiuchus cried silently. We stood before the pyre for a long time, even after the warmth from the sun had vanished. Even after the fire died down and the smell of ash suffocated the air. Ophiuchus's cries were the only thing that broke through the swirling darkness. Now he could truly mourn for his daughter—the daughter he had failed to save.

CHAPTER 49

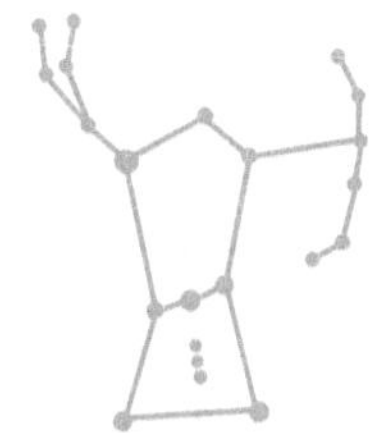

I HAD NEVER KNOWN that numbness could be painful. It wasn't supposed to hurt—numbness was supposed to be the absence of pain. But to me it felt like the opposite. It was a passive sort of pain, one that hollowed me out slowly like air leaking out of a balloon.

"Thank you," Ophiuchus whispered as we stood next to the ocean, waiting for Argo. The waves beat loudly against the shore, spraying cold drops on my face.

"I'm sorry for your loss," I said.

"I lost her a long time ago," he whispered. "I lost everything a long time ago. But thank you for helping me end the horrors I started."

"This wasn't your fault," I said.

"That's what I've tried to tell myself for the last few thousand years. But if I had just died instead of begging Centaurus for my life . . ." He exhaled. "I didn't know what staying alive would cost me. It ended up destroying everything, bringing ruin to all we had built." Ophiuchus was silent for a few seconds. "If you want to defeat Perseus, give him Love."

My heart contracted at that thought. "I . . ." I nearly choked on my own words. "How does that even work?" I asked. "Do you fall in love with the first person you see, or—"

"Yes," he answered. "You must be very careful when shooting, making sure that he's looking at the person you want him to fall in love with. He will *never* hurt that person."

A moment of silence stretched between us, full of understanding.

"Are you sure?" I asked.

Ophiuchus chuckled with bitterness. "It took me a long time to discover Cassiopeia had killed my daughter, and even after I knew the truth, I couldn't kill her." His voice caught. "I didn't *want* to love her, but the Arrow's power is too great. She knew I couldn't kill her. She . . ." He trailed off, taking a deep breath. "I know of the Prophecy between Andromeda and Perseus. If he loves her, he won't kill her—no matter what happens. Trust me." He paused. "Which means that Andromeda will be the one to kill him and fulfill her Prophecy."

Revulsion washed over me. I couldn't let Perseus love Andromeda. Perseus had used her to steal the Prophecies, and had played on her feelings. I wouldn't let him use those feelings to manipulate her again.

But what if it was the only way to save her?

Ophiuchus slowly walked away from me, leaving me alone with decisions I didn't want to consider. I had promised myself that I would do anything to protect Andromeda, but was this a curse I was willing to bring upon us? I breathed out. If Perseus didn't love Andromeda, he would surely kill her—maybe Love and Death did balance each other out.

Argo arrived shortly after, and we quickly climbed aboard the

Ship. I went straight to my room, too drained to talk to anyone. Andromeda guided me there without a word, then left to sleep in her own room. I hadn't even asked her if she had Corona Borealis, but assumed she did. I took off my shoes, then my pants, coat, and sweater. I climbed inside the blankets and lay on the bed. My head hit the pillow at the same time the door squeaked open.

Leo's paws scraped against the floor as the Lion walked next to my bed. I opened the Portal in my chest.

"How are you feeling?" Leo asked.

"How are *you* feeling?" I asked.

Leo didn't respond right away, as if the words were too heavy to lift. *"Cassiopeia killed the girl, didn't she?"*

"Yes," I said. "You didn't know?"

Leo exhaled. *"I didn't."* He paused. *"Or maybe I did but I didn't want to know."* The Lion let out a whine—I had never heard him make that noise. *"I loved Cassiopeia. We grew up together. She was my sister and I thought I knew her better than the others—better than Cepheus himself, but I didn't. I knew her the least because I was fooled too easily by her smile and her beauty, by her laugh and her charm, to notice what hid underneath."*

"She was a monster," I said.

"Yes," Leo responded.

I hesitated before my next question. "Do you think I'm a monster too, Leo?"

"Why would you think that? Who said that to you?" he asked in a defensive tone.

I shrugged.

"You're not a monster, Orion," Leo said, then added, *"You're not like Cassiopeia."*

"If you knew the things she made me do, maybe you would think differently," I said.

"*Oh, child,*" Leo said. "*I can only imagine the horrors you have lived through, but that doesn't make you a monster.*" Leo stepped closer to me, his breath sliding over my cheek. "*If you knew all the things I have done, you would think me a monster too. Everyone here would be a monster, I think, for all the deeds we've done to survive. Is Virgo a monster for her past? Is Draco? Is Andromeda a monster too?*"

"No," I immediately said.

"*Why?*" Leo asked.

"Because . . ." I trailed off while I gathered my thoughts. "Because Zia used her pain to hurt others, but we can use our pain to grow stronger and fight for each other."

"*You have your answer then,*" Leo said.

I *could* be better than Zia. I would be. She had never loved anyone but herself, never fought for anyone else. But I would fight for the people I cared about, regardless of what it cost me.

Leo's claws scraped against the floor as he exited my room. I closed the Portal in my heart and simply lay on my bed, letting my thoughts drift in the darkness. Weariness weighed me down, and I closed my eyes to go to sleep, but it didn't come as easily as I had hoped. My body was still tense and aching, ready to fend off any attack. I twisted in my bed for a long time, floating through the dark, trying to fall asleep.

"Hey," Andromeda said. I startled awake, not remembering I had fallen asleep. "It's me."

Andromeda's warm hand was on my arm.

"Hey." My throat felt ragged.

The bed shifted as Andromeda sat on the edge. "Can I sleep here?" she asked hesitantly.

"Sure," I said.

Andromeda stepped over me and settled on my right.

"We were in the Castle for five days," she said.

"What?" I nearly choked on my own saliva.

"I think time passes differently inside the Castle," she said. "The Twins were watching the news and noticed that several days had passed since we were last at Argo."

"But that means . . ." I tried to count the days inside of my head.

"That we have five days before Perseus's next rising," Andromeda said. My heart shrunk. Five days was not enough. We needed to recover our strength, get some rest, and train. I knew I wasn't the only one feeling exhausted—the last few weeks had been a string of battles.

"We'll figure everything out tomorrow," Andromeda said, pulling the sheets closer to her. "Let's just try to get some sleep."

Even though exhaustion clung to every cell of my body, sleep evaded me. The darkness around me didn't let me rest. I traveled from one dark landscape to another. I swam in an obsidian ocean, kicking my feet madly to stay afloat. The sharp waves pulled me back and forth, reflecting dark light from a moon that sparkled like a black mirror. I walked through a strange forest with onyx trees and leaves of black diamonds. Ravens cried as they stood on the branches, fluttering their wings but never taking flight. A black opal moon shone above like a giant eye spying on me. I stood on a meadow under a moonless night without stars. Pearls the color of shadows rained down on me, shattering to pieces.

I awoke at some point and noticed Andromeda was gone. Cold sweat covered my chest and back, and I absently wiped it away with the sheets. Had I dreamed of her coming into my room?

I thought again of what Ophiuchus had told me. I had the power to protect Andromeda from Perseus. He wouldn't be able to kill her, so she would be the one to kill him. But was that a decision I was willing to make for her?

No.

I had made too many decisions for her in the past few years, thinking that keeping her in the dark would protect her. But I wouldn't do that anymore—I could be better than what Zia had made me. I would tell her and we could make a plan together.

Someone entered my room. My scars burned.

"Just came to check in on your wound," Ophiuchus said.

I dragged myself to the edge of the bed and sat up as the doctor came closer.

"It's healing well," he said as he gently placed a hand on my left shoulder. "The poison is out of your system, but that wound may take a bit longer to heal." He pulled his hand away. "You should take a shower before I bandage you again. I can give you an ointment that will mostly numb the pain. That's the best I can do right now."

"That's more than enough," I said. "Thank you."

Ophiuchus stepped away, then stopped. "I don't want to get your hopes too high on this," he said carefully. "But I think I may have found a way to cure your eyesight."

My hopes immediately soared into the air. "You did?"

"Yes, but it's not a cure I can create right now."

"Why not?" I asked.

"I will need Taurus's blood to heal your eyesight," the doctor said. "The Pleiades are part of the Bull—they were born from it. The Bull's blood may be the only thing powerful enough to break the curse of the Seven Sisters. If someone can get the Bull's blood in the battle, I could use it for the cure."

"Shouldn't be too hard," I said sarcastically.

"Won't be harder than killing Perseus," Ophiuchus said as he walked out of the room.

I remained sitting on the bed for a while. I didn't know how we would get the Bull's blood during the battle, but I knew we could probably come up with a plan. Hope fluttered inside of my chest—I would soon be able to see again if I survived Perseus's next rising.

I smiled.

I took a quick shower and then left my room to find Leo—I had to tell him the good news. The Lion sat in the living room, his head raised as he presumably stared at something.

"Ophiuchus said he might have found a cure for my eyes!" I exclaimed. "He says that the Bull's blood can heal me, so we'll have to find a way to get Taurus's blood during the battle."

Leo was silent for a moment, although I would have expected him to be excited. He stood and turned to face me. *"Be careful,"* he said. *"If you recover your eyesight, you may lose your sensing."*

Ice swept over me. "What do you mean? Why would I lose it?"

"You cannot have everything at once," Leo said.

"Why not?" I asked defensively.

Leo sighed, stepping closer. I could imagine his bright golden eyes looking straight at my own.

"True power always comes with a sacrifice," Leo said.

"But why? What's wrong with seeing and sensing at the same time?" I asked as my heart echoed louder inside of my ears.

Leo's voice was gentle. *"Power corrupts, Orion. It is like poison to the minds of men. Even the kindest and the wisest will eventually be corrupted by it—that is simply its nature."* He paused. *"That is why true power always comes with a sacrifice. If you are always reminded of what you lost to possess it, you are less likely to become corrupted."*

"I . . ." I didn't know what to say.

Was losing my eyesight worth the power I had gained? Was it better to keep the rhythms and the sensing at the expense of my vision?

"Power is a choice, Orion," Leo said. *"You don't need to take it; you don't need to make that sacrifice. I didn't tell you the full truth about why I turned into a lion."* He growled sadly. *"Cassiopeia drank too much Light from me, drained too much strength, and she didn't give it back. So I didn't have enough power to stay in human form when the influence of the Stars in my Constellation shifted—not unless I lost all of the power I had."* Leo exhaled. *"I chose to shift into a lion and keep part of my power, instead of remaining human and losing all of it. I made that sacrifice."*

Silence stretched like a taut wire about to break.

"Was it worth it?" I finally asked.

"I don't know," Leo said.

I imagined the human form I had seen in the vision. Leo had been a Golden King. He still *was* a king, but a different one now.

"That's up to you to decide."

Leo walked out of the room slowly, leaving me alone with my thoughts.

●————●————●

Yellow stars danced in my vision as I fell to the ground.

"Get up," Zia ordered.

She pulled her loose hair into a ponytail. She wore a grey tank top, her white belt, and tight sweatpants. Her blue eyes were like a hurricane—they always looked like that when we trained. I groaned as I pushed myself to my feet again. I was getting taller, but was still not as tall as she was. The scorching sun made the air vibrate with heat. I wiped the sweat off my forehead.

"You need to do better," Zia said.

"I'm trying."

Her fist hit me squarely on the stomach and I doubled over, my intestines contorting into knots. It took me a couple of seconds to recover my breath and stand again. Zia threw her fist at my stomach again, but I lunged out of the way to the left. I held Zia's arm and pulled her down. She slipped from my grasp like butter. Pain exploded from my side as she kicked me. More stars blinded me, and I was on my back again.

"That's not good enough," she said.

"Not good enough for what?" I asked. Who was I supposed to be fighting?

As soon as I stood up, my leg burst with pain as Zia kicked me again. I screamed, but she didn't relent. I threw myself to the left, my head barely avoiding her fist. I landed on my knees and quickly pushed myself to my feet. I deflected one of her punches with my right arm, but didn't see the other fist as it came from the side and hit me in the chest. I crumpled to the ground, gasping for breath. The food I had eaten earlier erupted from my mouth, searing my throat. My nose burned with pain as if I had inhaled a flame. I coughed, then wiped my mouth, shaking.

Zia let out a breath behind me. "Get up."

I did as she said and followed her back to the two-story house. I thought Zia would take me back inside, but instead we walked around it. Zia headed to the tall ladder placed against the wall and began climbing it. I climbed the ladder after Zia, gripping it tightly as it shook. She would probably make me clean the roof again as punishment.

The forest covered a long distance on the right but seemed to have been cut in half by the path that led to the neighboring town where Andromeda was currently buying groceries.

Zia walked to the edge of the roof and looked down. I hesitantly stepped next to her. She was silent for a second, staring out at the horizon. She kicked my leg. For a terrorizing second, I was in the air, sure I would fall to my death. Zia grabbed my wrist and gripped it tight as my legs dangled over the edge of the house.

I screamed.

Zia pulled me up and I was able to grab the edge of the roof before she let go of my other hand. I gripped the edge with both hands.

"What are you doing?" I asked Zia, my voice weak with terror.

"Pull yourself up," Zia ordered.

"I . . ." I tried to pull myself from the edge but couldn't. I wasn't strong enough. "I can't."

"Yes, you can. Do it."

My fingers burned and my arms strained with fire, trembling as I held on for dear life.

"Zia, help me!"

Zia didn't move, simply stared down at me with those cold eyes. I knew she would let me fall if I didn't pull myself up. I would probably die if I broke my head with that fall. The mere thought of dying sent an electric wave of panic through me. I couldn't die. I couldn't leave Andromeda behind. If I died, I would never see her again.

My muscles strained like taut wires as I tried to pull myself up, but it wasn't enough. My arms ached even more painfully, as if my muscles were tearing like ripped fabric. I tried to find a footing on the bricks. My feet scraped against the wall until my left foot stepped on a brick that jutted out from the wall. I gripped the edge of the roof tighter, then jumped up.

I dragged part of my body onto the roof. But my legs still dangled in the air. I clawed at the concrete as I pulled myself away from the edge, then stopped. I let my head rest on the roof—it felt warm against my cheek. A large dead mosquito lay a few inches from my face. Its wings were twisted, and so were its legs.

"Good," Zia said somewhere behind me.

I heard her climb down the ladder. I stayed on the roof for a long time, trembling. I could have died. I had come so close to it. Thunder rumbled in the distance, but I ignored it. What was Zia training me for? The way she spoke made it sound like she was preparing me for a war. She had become more paranoid, always traveling with weapons, her gaze always alert as if a dangerous enemy would burst into our house and murder us. What was she so scared of?

Something cold dropped on my neck, as if Zia had pressed her finger into my skin. More raindrops fell on me, clattering softly on the roof. One drop hit the mosquito next to me, making one of its wings whither like a crumpled piece of paper. In a matter of seconds, the light drizzle became a torrent of rain. The mosquito flowed away in a river of rain. A few seconds later it fell from the roof as if it had disappeared down a waterfall.

I hadn't heard Andromeda come back home yet. The single scar on my back burned as if I had ignited it on fire. I screamed—I still wasn't used to the pain. Lightning lit the clouds above me, and thunder rumbled a second later. I pushed myself to my feet, my arms burning painfully. I managed to make my way down the slippery ladder. I raced around the house and looked out at the road, standing in the rain.

Andromeda burst from the forest a few seconds later, running towards the house as she clutched something to her chest. I ran up to meet her even though my body felt like wet clay. Andromeda's hair was plastered to her face, her back bent as she tried to protect our groceries from the rain. Her eyes seemed opaque as they reflected the clouds above us. Andromeda huddled close to me, as if I were an umbrella. I was glad that she was back home, and was happy that the rain meant Zia and I couldn't train more that day.

"Come on," Andromeda said.

Together we raced back to the house.

Chapter XV, Verse IV

Death will meet the Hunter at the edge of the door,
One he will be too afraid to cross through alone.
The Ruler of the Hunt will find his true power,
Only when he has surrendered all of his sorrows.
But Death he shall not be able to escape,
When it calls him to his rightful claim.
Only one he will be able to bring back to the Light.

CHAPTER 50

"STEADY," CASTOR SAID. "Keep it steady. Pull back until you feel the tension in your arm."

I pulled back the arrow as far as I could.

"Shoot."

I released the arrow and felt it zip through the air.

Castor laughed. "Bull's-eye!"

I smiled, walking forward to retrieve the arrow. I wasn't practicing with Sagitta—the Arrow hadn't let me. Since a dummy couldn't die or fall in love, Sagitta wanted nothing to do with it. I would have preferred to use Sagitta to get a feel of the Arrow, but I would have to make it work with the arrows that Castor and Pollux had given me earlier. For the first time, I had been able to distinguish between the Twins without hearing their rhythms. I could tell them apart because of their haircuts, which I could now sense clearly.

Pollux walked closer to his brother. "That was a nice shot."

"Thanks," I said.

I had never tried archery before—it wasn't something that Zia had ever emphasized. But it seemed instinctive to me when I used my powers. I could sense the bow, the arrow, and the target as easily as I felt my own body—they were an extension of me.

I could sense the trajectory of the arrow too, so when I aimed, I knew exactly where it would land. But I still kept practicing. I didn't want this to be easy—I wanted it to feel natural so when I was in the heat of the fight my body would know what to do even if my mind was distracted. I also had little else to do until we arrived at the battle. We were two days away from the solar eclipse that would herald Perseus's second rising, and we would arrive at our destination a day before. During his last rising, Perseus's powers had caused a massive earthquake in Italy, and we knew we had to be prepared for another similar event to happen even before the fight began.

Virgo had found the location where the solar eclipse would hit totality and last the longest—where it would give Perseus the most power. She had used the Atlas maps in Argo to pin the location to Lake Titicaca, a sacred lake at the border between Peru and Bolivia surrounded by ancient Incan ruins.

The Twins had consulted Argo and had determined that we could cross straight from the Pacific and appear in the middle of the lake. Apparently, the lake was also connected to the ocean through underwater tunnels the Twins had mentioned earlier. Our only problem was that we wouldn't know exactly where Perseus would be. Lake Titicaca had an area of over eight thousand square meters with numerous ruins around it.

"Surprise will be our only advantage," Pollux had said the day before when we had planned our attack. "I don't think Perseus knows about the subterranean tunnels, so he won't be expecting us to come from the lake. Most likely he'll be expecting us to attack from the west since that's where we would dock Argo and then move inland."

"This is Perseus we're talking about," Draco said. "He's never surprised."

"But then once we get to the lake, how will we find Perseus?" Andromeda asked, ignoring Draco's comment. "He'll definitely be at one of the ruins around the lake. Perseus loves them, but how will we know which one to look for?"

"Orion can find him," Leo said.

"But Darkness is protecting him," I said. "I've never been able to track down Perseus or the Pleiades."

"Darkness cannot cloak the rhythms completely," Leo said. *"If we get close to them, you might be able to discern their rhythms."*

"I've tried doing that but haven't sensed anything," I said. "But maybe if we're closer it could work."

"Okay then," Castor said. "Assuming Orion can find where they are, what's the plan of attack?"

"We will need to stay inside the Silver Circle," Leo said. *"It will protect us from Typhon's influence, and it can also protect us from Corvus's lies and Arianna's power."*

"But Andromeda is the only one who can kill Perseus," Virgo said. "How will she protect us and fight Perseus at the same time?"

"She can leave the Silver Circle with us if she needs to," Leo said. *"She doesn't need to be holding it physically for it to remain in place."*

"How big is the Silver Circle again?" Pollux asked.

"The largest Cassiopeia ever stretched it was about a hundred yards in diameter," Leo said. *"We can move with the Silver Circle if needed but just need to make sure we remain inside of it."*

"And you said it's like a force field, right?" Virgo asked. "So we would be safe from any physical attacks too?"

"Yes."

"If we only stay inside the Circle we'll be limited in how much fighting we can do," Pollux said.

"But this is our best bet at defeating them," Castor chimed in. "Taking an offensive stance at the cemetery nearly got us killed, so a defensive attack might be our best chance at outsmarting them."

"At least until we kill Typhon," I said. "Once I kill him with Sagitta the fight should be easier."

There was a short silence, and I sensed people nodding.

"Perseus's allies will know we're there to kill him, so they might try to keep him as far away from us as possible," Virgo said. "What if Perseus flees while we're in the Circle? We won't be able to go for him unless we leave the Circle."

"Perseus has never run away from a fight," Draco said.

"I know," Virgo said. "But this battle will be crucial, and they'll know he's our main target. If Perseus dies, they lose. So they'll keep him safe at all costs so he can complete his rising." Virgo paused. "When he has attained full power after the rising, he might come back into the battle."

"I can stay out of the Circle," I said. "Perseus made the Pleiades blind me. He probably won't expect me to be in the fight if I can't see, and he doesn't know about my new powers. I can use the rhythms and my sensing to follow Perseus once he runs away from the Silver Circle. I can make sure he doesn't escape too far."

"That—" Virgo started.

"Is brilliant," Pollux concluded. "Once they see the Circle, they'll know we can't leave it, so they'll try to keep us in there and as far away from Perseus as they can." Pollux paused. "And Orion's right, the others won't expect him to walk into the fight. So he's perfect for a surprise attack on Perseus."

"They won't leave Perseus alone," Draco said. "Most likely someone will go with him, maybe one of the Pleiades, or possibly Corvus. If Orion is outside of the Circle, Corvus's lies will still influence him."

"And assuming you manage to find Perseus away from the Circle, then what?" Andromeda asked.

"I know you're the one who's Prophesized to kill him," I said. "But I can fight him and prevent him from running away. I can weaken him and tire him out until you get there."

And once he saw Andromeda, I would shoot him with Sagitta. I hadn't shared my plan with anyone, but planned to talk to Andromeda in private later.

"I would have to slip out of the Silver Circle at some point to fight him," Andromeda said.

"I can help with that," Virgo said.

"How?" Andromeda asked.

"I . . ." Virgo trailed off. "I think I can create an underground tunnel that could take us to where Perseus is. We would have to be fast though, before the others realize what's happening."

"We can create a distraction while you escape," Pollux said.

"Shouldn't be too hard," Castor said. "For once I think we might be able to defeat Perseus."

"Just to summarize," Draco said as he cleared his throat. "We all stay in the Silver Circle, except Orion. Perseus will likely run away from it as he waits to gain full power from Algol's rising. Orion will make sure that he doesn't make it very far. Once Perseus is distracted fighting Orion, Virgo can take Andromeda directly to Perseus and Andromeda will kill him. And once Andromeda and Virgo are with Perseus, Orion can come back to the Circle and use Sagitta to kill Typhon. And then we take care of the rest of them."

"I don't like the idea of Orion being alone with Perseus," Andromeda said. "Perseus could take one of the Pleiades or Corvus with him. Maybe one of us should be with Orion?"

"Perseus will be suspicious if one of us is not in the Circle," Pollux said.

"I'll go with Orion," the hissing voice pierced through my head.

"What?" Ophiuchus asked, as shocked as I was. The Serpent had never spoken to me. "Serpens, you shouldn't—"

"I am immune to the Crow's lies," Serpens said. *"As long as I am touching Orion, he will be immune too."*

I wished I could have seen Ophiuchus's shocked expression. I translated Serpens's words to the others.

"Are you sure, Serpens?" Leo asked.

"Yes," the Serpent hissed.

"I'll stay here at Argo," Ophiuchus said. "I'm not a fighter, I never have been, but I'll be here waiting to heal whatever wounds you get from the fight."

A few moments of silence followed.

"I guess we have a plan then," Pollux said.

"But we should still be ready for anything," Virgo said. "Perseus always seems to be one step ahead of us."

"I think we're giving him too much power," I said. "He wouldn't have blinded me if he had known it would make me stronger."

"Unless it somehow benefitted him," Virgo said.

"Orion's right," Castor said. "Perseus is just a guy. The Prophecies are hard to interpret and translate. He can't possibly know everything that's going to happen."

"But we'll still be careful," Draco said.

"And if possible," I added. "We should try to get Taurus's blood so Ophiuchus can heal my eyes."

The doctor nodded. Leo tensed.

"Sure thing," Pollux said.

"This is it then," Andromeda's voice was steady. I sensed the nods of agreement around the room, then the others began discussing specifics about the fight and what everyone would do once inside the Silver Circle.

I drew back the arrow another time, pulling myself out of my thoughts. I was confident our plan would work. I sensed the dummy fifty yards in front of me—the outline of a head, arms, torso, and legs; the ragged hole on the chest where my last arrow had pierced it; the tension in the string as I held the bow; the sharp tip of the arrow. I aimed the tip to the ragged hole and *sensed* how they came in perfect alignment. I fired, and the arrow went straight through the hole.

"Nice!" Pollux said.

Footsteps echoed behind me as Andromeda walked into the room. She didn't comment on my perfect shot as I turned to face her.

"I just wanted to practice a bit more with Corona Borealis," she said.

"That's a good idea," Castor said.

The Twins moved closer to us and we all stood in a small circle. Andromeda stood right before me. She pulled the small ring off her index finger and placed it on her palm. Corona Borealis could shift into rings, bracelets, and crowns, which made it easy to transport. The silver ring had carvings inside of it, but I didn't know what they said—they were written in a language I didn't understand.

For a moment, nothing happened as Andromeda closed her eyes and breathed deeply. And then I felt it—a wave pouring out of the ring. My body vibrated as the Circle passed through me and created a small dome around us. The surface of the dome was impossibly smooth, humming with energy. I sensed it as a solid wall, yet I knew I was able to walk straight through it. Andromeda could choose what went in and out of the Circle, and anyone or anything that she didn't let in would simply bounce off the surface.

"How does it look?" I asked.

"Like a dome of silver light," Andromeda said. She sounded awed. "It pulses slowly like . . . like my scars."

The Circle expanded, creating an even larger dome. I measured the diameter of the Circle to be about fifty yards in length. It was large enough to hold everyone inside.

"And you're sure you can keep the Circle up as long as we need?" Pollux asked.

"Yeah," Andromeda said. "Even if I'm not inside the Circle, it'll stay there as long as I want it to. I practiced with Leo a couple of times, so I know it works." Andromeda pulled the Silver Dome back into the ring, and my body vibrated as the Circle passed through me again.

"Neat," Pollux said.

"It's almost dinnertime," Castor said. "I'll go see what we have in the kitchen. Hopefully Cancer hasn't eaten it yet."

A smile stretched across my face. The Crab had managed to keep hiding inside the submarine, making us forget him, and had only resurfaced the day before to steal some pizza from the fridge. I wasn't sure if it was healthy for crabs to eat pizza and tacos, but I wouldn't argue with Cancer. The Twins walked out of the training room, leaving me alone with Andromeda.

"How are you feeling?" I asked her.

She shrugged. "I'm fine." I let the silence stretch between us until Andromeda finally exhaled. "I'm nervous, stressed, and a bit scared."

"Only a bit?" I asked.

I didn't sense Andromeda smile.

"We'll be all right; we always are."

"But what if we're not this time?" Her voice was thin, like a sheet of ice about to break.

I walked closer to Andromeda and placed a hand on her shoulder. "We will be," I assured her. "I . . ." I trailed off to take a deep breath, trying to calm my battering heart. "I have a plan that will keep you safe from Perseus no matter what happens, but I won't do it unless you're okay with it."

"What is it?" Andromeda asked hesitantly.

"Sagitta can kill anyone with one shot, and even a scratch would be fatal. But in mythology, Sagitta was also Cupid's arrow and could make anyone fall in love with the first person they looked at. Ophiuchus was shot with Sagitta, and that's why he fell in love with Zia. Even after she killed their daughter, he couldn't kill her—couldn't hurt her in any way—because the Arrow's power is too great." I paused. Andromeda must have known where this was going. "If I shoot Love at Perseus and he sees you, you'll be safe from him, and then you'll be the one who fulfills the Prophecy."

Andromeda didn't say a word.

"I am repulsed at the idea of Perseus loving you, but if it's the only thing that will keep you safe from him, then I think it's worth the shot." I chuckled nervously. "Pun intended."

Still, Andromeda didn't respond.

"What do you think?" I asked, my hands sweating with nervousness. "I won't shoot him unless you give me the green light on this."

Andromeda continued to breathe silently.

"Do it," she finally whispered.

I nodded as relief swept through me. This plan couldn't fully ensure that nothing would happen to Andromeda, but if I shot Perseus then he would never harm her again. If Death couldn't take Perseus first, then I would let Love destroy him.

Andromeda stepped closer, and I hesitantly pulled her to me. She rested her head on my chest. I hugged her tightly, and after a second, she hugged me back.

"Thank you," Andromeda said.

"For what?" I asked.

"For asking for my permission."

I exhaled as I rested my chin on her head. "I know I haven't been a good brother to you in the last few years. But I promised you I would be better, and I am trying."

Andromeda hugged me tighter. "I love you."

My eyes burned with tears. "I love you too."

We remained hugging for a long while.

CHAPTER 51

ARGO LAY MOTIONLESS at the bottom of Lake Titicaca. I breathed deeply as we all stood next to the hatch, ready to disembark. The bow and Arrow hung heavily from my shoulders. The Twins had given me more arrows made from Cetus's bones, which would be effective weapons, and I carried those along with Sagitta. A sword hung from my waist in case I needed that too.

Perseus's rising would occur in a couple of hours. So far, we hadn't detected any mass catastrophes raging outside. Algol was completely unpredictable, and we knew that the Demon Star would create some sort of cataclysm, but it was impossible to tell when.

We had made it to the lake hours ago, but I hadn't been able to detect Perseus and the others until now, when I had sensed the distant echo of their rhythms. We still had enough time to find Perseus and fight him before the eclipse started and hoped that we could defeat him before that. But our time window would be narrow.

The darkness around me seemed restless as I opened the Portal in my chest and let the rhythms pour in again. I sensed my friends around me, but I pushed away from Argo and submerged myself into the water outside. I took in deep breaths as the rhythm of the lake pulsed against me—it was cold and weeping, crying for all it had lost. I pulled away from it, moving towards the land. *Perseus.* I thought, imagining his black eyes and hair like fire. We were Connected, even if only through hatred. I imagined the silver thread that united us.

Perseus's rhythm pierced my heart. I knew it was his as soon as I sensed it. Perseus was pure chaos—a cacophony of blood, death, and violent murder. The beats were jarring, like hammers pounding on stone and metal. And there was a continuous buzz in his tune like a swarm of flies eating from piles of dead bodies. I clenched my teeth and tried to find where that rhythm was coming from.

"He's in that direction." I pointed to the left.

Argo pivoted to the side.

"Can you sense the others?" Virgo asked.

I moved beyond Perseus's rhythm towards his surroundings. A chorus of different rhythms rang around me, but I separated them one by one. One rhythm was silent, as if trying to hide among the others—it beat with trickery and deceit. That must have been Corvus. The next rhythm was like a howl to the moon, drumming in a maddening pattern that made me feel dizzy. Lupus. Next to the Wolf was a vibrating pulse like a stampede about to trample me. Taurus. Then I sensed the choir of different rhythms—they all played together like seven strings in a lyre. The rhythm was enchanting, a beautiful tune that flowed as smoothly as silk. The Pleiades. Close to them was a rhythm like clouds drifting in the sky. A flutter of wings. A gust of wind. Was that Pegasus? The next rhythm was unmistakably Typhon—it was provocative and wild, lawless and chaotic, threatening to disrupt everything around him. It felt like inhaling drugs that suddenly made the world around me spin like a broken kaleidoscope. I searched around them, hoping to find another rhythm, but couldn't sense anything else.

"Arianna is not there," I whispered. I pushed all of the rhythms away and focused on Arianna. Even if she was Darkness itself, I was still Connected to her. She had a physical form now, one that was inextricably tied to all of us. I sensed her then. Her rhythm was beyond anything I could have explained with words, but it was rebellious, unruly, and made out of the purest beats of Chaos. "She's further inland, a couple of miles away from the lake."

"That doesn't seem right," Virgo whispered.

Pollux clasped his hands together. "Let's just focus on Perseus and try to kill him before the rising. We should disembark soon."

"Yeah," I said. "Could someone help me fasten my weapons so they don't fall as I'm swimming?"

"I can help," Draco immediately said. He pulled me backwards, away from the others. Draco stood behind me and tightened the straps at my back. "I know we're safe from Typhon inside the Silver Circle, but if it fails and Typhon takes control of me, I want you to keep your promise."

I bit my tongue. "I won't have to, Draco. We'll be all right."

I focused on Draco's rhythm, on the sharp contrast between him and the Dragon. Draco's rhythm was still stronger, and I hoped it remained that way. Draco exhaled, but he didn't say anything else.

I took in deep breaths to calm my nerves as I stepped closer to the others, my heart pounding loudly.

"I guess this is it," Pollux said.

Andromeda's hand slipped into my own. I squeezed it. She squeezed back hard.

"We'll celebrate with some tacos after this," Castor said. Something clanked against the metal ladder as Castor gripped it tightly. "Good luck, Orion," he said. "Kick Perseus's ass for us."

"Will do," I promised.

Castor moved up the ladder, followed by his brother.

"I'll see you soon," Andromeda said.

I squeezed her hand again. "See you soon."

She let go and my heart twisted in pain. I would see her soon, I told myself. Just a few hours and we would all be back together, eating tacos. Andromeda climbed the stairs and disappeared through the hatch. She was followed by Virgo and Draco, then by Cancer, who had decided not to make us forget him again.

"Orion," Leo said. The Lion's fur brushed against my shoulder as he stepped closer to me. *"I just wanted to say that I'm proud of what you have achieved in the last few weeks. You turned weakness into strength, which is not something everyone can do."*

"Thanks, Leo," I said as a knot formed in my throat. "I'll see you soon."

Leo roared.

I wasn't sure how the Lion managed to climb the ladder, but he figured it out. Sirius went after him, then Aquila. And just like that all of my friends were gone to start the battle. My heart beat like a galloping horse inside my chest, and I tried to calm my breaths.

A hiss echoed behind me as Serpens slid through the floor towards me.

"I'll be waiting here," Ophiuchus said.

I nodded. The Snake climbed my leg. "Can you breathe underwater, Serpens?" I asked.

"*Yes,*" the Snake answered as it slid into my shirt and wrapped around my torso. Its head snuggled close to my belly button.

"I'll see you soon," I said to Ophiuchus.

"See you soon," he responded.

I walked over to the ladder with Serpens wrapped around me like a belt. I gripped the ladder tight and climbed the steps. "Argo," I said, "move somewhere where I can take cover while I get out. I don't want anyone to see me."

The Ship began moving again, away from the others. They stood at the edge of the lake, then slowly began walking inland, closer to Perseus and his allies. Their rhythms beat loudly, like a synchronized band playing for a large concert. Argo stopped again. Before exiting, I quickly scanned my surroundings. There was something large to the right, probably a boulder. I couldn't sense anything else inside the water surrounding me.

I climbed out of Argo and into the approaching dawn. I crouched to keep my balance on the slippery surface, the sword scraping against the metal. The air was crisp and still, holding its breath. My friends were still two hundred yards away from Perseus and the others. I hoped Andromeda had already made the Silver Circle. I had to trust that my friends could take care of themselves.

I took a deep breath and jumped into the water. Ice swept across my body. I held back a grunt as my muscles numbed and my skin burned. Serpens tightened around my torso. I let myself sink a few feet deeper, sensing the smooth surface of Argo right next to me. I couldn't sense the bottom of the lake, so I assumed it must have been deep. I searched for Perseus's rhythm, which came from the left, and began swimming in that direction. Argo had left me about twenty yards away from the land, and I tried to swim parallel to the edge of the lake.

The two rings pressed into to my chest as I swam forward. My lungs didn't tire as I held my breath, swimming silently in the freezing water. I wondered why I was able to hold my breath for so long. It had always been something normal for me, but maybe it was part of my Constellation's power. Hadn't Virgo said that Orion was the demigod son of Poseidon?

As I kept swimming, I imagined the Silver Circle. It would have been an incredible sight—a silver dome shining against the darkness, pulsing with Light.

Perseus moved.

The others must have spotted my friends. Perseus began running parallel to the edge of the lake, in the same direction I was heading. We had been right—he wanted to be as far away from us as possible so we couldn't stop his rising. His tumultuous rhythm beat loudly as I swam faster. The Darkness around me was a churning black ocean as my muscles strained.

Something jutted out of the darkness on my left—a structure with sharp, rectangular edges. Did the lake have underwater ruins? If the site was as ancient as Virgo had said then it probably did. I continued forward, letting Perseus's rhythm drive me. He was about three hundred yards ahead of me, running faster than I could swim.

After a minute, Perseus stopped. I was too far to know if there was anything else around him. There were no other rhythms beating around Perseus, not even Arianna's. Maybe someone else would soon join Perseus? I hadn't expected the others to leave him alone, but maybe Perseus was confident that no one would find him. He was far from the fight, but he wasn't moving to get further away.

I searched for my friends—their rhythms were clustered tightly, all of them still beating. They were already surrounded by rhythms of Chaos, so I assumed the fight had started. Arianna was still far away. That made me nervous—I wondered why she wasn't in the thick of the fight, as she usually was, but I didn't have time to consider that.

The water began to move backwards, like a flowing river. The pull stopped after a second, and the water pushed me forward. Then it went still, and I floated in the water for a few moments as a muffled shriek echoed above me.

I continued swimming towards Perseus. He was so close, only a hundred yards ahead. The water around me vibrated, as if something had struck the earth. I continued forward, a bit slower than before, my senses sharp. Perseus was fifty yards away. Something small swam right next to me—it had a big round eye and soft scales. It stopped for a second, close to my legs, then rushed away. I kept swimming as my heart drummed inside of my chest to its own rhythm.

I stopped when Perseus was directly on my left. I turned and slowly swam towards the edge of the lake. Sharp edges and crumbling steps lay ahead of me. I stepped on a flat surface, then floated up the steps, gripping the slimy moss-covered rocks as I pulled myself up. I stopped right before my head broke the surface.

Before me stood a crumbling block which would hide me from Perseus, who stood twenty feet behind it. The area around him became clearer as my senses sharpened. He stood on a cracked platform surrounded by broken pillars and crumbling walls. He had a long sword strapped at his back.

I wondered why he had stopped here. He could have run further away from the fight. Why risk being so close if he knew we were coming to kill him? And why would he have escaped alone? I pushed those questions aside. I just had to focus on making sure he didn't run further.

Serpens tightened around me as my head broke through the surface. A deafening shriek broke through the darkness as I breathed. A roar came next, followed by crashing lightning. The earth shook and trembled as another growl exploded somewhere in the distance.

I focused on Perseus again. He stood like a forgotten statue. There was no one hiding behind the broken pillars that surrounded the platform, no hidden weapons.

It was just him.

Except . . . another rhythm, faint but noticeable, vibrated around him. It took me a few moments to realize it was coming out of Perseus, overlapping with his own rhythm. It felt as if one instrument in the orchestra of Perseus's Chaos was taking center stage, trying to eclipse the rest of the music. That sinister tune could have belonged to a horror movie. It had a feel of suspense about it, like a demon hiding in the night moments away from breaking free. Was that Algol's rhythm gaining strength before the rising? Only one way to find out.

I grabbed the edge of the broken stone in front of me and pulled myself out of the water. A vein in Perseus's forehead popped out as he tensed. I walked towards Perseus as water dripped from my clothes. He didn't back down. He didn't even reach for his sword. I could make out the gloves that reached up to his elbows. I stopped ten feet away from him.

"Hello, Orion," Perseus said. His lips pulled back into a smile. "I was hoping to see you here."

Chapter IX, Verse II

The Silver Circle will reveal the secrets of the Queen,
But the Princess will keep them hidden after a vow has been made.
Many other secrets and powers the Castle still hides,
But they won't be shown until the Crown sits on her head.
After the White Throne has risen from the stone,
And she pardons the sins born from hate.
Only then will the last battle be fought.

CHAPTER 52

I CLENCHED MY JAW. That was a lie—Perseus was trying to throw me off balance, making me think he had planned everything. He would never admit I had surprised him. I pulled the sword from my side. I couldn't use the Arrow yet. Perseus pulled his own sword from his scabbard.

He lunged forward, the tip of his sword aimed at my left arm. I stepped to the right and blocked his strike. Our swords met in a clang as thunder raged above us. Our swords clashed again, locking with each other as we both pushed forward. Perseus dropped, and before I had time to react, his leg kicked out. I felt the impact on my right thigh a second later. I lost my footing and stumbled down, the sword clattering out of my grip. Perseus jumped back to his feet and grabbed my sword from the ground. I shot back up, clenching my fists as my heart thundered.

A shriek boomed in the distance, followed by the sound of rushing water in the lake. Serpens tightened around my waist. Perseus took a step forward as he faced me, holding both swords in front of him.

Before I could reach for my bow and one of the normal arrows, Perseus threw my sword back to me. I caught it with ease, tightening my grip on it.

"You're fast with your arms, but slow on your legs. Try bending your knees a bit more, and practice stepping to the sides—that will make your movements more fluid," Perseus said.

A shriek like a thousand cows being slaughtered erupted around us and the earth shook again. The ground splintered on my right as a crack boomed around me. Perseus lunged forward again, bringing his sword down on me. The bones clanked as they met again. Perseus brought his knee up, aiming at my groin. I spun, and Perseus's knee hit the air. Our swords slid away from each other as I stepped back.

"Good," Perseus said.

"You couldn't have expected me here," I said. "You blinded me because you wanted to cripple my power."

"I didn't," Perseus said. "I knew that if I forced you into the Darkness, you would find a new Light. You can see everything around you, just not with your eyes."

I gripped the sword so tightly my hand ached. "And how does that benefit you?"

Perseus's lips pulled back into another smile. "When you're on the defensive, don't hold your sword like that. Position it vertically, like I'm doing now. It will allow you to block strikes more easily."

As soon as I moved my sword, Perseus surged forward and struck again. The impact made my bones shudder. Perseus pulled his sword away and I swung mine forward, aiming at his head. I only grazed his hair as he arched backwards. As soon as my sword had passed over him, Perseus shot forward like a spring. His leg connected with my stomach before I could step to the side. I crashed on my back but kept my grip on the sword. I sensed a broken column on my right, a few inches from my head. I placed my hand on its ragged surface and pushed myself up.

"You're not as good as I hoped you would be," Perseus said. "But this will have to be enough, I guess. All you really need is Sagitta."

How did he know I had the Arrow? The earth shook again. Water rushed as if a tornado had formed in the middle of the lake. Thunder exploded in the sky. Where was Andromeda? I wasn't sure what Perseus was playing at, but the sooner she got here, the better.

"I'm surprised none of you figured out why I blinded you," Perseus said.

"Because you didn't want me to find Sagitta or Corona Borealis," I said.

"I wanted you to find Sagitta," Perseus said. "I wanted you to train with your new power, to become as good a fighter as I am."

"Why?"

Perseus paused. In the silence, his new rhythm seemed to become stronger, like a rebelling musician trying to break away from their band. No, more like a band member killing the other players to take all the glory themselves.

"Do you know what will happen during this eclipse?" he asked.

"Algol's second rising," I said.

"It's more than that," Perseus said. "Today, Algol will be born."

That had to be the new rhythm then.

A roar cut through the air as the earth shook again.

"Do you know what Algol represents in mythology?" Perseus asked.

I quickly searched my memory. My body went numb. "Medusa's head."

Serpens tightened around my torso.

Perseus's voice darkened. "*The blinking demon shall rise when the sun goes back into the night. Into flesh and bone the demon will be born, with a glare that will turn everyone into stone.*"

I nearly stumbled backwards as everything fell into place.

"Anyone who looks at Medusa's eyes will turn into stone— even me. But not you, Orion." He paused. "Her glare can't turn you into stone if you can't see it."

I struggled to breathe, feeling as if Perseus had punched me in the gut.

"I blinded you so she wouldn't be able to kill you. I wanted you to discover your new powers, to sense everything, so you would be able to fight her." Perseus walked closer to me, his chin raised high.

"I won't kill that monster for you," I spat out. Maybe Algol in the form of Medusa would kill Perseus for us and end all of this.

"Corona Borealis won't protect them from Medusa," Perseus said, as if he had read my thoughts. "Not when she's at full power during the eclipse. Her glare will turn *everyone* to stone today unless you stop her—unless you use Sagitta. Normal Star Weapons won't be able to kill her during the rising. Only a shot of Death will be able to destroy her." Perseus paused. "You may be tempted to let Medusa turn my family to stone first, to let her take us down before you kill her. But are you willing to risk your friends' lives as well? If we die, they die with us."

The implications of that question tore through me. Was I willing to sacrifice the only people I cared about to destroy Perseus? I tightened my grip on my sword.

"You played me." A laugh rumbled out of my chest. "You planned everything."

"I always do."

A soft warmth grazed my skin—dawn was here.

Perseus sped away from me, and I barely had time to register that before I instinctively raced after him. He was heading back to the fight, back to my friends. If he got closer to them, and Medusa broke out of him, then they would be directly exposed to her glare.

No, no, no, *no*. We hadn't prepared for this. If we all died, then we could literally save the Universe from Perseus. But was that a sacrifice I was willing to make?

Sagitta vibrated at my back.

"Who are you?" the Arrow had asked.

I had told Sagitta that I needed its power to protect the people I cared about and save the Universe. But I wouldn't be able to do both today—Perseus had forced me to choose one. Maybe someone nobler would have chosen to sacrifice themselves and their loved ones to save the world—but that's not who I was. I would protect Andromeda, and my friends, no matter the cost.

My surroundings became a blur as I raced up broken steps, ran over patches of grass and dirt, and avoided crashing into random walls, boulders, and broken columns. Perseus was fast, and I couldn't catch up to him as he raced back towards the battle.

My heart shrank as the new rhythm gained intensity. It was a rhythm of brutal death, dripping blood, and burning bodies.

Algol was coming.

Raw fear shot through my veins. Would I be able to kill Medusa and Typhon, *and* stop Perseus with a shot of Love? I would need three shots to make it work and balance out the conditions Sagitta had given me. Death. Love. Death. Every Death was followed by Love, but would I be able to make that order work? I would have to kill Typhon or Medusa first. But if I didn't, and if I could only shoot Death at Medusa *or* Typhon, who would I choose?

Ahead of me, something surged out of the earth, like the dead clawing out of their tombs. Perseus stumbled down as the ground beneath him swayed. I stopped a few feet behind him as two figures emerged from the earth. Virgo kept her palms open and aimed downwards as Andromeda raised her sword high and brought it down. Perseus, who still lay on the ground, blocked it. The swords clanged. Perseus kicked Andromeda in the leg and she staggered backwards.

Love would come first then.

I was about to unhook the bow from my back and grab Sagitta when something wrapped around my shoulders. I screamed as my feet left the ground. The swoosh of air drowned the raging screams of the battle. I braced myself to crash on my back, hoping the bone arrows wouldn't break, but was surprised when I landed on my feet.

For a moment I just stood there, stunned, then her voice broke through the dark. "We meet again, Hunter," Arianna said. Her tendrils of Darkness wrapped around my arms. Serpens was very still, and I wondered if the Serpent would get out of my shirt at some point or if it was just enjoying the ride. "No need to have you in the midst of battle, where you could get hurt."

"You want to keep me alive so I can kill Medusa," I hissed.

"That is the plan," Arianna chanted. I could imagine her shining blue eyes staring at me. I clenched my hands, then realized I didn't have the sword anymore. When had I lost it? The tentacles of Darkness wrapped tighter around my arms as I tried to reach for the Arrow. My hands clapped together as Arianna bound them. She wrapped around my chest and my legs too. I screamed in rage.

"Don't despair," Arianna said soothingly. "It shouldn't be long before Algol rises." Arianna paused. "Your friends seem to be holding up all right inside the Circle, and Andromeda is giving Perseus a savage sword fight. And Virgo . . . it may take her a while to break away from that lie."

I tried to sense my surroundings but could only sense the Darkness around me like a slithering cage.

"Did you really think you could outsmart Perseus?" Arianna asked. "He has planned every step of the way until his final rising. Everything you do will lead us there—you can't escape."

The earth shook, and it kept shaking. There was no way to know if Virgo, Perseus, Typhon, or something else was causing it. Shrieks, roars, and shouts composed a hellish song around me as Darkness tightened her grip on me. Beyond me, Algol's rhythm became stronger. It seemed to come from everywhere at once—from the sun, the moon, the rocks, the lake. The sun bled and the moon wept. Fire froze and water blazed. The rhythm was unnatural—something that should never have been created. Something that didn't belong in this world.

"ANDROMEDA!" I shouted. "RUN!!! Don't look at—"

Something wrapped around my mouth, cutting me off. "Shhh," Arianna said.

I was able to break through the Darkness and sense beyond Arianna. Perseus and Andromeda were fifty yards away from us. Andromeda was on her knees, and Perseus lay on his back a few feet away from her.

I could sense Algol being born out of Perseus, growing from his chest like a cancerous tumor. The rhythm intensified, drowning out every other rhythm around me. Andromeda screamed and stumbled backwards as a blob began to swell out of Perseus's chest.

Serpens shot out of my shirt, ripping through the fabric. The Snake lunged at Arianna and sank its fangs in her neck. Arianna let out a shriek and vanished like a puff of smoke. Serpens dropped to the ground, then quickly slithered to me, climbing my leg.

I sped towards Andromeda. Serpens continued to climb my body, wrapping itself around my torso again. The earth shifted beneath me, and I stumbled forward. My hands broke my fall and I scrambled back up. My mind couldn't process my surroundings fast enough, but it didn't need to; my body knew what to do.

Ahead of me, the violent rhythm intensified. The squirming blob growing out of Perseus's chest had doubled in size. Andromeda stood next to him, probably frozen in shock. There was no time for Love—Andromeda needed to be as far away from Perseus as possible.

"Andromeda, run!" I shouted. "Get back into the Circle and close your eyes!"

Virgo ran towards Andromeda and grabbed her arm. Virgo extended her hand to me, but I stopped a few feet away from her.

"Orion, come on!" Virgo shouted.

"No!" I said.

A figure began twisting inside the bleeding tumor.

"I'm the only one who's immune to Medusa's glare. GET BACK TO THE CIRCLE!"

"Wait!" Andromeda shouted.

She didn't finish. The earth swallowed her and Virgo like a gaping mouth. Perseus twisted on the ground, hollering in pain. I was about to pull Sagitta from my quiver when one of Arianna's tendrils wrapped around my wrists and pulled me to the side. I fell on my face. Serpens squirmed as I squashed him beneath me.

"Patience," Arianna sang into my ear. "The demon is nearly here."

Arianna pinned me to the ground, my face against the wet mud. Roars, shouts, screams, shrieks, and thunder exploded around me as the battle raged on. The bloody rhythm became even louder, growing like a parasite out of the earth. It was as if the gates of Hell had opened, and a marching band of demons was coming out of it. Arianna let go of me and vanished again, but it was too late.

As I lay on the ground, the figure broke out of the blob. Its head twitched with hissing snakes. The creature had the upper body of a woman and the lower body of a snake. Perseus lay immobile, but I knew he wasn't dead. His heart was still beating, and his chest rose with ragged breaths. I didn't know how badly Medusa had injured him, but the monster must have taken flesh from him to build its own body.

I didn't need anyone to tell me that the eclipse had started— the warmth from the sun disappeared abruptly, and a rhythm of pure Chaos exploded through the land like a bomb. Medusa shrieked as she stood over Perseus.

Algol had risen.

CHAPTER 53

THE DEMON LUNGED AT ME. I didn't have time to react before I was knocked down, the quiver of arrows digging painfully into my back.

"Orion!" Andromeda screamed in the distance.

I held the demon's shoulders and pushed the creature back. The demon's skin was blazing hot. Algol hissed at me. Hot drops of saliva splattered on my face. The demon's clawed hands sank into my upper arms. I screamed as warm blood slid from the wounds. The demon pushed me down, as if intending to bury me into the ground through sheer force.

"The demon is too strong," Arianna said.

My arms strained as Algol tried to lean down closer to my face, the snakes hissing and snapping. Pain stung my arms as the demon's claws sunk even deeper into my flesh.

"I can lend you the power you need."

"No!" I shouted.

With a burst of strength, I pushed Medusa to the side. Wind buffeted my face as something landed next to Perseus a few yards in front of me. It was one of the Pleiades, but I couldn't sense which one. She reached down to grab Perseus by the waist, but the demon immediately leaped at her. She screamed, and I recognized her tone as Maia.

Maia slashed her sword in front of her, but her arm shook. She swung it wildly, and I realized she must have had her eyes closed. The demon's snake tail wrapped around her legs with inhuman speed and pulled her down. Maia fell to the ground, her sword tumbling away. I swallowed down my pride, staggered to my feet, and threw myself at the demon. We both fell to the ground with me on top of the monster. I pressed down on the monster's bare back, keeping her face down. The monster's blazing skin burned my palms. Algol clawed at the ground, and I knew I wouldn't be able to keep her down for long. I should have grabbed the Arrow before throwing myself at the monster. If I removed one of my hands from her back, she would spring back and kill me.

Maia screamed, and I heard a sickening crack as the monster wrapped more tightly around her legs. More wind buffeted my face. Someone landed next to me with a thud. Another one of the Pleiades pulled a sword from her back and slashed it down on the monster. The sword didn't cut through the snake tail, only made a shallow wound, but it made Medusa loosen her grip on Maia.

"Come on," Aster said.

Maia whimpered as Aster pulled her away from the monster. Maia's legs were not moving as she cried out in pain. Algol went still and the snakes dropped to the ground. For a moment, confusion took over me. That cut couldn't have killed the demon. Then she planted her hands firmly on the ground and pushed upwards, knocking me backwards. I was thrown into a backflip and landed on my side with a grunt.

"NOO!" Maia screamed. She fell to the ground as Aster went very still. "ASTER!"

Aster's soft skin solidified. She froze with her mouth open in surprise, her eyes wide. Rage swept over me. I screamed as I pushed myself back to my feet.

"Hey!" I shouted at Medusa.

The demon turned to face me, and I could imagine her deadly gaze on me. But the monster couldn't hurt me, at least not with its eyes. Algol seemed to realize this, and the demon gave a confused hiss as it cocked its head to one side.

I pulled Sagitta out of the quiver. The Arrow vibrated in my grasp. I didn't even bother to unhook the bow from my shoulders. I lunged forward at the demon, both of my hands tightly gripping the Arrow's shaft. The demon caught my wrists with its hands, and its claws dug into my skin. Thin streams of warm blood slid down my arms. I pushed my hands down towards its chest as the monster pushed them up. The snakes on its head pulled back, away from the Arrow's deadly tip. The demon's tail arched on my left, but it was too late. The tail swept me off my feet and made me crash to the side, but I didn't lose hold of Sagitta.

The demon slithered away from me. My heart jumped into my throat as it headed towards the Silver Circle. I wasn't sure if Medusa had the power to break through the Circle's protection, but I didn't want to find out. Behind me, I heard the flap of wings as more Pleiades swooped down from the sky. One of them let out a grieving cry.

I raced after Algol as it slithered down a hill. I descended as fast as I could without stumbling forward. I grasped Sagitta tightly, the Arrow still vibrating warmly in my hand.

"Close your eyes!" I roared as the demon moved closer to my friends. Typhon's vexing rhythm beat to my right, but the giant monster was hidden behind a cracked wall. What a coward. I would take care of him later.

Algol's chest scraped against the ground as if it were fully a serpent. I ran even faster, the tip of the demon's tail only a couple of feet in front of me. I bent my knees and jumped forward. I landed on Medusa's bare back with my knees, my bones jarring with the impact. The demon shrieked. It didn't stop slithering, and I felt as if I were riding a very slippery skateboard.

I held Sagitta tightly. *Give the demon Death.* I brought the Arrow down. It never pierced Algol's skin. I was thrown to the side and my body left the ground. I tried to grip something, and managed to get a hold of the demon's arm. I held it tightly and we both rolled down the hill in a painful tumble. Darkness spun around me and my senses blurred with pain.

"I can give you the strength you need to defeat the demon," Arianna whispered. "You only need to drink a little bit of—"

She cut off as I splashed into the water. I hadn't sensed the lake, and the cold wrapped around me in an icy embrace. Medusa slipped from my grasp, but instead of going back towards the surface, the monster dove deeper. I kicked my legs and followed it. Medusa was a lot faster than me, but I used all of my strength to catch up. The demon's tail slithered right ahead of me. Serpens was still wrapped around my waist, its head brushing against my stomach as we swam down. The pressure from the water should have become unbearable, but it didn't. I placed Sagitta back in the quiver.

Sharp edges and flat surfaces rose ahead of me—Medusa was heading towards the underwater ruins. She slithered into a gaping hole on the side of a wall, and I followed her inside. The rectangular room had cracked walls with algae or other marine plants dripping from it like torn skin. A few feet in front of me, Medusa scraped at one of the walls, trying to move a large boulder to create another opening that led further down into the ruins.

I placed my foot against the rock behind me and pushed myself forward. If the demon disappeared inside that narrow opening, I wouldn't be able to fit through to follow her. I gripped its shoulders and pulled her back. Medusa spun around and slashed her claws at me. I let go of the demon and pulled myself backward as they cut through the water like curved scythes. Medusa lunged forward, grabbed my wrists, and pressed me against the wall behind me. It took a concentrated effort not to open my mouth and scream. I pulled my knees up and kicked Medusa in the chest. She let go of me as she shot backwards. She shook her head wildly, as if something had caught in her hair. Then she slithered past me, out of the hole we had come through.

I swam out of the ruins. Medusa floated twenty yards in front of me, her hair twisting as the rest of her body floated still. For a moment, neither of us moved, then she lurched forward. I pulled Sagitta from my back, but Medusa grabbed my wrist and pushed me backwards. My hand was locked in her grip as she pinned my arm to a jagged rock. Before I could fight back, she used her other clawed hand to slash at my wrist. Pain burned in my arm, and I bit back another scream. The demon let go of my wrist, and I realized that Sagitta wasn't in my hand anymore. Another burst of pain erupted on the side of my neck, and warmth seeped out of my skin.

Medusa slowly swam away from me. My head felt light, as if it was about to float back into the surface. I sank deeper into the lake. My thoughts were distant, as if Medusa had sliced them away. I knew I had a severed artery in my wrist, and probably one in my neck too. If I didn't stop the bleeding, I would die. Those thoughts passively crossed through my mind as the cold numbed my body. The weight of the two rings around my neck pulled me further down. I was vaguely aware of Serpens unwrapping from my waist and instead wrapping around my bleeding wrist. I numbly felt the Serpent's pull as it tried to drag me upwards, but I only fell deeper and deeper into the darkness.

●————●————●

I jumped, and as soon as my feet touched the ground, water splattered around me. Andromeda burst out laughing. She jumped next, and the puddle seemed to jump to the side. A few drops of water hit me in the face as I giggled. Thunder rumbled in the distance, but I didn't see any flashes of lightning.

The dark alley behind the apartment was lit only by light pouring from a window on the third floor. The yellow light reflected blurrily on the water, as if each puddle had caught a yellow flame and was trying to keep it trapped inside.

Andromeda laughed again as she jumped in another puddle a few feet to my right. She gave me a wide smile. One of her front teeth was missing—it had fallen out a week ago, and when I had examined her mouth, I had seen a new tooth growing from her gums. My front teeth had fallen out a couple of years before, and I remembered how much it had hurt. But Andromeda hadn't even cried.

I looked up at the sky above us. The black clouds made it seem like it was night even though the morning sun had shone brightly only a few hours ago. The door behind us burst open. The woman, Zia, came out of the building.

"You shouldn't be outside during a storm," she said.

She held a pair of towels, and immediately wrapped one around Andromeda, then placed the other towel over my shoulders. She pulled us inside the building. Andromeda's black hair splattered rivers onto the floor, but Zia didn't seem to care. We quickly ascended the stairs with yellow walls. The color had faded, and in some sections it had scraped off. Zia had said we would be moving somewhere nicer soon, but this place didn't bother me. It was much better than the places Andromeda and I had been living in anyway.

Zia pulled us into the second-floor apartment. The square table didn't leave much space in the kitchen, and it was usually cluttered with pans and pots. The bed where Andromeda and I slept stood against the wall. Zia slept on the couch next to it. Past the bed was the door to the small bathroom.

Zia guided us towards the couch right across from the front door and I hesitantly sat down. I didn't want to make the couch wet if she was going to sleep there. Andromeda sat down next to me, her head leaning on my shoulder. Zia walked to the bed and crouched down. There was a click, and light cut through the darkness like a sword. Zia walked back to us with the flashlight and sat on the floor in front of us. She left the flashlight next to her, and the beam of light pointed towards the right, illuminating one of the table legs. Zia's light-blue eyes examined us worriedly.

"You shouldn't be out during a storm," she repeated.

"Why not?" Andromeda asked, wrapping the towel tighter around her. "Will we get sick?"

Zia raised a brow. "No. Who told you that?"

"A lady at the park," Andromeda said.

I couldn't recall any lady at the park.

"You can't get sick," Zia said, her eyes tracing over us. "We almost never get sick."

"Then why are you worried?" I asked.

Zia didn't answer. She pulled out something from her shirt and held it tightly. It must have been the ring. When I first saw it a few weeks ago I had thought it was a necklace, but had soon realized that it was a golden ring around a chain. Shouldn't she have worn that on her finger? Why would anyone wear a ring like a necklace? Zia was a strange woman, but I liked her. She always made sure we had food three times a day, and she let us sleep on the bed with warm blankets.

Zia rubbed her forehead, closing her eyes. Deep lines cut through her skin, which made her look like an old lady. She seemed tired, which confused me, since she slept most of the day. Maybe she was sick?

A flash of white light burst in front of me, and I felt a pull inside of my chest. I blinked, and the light disappeared. Had I imagined that? I turned to Andromeda, who was blinking confusedly. Where had that light come from? The flash had only lasted a second, but I had seen it clearly.

"So what do you want to do tomorrow?" Zia asked. I turned back to her. Her eyes seemed to be brighter, and the deep lines that had cut through her skin only a few seconds earlier were gone. Had I imagined those too? Zia didn't look like an old lady anymore—she looked like a young woman with flawless skin. "We could go back to

the museum so I can teach you more history. Or we could go to the bookstore to pick some new books." Her smile widened. "You're both getting better at reading."

"Can we go to the movies again?" Andromeda asked. "I want popcorn."

"Or can we go ice skating?" I asked.

"We could do both," Zia said.

Andromeda giggled.

Living with Zia was definitely better than being on our own. No one stopped us on the street anymore to ask where our parents were. We also didn't have to worry about people calling the police and having to run away and hide.

"But we should also do some reading," Zia said. "It's important that you learn that."

"Can we read the dinosaurs book again?" Andromeda asked with her toothless grin.

"Sure," Zia said. She glanced under the bed, and I could spot the outline of the book Andromeda wanted. It didn't have a cover page, so I didn't know the title of the book.

A tear fell from Zia's eye, and she quickly wiped it away.

"Are you okay?" I asked shyly.

Zia laughed. "Yes." She looked at me, then at Andromeda, and her smile softened. "I've just been alone for a long time, and I'm glad to have found you."

"I'm glad too," Andromeda said. "I like eating ice cream together."

Zia's smile widened. I wondered if she would let us stay with her. I wished she would, but even if she didn't, I knew Andromeda and I would be all right on our own—we always had been.

White light exploded through me, so hot it burned into my soul. Then the Light vanished, and the cold rushed in around me. I held my breath as I realized I was underwater. Someone held my arm tightly, pulling me sideways. My memories came back to me in a flood, and I pulled away. For a second, I just floated. The Portal in my heart opened instinctively—Ophiuchus was right next to me.

The world around me came into focus as my senses sharpened. Something large and oval hovered above me—Argo. It lurched forward, hitting Medusa straight on. The demon shot backwards in the water.

Sagitta. I needed to find the Arrow and shoot Algol dead. I grabbed Ophiuchus's shoulder and squeezed, hoping that my gratitude would transmit through that small gesture. He had saved my life again, and I would have to thank him later. My body felt renewed, and I knew the doctor had healed all of my wounds.

Ophiuchus swam back towards Argo, which lay still as it waited for him. Serpens tightened around my arm I was glad the Snake had chosen to come with me.

As soon as I focused on Sagitta, its rhythm cut through the water and reached me. The Arrow had fallen to the bottom of the lake—it lay unmoving about sixty yards below me. Argo blasted forward once more, heading towards Medusa, who frantically swam away from the Ship. I hoped Argo was able to distract the demon long enough for me to recover the Arrow. I kicked my feet and dove further down. Serpens shifted on my arm, getting thicker. The Snake must have been adapting to the pressure. I didn't feel it though, as if my body had been built to be underwater. I had probably spent a considerable amount of time below the surface, but my lungs didn't even burn.

My arms and legs strained with the effort as Sagitta's airy rhythm called desperately at me, whistling loudly. The cold water began numbing my muscles, but I pushed forward. Serpens shot from my arm, heading for the Arrow. Serpens gently bit the Arrow's shaft and pulled the tip out of the ground. The Serpent swam back to me and held the Arrow next to my hand. I grabbed Sagitta and Serpens wrapped around my torso again. I kicked my feet and propelled myself upwards.

Argo moved closer to me and stopped at my side. I searched for Algol's rhythm again and my heart nearly beat out of my chest when the demon's head broke through the surface. I grabbed onto the submarine's hatch with my free arm and gripped it tightly as Argo surged up. In my other hand, Sagitta vibrated hotly.

We broke through the surface with a splash, and I clung to Argo as I took in a deep breath. The Ship moved closer to land. Deafening thunder crackled above me, accompanied by a powerful wind. The lake's surface rippled with waves that splashed against one another.

A frightful shriek cut through the air. Algol's rhythm moved closer to my friends. I hoped they had their eyes closed. The Ship stopped right next to the edge of the lake. I let go of the hatch and dropped onto dry land. Argo backed away, disappearing below the waves. My friends were huddled in a tight group as the Silver Circle hummed around them. The demon slid closer to the Circle, standing right before it.

"Don't open your eyes!" I shouted.

I pulled the bow from my back and nocked Sagitta. My arms strained with the tension. Medusa went still before reaching the Circle and slowly turned to face me. I aimed the Arrow directly at Algol's face.

Give her Death.

I shot the Arrow.

With frightening speed, Medusa snapped Sagitta from the air. The Arrow's tip had stopped an inch away from the demon's forehead. Algol pulled its lips back into a snarl, baring its sharp teeth. The demon threw the Arrow to the side. Sagitta sailed through the air once more before landing on the ground fifty yards away.

The rhythm of violent Chaos and carnage intensified, as if the sun was dripping blood over us. Medusa placed her clawed hand on the Silver Circle. The humming stopped abruptly, and the dome shattered like glass.

Chapter XXI, Verse II

First owned by the Wise One, then by the Healer,
The Arrow shall be used to avenge their bleeding hearts.
Much destruction the Arrow has caused, its purpose misunderstood.
For Love and Death were never meant to be shot separately,
But only together will they bring an end,
To the war that for so many ages has raged.
Only the Hunter will understand after Death he has traversed.

ANDROMEDA SCREAMED as the Silver Circle burst.

"NOO!" I shouted as I raced forward.

"I can help you defeat the demon," Arianna whispered.

I ignored her as I kept running forward—fifty, forty yards away from my friends. Algol hissed and lunged at Andromeda. Pollux stepped in the demon's path, his sword raised in front of him. He waved the sword in an arc, but the demon used its tail to swipe at his legs and throw him to the ground. Pollux landed on his side, a few feet in front of Andromeda, and the sword skittered out of his grasp. Before Pollux could stand again, the demon sank its claws in his stomach. Pollux screamed as the snakes on the demon's head snapped at him, trying to take a bite off his face.

Serpens shot from my torso and slithered towards the demon. The Snake jumped and sank its teeth into the demon's arm. Algol let out a furious shriek, pushing away from Pollux. Serpens dropped from the demon's arm and slithered away from Algol, snapping its head from side to side as if trying to spit out venom.

Twenty yards, ten. I threw myself at Algol and fell on top of it. Andromeda dragged herself away from us, clutching the silver ring in her right palm. Algol used its tail to push me away, and I landed next to Pollux.

"Come on, Corona," Andromeda said.

The ground trembled underneath me as I pushed back to my feet.

"Draco!" Virgo cried out behind me.

Draco's fiery rhythm dimmed as something more savage and violent began to beat out of him. Algol hissed at Pollux as he lay on the ground, but Pollux only pressed his hand to his stomach.

I threw myself forward at the demon again, intending to push it away from Pollux. Medusa's fist hit me in the side, and I heard a loud *crack*. I crumpled to the ground, the air knocked out of my lungs as my side flared with burning pain.

"Hey!" Castor shouted as he raced towards us.

He swung his sword. The tip cut the head from one of the snakes in the demon's hair. Medusa let out a choked scream. Just as Castor brought his sword back in another arc aimed at her neck, he went still.

"Castor!" Pollux cried.

Castor froze in place with his sword inches away from the demon's neck, his eyes wide in surprise.

"Leo, please!" Virgo pleaded.

The Lion roared savagely. Typhon's rhythm pulsed from the left. He must have still been hiding behind that wall, but his mere presence was enough to disrupt my friends' sanity. Leo's rhythm, instead of beating like a coordinated army, became a chaotic battle, warring with itself. I pushed myself to my feet with a roar of rage.

I pulled out a normal arrow from the quiver, aimed at the demon's chest, and shot it. Algol snatched the arrow out of the air and snapped it in half. I cursed and lunged at the demon once more. Algol's tail curled, then uncurled as it slapped me away. My chest exploded with pain as my feet left the ground. I landed on my side with a grunt, the bow tumbling away from me.

Algol hissed, turning its head to Andromeda, who still lay on the ground, clutching the ring. She had her hood pulled over her head, shielding her eyes.

"Let me help," Arianna said.

"Orion!" Draco shouted as his rhythm turned more violent, beating with cruel pulses. "Stay away, Virgo! ORION!"

Algol advanced closer to Andromeda, baring its sharp teeth. The demon hesitated just before reaching her. It cocked its head to the side as its deadly gaze settled on an empty patch of grass. Cancer's deceptive rhythm rang around me, but I knew the Crab wouldn't be able to distract the demon for long.

"I can give you the strength you need to save her," Arianna whispered, knowing I had no other option.

Andromeda had paid the price of using Darkness to save me. I could do the same for her and the rest of our friends—even if I ended up drowning inside of it. I didn't care. No price would ever be high enough to stop me from saving her.

Arianna smiled.

I surrendered to the Darkness, letting it pour into my heart and flow into my veins—it had been waiting for a long time and greeted me like an old friend. My scars burned fiercer than ever, as if they were tearing open again. They ripped into gaping wounds, revealing what lay in my core.

My sensing expanded all around me. Perseus and the Pleiades were at the top of a small hill surrounded by crumbling ruins of what once could have been walls and pillars. I sensed every crack in the stones, the blades of grass pushing in between the rocks, the vines crawling over the ground. One of the Pleiades held up Perseus as blood dripped from his chest. Ten feet next to him, Aster still stood frozen with her mouth open in shock. One Pleiad wept at her feet—the tears hot as they slid from her cheek. Her wings sagged down at her back, the soft feathers drooping onto the ground.

Twenty feet in front of me was Medusa, who had stopped her advance and had turned to look at me, her snakes stiff. Andromeda lay on the ground next to the demon, gripping the ring as it dug into her palm. Hot breath came out of her mouth as she whispered something to Corona. Castor stood frozen in place with his sword still cutting in an arc, his eyes wide. Pollux hugged his brother's legs tightly, his forehead pressed against the stone as he avoided the demon's glare. Virgo had fallen to her knees, facing Draco as he squirmed on the ground. Sirius's three heads dripped foam as they barked madly, snapping at an invisible enemy in the air. Aquila had taken flight and circled around us in turbulent circles. Leo moved closer to the wall where Typhon hid. The giant Lion bared his teeth and roared. The powerful muscles in his legs twitched and he shook his head wildly, as if trying to get a snake off his mane. Typhon still hid behind the wall—the monster afraid of the demon. He knew he didn't need to come out; his mere presence commanded my friends to obey him.

Light exploded from me like a bursting Star, propagating around me like a wave. Something hollowed up inside of me, but Darkness was there to fill the void. Then I sensed something beyond the Light, something that came from the very core of my soul. A rhythm—strong, powerful, mighty. It beat to the sound of the Wild. It called on the beasts and monsters, warning them, threatening them. It was the rhythm of the Hunt, one that danced between the hunter and its prey.

It was *my* rhythm.

It blasted out of me, traveling with the Light.

"Stop!" I roared.

Typhon trembled.

Leo, Sirius, and Draco went still. Aquila landed on the ground, shaking its head. I was the Hunter, the wild obeyed *me*.

"Medusa!" I shouted as I got back to my feet. The white Light still shone out of me, humming inside every cell in my body. "Fight *me*!" I commanded the demon. Serpens slithered back to me with Sagitta in its jaws. I opened my right palm and felt the shaft of the Arrow as Serpens dropped Sagitta in my hand.

I sprinted forward. Algol hissed at me. I was three feet in front of it when the demon extended its claws, aiming at my chest. I spun to the side and the claws grazed my arm. I tensed as my elbow smashed into the monster's stomach. I knocked down Medusa and we fell to the ground. I landed over the demon, but Algol squirmed underneath me and pushed me to the side. I tumbled on the grass, then scrambled back to my feet at the same time as the demon stood on its tail.

I lunged forward, Sagitta in my right hand, aiming at the monster's head. Medusa grabbed my right arm, digging her claws into my flesh. The Arrow was inches away from her face, but I couldn't move it closer. Behind the monster, Andromeda stood. She gripped her sword tightly. Serpens slithered behind me, tense and ready to strike.

Medusa swung her free hand towards me, her sharp claws like daggers aimed at my neck. Andromeda brought her sword downwards. One of Medusa's claws made a small cut in my collarbone before Andromeda's sword sliced her arm. It didn't cut through the bone, but it was enough to make the demon's hand loosen its grip on me.

Algol shrieked.

I let Sagitta drop from my right hand. Medusa turned to look behind her as the snakes in her hair hissed. Andromeda pulled the hood over her face. Serpens shot forward, catching Sagitta by the shaft before it touched the ground. I extended my left hand and Serpens placed the Arrow in my palm. I gripped Sagitta tightly and raised it above my head, the tip pointing downwards.

Death.

The snakes in Medusa's head hissed in alarm. Algol's head snapped back to me. I screamed as I buried the Arrow into the demon's eye, piercing its skull.

Medusa let out one last shriek. The demon gripped my right arm tighter, sinking its claws deeper into my flesh. The rhythm of Chaos stopped at the same time the demon's hand went limp and the upper body dropped to the ground. I stumbled to my knees as the claws still buried in my arm ripped through my skin. I grabbed the limp hand, still warm, and pulled it away. Pain exploded through my arm in a wave, and I bit back a scream.

I pulled Sagitta out of the demon's eye, then grabbed Medusa's feverish shoulder and turned the monster around so its gaze would face the earth. I wasn't sure if its glare could still harm my friends, but I didn't want to find out.

Darkness flowed around me, grazing me softly. I tried to ignore it. But a hollow cavity inside of me demanded more. A deep hunger slashed through my body, one I knew wouldn't be satiated until I took in more Darkness, but I refused to give in to that power.

The frantic flap of wings pulled me out of my thoughts. My senses expanded again. Pegasus landed right next to Perseus, its hooves pounding on the ground. Perseus scrambled on top of the Horse.

"He's escaping!" Andromeda shouted.

She hurried back to me, holding the bow I had dropped. I took it from her hand. The Arrow vibrated with anticipation. I raised the bow and pulled the Arrow back as far as I could. Its dark feathers brushed against my cheek.

Pegasus jumped into the air with a whine. I sensed the force in those massive wings, the soft texture of the feathers. Perseus grabbed the Horse's mane tightly as the Pleiades flew behind him. Two Pleiades carried Aster's statue, and two other Pleiades carried Maia, whose body was limp, but her heart still beat.

Andromeda rushed away from me, away from all of us, until she stood alone without anyone else around her. I aimed Sagitta at Perseus, aligning the deadly tip with his beating heart. Perseus turned back one last time. His gaze settled on Andromeda, who raised her chin defiantly. The Arrow burned in my grasp—it knew what to do.

Sagitta shot forward.

CHAPTER 55

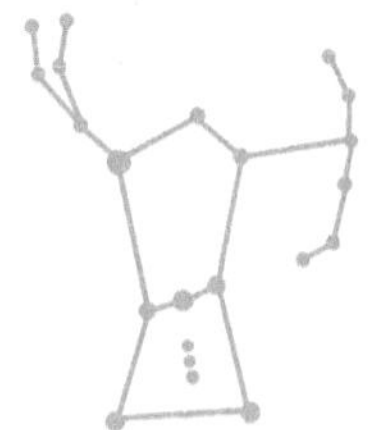

THE ARROW CUT SWIFTLY through the air. It flew high, sailing directly towards its target. Pegasus whined and swerved to the side. But it was too late. Sagitta cut through Perseus's arm, leaving a deep gash. Blood spilled from it, dropping onto the Horse's mane.

Sagitta continued to fly through the air, going beyond Perseus and landing somewhere far beyond my reach. I clutched the bow tightly, breathing raggedly, then swung it around my shoulders again.

A monstrous shriek exploded like an erupting volcano. Typhon emerged from behind the large wall, the multiple wings propelling him into the air. He had been waiting—but now that a shot of Love had been spent, I had another one for Death.

"Andromeda! The Circle!" I said.

"It's not working," she said desperately.

Typhon landed at the edge of the lake, blocking our escape to Argo. Behind me, Leo's rhythm intensified, like swords clanging in the midst of a battle. Draco screamed, his new rhythm savage and cruel.

"Stop!" I commanded them again.

But they didn't yield to me. Typhon was more powerful than I was—he had much more Darkness inside of him.

"Orion, no!" Andromeda seemed to have guessed my thoughts.

I let more Darkness pour inside of me. That made the whiteness around me brighter. I craved that Darkness as if it was the only thing that would sustain me. I felt its power coursing through my veins, lighting me up.

"STOP!" I roared.

For a moment, they did. Draco's rhythm flowed back around me, warming me like a hearth. Leo's rhythm organized into a coordinated battle, marching in unison. Aquila thundered back to normal, and Sirius's stringing rhythm flowed like a sweet chant around us.

Typhon was still for a moment. Then he gave me a feral grin.

Draco's rhythm burst like a wildfire, Leo marched into Chaos, Aquila smoked with thunder, and Sirius pulsed with Death. I let more of the Darkness rush into me, welcomed it as a friend. I needed it—my friends needed it.

"Orion, stop!" Andromeda shouted.

I was lying on my back, Andromeda kneeling next to me. "Please stop! You can't beat him. The Darkness will kill you!" I traveled beyond the Light, and sensed my rhythm again, but it had changed. The hunt had become chaotic, the hunter falling into the prey and the prey becoming the pursuer. Madness drummed inside of me in chaotic pulses.

Then I sensed something else, a silent rhythm that seemed to be just beyond my grasp. It was a portal that transformed one life into another. Death reached out a skeletal hand to me, but it wasn't going to help me defeat Typhon. It would pull me to the other side, but I wasn't ready for that journey. I turned away from Death and returned to the Hunt.

"STOP!!!" I shouted.

But Typhon's power was too great.

"Please," Andromeda begged.

I stopped, shutting off the Darkness abruptly. Everything inside me ached. I needed Darkness. I *wanted* it. It wasn't just an addiction, it was a raw and primal need that required more. The pulse of Death vanished, but its smoky taste lingered behind, beckoning me to follow it.

No matter how much Darkness I consumed, there would never be enough for me to compete against Typhon's power. That monster was ancient. It had been born long before humanity and had been feeding on Darkness for hundreds of thousands of years.

"Draco!" Virgo cried out.

"Run!" Draco roared. "Orion, now!"

Andromeda pulled me back to my feet. My senses sharpened once more. Pollux was wrapped around his brother's stone legs, weeping. Draco squirmed on the ground as he screamed in pain. Virgo kneeled over him, saying his name over and over again. Leo savagely scraped at a rock as if trying to rip it apart. Aquila flew in circles above us. The three heads on Sirius's neck barked as they tried to bite off each other's ears.

Typhon's maddening rhythm echoed around me, and I vainly tried to suppress it, to let the rhythm in my chest beat louder. But it was like trying to listen to someone's voice in the middle of a concert. Typhon's power was too great. A hundred yards behind me I sensed fast movement—Serpens. The Snake was carrying

Sagitta again. But it was too late. Something snapped inside of me as my friends' old rhythms disappeared completely, replaced by a terrible vibration.

The earth trembled as Typhon flew into the air with a shriek, retreating quickly from the battle and crushing my hopes of killing him with Sagitta.

"Get the Twins back to Argo!" I shouted to Andromeda.

I didn't wait for her to respond as I raced towards Virgo and Draco.

"Kill me, Orion!" Draco shouted.

Leo's roar reverberated in my bones as the Lion charged at me. Before I could throw myself sideways, Leo's paw smacked against my chest. The Lion pushed me onto the ground, and I had no air left in my lungs to scream.

"The Weavers," Leo said in a distorted voice. *"Find the end of Eridanus. Find the Well of—"* Leo roared, his sharp teeth dripping with saliva. *"Shadows. Blood. I need—"* Leo gave a deafening roar as he pulled back. The Lion ran away from me.

"Leo!" I shouted, but the Lion ran even faster, and seconds later he was out of my reach.

My ears rang as lightning crashed somewhere near me, making my bones shudder. I tasted iron in my mouth, and for a few terrifying seconds I couldn't hear anything, only a high-pitched ring. Then the giant Eagle flew away from us, opposite from where Leo had gone. Noise returned to me in a wave. Andromeda was shouting behind me, but I couldn't understand what she was saying. In front of me the earth shifted. Roots surfaced from the ground and wrapped around Draco, tightening around his horns and clawed hands.

"Please, Draco." Virgo was crying.

Something large flew above us. One of the Pleiades landed silently behind me. She raised a sword, then brought it down, severing Medusa's head. She dropped something over the head and wrapped it up. I didn't have time to get back to my feet before the Pleiad flew back into the air.

I couldn't sense Sirius around me anymore. At some point the three-headed Dog had left.

"Please," Virgo pleaded. "Don't go."

The tree roots tightened around Draco's legs, pulling him down into the earth. Serpens finally reached me, and I grabbed Sagitta.

"Orion!" Draco's voice was shrill.

I unhooked the bow from my back, my right hand trembling and wet with blood. Draco's flaming rhythm had almost sputtered out, reduced to smoke, as a brutal pulse took strength. It burned like a wildfire.

I notched the Arrow.

"I'm sorry," Draco said.

"I'm sorry too," Virgo responded. Tears slid down her cheeks.

I steadied my shaking grip and aligned the tip of the Arrow with Draco's battering heart.

The Dragon awoke.

A wave of heat smashed against me, and even when the Arrow shot forward, I knew it had missed its mark. I managed to keep a hold of the bow as I crashed on my back. A roaring shriek made the earth shake. It was ancient, deep, dangerous. Fire engulfed Draco, the flames licking his body. Draco's rhythm extinguished, and a violent blaze sprang forward. I scrambled back up and raced to Virgo. I pulled her to her feet. Sagitta's rhythm called me—it was beyond Draco, forty feet behind him.

"Get back to Argo!" I shouted to Virgo.

I sprinted towards the Arrow, my feet burning as if my shoes were melting. The Dragon pushed out of Draco's body like a butterfly exploding out of a cocoon. The Dragon squirmed inside the fire, its body twisting into life. Scales grew from the Dragon's skin, solid and smooth. The horns grew like curved swords. Its claws extended like lances. The wings unfolded, big enough to cover a house. The Dragon was about ten stories tall.

I reached down and picked up the Arrow. I notched the Arrow in the bow as I turned and pulled back the string. Draco was gone—this monster was not my friend.

The Dragon roared. Its tail lashed out at me. I jumped out of the way. The stone pillar behind me crumbled to pieces. Heat built up in the Dragon's chest, traveling up to its head. I scurried away, sensing frantically around me. I jumped over a large boulder and landed on the ground just as a wave of heat exploded from the Dragon's mouth. The rock trembled as it heated. For a moment, I couldn't breathe. Then the fire stopped.

I had only taken a gulp of air when the Dragon surged forward. I jumped forward as the Dragon stepped on the stone behind me, flattening it to dust. I turned on my heel, but the Dragon's tail lashed at me again before I could notch the Arrow. I jumped above the Dragon's tail, my shoe grazing against it before I landed on the ground again. The Dragon's tail rose high, then smashed onto the ground before me, making it crack and shatter under my feet. I screamed as I fell, my senses blurring. My body exploded in pain as if I were being hit by a hail of stones. The movement stopped.

Ragged surfaces surrounded me on all sides. I sensed for Sagitta, and the Arrow's rhythm came ten feet to the right, next to the smooth curve of the bow. I tried to push away from the rock across my torso, but my body burst with dizzying pain.

The Dragon stepped closer to me. Its claws buried in the broken stones as if it were walking on sand. The monster emitted a shrill roar. I imagined the Dragon's bright red and orange eyes glaring at me. Fire built up in its chest.

"DRACO!" Virgo shouted.

The fire died in the Dragon's mouth as its head snapped to the side. The Dragon moved away from me and slowly approached Virgo, who stood above a broken pillar fifty yards in the distance. She stood with her chin raised defiantly as she faced the monster. Virgo moved her mouth, but I was too far away to hear anything. The Dragon recoiled as if Virgo had spoken a curse.

The stone across my chest slid off me and pain flared up from every inch of my body. I let out a groan as I kneeled. My bones probably had more cracks than the ruins, but I pushed my body beyond the pain and rose once again to my feet. The Dragon extended its wings. I stumbled through the rocks, limping. Every time I stepped with my right foot it felt like a hammer was banging on it. The earth trembled as the Dragon jumped into the air. I hopped forward a few more steps and fell to my knees, which burst into nauseating pain. I picked up Sagitta and the bow. My right shoulder burned as I notched the Arrow. My left arm trembled as I held the bow. The Dragon's fierce and vicious rhythm blared somewhere to the right, and I aimed the Arrow in that direction, but the creature was already too far away. I let the bow and Arrow fall limply at my sides as more pain engulfed me.

"I'm sorry," I whispered to the air.

I had failed Draco. The pain obscured the whiteness around me, engulfing me once more in black waters.

"It will be all right," Arianna whispered. "My dear child."

The hunger smashed against me like an avalanche. I needed more Darkness. Needed it as if I had been under the desert sun for a day without water.

"No," I said.

The Dragon roared once more before my consciousness was devoured by the Darkness.

Chapter XIX, Verse IV

The Lion was never able to reveal,
The true might and power owned by the Hunter.
After the Lion an enemy has become,
The Hunter his own secrets will have to discover.
Through the doors of Death he will have to traverse,
And find a truth only the Weaver can bear.
To put an end to the war that for so long has been waged.

CHAPTER 56

I OPENED MY EYES, but the darkness was all the same. I groaned, my head heavy, but I didn't feel any pain. I tried to sit up, but a dizzying nausea sent my head into a spiral.

"Lay back down," Ophiuchus instructed.

I did so with another groan. "What . . . ?" Then my memories came back to me in a rush.

"They're gone," I whispered. "Draco, Leo, Sirius, Aquila, and Castor."

Ophiuchus responded after a second. "Yes."

"The others?" I asked.

"Pollux brought back Castor's statue intact, but I couldn't fix him," Ophiuchus said. "Virgo and Andromeda had some wounds, but they have healed now. Cancer has disappeared somewhere in the Ship, and Serpens is all right."

We had lost so many. Their absence felt like a void in my chest—I hadn't realized how much they meant to me. It had always been Andromeda and me, with Zia, but in the last few weeks I had become part of something more. But now I had lost it all. My throat tightened as tears threatened to burst from my eyes.

"Did you shoot Perseus?" Ophiuchus asked.

"Yes," I said.

"Then we might still have a chance at defeating him," Ophiuchus said. "That's our only chance, really."

That didn't bring me any relief. Leo, Sirius, and Aquila had become wild, Castor was a statue, and the Dragon had killed Draco. That sent a deep throb of pain through my chest.

My scars flared instinctively. Aquila had flown all the way to Brazil, Sirius seemed to be moving to northern Peru, and Leo was now in southern Chile. Their rhythms were still in Chaos, a wild chorus of savageness. If we found them again, they probably wouldn't recognize us. Typhon had turned them into fierce monsters, and if we encountered them again, they would tear us to pieces. They had run away to protect us, and even though I desperately wanted to find them, I knew it would be suicide. I didn't know how to break their Connection to Typhon, not unless I took any more Darkness. Until we discovered another way, our friends were gone.

At the thought of Darkness, the familiar hunger came back. The craving pulsed all throughout my body, demanding to be satiated. I gritted my teeth. Andromeda had lived with it for the last couple of months—I could do the same. But now I understood why she had been afraid to face Arianna again. The pull of Darkness was intoxicating. It *would* give me all the power I wanted, but it would end up destroying me eventually while it made Arianna more powerful.

"Did anything else happen?" I asked. "During the rising. Any disasters?"

"Several volcanoes erupted in South America," Ophiuchus said, then after a pause added, "Try to get some rest."

He didn't mention how many volcanoes had erupted, how many people had died, or how much destruction they had caused. But I knew it must have been catastrophic. Perseus once again had destroyed entire countries with a power he couldn't control.

Ophiuchus left my room, making the silence around me more pronounced. Leo wouldn't be coming in to check on me, and I wondered if I would ever get to talk to him again.

I pushed the sheets away, and despite the dizziness managed to stand up. I opened the Portal in my chest until my senses sharpened. I left my room, wandering through the hallways. I hadn't made it far when I heard Pollux's muffled cries through his door. I tried to ignore him, but I bit my tongue and stopped walking. I exhaled and stepped towards his door, opening it slowly.

"Pollux," I said gently as I walked into the room.

Castor's stone sword was still in an arc, right about to cut off someone's head. Pollux was curled on the floor, lying next to his brother's feet. I kneeled down next to him as he sniffed.

"This wasn't supposed to happen," he said. "This wasn't in the Prophecies Perseus gave us." He sniffed again. "This wasn't how one of us died."

"One of you was prophesized to die?" I asked, surprised.

Pollux nodded slowly. "But not like this. Perseus, he . . . he must have kept some of our Prophecies from us. But . . ." He began sobbing again. "There has to be a way to bring Castor back. This wasn't how one of us was Prophesized to die."

"Maybe you misinterpreted the Prophecies?" I asked, which I knew weren't very comforting words.

"No, we . . ." Pollux trailed off. "This wasn't the plan," he whispered, then began crying again. "This wasn't part of the plan. He's left me no choice." I sensed the tears streaming from Pollux's cheeks.

I wanted to ask what he meant by that, but didn't find the strength to do it. Pollux needed to grieve—he could explain later.

"Maybe there's a way to bring him back," I said. "Maybe Medusa's power is reversible."

"Maybe," Pollux cried.

"We'll find a way," I said, although I wasn't sure we would.

"We will," Pollux whispered. "I'll bring Castor back."

I took a deep breath and stood up again. I knew Pollux needed some space, and I needed my own time alone. I closed the door behind me and continued to make my way through the hallways. Even Argo seemed to be mourning—there was a grieving silence that filled the space around me. I made it to the living room, which I realized wasn't empty.

"Hey, Virgo," I said as I sat next to her.

"Hey," she said in a hollow voice. "How long had you known about the Dragon?"

I exhaled slowly. "He told me after the cemetery."

"He's gone, isn't he?" Her voice was almost a whisper.

"Yeah." My throat tightened painfully.

Virgo tried to stifle a sob. "It's over," she cried. "Perseus won."

"No, he didn't," I said. "I shot him with Love, so he won't be able to kill Andromeda. She's the one who will fulfill the Prophecy." I paused. "We still have a chance."

Virgo sniffed again. "Even then, they took Algol's head, and we're badly outnumbered."

Leo's words echoed inside my mind.

"Find the end of Eridanus," I said. "That's what Leo told me before he ran away. He told me to find a well, but I'm not sure which one he was referring to."

Virgo tensed, wiping her tears. "There are Three Wells at the end of Eridanus." She paused. "That's where the Weavers live."

"Do you think they might be able to help us?" I asked.

"If there's anyone who might know how to help us defeat Perseus and his allies, then it's the Weavers of Fate themselves." Virgo cleared her throat. "If those were his last words, then he must have had something in mind."

"Yeah," I said.

"I haven't seen the Weavers in years," Virgo said. "I haven't dared to swim through Eridanus again. But Argo should be able to take us there. I know the way to them, but it's a dangerous journey."

"I didn't imagine it would be easy," I said. "How long do we have until Perseus's next rising?"

"I don't know," Virgo said.

"What do you mean?" I asked. Virgo always knew.

"We don't know what will cause Perseus's last rising," Virgo said. "The Prophecies said that it would happen *when the sky goes full dark,* but I don't know what that means so I don't know when it will happen."

Silence settled in between us for a few tense moments.

"Then we just have to be ready for anything," I finally said. "And in the meantime we can visit the Weavers to ask for help."

"Before we set out through Eridanus, though, I have to map out the exact path," Virgo said. "The last thing we need is to get lost on our way there."

"That sounds like a good idea," I said. It would keep Virgo's mind busy. I couldn't imagine the loss she must have been feeling. Andromeda and I still had each other, but Virgo had lost all of her old friends, and Pollux had lost his only brother.

"Yeah," Virgo stood up from the couch. "I'll start working on that."

"Virgo," I said before she exited the room. "Do you know if the Constellation of Orion is connected to Death?"

I could still sense its smoky taste within me.

Virgo answered after a couple of seconds. "In Egyptian mythology he is." She paused. "Orion represents Osiris, the god of Death and the Underworld. Didn't Leo tell you that?"

"He didn't," I said.

Virgo didn't respond. She walked away without another word. I leaned back on the couch. Leo had only said that I was a Portal to other worlds—but could I also be the Portal between Life and Death? At the thought of Death, its smoldering rhythm intensified. It beckoned me to follow, to open the Portal in my chest and see where it led. Fear tightened around my heart—was Death a path I wanted to follow?

I wished Leo was here to guide me. For the first time since I had lost my vision, I felt utterly lost. Without Leo, I would never have discovered my new power. I was terrified to explore Death on my own and see where it led. He must have known the Egyptian myth that connected me to Osiris. Why hadn't he told me then? Had he been trying to protect me from something? Maybe Death wasn't a door I needed to cross. But even as that thought crossed my mind, Death's rhythm delicately brushed against me, as if trying to tell me that it would be waiting for me—it felt like a promise.

I sat on the edge of a low cliff, hearing the waves beneath me. The water splashed rhythmically against the coast like a giant, beating heart. My bare feet were already wet, but I didn't mind. The birds and seagulls sang happily as they flew around me. The air was still cold, but I knew that once the sun rose its warmth would cloak me.

I held the vial tightly in my right hand. It had become warm in my grasp, but I remembered the cold emanating from it when Ophiuchus had given it to me two days ago.

"This will cure your vision," he had said. "Taurus's blood will break the curse of the Seven Sisters."

Serpens hissed happily.

At some point during the fight, before Perseus escaped, Serpens had bit Taurus and sucked its blood. I had been so focused on fighting Algol that I had completely forgotten about the Bull's blood.

Ophiuchus handed me the vial.

"Thank you," I said.

Ophiuchus nodded. "Taurus's blood will rot soon, so you should place a few drops in each eye before two days pass if you want the cure to be effective. Do it while staring at the rising sun."

"The rising sun?" I asked.

"The Light from the sun has healing properties," Ophiuchus explained. *Click, click, click.* "I know that if you recover your sight, you may lose your other powers."

I gripped the vial tighter.

"Great power always comes with a sacrifice," he said. "But I wanted to let you make that choice for yourself."

Was power a sacrifice I was willing to make? If I lost the rhythms, then I wouldn't be able to sense Perseus and his allies. I could sense their rhythms strongly now, coming from southern Colombia. I was keeping track of them and noted their every move. Arianna couldn't hide them from me anymore—after having drunk her Darkness, I had been able to pass through it.

The smooth vial dug into my flesh as I held it tighter. A cold wave brushed against my feet. If I lost my new powers I wouldn't be able to help Leo, Aquila, and Sirius. I had almost saved them from Typhon. If I had been a bit stronger than the monster, I could have kept their rhythms normal. I knew I could find a way to help them using the rhythms. I just needed time to figure out how.

Another cold wave splashed against my feet and then pulled back. If I recovered my vision, then I wouldn't be immune to Medusa's glare, which Perseus would definitely use against us. I was the only one who had an advantage over the demon's eye—the only one who could fight against its power.

Yet a part of me was desperate to see again. I wanted to stare at the blue waves below me and the Stars over my head. I wanted to see another sunrise. If I threw the vial away now, I might lose my sight forever. I didn't know when we would see Taurus again, or if we would be able to get his blood for another cure. Next time we faced the Bull, it would be during our last battle—one where we were all likely to die.

Pebbles crunched as someone approached me. Andromeda silently sat next to me. I wanted to see Andromeda again. I wanted to see how her hair had grown, how her wounds had healed. I wanted to see her brilliant blue eyes.

I clutched the vial tight.

"How does the sky look right now?" I asked.

She took a few seconds to answer. "It's marine blue right above us, but lighter at the horizon. The moon is also bright—it seems a lot bigger than normal." She paused. "It's like a pearl embedded in a dark fabric, and the few Stars that are visible are like tiny jewels sewed into the night. The ocean is still dark, but it glitters with the light of the moon in silver sparks."

"Thank you," I breathed out.

Andromeda leaned closer to me, her breath brushing against my cheek. She placed her hand on my chest, and the two rings dug into my skin. Andromeda pulled her hand back.

"Could you hold this for me?" I said.

Andromeda held the vial, wrapping it tightly in her palm. I pulled the chain over my head, the rings clanking softly against each other. I pointed at the smaller ring. "This was Zia's," I said. "And this one belonged to Cepheus."

Andromeda didn't answer.

Another wave splashed onto my feet. I took a deep breath and held the rings tightly in my right palm. Zia had hidden so many secrets from me, and there was still so much about her to discover. I let the circular metal dig into my flesh as I held the rings tighter. I imagined the smaller ring sliding onto Zia's finger, her delicate hand with the beautiful golden band. Zia had lived a long life, one that stretched back thousands of years. Her secrets were buried but still alive, waiting to be uncovered. But she was dead now, and some secrets were better left buried.

"Goodbye," I whispered, letting the wind carry my farewell.

I opened my palm and let the rings drop. They splashed into the water. Then the darkness engulfed them and the two rings sank beyond my senses. Andromeda slipped her free hand into mine and squeezed. For a while we just remained like that, holding hands as we heard the waves splash around us.

"The sun is coming up," Andromeda said.

She handed me the vial, and I gripped it tight. My heart thundered inside of my ears. *Power corrupts. That's why true power always comes with a sacrifice. If you're always reminded of what you lost to get it, then you're less likely to corrupt.*

Was I willing to pay that price? But it wasn't the price of power that I was paying for. This was more than that. It was the slim chance to defeat Perseus. It was the only way to help our friends break free from Typhon. It would be our best bet at surviving and living to see another day after his last rising.

No matter what you do, in the end it will lead us all into the future I have planned for.

Perseus's voice echoed through the darkness. He had outsmarted me too many times to count. But Perseus was no god. He was just a boy, a man, and every man could be destroyed no matter how smart. I would find a way, and I knew that my new powers would lead me to his destruction.

Only in the Darkness I would be able to find the Light.

I gripped the vial tighter, then threw it away. I didn't sense where it landed, or even heard a splash. The sun pulled me into a warm embrace a second later. It softly grazed my skin like a delicate caress. Andromeda let her head rest on my shoulder. I wrapped my arm around her, pulling her close.

As the warmth on my skin grew hotter, I summoned an image of the sun peeking from the horizon, tainting the ocean orange. I pictured the sky lightening, becoming as bright as Andromeda's eyes. I let my body relax, imagining the most beautiful sunrise my mind could create.

ACKNOWLEDGEMENTS

I AM DEEPLY GRATEFUL to the many people who have supported this series over the past few years, helping me bring these stories to life and share them with the world. Your encouragement and belief in my work mean more than words can express.

Harrison Demchick, thank you for being the best editor I could have asked for and for always helping me learn how to become a better author and improve my characters and plot with every draft. Ally Machate, for all your advice and support throughout all these years. Julie Haase, thank you for supporting this series so much and always keeping the publishing process on track. Amy Handy, for your careful eye editing this book.

Emily Hitchcock, thank you for being so responsive to my many questions and helping me navigate the publishing journey. Clair Fink, thank you for all your work on the interior design and getting this book to its final form.

I am grateful to have met some very amazing friends who have supported my writing for years and are always there to listen and read my next crazy story. Daniel, thank you for being the best O-Week dad and an awesome friend. Gargi, thank you for your endless support not only with these books but also for always being there for anything else, and for being such an awesome quadmate, friend, and O-Week sibling. Abby, thank you for your friendship and all your support. Sam, for being the first beta reader of this book. Josselyn and Yessenia for being such supportive and fun friends and housemates and for all our crazy adventures (wishing us all mucho pan). To my friends in Mexico who have been there from the very first book I published: Pam, Denise, Mel, Alejo, Ana Sof, and Val, thank you for everything. Rosa, Eric, Daniel, Mario thank you for being great lab mentors, and I'm grateful that we became great friends even after I left the lab.

Augusto Aguilera and everyone at D'signLab, thank you for another brilliant book cover, and for your endless support and creativity to help me bring these books to life.

Mom, for supporting me from the very first day I started writing and for all the unconditional love you have given us. Thank you for helping me find my passion and nourishing it when that little flame was becoming a fire inside of me. Dad, not only for being the biggest fan of anything I write and publish but also for your support to get these books out into the world and for your love and support. Caro, for being my best friend and sister. For all your fun ideas to incorporate in my book, and for always being there to support me. I'm so proud of you and am grateful that we can both grow and succeed together. Abu, for being the kindest person I know and always being present and so willing to support us with anything we need.

And thank you, dear reader, for following me and the Star Children along in this journey.

BOOKS BY SOFI AGUILERA

Star Blood
Andromeda

Corvus

Orion

The Fragmented
An Echo of Oblivion

ABOUT THE AUTHOR

AT 17, SOFI BECAME Mexico's youngest published author. She is the author of *The Lost Origin*, *Star Blood,* and *The Fragmented* series. She won the award "Writers of Tomorrow" and was named one of the most influential women in Mexico by Quién magazine at 19. Sofi wants to keep one foot in the future and get involved with technologies that are making fiction turn into reality through science. She holds a B.S in Bioengineering from Rice University and has worked at Hilton Lab doing research in epigenetic engineering and synthetic biology. Sofi currently works in Venture Capital looking to find startups working to transform the world.

9 781633 378377